The Dark Ruler

Book Three in the
Camilla Crim Series

Edition: 1/2022

ISBN: 978-0-9966824-9-7

Cover Design by: www.ebooklaunch.com

Editing by: www.ayersedits.com

Find Emily online at www.emilyfortney.com

TO NOAH.
YOU ARE THE JOHNNY TO
MY CAMILLA.

Elmyra

Siourious

Otsana Wood

Rose Sea

LilyAye

Bear Gap

The Dark Ruler

CHAPTER ONE

HEAT RISES FROM the sunbaked clay roof tiles and warms the backs of my legs. I sit atop the Bear Gap House, leaning on the palms of my hands, and stare out across the farm. Villagers dot the fields as they crouch to harvest the last of the onions and cabbage. The sun hangs like a great fireball, resting on the treetops. I love these long days, but sadly, the summer is waning fast.

Bear Gap is a different territory than it was three months ago. The villagers are here by choice. Soldiers and whips are nothing more than a part of our history. A wooden stockyard fence still encompasses the property. Its pointed tips are reminiscent of a time when they were meant to keep us corralled inside. Now, that very wall is our main defense against the man who had it built: Quinten Warwick.

Finding order after the Warwick government was disbanded in Bear Gap was difficult. The national farm, which resided in our territory, had to be restructured. No one was forced into slave labor anymore, but we still had to eat. The whole country needed to eat. Part of our agreement with Quinten is that we'd keep the farm running, but the crown would pay us for the fruits and vegetables we produced. Once a month we have a tense meeting with some Warwick soldiers at the territory border where we make the exchange of goods.

Laughter draws my attention to the ground just below me. I lean forward, peeking over the edge of the roof, and catch a glimpse of Tuor's narrow face. He stands in the spot where once he languished in the stocks. The stocks are still there, but they're no longer used to satisfy a Warwick whim.

Tuor leans against the wooden contraption. Another boisterous laugh escapes his lips. He runs a hand nervously through his messy hair. I squint to see who he's talking to. A petite woman walks into my line of view. Eve . . . I sigh audibly and lean back on my hands.

What is she doing with my brother? I've seen her hanging around a lot over the summer. Although she's technically on our side, a rebel, our personalities don't blend well. I endured her company during the Bear Gap occupation but don't care to socialize with her anymore. I shake my head to put Eve out of my mind. I'm happy at the Bear Gap House, and I won't let this slight annoyance get in the way of that.

The murmuring voices of the villagers drifting in from the fields are evidence of a peaceful territory. Sure, The Supreme Ruler could come back here at any time and try to claim what's his, but he hasn't yet. We've spent the last three months building our defenses and putting spies on the road leading in and out of Bear Gap.

It's been quiet, and I like it like that. I run my fingertips along the mutilated Warwick brand on the inside of my arm. It's a relic of my past life when I was just a cog in Quinten's wheel. I look at it often and remind myself that I'll never go back.

Maybe that's why I've been spending so much time on the roof. Something about being at the highest peak puts me at ease. Being able to see the treetops and feel the wind gives me clarity. I lift my face to the darkening sky. Closing my eyes, I breathe in the fresh air. Maybe this is Tuor's and my opportunity to finally be safe and *free*.

My name catches on the light breeze. I open my eyes just slightly, suspicious if what I heard was real. The voice comes again. It's far off and muffled, but there's no doubt someone is calling for me. Hoping to not be found, I stretch out my legs and lay flat with my hands on my stomach. I just want to enjoy one of the last days of summer.

"Camilla." The voice is soft and timid.

I groan, letting my eyelids slowly open. Penelope stands on the ladder at the edge of the roof. Her face twists into a cringe.

"Hey . . . I'm sorry to disturb your . . . alone time, but he really wants to see you," she says.

I prop myself up on my elbows. One of the young farm workers from the Warwick regime, Penelope stuck around the Bear Gap House after the rebels took over, mostly because she didn't have anywhere else to go.

"He says it's important," Penelope adds, gnawing on her lower lip.

I gaze at the reddening skyline. "He always says it's important."

"Sorry . . . I could tell him I couldn't find you."

"No, it's okay. I can't ignore the chief forever," I say with a grin.

Penelope's cheeks blush as she lets out a chuckle.

"I'll be down in a minute," I say.

"Okay. See you at dinner!" Penelope says cheerfully before starting her descent down the ladder.

It's true that I've been avoiding Reed. I know what he's going to say, and I'm not ready to hear it. We were supposed to leave for our mission three months ago. I've continually come up with an excuse to wait just a few more weeks, but I can't ignore him forever. He's a Warwick. It's in their nature to be demanding.

Setting my foot on the first ladder rung, I lower myself down the side of the Bear Gap House. My view of the farm and the fields slowly shrinks as I scale the side of the five-story building. I stop just a few feet down and reach out to grab a nearby window that leads to the fourth-story stairwell.

I stretch my leg across the space from the ladder into the open window, then make a quick jump to pull the rest of my body through. I tumble into the spiral stairwell and brush dirt from my loose cotton shirt. One of Ralf's soldiers walks past me while heading downstairs. He gives me a curious look.

"Good evening," he says with a nod.

I plaster an awkward smile on my face. There's no point in taking the ladder all the way to the ground just to climb these stairs again, I reason with myself. Down the hall, footsteps click across the hard floor.

"There you are." Reed stands at the threshold of his office. "Come," he beckons before disappearing through the door. I reluctantly follow.

When the rebels gained control, Reed took over the governor's old office. Even though Ralf is technically in charge of the territory he had no interest in calling this room his. He muttered something about the ghosts of them who used to occupy it. Reed however, seemed eager to take the best room in the manor.

A thick mahogany desk sits in the center of the room. Reed stands behind it, poring over stacks of parchment. Behind him is a set of glass double doors leading out onto the balcony that overlooks the fields.

"I've been trying to meet with you for days," Reed says, taking a seat in the high-backed leather chair.

"This is a big place. I guess we just didn't cross paths."

I move into the room, resting a hand on the back of one of the chairs facing Reed's desk. He glances at me from under heavy eyelids. His crystal-blue eyes and dark circles still make me uncomfortable, no matter how long I've known him.

"Sit. I received word from one of our spies in LilyAye. Quinten is planning to travel soon. As you know, he hasn't left his castle since the rebels took over Bear Gap. This is a big deal, Camilla. He'll be vulnerable. This is our chance."

My chest tightens. I ease into the chair. *Our chance.*

"We've known since the day we took over this territory that my uncle would be back," Reed says. "Even with the deal we made, the whole country is still suffering with Bear Gap's now limited resources."

"So you think he's planning an attack on Bear Gap?" I ask, a lump forming in my throat.

"I know he is." Reed locks his gaze with mine. "This is our opportunity to not only save Bear Gap, but to secure my position as the new Supreme Ruler."

"Do you think now is the right time?"

"It's the perfect opportunity. He'll be out of the protection of his castle and the walls of LilyAye. We'll get him on the road and stop him before he can make it here. This won't be like the last attempt."

A few weeks after the rebel take over Reed and I and a small company saddled up and headed to LilyAye, thinking we'd be able to cut down Quinten easily. We barely made it to the territory border before we were met with hostility and had to retreat.

Reed continues. "With me being the rightful heir to the Warwick fortune, once he's dead, I'll claim the throne." Reed studies a map on his desk. I nod, unsure of how to respond. "Quinten's planning this attack in a month, maybe six weeks, at least that's what our spy has heard. It will take several days, perhaps weeks for us to get to LilyAye. If we leave tomorrow, that should give us enough time to take the LilyAye Road, barring any incidents. Then we'll connect with the rebels in LilyAye and shore up our plan before Quinten ever mounts a horse. I've already spoken with Ralf and informed him that you and I will be leaving our posts."

"You told him *what*? I haven't agreed to this."

Reed tilts his head, confused.

"What about Ralf? Can he carry on here without us?" I ask.

"It's not going to be easy for him running Bear Gap in our absence, but killing my uncle is more important," Reed says matter-of-factly. "You should be a part of this mission, Camilla."

Turning his attention back to his desk, Reed says, "I'd like you to get your horse readied in the morning. Pack light. Everything you'll need can be provided in LilyAye."

I stare across the desk at Reed, my lips parted in hesitation.

"I don't think I want to come to LilyAye with you." The words tumble from my mouth.

Reed's face contorts into an angry scowl as he clenches his jaw. "You don't wish to see my uncle dead anymore?"

"No, I do. I want him dead more than anything. I just don't want to be the one to do it."

The more I speak, the more confident I feel about my decision. The wrinkles on Reed's forehead deepen.

"Explain yourself," Reed demands.

"I like the way things are right now. The territory is thriving. Things are peaceful, and I get to see my brother every day. I've never lived like this before, without fear or desperation. I don't want it to end."

"The reason you're living such a good life is because of what I—what *we* did to take this territory from Quinten. We have to make sure we don't ever have to deal with him again."

"I know." I look down at my hands. "I know all of that. I think someone should travel to LilyAye and assassinate him. It's just, why does it have to be me?"

Reed's expression softens. "It has to be you."

"Why?"

"You're . . ." Reed searches for words. "You're the passion behind this rebellion. You built it from the ground up, and you and I outwitted the Supreme Ruler together. We must do it again."

I lean back in my chair and slowly shake my head. "I think I'm done with that life. All I wanted was my brother. Now I have him. Why can't you and Ralf finish the job? I'll stay here and run Bear Gap."

Reed leans across his desk and locks eyes with me.

"At the beginning of the summer, after we took over Bear Gap, you agreed to go to LilyAye with me. We made a deal. We shook hands."

I let my gaze wander around the room. The paintings, the furniture, nothing has changed since I sat in this very room with Governor Leo and argued for my brother's life.

"I'm aware," I say.

Reed stares at me intently.

"Just give me a little time to think about it."

"What is there to think about?" Reed lets out a slightly hysterical laugh. "This is the opportunity we've been waiting for!"

I stand abruptly. The chair screeches against the floor. "My life has been dictated for me since the day I was born." I point to my chest. "After everything I've done for this territory, I get to choose my life now."

"Fine," Reed says, his voice back to his normal tone. "Take the evening to think about it, but I need an answer. We leave tomorrow." He points his quill pen at me. "And Camilla, remember that if you don't come with me to take care of Quinten, who knows how much longer you'll be able to live your life here in peace?"

CHAPTER TWO

REED'S OMINOUS WORDS swirl around in my head. The Bear Gap I've come to love is an hourglass, slowly draining away. I stalk down the hallway, into the stairwell, but my feet suddenly stick in place and I feel paralyzed. I hate coming to the upper floors. Slowly twisting my body, I glance up the stairwell, toward the fifth floor. In a moment, I'm transported back to when I was dragged up these steps to Karla's bedroom.

Moaning and rattling chains clang in my ears. I blink, and Karla is standing at the top of the steps. My hand grapples for the stone wall to steady myself. Karla holds a knife in her hand. A shiver runs through my core. I squeeze my eyes closed and try to shake away the hallucination.

The beat of my heart doubles in speed. The tiny scars on my body, from where Karla poked me with her knife, tingle and burn as if the cuts are happening anew. *Stop it*, I command myself. Just stop thinking about it. It was months ago. I open my eyes. Karla is gone. All that remains is the hollow echo of the stairwell. Maybe getting away from Bear Gap wouldn't be the worst thing to happen to me.

I take the spiral staircase quickly, practically running down the steps. They empty me into the sitting room. The fanged teeth of the bear rug seem to be pointed toward me. I rush past, pushing open the kitchen door. A stark comparison to the upstairs, the kitchen bustles with activity.

Residents of the house make their way in for dinner. I pause and search for Tuor. A tall stockpot boils on the stove, while one of the kitchen help stirs it with a big ladle. No one is a slave anymore. Instead, we all have jobs. Some work to keep the house running while others continue to work on the farm, this time for a fair wage.

Penelope stands over the counter, fixing bowls for everyone. An aroma of broth and root vegetables fills the air along with a steamy haze. Six long tables fill up the space that was once used to store the governor's extravagance, things like hams, mutton, and barrels of wine. Ralf sits with a few of his men at a table. He waves at me as I pass.

I spot Tuor. Eve is sitting across the table from him. Her mouth is cinched into its typical sour expression, but a laugh seems ever present on Tuor's lips. My stomach drops. I slide onto the bench next to Tuor and force a smile on my face.

"Hey, sis," he says, surprised to see me. Tuor's face is flushed with delight.

"What are you laughing at?" I ask.

Tuor drops his voice. "Have you ever noticed how Theodore's bald spot is getting bigger, and he just keeps combing over more hair to cover it up?"

I glance at Theodore, who's sitting at Ralf's table. Tuor can't help but guffaw. I turn back to my brother and shake my head. Eve holds back a smirk. She folds her hands neatly together on top of the table as if resisting my brother's silliness. My eyes light on Eve's fingers. She's no longer wearing the gold wedding band that symbolized her first marriage. I swallow hard. *Why did she take it off?*

"You could look like that one day," I say trying to maintain my composure.

Tuor's mouth hangs agape. "No! Don't say that!"

"You're being mean to Theodore," Eve tells Tuor. She seems to be forcing a stern expression because a smile still plays at her lips as she scolds him.

"Oh, come on. You both were thinking it. You just didn't say it."

"I have more important things to think about," I mumble.

Tuor huffs at me. "You're no fun."

A low rumble of chatter echoes around the kitchen's tall stone ceiling. The brick hearth whirs with a crackling fire.

"Eve, who's looking after Lindon Place?" I ask, hoping she can't tell I'd rather she were there than here.

Eve takes a sip of water and lifts her chin. "My sisters can run things without me now. I've trained them well. I want to be free to be more instrumental with the rebellion."

"So you'll be helping around here now?" I ask.

"Yes," Eve says, straightening her back. "I've already spoken to Ralf."

Great. I guess my hope of ridding the Bear Gap House of Eve is dead. Tuor and Eve exchange a look. Penelope comes to our table with a tray full of bowls.

"Ah yes!" Tuor says, taking his food excitedly from the tray. He sucks in air as his fingertips touch the hot bowl. Barely able to hold onto it, Tuor nearly drops the bowl, letting a wave of broth slop over the side and onto the table.

"Are you mad?" Penelope shrieks.

Using a dish towel, she carefully sets a bowl of steaming cabbage soup in front of me.

"How was your meeting with Reed?" Penelope asks in a hushed tone.

"You met with Reed?" Eve asks. Her face lights up with interest.

Suddenly, Tuor, Eve, and Penelope all have their eyes pinned on me. I pick up my spoon and swirl the contents of my bowl.

"Yes. We spoke. It was . . . fine," I say as Penelope sets the last bowl in front of Eve.

"What did he want?" Penelope presses.

"It was nothing." I wave her off. "Just some farm business. You know how intense he can be."

"I know." Penelope tucks the tray under her arm and hurries from the table.

"You're a bad liar," Eve says as soon as Penelope is out of earshot.

I sigh, looking down at my bowl of cabbage soup. I then glance across the table at Eve and debate whether I should tell them both about my conversation with Reed. I had hoped to talk with Tuor tonight . . . *alone*.

"Out with it!" Tuor says, taking a spoonful of soup into his mouth.

"Reed said there are rumors that Quinten will be traveling to Bear Gap in a month and bringing an army with him."

"Is he sure?" Tuor asks.

"Yes, pretty sure. Reed wants to make an assassination attempt while Quinten's vulnerable. Kill him before he can make it here."

"Hm . . . risky move." Tuor turns back to his dinner.

A spoon falls from the table next to ours, hitting the floor with a clang. Eve crosses her arms across her chest.

"That's his plan?" Eve asks. "What about the army that's coming with him? Shouldn't we be building an army of our own?"

"He says that, with Quinten dead, he'll have immediate claim to the throne and be able to control the Warwick Militia," I say.

Eve raises her eyebrows. She picks up her spoon with a frustrated groan. "Some of those soldiers will be loyal specifically to Quinten. Who's to say they won't just turn around and kill Reed?"

"I don't know. We didn't get that detailed in our conversation."

"Sounds like a suicide mission to me," Tuor mumbles as he slurps more of his soup.

"He's leaving for LilyAye tomorrow. He wants me to go along," I say, daring to meet Tuor's eyes.

He pauses mid-bite. "What did you say?"

"I told him I'd have to think about it."

"I'll go," Eve says.

"Wait, what?" Tuor says quickly.

"I want to go. This is what I've been waiting for," Eve says.

"You'd leave Bear Gap?" Tuor asks, a note of despair in his voice.

"To kill Quinten Warwick? Yes." Eve glances from Tuor to me and then back to Tuor. "But I think you should come too."

"Okay," Tuor says. The two of them gaze dreamily into each other's eyes. "I'll go."

"Now, you're going too?" I ask. "You just said it was a suicide mission."

"Well, Eve's right. We've been waiting for this opportunity all summer," Tuor says.

"But things have been so good here. We're safe."

"We're not safe for long if there's an army on its way," Eve says.

I push the cabbage soup away from me and rest my chin in my hand.

"Camilla, I thought you'd jump on an opportunity like this." Tuor pauses and leans in a little closer to me. "Is this about Mirabelle?"

"No," I snap.

Mirabelle. I haven't seen her since we stood at Knox's deathbed. She knew he betrayed Tuor and me but never told us. I'd be perfectly happy to leave her behind.

"I just like my life here," I say defensively.

Eve eyes me suspiciously. "Maybe you don't want to leave because of Johnny."

Her words hang in the air. Anger stirs in the pit of my stomach, and I remember why I dislike Eve so much. She's so annoyingly perceptive. I press my lips firmly together. I also haven't seen Johnny all summer, and it's bothering me more than I thought it would. I maintain a calm expression and take a deep breath.

"Why is it such a surprise that I would enjoy living in Bear Gap? All I ever wanted was for Tuor to be safe, and to live in a free territory. Now, I have both of those things. I don't need to go fighting all of Elmyra's battles."

Eve straightens her back. "That's understandable. You should live the life you want," she says, drawing her hand up to inspect her fingernails.

"Thank you," I say, surprised to be agreeing with Eve.

Tuor fills his mouth with more soup. I tap at the side of my bowl. Penelope giggles as she carries a tray of food to the table next to us.

"But . . ." I say with trepidation. "Have any of you heard from Johnny?"

Eve shakes her head, a smug expression on her face.

"Nah," Tuor says.

"I wonder if he's okay."

"I'm sure he's fine. He's probably just busy helping his family." Tuor lifts his bowl and slurps the last of the cabbage soup. "We should stick together. Whatever it is we do."

I nod, feeling the calm returning to my body.

"But if we leave . . . we won't have poor Theodore to tease anymore," Tuor says with a mock frown.

"I think we'll make do," I say.

A tall, lumbering figure approaches our table. His husky frame and broad shoulders are undeniable. My father clears his throat.

"Can I eat here?" Malcolm asks awkwardly.

"Sure," Tuor says.

Malcolm squeezes into the bench next to Eve. It truly is a new territory, I think to myself. My own father has taken to living and helping at the Bear Gap House. Tuor and I are actually on friendly terms with him. It's odd when I think about it, but I see now how Malcolm tried to protect us from our mother. I have to give him credit for that. He's also a different person now that he's done with the drink.

"I think I'm done eating," I say.

"But you barely ate anything?" Tuor says.

"You want the rest of it?" I ask sliding my bowl over to Tuor.

I stride from the kitchen, thinking about how right Eve is. She can see what I can't even admit to myself— that I can't get Johnny out of my head. Where is he? Why hasn't he come to see me, or at least see how the rebellion is doing? I expected Johnny to stick around with Knox until he died, but I thought he'd come back to the Bear Gap House and rejoin the rebels. He hasn't done that yet . . . In fact, I haven't seen or heard from Johnny all summer. I have to remind myself that Johnny and I parted as friends, and nothing more. But don't friends check up on each other?

Hurrying through the sitting room, I pass two more rebel members on their way to the kitchen for dinner and tear out the back doors. A few villagers still toil away in the fields, but most people are packing up and heading home. I walk past the low fields to the stables. There, I saddle up Shae and kick off, galloping through the open gate. If I'm going to leave Bear Gap with Reed, I have to know there's nothing left for me here.

I push Shae down Reaper's Way, but before emptying into Rande Square, I turn off the road and into the woods. I try to remember the way. It's been months since I've traveled this route. I pull Shae to a slow walk and lead her through the dense woods. With the sun setting and the thick trees, it already feels like nightfall. We crest a small incline, then drop back down into a creek. The air is muggy yet cool. I pull my vest closer to my chest as we ride.

"Whoa . . ." I mutter as I tug on Shae's reins, bringing her to a stop.

Scanning the woods, I hope to find something familiar. A squirrel zooms up the trunk of a wide, gnarly tree trunk. A plume of smoke rises into the tree branches off to my right. *I found it.* I hop off Shae and leave her tied to a low-hanging branch. I move through the woods toward the smoke, groping in the darkness.

My feet crunch the branches and dried leaves that cover the forest floor. I climb a small hill and pause at the top. Johnny's house lies in front of me. It's a squat, rustic cabin with just the essentials. The memories I have of this place are sweet. I recall training sessions with Johnny over there in the clearing, which would often divert into time in each other's arms and tender kisses.

That's definitely Johnny's horse tied up out front, but there's another horse there too. I scurry down the hill to get a closer look. Hiding behind a nearby tree, I look through a window. It's dim inside except for a few candles flickering through the glass. I search for movement, but see none. I need a closer look. Quietly, I creep up to the cabin and peer inside. Nothing. Could Johnny be ill? Or injured? Maybe that's why he hasn't come to the Bear Gap House. What if he's stuck inside with no one to help him?

I'm overwhelmed with a feeling of both relief and panic. If I'm right, it would explain a lot. I rush over to the front door, determined to rescue Johnny. I'm about to burst through the wooden door when, through the front window, I catch a glimpse of Johnny. He carries an armful of wood to the fireplace and sets it on top of a pile of glowing embers. He stands and brushes wood chips from his pants.

He's all right. He looks fine, perfectly healthy. He's the same Johnny I knew before, broad shouldered with soft blond hair. He moves to the couch, taking a seat. Voices seep through the open window. I shift to get a better look. A woman sits on the couch next to Johnny. She's tall with tan skin and delicate features.

They laugh easily together. The woman reaches down and squeezes Johnny's hand, giving him a knowing glance. An ache grows in the center of my chest. I stumble backward from the window and force myself to look away. He's found someone else, I realize with a sudden burst of queasiness.

What am I doing? I've just ridden here to spy on a man who obviously hasn't had a single thought about me. He's already replaced me. I practically smack my hand onto my forehead. I've been so stupid. I've been hanging around Bear Gap, hoping that Johnny would come back to the rebellion, hoping that maybe he and I could be something more than friends, and hoping that we could live together in peace.

I'm a fool.

Reed is right. I'm not meant to sit around Bear Gap in this comfortable life. There's still an evil ruler sitting on the throne in LilyAye, and I might as well be the one to kill him.

CHAPTER THREE

JOHNNY HAS MOVED on. Realizing that truth stings worse than a hornet. That's all right, I tell myself. I have more important things to do anyway. I urge Shae forward, not even giving a backward glance at Johnny's cabin. Darkness has fully engulfed Bear Gap by the time I stumble out of the woods and onto Reaper's Way.

The windows of the Bear Gap House glow amber, warm and inviting. Soft plumes of smoke billow from the chimneys. I pass through the front gate. Shae's hooves crunch on the stone road that leads to the farm. The villagers have gone home by now. All that remains are those of us that reside here.

On my way to the stables, I notice a slender, soldier-like figure standing at the back of the house at the edge of the fields. Pulling on the reins, I pause and squint in confusion. Light pours through the floor-to-ceiling windows in the sitting room, illuminating the man's image. A low murmur reaches my ears. It sounds like he's talking to himself. I dismount and tug Shae over as I approach the mysterious figure.

"Reed?" I ask.

Reed's head spins around to face me. His self-talk stops immediately. "You've been gone for a while."

"Yeah. I went for a ride. I needed to clear my head."

With Shae by my side, Reed and I survey the fields. A hazy moon hangs in the sky.

"What are you doing out here?" I ask.

Reed sets his hands on his hips. He looks out over the property with an expression I'm familiar with. Governor Leo used to stare at the farm like that, as if it were his, and his only, to rule.

"Just taking it all in," Reed says. "We've done an amazing job saving this territory. Bear Gap is a healthy, pleasant place to live. We need to do it for the rest of Elmyra."

"I know," I say.

The cool nighttime breeze carries the crickets' song over the rolling fields. Reed tilts his head to face me. "This is why I need to be Supreme Ruler. I can do for the whole country what I did for Bear Gap. But we have to kill Quinten first." He pauses, staring quietly out over the farm. When he speaks again, I sense the trepidation in his voice. "Have you decided?"

"Yes, I've decided."

Reed's shimmering blue eyes sparkle in the low light.

"I'm coming with you. Under one condition."

"Granted," Reed says.

I cock my head curiously. "You don't even know what my condition is."

"I need you on this mission. I'll agree to whatever is required to entice you to come."

I'm taken aback by Reed's fervency. Perhaps I should have demanded more.

"My condition is to bring Tuor and Eve along. Tuor has to come. I won't be separated from my brother, and Eve . . ." I take a deep breath. "I can't believe I'm saying this, but she should come with us too. She's passionate and clever, and she could be a real asset."

Reed's face is stern, and he keeps his gaze on the horizon. "Fine," he says with a nod.

He turns suddenly and places a hand on my elbow. I shudder at his touch. I still haven't gotten used to how freely he embraces me.

"I'm happy to hear you made the right decision, Camilla. I've been wanting to tell you for some time how impressed I am by you. Bear Gap would still be in Quinten's hands if it weren't for your help."

His compliment surprises me. Confidence blooms in my chest.

"Thank you," I say softly.

"Camilla, do you trust me?"

I speak quickly. "Yes, of course."

"Good, good. We would be foolish to go on this mission together if we didn't explicitly trust each other."

"I wouldn't be here if I didn't trust you."

In the distance, an owl hoots. Reed's hand slides from my elbow to lace his fingers with mine. I shiver, wondering if Reed has forgotten himself.

"My feelings for you go deeper than just trust on the battlefield," he says.

My heart thrums. "Oh . . ."

"I've been strategically holding back my feelings from you. I wasn't sure of your full commitment to the rebellion. Plus, I've been so focused on planning the demise of my uncle. Now that I know you're coming with me to LilyAye and leaving this life behind, you should know that I've grown to care for you."

Warmth floods my cheeks despite the stiffness of his words. Reed searches for my eyes, but I can't look at him. I stare at the ground. My head spins. Reed has feelings for me? When did this happen, and how did I miss it? Maybe I was too busy waiting for Johnny.

"Once all of this is over, you could stay with me in LilyAye. Perhaps you'd like to rule by my side?"

A nervous chuckle escapes my lips. "I can't think past what I'm going to pack for the trip, let alone what I'll want to do if we manage to kill Quinten." I pull my hand from Reed's grasp. "I appreciate all you've said, but my heart is pretty undecided when it comes to that kind of stuff."

Reed appears unfazed by my rejection. He places his hand back on his hip and looks across the dark horizon again. "No need for apology. Perhaps in time your heart will change. We don't need to let this impede our plan."

"Oh, good." Shae shakes her head next to me. I stroke her mane to calm her.

"We'll leave tomorrow evening. I'm sure you understand that it would be best to tell as few people as possible what we're about to do."

"I understand."

"Camilla."

"Yes?"

Reed fully turns to face me now. He touches a hand to a lock of my hair lying on my shoulder. He studies my face as he rubs my hair between his fingers. "There is just one more thing I need you to do before we leave."

***

The mirror in my bedroom is an old one with splotchy black cracks running through the glass. It sits atop an ornate yet dilapidated dresser that's been tucked away in one of the many extra bedrooms in the Bear Gap House. I stare at my reflection. Long dark tendrils crown my face.

The midmorning sun pours in through my open window. A cool breeze tells me that fall is as inevitable as my leaving Bear Gap. I pull out the dagger that I keep always on my hip, the dagger that Knox gave me. I run my finger along the cool blade and squeeze the handle tightly.

I'm glad he's dead, I say to myself, thinking of Knox. I just wish I had stuck around to see it for myself. As much as I hate him now, I can't find it in me to give away his dagger. The smooth leather handle fits my hand well, and it has never failed me in battle. It won't fail me in this morning's task either.

I hesitate. Reed is right. I should cut it off, but it's hard to say goodbye to something you've had your whole life. I let my thick, wavy hair hang over my shoulders. Running my fingers through it one last time, I fill my lungs with a deep breath. You've got much harder things ahead of you, I remind myself.

With a shaky hand, I pull a chunk of my hair away from my head. Using the dagger, I run the blade along my hair within a few inches of my scalp. I grab another bundle of hair, and with a quick swipe, I cut off more. Blobs of dark brunette hair fall onto the dresser and floor. I continue until my head is nearly bald, except

23

for a few inches of hair. The breeze tickles my neck. At least my head feels lighter.

Once the hair is gone, I secure the dagger on my belt and toss my beautiful hair out the window. The thought of some bird using it to build her nest comforts me. I touch the back of my head. Where there used to be thick tendrils, I now feel nothing but short tufts of hair. I swallow the loss. It's just hair. I won't let myself be sad about it.

Crawling onto my bed, I grab a piece of parchment and a pen that I stole from Reed's desk. I've been debating all morning if I should write this letter or not. I'll just write it, and I can decide later if I want to do anything with it. I stick a book behind the parchment to use as a hard surface. Holding the pen over the paper I pause.

Johnny, I write. *I'm leaving Bear Gap today, along with Reed, Tuor, and Eve. We're not allowed to tell anyone, because we're going to free Elmyra from Quinten's grasp. I don't know for certain if we'll ever make it back, which is why I'm writing you this letter. Perhaps you don't care at all, but in case you do, just know that I think about you often. I keep imagining what this trip to LilyAye would be like if you came along. Remember when you pulled me inside the Justice House? We left Governor Leo with quite a shock. I miss those times, you and me, fighting together. I think I made a mistake telling you I wanted space. I miss you. Anyway, we start our journey to LilyAye today. I don't know exactly what waits for us there, but I hope we can make a better Elmyra for everyone.*

My pen hangs poised over the paper as I consider the ending of my letter. There's a good chance I'll never see Johnny again, I remind myself.

I love you,
Camilla

I quickly fold the paper as if that will make the words I just wrote less real. I wipe a stray tear from my eye as I pop off the bed. I shove the letter into my pocket. I'll decide what to do with it later. Throwing my bag over my shoulder, I look around my room one last time before slipping downstairs.

We won't get much food on the road, so I force myself to eat lunch in the kitchen. Penelope compliments my hair, even though there's no way she can mean it. She asks what I'm doing today.

"Traveling to Rande on some farm business," I lie.

After lunch, I tell her goodbye even though she doesn't realize it's for the last time. Reed, Tuor, Eve, and I spend the afternoon packing up supplies and preparing our horses. I tighten the strap on Shea's saddle. A plume of dry hay dust fills my nose.

"Let's go over our plan," Reed says when the stable is emptied of villagers.

We gather in Shae's stall while I continue to pack my saddlebags. Tuor tuns over a bucket and sits on it while Eve stands behind him.

"How are we even getting to LilyAye? Surely Quinten has the road well guarded," Eve says.

"He does," Reed says. "Our spies have told me he has soldiers and checkpoints all along the LilyAye Road. No one gets in or out of Bear Gap without him knowing who it is."

"So how do you expect to get *me* there?" I ask.

"I know this road. It's long and covered with woods on all sides. It's a hard stretch to properly guard. Quinten has had his eyes on me most of my life, and I've still managed to travel it without detection. Some disguises should get us through. Camilla, you're the most recognizable in this area. That's why I had you cut your hair. When we get to LilyAye, I'll be the most at danger of being identified, but I suspect that Camilla is quite famous there too."

"So, what's our rouse?" Eve asks.

"We're leather merchants," Reed says. "I gathered what leather supplies I could from Billage and packed them up in case we're searched. We can't dress like rebels either. We have to hide all of our weapons. We can't wear anything that looks like we're ready for battle. Tuor and I will wear simple pants and a tunic, and I have plain dresses for you two."

Tuor points at me and guffaws. I look down at the boots and animal-skin pants I've grown accustomed to. "I have to ride Shae all the way to LilyAye in a dress?"

"It's only a couple days' journey," Reed says.

"Some of us are used to riding a horse properly in a dress. It'll be no problem," Eve says.

I roll my eyes.

"What happens when we get to LilyAye?" I ask.

"Once we make it through the gates of LilyAye, we'll still have to be on guard, even more so. Quinten knows I have many supporters there. We'll immediately secure ourselves in one of the rebel safe houses. I'm hoping my people have more information on when Quinten is traveling and what size army he's taking with him. From there, we'll mount an attack plan with the LilyAye rebels."

I stop my work on Shae and move closer to the others. A horse at the end of the stalls whinnies.

"Let's say we manage to murder Quinten as planned, then what?" Eve asks.

"I have full claim to the throne," Reed says. "Despite his many wives, Quinten only managed to have daughters, and with my father dead, all of

Quinten's wealth transfers to me when he dies, which in turn makes me Supreme Ruler. He knows this, of course. That's why he's been trying to kill me before I kill him."

Reed speaks of the death of his father and uncle so plainly. His message is clear: the road to the throne is certainly a bloody one.

Tuor speaks. "When I was stationed in LilyAye, most of the boys in my militia troop were Quinten supporters. They at least said they were. Who's to say your reign won't be challenged?"

Reed tilts his head and gives Tuor a quizzical look. "I am to be Supreme Ruler, either now, or when Quinten dies of natural causes. We can't wait for the latter. Elmyra can't wait. The only thing that could be contended is if they could prove that I murdered Quinten or was a part of the plot to murder him."

"But you are a part of the plot," I say.

"That's why it's critical that I not be seen as guilty in this. If it can be proven that I had something to do with his assassination, then Quinten's supporters could attempt to have me imprisoned for treason. It will have to appear as if a rouge group of rebels killed him, and that I had no association with them," Reed says.

"What happens to us if we're arrested for his murder?" I ask.

"Hopefully I'll be crowned ruler in short order and have you delivered from the dungeons," Reed says.

Eve straightens her back and looks intently at Reed as if she's not fully pleased with this plan.

"Do all of you want Quinten Warwick dead?" Reed asks, irritated.

"I want him dead," Tuor says.

"This is what it takes. I assure all of you that once I'm Supreme Ruler, each of you will be treated with more riches than you can dream of. The governor's house will look like a house built for a stray dog. You'll have your own land, and you'll each have a seat on my council." Reed looks right at me. "Imagine having a say in how all of Elmyra is run."

I nod in understanding. "This isn't going to be easy."

Eve lifts her chin. "I'm on board. I've already decided I'm in this."

"Me too," Tuor says.

"Good. Get changed into your new clothes, and let's get ready to go," Reed says.

We load up our horses with water and food enough for a week. I change into Reed's horrid dress. It's periwinkle blue with a white collar and matching white apron and cap. I audibly groan as I run my hands down the skirt. Tuor giggles from the other end of the stall.

"The sleeves are huge," I whine. At least the hat covers my ragged hair.

As evening settles in, Ralf appears at the stable door. He stands tall at the threshold like the Warwick soldier he used to be. "Well, my sincerest good luck to all of you."

"What will you tell people if they ask about us?" Eve asks.

"That I sent the four of you down to Hanover to help the people with their gardens and food supply. That should be a good enough reason for a few weeks at least. Hopefully, by then, I'll be able to tell them the truth."

"Take care of Bear Gap," I say.

Ralf nods slowly. "Yes, I have a job ahead of me, losing all of you. We'll still prepare in case you fail. I'll continue to build up our defenses and train our men."

"We won't fail," Reed says, tightening the strap on his horse's saddle.

"Of course." Ralf looks behind him at the Bear Gap House. "I've called everyone inside for a meeting. If you leave now, no one should notice you riding out."

"Let's get moving then," Reed says.

Ralf turns to exit the stables. I follow after him and grab his attention just a few paces outside.

"I need you to do something for me," I call.

"What is it?"

I pull Johnny's letter from the pocket of my apron. "You remember Johnny Bennette, right? Knox's nephew. He helped us the day we occupied Bear Gap."

"Yes, I recall."

"If he ever comes here looking for me, can you give him this?" I nervously pass the letter to Ralf. He stares at the parchment curiously.

"What if he never comes?" Ralf asks.

"Then just hold on to it for me. Burn it if I don't make it back."

"I can have a man deliver this to Johnny for you," Ralf offers.

"No, no. Only give it to him if he comes here asking after me. Do you understand?"

Ralf gives me a stiff nod as he places the letter in his breast pocket. "I will keep it in a safe place. Again, good luck to you, Camilla. It's been a pleasure fighting alongside you."

"You too. Oh, and please don't read the letter."

"I wouldn't dare."

The Bear Gap House grows quiet as the villagers

head inside for Ralf's meeting. Reed, Tuor, Eve, and I mount our horses and ride through the iron gate for possibly the last time.

CHAPTER FOUR

I PULL MY jacket tightly over my chest and lean into the cool wind as the sun begins to set. Massive pine trees line the narrow LilyAye Road. The gentle clip-clopping of Shea's hooves on the rocky trail makes it seem like we're alone, but I'm constantly peering into the dark shadows between the trees. To our left is the mountain range that creates the northernmost border between Bear Gap and the LilyAye territory. I'm officially farther from my home than I've ever been before.

"Your hair is shorter than mine," Tuor says as he rides a few paces ahead of me. He twists in his saddle and cringes.

I adjust the scratchy bonnet on my head. "And your hair looks like a dirty mop."

Suddenly self-conscious, Tuor musses his wavy hair. He looks over at Eve to catch her reaction. She sits sidesaddle on her horse with her back as straight as a fence post and her eyes focused ahead. The thick skirts of my dress bunch up around my knees, and my boots awkwardly stick out, as I refuse to ride sidesaddle.

"You kind of look like Theodore if he were an angry kitchen maid," Tuor adds with a laugh.

"I didn't cut my hair to look pretty, you know."

Tuor smirks. "That's obvious."

I grit my teeth, then quickly nudge Shae so she gallops right up next to Tuor's horse. I swing and punch him hard in the arm.

"Ow!" Tuor exclaims. "You're a burly kitchen maid."

Eve grips tighter to her reins as she smugly squints at Tuor and me.

"You're dead." I reach out and playfully try to pull Tuor from his saddle.

"Hey!" Tuor yelps.

"Are you children?" Reed barks from the front of the line. "The tavern is just ahead. Compose yourselves."

I give Tuor a final shove before nudging Shae up next to Reed. "Sorry about that. It could seem more realistic if we just act normal."

Reed's gaze is fixed on the road. "I don't want to draw any attention to us. Let's stay focused."

"Okay." I try to catch his eyes, but he's deep in thought about something else.

The sun touches the horizon. The woods darken and those same fir trees start to look like stalking giants. Up ahead on the LilyAye Road, the thatched roof of a tavern comes into view. Thick gray smoke billows from the stone chimney. We pull our horses to a trot and ride up to the front of the tavern.

It's nestled among the trees, with the foothills of the mountains right behind it. A stone foundation holds up the square building. Wooden steps lead to a canvas-covered porch. The windows are foggy from soot, but a golden glow fills the diamond-shaped glass grids.

"We'll spend the night here, and then we should hit the first checkpoint by tomorrow," Reed says.

"I used to stare at these mountains," I say as I dismount Shae. I stretch my neck to peer all the way up the mountainside. "I can't believe I'm actually standing in the shadow of them."

"I think I know this place," Eve says as she gracefully steps off her horse.

"Have you been here before?" Tuor asks.

"I'm not sure . . ." Eve muses.

"It's getting dark. Let's get inside and secure our rooms," Reed says.

"It doesn't look like anyone is here," Eve says, pulling off her leather riding gloves.

I glance around and realize she's right. The tavern is quiet. No other horses or carriages are tied to the hitching post.

"There's smoke," Tuor says. "Someone's home."

"Come on," Reed says. "It looks like there's a stable out back. Tuor, Eve, you tend to our horses. We'll get the rooms."

Reed and I gather our bags and enter through the tavern's front door. Warm candlelight envelopes us from the huge circular chandeliers that hang from the tall pitched ceiling. Square tables sit neatly in the dining room, each set with its own candle, stack of cloth napkins, and thick metal utensils. It's quiet, eerily quiet.

"This is curious," I say with a whisper. "They look ready for business, but no one's here."

Reed glances around the room with tightly knit eyebrows, as if he were scowling at the tavern. With an unsatisfied grunt, Reed approaches the long wooden bar. He knocks on its surface and calls out for assistance.

Fat mead barrels sit propped against the thick columns. More are stacked behind the bar.

"Hello?" Reed says, a note of irritation in his voice.

A gaunt man with deep wrinkles emerges from a dark hallway at the end of the bar. He grimaces as he slowly comes into the light.

"It's about time," Reed says, reaching for his pouch of Catahli rings. "We need two rooms for the night."

"I don't have any rooms for tonight." The old man's voice is throaty.

Reed arrogantly tosses a handful of rings onto the bar top. "Find some."

"I don't have any rooms for tonight." The man's voice rises.

"This is a tavern, is it not? I have rings, so you'll find us some rooms." Reed's Warwick entitlement oozes from his every pore, and I wonder if it will actually work.

"I said, no room. Go somewhere else." The man growls as he points a finger to the door.

"There's no one here," I say, moving into the dining room. I adjust the bag on my shoulder.

"Camilla, don't bother," Reed says as he swipes the rings back.

I furrow my brows, wondering why the man would leave the door unlocked if he didn't want business. The tavern door opens with a groan. Tuor and Eve stand at the threshold.

"Go back down the road and find camp somewhere else," the man says, turning his back on us.

"Wilson?" Eve says approaching the bar. "Is that you?"

The man half turns back to us.

Eve smiles pleasantly. "I'm Eve Lindon, Peter's daughter. We own Lindon Place down in Rande. Do you remember me?"

Wilson's eyes soften as he nods. "Yes, I remember you," he says solemnly.

"My father used to do business with Wilson years ago," Eve says, addressing the rest of us. "I was just a little girl at the time, but I remember you."

"Yes," Wilson says. "Not much business going on here now."

"What's happened?" Eve asks. "You have a lovely tavern."

"No one travels this road much anymore, and I'd advise you all not to travel it either. Find another place to lodge."

Wilson turns again to walk away as if to wash his hands of us.

"Please," Eve calls. "We'd be grateful if you gave us a room tonight."

"I can't," Wilson says.

"I don't understand," Reed says gruffly. "Don't you want the business? Here you are complaining of no customers, and I've brought you four." Reed glares down at the man. "Maybe you've got no business because you treat people this way."

"Fine," Wilson growls, his jaw set. He looks straight at Reed with burning eyes. "If you insist. I'll give you the rooms you so desire."

Wilson pulls two sets of keys from the hooks behind the bar. Reed reaches back into his bag of rings.

"Keep it. No charge for a Lindon girl."

"Thank you," Eve says.

"Follow me."

Wilson leads us across the dining room to a set of wide wooden stairs. They creak as our heavy boots take each step. Upstairs, he leads us down a dark hallway.

"Room one," he says, turning the key in the lock and swinging the door open. He then takes a few steps down the hall and does the same thing to the next door. "Room two." Without meeting our eyes, Wilson passes us swiftly walking down the hall.

"What about some dinner?" Tuor asks.

"Kitchen's not open tonight."

"That's an absolute surprise," Reed says sarcastically.

"Good night," Wilson says.

"Good night," Tuor says as Wilson disappears down the steps. "That was odd."

"Rude is the word you're looking for," Reed says. "Everybody, get some sleep. We have a long day ahead of us tomorrow."

Reed and Tuor take the first room while Eve and I settle into the second. Two narrow beds, their frames made out of tree branches, sit up against the wall. A woven tapestry hangs above them, and a simple porcelain wash basin rests on a table on the other side.

Immediately, I drop my bag and move to the window, drawing the thin curtains open. Our second-story bedroom looks down on the LilyAye Road. Only the cool blue light of the moon distinguishes the road from the tree line. I push open the window, letting a chilly breeze fill our room.

"Leave it open," Eve says. "I sleep better with fresh air."

I close the curtains but leave the window half-open.

Eve sits on the edge of one of the beds and rummages through her bag. "He was acting strange, wasn't he?"

"Who? Wilson?" I rip off my bonnet and toss it onto the quilted bed cover. "Is he not normally like that?"

Eve slowly shakes her head. "I haven't seen him in near twenty years. It's hard to say."

I gather up the skirts of my dress and shimmy it over my head. I dig my dagger out of the deep pocket in the apron and roll the dress up into a ball.

"Maybe he's just upset that his business is dying," I say. "It's no surprise that there would be less travel between Bear Gap and LilyAye now."

"But that's just it," Eve says, twisting to face me. "He complained of no business, yet he seemed eager to push us out. He didn't even want to give us a room."

I kick off my boots and slip on one of my loose cotton shirts before plopping into bed.

"Reed wasn't exactly being nice to him. Maybe he just didn't want to help him," I say, placing my dagger on the nightstand.

Eve tilts her head as she looks over at me with a disapproving gaze.

"Your hair is very short," she says.

"Good night, Eve."

Rolling over, I shove my legs under the covers and ignore any further comments from Eve. The strange sounds of a new bedroom keep me from slumber. Eve blows out the last candle, and I listen to her nestle into her bed. The curtains flap gently from the open window.

I squeeze my eyes closed and eventually fall into a deep sleep. Soon, my head is engulfed by the ominous droning of horses' hooves. In my dream, I picture Portia atop a tall horse, riding down the LilyAye Road toward us. She's a vision in her long cape and pointy fingernails. Her shiny lips shimmer in the icy moonlight. I want her to leave, but the pounding of her horse riding toward me grows louder and louder.

I kick the blankets off my legs and groan; another dream about my mother. Karla torments me during the day, while Portia still visits me in my dreams. Only the nightmares aren't due to one of Portia's incantation. It's simply my own mental torment that keeps my mother in my thoughts.

Lying in bed, I stare at the pitched ceiling. I cock my head when I realize I still hear horses, and voices too. I go to the window and search the road. To my left, a small army of men and horses ride down the LilyAye Road, carrying torches. They wear black vests. A maroon *W* is burned into the breasts. They're Warwick soldiers.

CHAPTER FIVE

"EVE!" I GROAN, running to her bedside and shaking her awake.

I pull on my pants and throw my bag over my shoulder. Eve rolls over and rubs her eyes.

"Warwick soldiers," I say firmly. "They're coming down the road. We have to leave now!"

I grab my dagger from the nightstand and fly out the bedroom door. Bursting into Reed and Tuor's room, I practically rip Tuor from his bed.

"Wake up!" I say urgently yet quietly, not wanting to alert the soldiers of where we are.

"What's going on?" Tuor groans.

"Get your things."

I violently shake Reed. He swings over in his bed and pulls a knife on me.

"It's me. It's Camilla. There are Warwick soldiers outside. We have to go."

I rip the covers from Reed's bed.

"Now!" I moan.

Reed stumbles out of bed. I toss him his bag and push Tuor out of the bedroom door. Eve is in the hallway.

"I saw them," she whispers. "They're coming in here. Someone must have told them we're here."

"Come on," Reed says.

He leads us through the hallway and down the steps, pausing halfway down. Voices murmur outside the front door.

"The horses are in the stable. We have to get to them," Eve says.

I glance to the bar and catch Wilson standing in the shadowed corner as if watching what's about to take place.

"There," I tell Reed, pointing.

We fly down the steps, cross the dining room, and scurry behind the bar. Shock fills Wilson's face. He disappears through a door behind the bar. We follow, stumbling into the tavern kitchen. Tuor closes the door behind him as we hear the soldiers push open the tavern's front door. We listen as they take the creaky steps upstairs. Wilson stands with his back against the cast-iron stove.

"You did this," Reed spits. "You told them we were here."

Wilson sets his jaw but says nothing.

Eve's face twists in disgust. "How could you?"

"We have to find a way out of here," Tuor says. He walks the perimeter of the kitchen, searching for an exit.

Reed rushes across the kitchen and takes the old man's shirt in his hand. A pot behind him crashes against the stone wall. Wilson's face remains firm.

"Tell us how to get out of here!" Reed growls.

"How did you know who I am?" I ask.

Wilson looks at me curiously. "I don't know who you are. I only knew Eve's father from a long time ago."

"Then why did you turn us in?" I ask, walking a few paces closer to Wilson.

Upstairs, the soldiers march down the hallway, searching rooms.

Wilson's lips press tightly together. Reed squeezes harder on his shirt.

"Be careful," Eve says nervously.

"I turn everybody in," Wilson admits.

"What do you mean?" I ask.

The old man's face twists into a painful expression. His breathing quickens. "I have to tell them about everyone who stops here. They arrest anybody who gets close to the border. If I don't tell them, they'll kill me and my wife. Please, I'm sorry. I tried to get you to leave, but you insisted."

"You could have locked your doors if you really wanted to keep people from coming in here," I say.

"They make me keep the fires lit to attract travelers. I speak the truth!" Wilson says.

"Why not just arrest us at the checkpoint?" Eve asks.

"People escape into the woods, up the mountain. Hardly anyone travels the LilyAye Road anymore. It's too dangerous," Wilson says.

"What do they do with them, these people that they arrest?" Reed asks, pushing his face close to Wilson's.

Wilson turns his gaze downward. "I don't know . . ."

The soldiers upstairs shout to each other.

"They're gonna come down here," Wilson says. "I told them I have four people."

Eve stalks across the kitchen floor to Wilson.

"Do the right thing," she says firmly. "Get us out of here."

"How do people get to LilyAye if they're arresting everyone who comes through here?" I ask.

Wilson hesitates. He nervously looks from Reed to Eve. "There's a road. It's called Thieves' Road. It's the only way I know to get to LilyAye these days, but it's dangerous, very dangerous."

Reed loosens his grip, letting Wilson back onto his feet.

"More dangerous than the solders waiting out there for us?" I spit.

"You either get caught by the soldiers or the slavers," Wilson says. "The Supreme Ruler's dropped all slave-trade restrictions. There's been rumors they've taken people right off their own front porch."

The steps squeak as the soldiers empty into the dining room. I give Tuor a worried look.

"We'll take our chances with Thieves' Road," Reed says. "How do we get to it?"

"It's straight up the mountain behind us. Keep going. Eventually, you'll intersect a dirt road. Follow that over the mountain, and you'll see the walls of LilyAye."

"Let's go," Reed says, releasing Wilson's shirt.

The soldiers mill around in the dining room, their voices echoing through the whole tavern.

"Can you get us out of here?" Eve asks.

He nods. "If you go out this door, turn right. It'll take you into my apartment. There's a door that will lead you to the back of the tavern. I'll distract them."

Reed and I exchange an uneasy look. I pull my dagger, and we watch carefully as Wilson strides through the kitchen. He slowly opens the kitchen door and slips out into the dining room.

"Where are these people you told us about?" one of the soldier's barks.

"They caught wind," Wilson says calmly. "They turned around and headed back to Bear Gap."

"Is that so? And how'd they *catch wind*?" the soldier retorts.

"How should I know? I can show you which way they went," Wilson says.

We listen from the kitchen as Wilson exits the front door of the tavern. The soldiers slowly follow. We wait until the dining room sounds empty, then open the kitchen door slightly. Reed peeks out and motions for us to move. We push open another door at the end of the bar that opens into Wilson's room. An elderly woman wrapped in a blanket stands in the corner, shivering. She points to a thick wooden door at the end of the room.

"Please don't hurt me," she begs.

Reed pulls on the door, and we all scramble out the back of the tavern. Wilson's voice floats from out front as he tells the soldiers where we supposedly escaped to. We creep across the yard to the stables. I calmly stroke Shae's mane as I saddle her and untie her from the stall. The four of us pull our horses through the backyard, toward the tree line.

"They're over here!" a shrill voice screams. "Get them! They're going up the mountain!"

Wilson's wife stands at the side of the tavern, waving down the soldiers. She points in our direction. One of the soldiers turns and spots us.

"Move!" one of the soldiers yells.

We scurry into the trees like a nest of mice. I climb into Shae's saddle and push her up the foothills. Darkness engulfs us. Shae canters between the trees. I keep my head low and urge her forward. Below us, the soldier's lantern light bursts into the forest.

Although I can hear rustling on either side of me, when I quietly call out for Tuor, I get no reply. I sense distance growing between the four of us as we climb. Soon the soldiers' light disappears. The incline becomes too steep for Shae. I slide off and continue pulling her up the mountain. I grope through the woods, only hearing chirping and the wind through the trees.

The night wanes, and still I continue to climb. I tug on Shae's reins, begging her to move. I pause only for a moment to catch my breath. The soldiers could still be at our heels, so I keep going. My chest is tight from breathing in the cool, humid night air. I barely notice at first, but a golden morning glow begins to fill the woods. I search and find Eve climbing off to my left.

"I found the road," Reed calls from up ahead.

"Come on. Just a little farther," I tell Shae.

I join Reed and Eve, who are standing on a narrow dirt path that leads up the mountain.

"Has anyone seen Tuor?" I ask.

"He was right behind me," Eve says.

I look down the dewy mountainside and find Tuor scrambling up the steep incline.

"This is Thieves' Road?" I ask, settling my hands on my hips. "Not much of a road."

Tuor stumbles onto the dirt path, tugging his horse up the final step. He grabs the nearest tree and sucks in great gulps of air.

"Are you okay?" Eve asks, placing a hand on his back.

"Fine . . ." Tuor's voice is breathy. "It's been a while since I climbed a mountain."

"Should we keep going?" I ask.

"Yes. They could still be tracking us," Reed says.

Tuor moans as he wipes sweat from his brow. Eve hands him a canteen of water.

"No, please," Tuor begs. "We have to stop and rest."

"Hold on," Eve says. "Have we decided that we're going to take this Thieves' Road all the way to LilyAye?"

"What other choice do we have?" I ask.

"We should at least talk about it," Eve says.

Reed stands tall and scans the woods. He purses his lips. "We don't have time to talk about it. Besides the LilyAye Road isn't an option anymore. If they're arresting everyone, it doesn't matter how good our disguises are."

Eve leaves Tuor's side and comes to stand between Reed and me. "We could head down the road and back to Bear Gap. This may be a sign that we need to do more planning before taking this mission."

"No," Reed says firmly. "We're killing Quinten now. He travels in just a month. If we don't kill him then, we don't know when we'll get another chance."

"And what about these slavers that Wilson spoke of?" Eve asks.

"I'd heard the slave trade had worsened. We just need to be cautious," Reed says.

"We have to keep going regardless," I say. "We know about the slavers, so we can be on the lookout for them."

Eve lets out an unsatisfied sigh. Tuor joins us, taking another deep drink from Eve's canteen. His face is flushed red.

"Get it together, baby," I say, punching Tuor's shoulder. He hacks a cough and sucks in air.

"What about our food?" Tuor asks.

"Always thinking about food . . ." I tease.

Tuor lets out a fake chuckle. "We only packed enough food for a week. The LilyAye Road was supposed to take just a couple of days and we thought we'd be able to eat at the taverns along the way."

"Tuor is right," Eve says. "We don't know how long this road will take us to get to LilyAye. We should go back to Bear Gap, gather more supplies, and get some information on Thieves' Road. Send word to your spies. Find out what they know about it. We don't know what lies ahead."

Reed glares at Eve. "We're not going back to Bear Gap for a few loaves of bread. There is food in these woods. We can hunt."

Eve folds her arms across her chest and shakes her head. "Fine."

"Saddle up," Reed announces. "We'll ride a little farther up the road until we find a safe spot to make camp."

Eve's face is pinched into a sour expression as she mounts her horse. A part of me enjoys seeing her outranked by Reed.

"It's a shame you can't keep up with a kitchen maid," I say to Tuor as I pull myself up onto Shae, settling into her saddle.

"Ha-ha," Tuor says mockingly.

Reed leads the way up the mountain. The rugged trail is fraught with rocks and roots. It's bordered tightly on either side with thick trees so that we have to ride in a line. I continually scan the woods for signs of the tavern soldiers, but the mountain is surprisingly serene.

A yawn escapes my lips. The rocking of Shae's body could put me to sleep as the adrenaline from the night's escape wears off. We ride for another hour before Reed is satisfied that we've put enough distance between us and the soldiers. A few minutes' ride off the road, we stop and make camp. I yawn again as I unroll my bed mat onto the leafy forest floor.

"I'll keep watch while you all sleep for a few hours," Reed says.

"How are you gonna stay awake?" I ask, concerned.

"I'll be fine," Reed says nonchalantly as he sits himself up against the trunk of a tree.

The circles under his eyes are darker than normal, giving him away. I notice a slight tick in his hand, but I'm too tired to argue with him. I collapse onto my bed mat and fall asleep immediately. I wake to the noonday sun piercing through the leaves. Eve and Tuor lie motionless next to me. Their fingers are loosely linked together as they sleep.

My suspicions are correct. Tuor's sudden agreeability with Eve is because he likes her. By the looks of it, she likes him too. I bring my knees up to my chest and spot Reed still sitting by a tree, awake.

"How are you feeling?" I ask, taking a seat next to him.

Reed's eyelids hang heavy. "I've stayed up this long before."

"Thanks for getting us out of that tavern," I say.

"You're the one who saw the soldiers."

"Yeah, but you led the way out." I stare at a millipede as it crawls in front of my bare feet. "And I think you made the right decision continuing on to LilyAye. There's going to be trouble no matter which direction we go."

"Eve is scared. We can't have terrified people on this mission," Reed says.

He scans the woods with a determined gaze. Imagining Reed as the Supreme Ruler has always felt like a future dream but watching him fight sleep for our safety makes me see him as a true leader for the first time.

"I'll keep watch," I say. "You sleep."

Reed takes a deep breath. "Are you sure?"

I nod and watch as Reed grunts to standing and then drops onto my bed mat drifting off to sleep. Sometimes, I see Reed as just another entitled Warwick, but there's more to him. He was born to lead. I wonder if I spoke too soon when I rejected him back in Bear Gap.

After a few hours of sleep and a quick meal from our food reserves, we mount up and continue our climb. The sun warms my cheeks. The trees thin, and the mountainside becomes a rocky cliff. The footing grows too hard on the horses, so we're forced to walk. The pace up the mountain is slow and painful.

"Come on, girl," I beg, pulling on Shae's reins. My knees are bent sharply as I lean into the steepness. She shakes her head and snorts in disapproval. I'm achy and exhausted. The air thins, making it harder to catch my breath.

For two more days, we drag our horses up the steep, rocky mountainside at an agonizingly slow pace. Making camp is difficult on this incline. If it weren't for my extreme exhaustion, I would struggle to sleep on the rough terrain. The leaves have begun to turn red and golden. We inch up the mountain as it grows to a narrow peak.

The trail leads us to the edge of the mountainside to a rocky cliff. It's a narrow platform that curves around the mountain. There's no railing to keep from falling, and the trail looks no bigger than a few feet across. The four of us stand in a line, hesitating, staring at the cliff's edge.

"I am not walking out there," Eve says sternly. She pulls the lapels of her jacket close to her chest and holds her chin high over her scarf. "There has to be another way over this mountain."

"This is the way the road brought us," Reed says.

Eve's eyes widen as she pitches forward to catch a sight of the gorge below.

"It's not going to get any easier by staring at it," I say.

"Secure all your belongings," Reed tells us. "It looks windy out there."

I tighten Shae's saddle, check that my bags are attached, and even button my coat all the way up. Reed is the first to step onto the ledge. He leads his horse behind him. I follow, immediately feeling a cold breeze as I walk fully exposed onto the cliff.

The gray sky opens to reveal low-hanging clouds. A black raven soars around the mountain. He lands on an extended branch above us. His caws echo across the open cavern of space that exists between this mountain and the next. Wind swirls through the trees and funnels rapidly between the mountain peaks. I clutch Shae's reins and lead her forward one step at a time.

"This is insane," Eve says in a breathy voice behind me. "This is insane," she mutters again.

I peer down the mountainside. Being up this high doesn't frighten me, but when Shae knocks a rock loose with her hoof, I watch as it trips and tumbles down the tree-covered cliff and imagine that rock being me. I wait for the sound of the rock to hit the bottom, but that sound never comes. It seems the gorge is so deep it simply absorbs anything it encounters.

"Keep your eyes straight ahead!" Reed yells back to us.

I decide to take his advice. Instead of ruminating on how many people have probably fallen to their deaths on this cliff, I look forward and focus on the gentle curve of the trail. I take little toddler steps, putting one foot in front of the other.

The next step I take, I feel a tug on Shae's reins. She whinnies softly behind me. I stop and carefully turn around to see that Shae's hoof is stuck. I let out a shaky breath as I peer across the open gorge.

"Why aren't you moving?" Eve asks desperately from behind my horse.

"Shea's stuck," I announce to the whole group.

Reed stops on the ledge. "You have to pull her out."

Keeping my back against the mountain's edge, I inch my way to Shae. She skitters on her feet, knocking a smattering of pebbles loose. It feels like the whole mountain is moving.

"Steady girl," I mutter under my breath as I kneel to inspect her foot. Her leg is half-bent, and the tip of her hoof is wedged into a crevice. I grasp both hands around her leg. *Breathe*, I tell myself.

"Careful!" Tuor yells to me. "The wind is picking up!"

I pull on Shae's leg with a swift tug. Her foot doesn't break loose, and again she shuffles on her feet, getting ever closer to the edge. Terror builds in my chest as a tingly feeling emanates down my arms and fingers.

"Camilla, stop," Reed calls to me. "Try the hatchet. It's in my bag."

I slowly come to my feet and lean against the side of the mountain. An icy wind flows across my face and ripples Shae's mane. Reed unties a bag from his horse and sets it on the ground. He riffles through the bag where we keep our tools and the sacks of grain and dried meat.

He pulls out the hatchet, but his horse stands between us. I scoot as close to the rump of his horse as I can while still holding onto Shae's reins. Reed stretches the handle of the hatchet across his horse. I strain as I reach for it. Finally, I feel the wood handle and wrap my fingers around it.

A sudden gust of wind knocks me against the mountainside. My stomach drops. Shae whinnies loudly, and on the other side of Reed's horse, I hear something slide off the ledge and tumble down the mountainside.

CHAPTER SIX

"REED!" I FALL to my knees and peer through the legs of Reed's horse, expecting to see an empty spot on the ledge. Instead, Reed is hunched over, his face in his hand. He lifts his head and angrily chews on his lower lip. He curses under his breath.

"What was that?" I ask.

"The bag," he says without looking at me. "The bag fell."

Fear trickles down my spine. "The one with our food?"

Reed nods. He balls his hands into fists and looks around as if he might punch the mountain.

"Take care of your horse," he instructs. Finally, he lifts his head and looks at me. "Do *not* fall."

Standing, I inch my way back over to Shae.

"What's taking so long?" Eve asks in a hysterical high pitch.

"Is everyone okay?" Tuor calls.

"Yes." For now, I think to myself.

I bend again to Shae's foot and carefully wedge the blade of the hatchet into the crevice. The tingly feeling returns to my limbs as I picture Shae being thrown from the cliff's edge by another gust of wind.

Focus, I tell myself. Slowly, I wiggle the blade while gently pulling on her leg. She scuttles backward half a step. I dig the hatchet deeper into the crevice, and with one more tug on Shae's leg, her foot pops loose. I hold tight to her reins as she regains her footing. "I got it!"

Without a word, Reed continues his walk forward. I urge Shae along, now having to carry the heavy hatchet the rest of the way. The trail guides us off the cliff. We empty into a patch of thick pine trees.

Eve takes in deep gasps of air as she steps off the ledge into the safety of the forest. Tuor follows close behind her.

"What happened out there?" Tuor asks as the four of us gather.

Reed's fists clench as he cracks his knuckles in frustration. "We lost the bag with our food."

"What?" Eve shouts in a frenzy.

"The wind blew it off when he got me the hatchet," I say.

Eve puts a hand on her hip. She stares daggers at Reed as she says, "Aren't you the one who told us to secure our bags?"

"It was an accident," I say. "He was trying to help me."

Reed looks at Eve under heavy eyebrows. "There's nothing to be done about it now. It happened. We move forward."

"How do we move forward without any food?" Eve asks.

"What about the food you brought?" Tuor directs the question at Eve.

Eve stares at Tuor wide eyed as if he wasn't supposed to reveal that secret.

"You brought your own food?" I ask.

"Just in case," she says. "But my supply is for *me*. It's only enough for one person, not four."

"It will have to do," Reed says.

Eve breathes heavily through her nose like a snorting bull. She looks behind her at the terrifying cliff we just walked across.

"This is your fault," she says through gritted teeth.

"It's not his fault!" I shout. "You just can't move on. If this trip is too much for you, maybe you should go home."

Tuor looks at me with a ready reprimand. "Camilla—"

"I don't need you to defend me," Reed snaps at me.

Eve speaks. "You think you can restore Elmyra to a free land, but you can't even get us to LilyAye alive."

Reed clenches his jaw and looks down at Eve with an icy stare. "You forget yourself, woman. We're moving forward up this mountain. If anybody wants to turn back, they're welcome to, but Camilla and I are finishing this mission."

Reed mounts his horse as if to put an end to the conversation. Tuor shakes his head and gives me a disappointed gaze. A pang of guilt hits me in the chest. Tuor takes a fuming Eve by the elbow, and the two talk.

"Do you want to go back to Bear Gap?" Tuor asks in a low voice.

Panic bubbles inside me as I realize they're considering leaving, and that would mean being separated from Tuor.

"No, you can't leave. We have to stick together, or we will die up here," I say.

Eve glares at me. She goes to her horse, grips the pommel, and pulls herself into the saddle. "Don't worry, Camilla. I'm not abandoning this mission yet. You can't get rid of me that easily."

Tuor follows her lead. I stagger backward as they ride through the clearing and into the trees. I'm not giving up yet either. I secure the hatchet in my saddle bag, mount Shae, and continue up Thieves' Road.

We ride over a forest floor covered in pine needles. The fir trees shield us from the sun, taking away the midday warmth we'd become accustomed to. The air grows cooler as we climb. That night we find a soft place to make camp. The tension is thick as no one speaks. We sit around the fire in silence as Eve divvies out our share of her food supply.

Reed gnaws on his jerky, appearing completely unperturbed by the argument at the cliff. I wish I could adopt his steely demeanor. I glance across the fire at Eve and can't even manage to look her in the eyes.

The next day, we enter a forest so dense that we can barely see the sun. The trail weaves in and out of the trees like a wandering stream. The branches sway and rustle with the cold breeze. The mountain has grown quiet. Nobody seems interested in conversation. Two teams have formed: Tuor and Eve against me and Reed.

That night we eat another meager dinner. We've gotten into the habit of only eating a little in the morning and at night. It's just enough food to keep us moving. Between the bits of food and thinner air, it feels like we're crawling up this mountain.

A few days bleed into a week. We see nothing but those same dense woods. The trail continues to slope upward at a steady pace, and we get almost no relief from the incline. There isn't a muscle in my body that's not sore. My legs are like wet rags. Every step steals a breath from my lungs. I struggle to even put one foot in front of the other.

The low light of evening bathes the trees in a gray-blue haze. Tuor and Eve sit across the fire from me. Eve is wrapped in a woolen blanket. Her head rests heavily on Tuor's visibly bony shoulder. Reed tosses little sticks into the fire as he lays on his side. The flames illuminate his gaunt face.

"Should we forage again?" I ask with a scratchy voice.

"There's no point," Reed says quickly. "There's nothing up here."

I pull my jacket tightly around my middle and lean into the warm flames. "Then let's go hunting again. There are squirrels and rabbits—"

"No point," Reed says, punctuating each word. "It's too dark to see a tiny squirrel. None of us are that skilled. We live off Quinten's farm. That's all we know." Reed rolls over onto his back and rubs his eyes. "That's why we have to kill him. We have to kill him . . ."

"We don't have the energy to forage anyway," Tuor says in a flat voice.

The argument at the cliff diminishes each day we grow closer to starvation.

"How much food do we have left?" I ask Eve.

She lazily lifts her head and pulls her bag close. "Some stale bread, a touch of jam, and just a little bit of oats."

"That isn't going to last us past tomorrow," I say.

"We know that!" Reed moans from his spot on the ground.

"Then what should we do?" I ask.

"Ask Reed. He's in charge," Eve says derisively.

I look down at Reed, who's rocking back and forth on the forest floor as if he were writhing in pain. That bold image of a leader I saw in him at the beginning of this trip has faded.

"We have more strength now than we will in two days when we're eating nothing," I say. "We should use all the energy we have now to find more food. Maybe we can set a trap or—"

"Stop it!" Reed shouts. "Stop talking. My head!"

"I don't care about your head!" I snap back. "We're days from dying of starvation. Soldiers could still be at our back, tracking our every step. If they attack, we couldn't run or fight. We have to try something!"

Reed grunts as he scrambles to his feet. He staggers toward me.

"Everyone needs to silence their complaining. *I* am leading *you*." The twitch in Reed's hand is now an unsteady shaking. "You do as I say, and what I say right now is that we will continue up this mountain until we find food. We're not doing anymore hunting or foraging tonight. We sleep."

Reed staggers backward and places a hand on his forehead. He digs a blanket from his saddlebag and plops onto his bed mat, near the fire. His thin body soon turns still as he drifts off to sleep. I groan, resting my face in my hands.

"He can't stop me if he's passed out." I rise quickly, feeling a burst of lightheadedness.

"Where are you going?" Tuor asks.

"To look for food. I'm not dying up here."

I retrieve my bow and quiver from my bag and dive into the darkening woods. I grope from tree to tree, determined to shoot and kill something tonight. The rush of my anger pushes me a few minutes' walk from our camp, but soon I'm struggling for air.

My head swims. I stop and lean my back against a tree. My stomach rolls with hunger. The dissension in our group makes my heart ache. I bend and slide down the tree, dropping my bow next to me. Tears fill my eyes as I rest my forehead on my knees.

My mind turns to Mirabelle and the food she used to cook for me: stews, mushroom cakes, roasted parsnips. I consider what I'd do to have a plate of her mushroom cakes right now. Dying of starvation on this mountain is a reality I must face. Should I have ever left Bear Gap?

What if I never speak to Mirabelle again? The thought grips me. A tenderness blooms in my heart for her, and I actually consider forgiving her. What's the point of a grudge if I die burdened with bitterness?

Soft, wet flakes trickle through the trees. I hold out my hand and catch the falling snow. It's winter up here already. A soft dusting accumulates around me. I wipe my tears as darkness envelops me like a frosty hug.

When I reach down to grab my bow and arrow, my hand grazes a tuft of thick grass and twigs. A nest is burrowed next to me with a tiny round hole on the front. I recognize it. We used to get similar nests on the farm. I laugh audibly and lift my head to thank the heavens. We'll live another day.

***

At the break of morning, everyone gnaws on the bodies of the mountain mice I found. They're bigger than the field mice that infest the farm. I tell Reed that I found the nest near Shae, so that he doesn't know I went out hunting.

"I told you we'd find food," Reed says, tossing a mouse bone into the fire. "You all worry too much. We're nearly at the top. Let's keep going."

Reed is back to his old self, bossy yet in control. We load up and continue on. By midmorning, we're hiking straight up the mountain, through a thin layer of snow. Riding is impossible. My breath is heavy in my chest as I pull Shae up the steep mountainside. Days of hard travel have left me achy all over.

My legs burn. My shoulder spasms from tugging on Shae's reins. The blue sky peeks out as I approach the precipice. I take the final steps and nearly collapse at the peak of the mountain. I drop Shea's reins and walk through a small patch of thinning trees.

A foggy mist creeps across my feet. The air is nippy with ice crystals. The snow-covered ground turns into slippery rock and shale. Slowly, the trees open up to reveal an immense sky. Tuor and Eve stand on the edge of the cliff while Reed hangs back with his horse. Despite my weariness, a surge of energy rushes into my limbs. I jog to Tuor and stop just short of the mountain's edge.

"Careful," Tuor says, grabbing my elbow.

I take a deep breath as a gust of wind sweeps past us. We're in the clouds. White fog envelops us like a cool, damp pillow. I inch my toes to the edge of the cliff. The side of the mountain is speckled with pine trees and bushes. A magnificent gorge lies miles below us. The soft rumble of water rushing through the valley wafts to our ears.

"It's beautiful," Eve breathes. Her face is pale. No matter how many times she runs her hand over her hair to smooth it, frizzy strands pop up all over.

"It almost makes the climb worth it," Tuor says with a weak chuckle.

I take a deep breath and close my eyes against the misty breeze. Something about being up so high, and feeling so free, makes me burst with energy. I feel like I'm back on the roof of the Bear Gap House.

Eve shivers. "I'll get a fire going," she says before leaving Tuor and me alone on the cliff's edge.

"I should help her," Tuor says quickly.

"Wait." I reach for Tuor's arm. "Can we talk?"

"Fine."

We peer out across the open expanse. I suddenly feel awkward around Tuor. "I know about you and Eve."

Tuor stiffens his back. "So?"

"So . . . why didn't you tell me?" My tone is accusing.

"It doesn't concern you."

I tilt my head and give Tuor a look of insult. "You're my brother. Of course it concerns me."

"You didn't tell me when things were going on between you and Johnny earlier this year."

"That was different. We knew that Knox wouldn't approve and—"

"Doesn't matter. Camilla follows the rules she wants to." Tuor's gaze is focused straight ahead. The clouds around us swirl and twist from the wind. I imagine that it's Tuor's frustration causing the turmoil.

"This isn't like you," I say. "Secretive, angry."

"I don't have to tell you everything."

"I know that." I drop my head. "She's so much older than you, though."

Tuor gives me a disgusted look. "You don't get it. You've been nothing but unkind to her. Maybe that's why I didn't tell you."

The wind whistles as it rushes through the narrow gorge below.

"We're civil with each other."

"Barely," Tuor says.

"Okay, you're right. I admit that. We're not exactly friends."

Tuor turns to face me. "You don't like her. Just say it."

"Fine. I don't like her."

Tuor scoffs and turns from me again.

"But if *you* like her . . . I just don't want us to fight anymore."

"Is that your pathetic attempt to apologize?"

"I'm sorry. I am sorry for what I said at the cliff, and I'm sorry that I haven't been the nicest to Eve." I take a deep breath. "Can you forgive me?"

Tuor nods. "I guess."

I slip my arm around Tuor's bony frame and give my big brother a side hug. He tugs me close and squeezes my shoulders before releasing me.

"I'm kind of jealous of you two. Sometimes I wish things had worked out with Johnny and me." I pick at my fingernails. "I'm technically the one who ended it, but there are days that I think he'll come back and tell me that he still loves me."

"You need to let Johnny go," Tuor says softly.

"Why?" I protest.

"If he still loved you, he'd be here."

"Yeah, but he doesn't know—"

"If Eve were on this mountain, or in a snake pit, nothing would keep me from being by her side. That's how men are. If he still loved you, he would have never let you out of his sight."

Tuor's words wash over me as the sun settles behind the horizon. I never thought I'd be miles from home, standing atop a magnificent mountain peak, when I realized that Johnny truly doesn't love me anymore.

CHAPTER SEVEN

"WE SHOULD HELP set up camp," I say.

"Actually, there's something I wanted to talk to you about too," Tuor says. "Eve has some concerns with Reed, and . . . I share her concerns."

I take a deep breath. I was afraid of this. "About what?" I feign ignorance.

Tuor lowers his voice. "You know, just the way he's been handling the food supply, and last night he acted really erratic."

"He seems better today."

"I'm keeping a close eye on him," Tuor says as he pats the sword hanging from his belt.

My eyes widen. "He wouldn't hurt us."

"Are you sure?" Tuor says in a worried tone. "The way he yelled at us last night . . . Eve is worried, and I don't blame her."

I open my mouth to speak but find myself at a loss for words. I turn around and peek at Reed. He stokes the fire and slowly adds sticks to bring it to life.

"We can't forget that he's still a Warwick," Tuor says.

"He fought on our side during the Bear Gap rebellion. He risked his life for us then. I have no reason to doubt him."

"Just stay vigilant," Tuor says.

***

After a meager dinner of stale bread and the scrapings of Eve's jam jar, I sneak back to the cliff alone. I sit on the edge and let my feet dangle. The night has grown dark, and I can't see much except where the crescent moon casts a deep blue haze on the edge of the mountains.

The wind whistles among the treetops. In the distance, a coyote howls. He chatters with his pack. A whole group of them run along the ravine below, then find some prey and chase the poor creature down until the yelping stops.

I pull my knees up to my chin and hug my legs. The peaceful feeling begins to morph into loneliness. I miss Johnny. Almost every minute of every day, I wonder where he is and what he's doing. I miss his arms holding me, and right now in the cold evening, I imagine those arms wrapping tightly around my shoulders.

Another howl from the coyotes pulls me out of my reverie. Dampness hangs in the air. Why did I ever turn my back on Johnny? At the time, it seemed like a good idea, the right thing to do. Now, tonight, I can't remember why. It doesn't matter anymore. I won't continue to love a man who doesn't love me. Tuor's words bounce around in my head. I sigh audibly and stare into the clear sky. A foggy breath leaves my mouth, and I symbolically let Johnny go from my heart and into the night air.

***

I open my eyes the next morning to a forest blanketed in a thin, silvery layer of snow. I gasp as I shake the mounds of white fluff off my quilt. My hands are like ice. My cheeks and the tip of my nose feel frozen. It's early. The sun is barely visible through the branches.

A fire crackles nearby. I stand and stretch. Eve squats next to the fire and balances a tin pot of water on the flames. Her petite body shivers despite the blanket she holds around her shoulders. Tiny bubbles form as steam rises from the pot.

"Finally, someone else is awake," Eve says.

I roll my eyes as I kneel next to the fire to warm my hands and face. Eve reaches into a bag that's lying next to the fire. She pulls out a small burlap sack that's nearly empty and proceeds to pour some oats into the now boiling water. She dumps what's left in the bag and gives the pot a stir. I watch with interest as the grains boil and slowly expand.

"I'm sorry about what I said at the cliff," I say, forcing the words out before Eve says something else to annoy me.

Eve keeps her eyes pinned to the boiling oats. She hands me a spoon and we eat straight from the pot.

"Holding a grudge right now would be pointless," Eve says.

I shove a spoonful of thick oats into my mouth. Eve stares at me from across the fire. Reed yawns loudly as he emerges from the fog and stumbles toward the fire. He brushes snow from his pants and rubs his arms with his hands to create heat.

"You have any of that left?" Reed asks, pointing at the pot.

She hands Reed a spoon from her bag and then passes over the pot. Reed dives into the porridge like a ravenous animal. I anxiously wait for Reed to hand the oats back to us. I've hardly satisfied my hunger, and Tuor needs to eat too.

Finally, Reed hands me the pot, and I shove another spoonful in my mouth.

"That's the last of it," Eve says, loudly. Her voice is crisp as it lands on the soft snow.

"Of the oats?" I ask.

"Of the *food*."

I swallow, but it doesn't go down as easily this time.

"We're out of food," Eve says. "We have nothing for dinner tonight."

I bite my lower lip and put my spoon into the pot and set it aside. I knew this was coming, the end of our food. I look to Reed. He says nothing, just flings bits of leaves and sticks into the fire.

"We're now trapped on the top of this mountain with no food," Eve continues.

Again, Reed says nothing. Eve stares at him, begging for a response.

"We need to make a plan," Eve says.

"I have a plan," Reed snaps back.

Eve laughs derisively. "And what is it?"

"We keep going until we find an inn or a town or somewhere we can find supplies." Reed's tone is annoyed. He walks to his horse and starts rummaging through his saddlebag.

I follow, feeling a sudden rush of blood pumping through my body. "You need to give Eve an answer. She's about to lose it."

"Camilla, I do not need advice from you."

I bristle, taking an insult from Reed for the last time. "You do need my advice since I'm the only one who's managed to find food for us."

Reed grinds his teeth. He flexes his hand in and out as if to stop the shaking. For a second, I think he's going to explode, but instead he turns to me and says, "Then what would you suggest?"

"We need to go hunting. We should stop traveling an hour before sunset. Two of us can go out hunting together while the other two set up camp. We have to try."

Reed drops the flap on his saddlebag. "Fine, we'll do it your way."

He walks away, and I'm left standing in the snow by the horses. I wake Tuor, and we quickly pack and start our descent down the mountain. The sun reflects off the snow in blinding shimmers. Thieves' Road follows along the edge of the mountain so that we have a view of the open expanse above the gorge. A crystal-blue sky surrounds us, and the warm sun is a welcome relief from last night's snowfall.

The surrounding mountains are like towering beasts compared to the peak that we're traversing. Patches of white cover the tops of some of the other mountains. Even with the beauty of our surroundings, we find the trail downhill almost harder than the climb up. The horses struggle to take the steep downward decline. The tops of my knees ache, and I trip constantly on the tree roots.

"All right, Camilla. Let's go," Reed says when we make our stop for the evening. "We'll hunt while you two set up camp."

Reed and I venture into the woods. A chilly mixture of snow and rain begins to fall. I pull a hood over my head and secure my jacket tightly around my neck. At least the snow will make it easy for us to find our way back to camp. My foot lands on a muddy spot. I slip. Reed grabs me under my arms and places me back on my feet. A flock of birds flutters from the tree above me.

"Thanks," I mutter.

"You have to be quiet to hunt," Reed says. "I at least know that much."

"Being quiet isn't my best quality."

Reed chuckles softly.

"Are you okay? You've been lashing out at everyone lately."

Reed softly steps through the slushy snow. "It's just the stress of our mission."

"You need to be careful, or you're going to start developing enemies."

Reed scowls at me. "Has somebody said something to you?"

"Just try to be more agreeable, okay?"

Reed's face softens. He stops and leans his hand against a tree. "I haven't been at my best. The closer we get to LilyAye, the more anxious I feel at the thought of coming face-to-face with my uncle. Remembering the things he did to me ... He humiliated me as a teenager and ever since then he's been trying to have me killed. It all comes to the front of my mind as this becomes more real."

I tug on the strap of my quiver and lean against the tree so our bodies are only inches apart.

"I hadn't thought of that," I say.

Reed shakes his head. "We've all been through hurt in our lives. I've let that pain turn me into an unpleasant person. It's not an excuse, just a reality."

Reed's words make the guilt I've been feeling over Eve lessen. There's something about the pain behind Reed's eyes that I see in myself.

"I understand. If you feel that way again, perhaps you could come and talk it out with me instead of fighting with others."

A flirtatious smile spreads across Reed's face. "I'd be all right with that."

Wet snowflakes plop on our heads. Our eyes connect. Reed leans in and places his cold lips on mine. He plants his hand firmly on the small of my back and pulls me close. My whole body jolts. I shove him off before I have a chance to register what happened. Reed gives me a gentle scowl. My breath comes quickly.

"Did you push me away because you were surprised or because you still don't have feelings for me?" Reed asks nonchalantly.

I hesitate, not sure of the answer myself. "You caught me off guard."

Reed slowly places his hand on my hip. He bends and kisses me gingerly. This time I allow myself to feel it and not be scared. His lips move softly yet passionately. It's different from Johnny, and I relish this new feeling. Satisfaction fills Reed's face as he emerges from our embrace.

"We should probably do some actual hunting before the sun sets," he says with a smirk.

We return to camp an hour later empty-handed. I'm intentional about keeping my demeanor resolute and not showing any hint of what took place in the woods. How can I feel so cheerful when I don't know where my next meal is coming from?

The next morning, I roll over on my bed mat and feel a hollow ache in my gut. I take a long drink from my waterskin just to have something to fill my stomach. I sit on my bed and massage a cramp in my calf. Eve digs out some onion grass she found in the snow. It's not a lot, but we eat it.

Reed calls us to ride again. We all mount up and continue our journey down the rugged terrain. For most of the day, we're able to ride the horses, but when again it becomes too steep, we walk our horses carefully down the mountain.

I catch Reed's eyes. He gives me a charming smile. I blush in spite of myself. It feels odd to have fallen into a tryst with Reed. He can be so condescending sometimes, but despite the troubles he's gone through, he still grew up wealthy and privileged. Maybe he just can't help but be haughty, I reason.

The morning disappears. All afternoon we hobble down the trail. Eve stumbles down a rocky hill and grips her horse's reins, coming to a stop at a small landing. She groans in frustration as she drops her hands to her thighs and breathes heavily.

"Blast these rocks!" she yells. "They're cutting right through my shoes!"

Eve rips off her right boot and reveals a bleeding toe. The blood drips onto the white snow. She grabs a piece of cloth from her bag and wraps it around her toe. Tuor comes to her side, holding Eve up by her shoulders. She winces as she places her foot back in her boot.

Tuor looks at Eve helplessly. "I'm gonna go look for some more onion grass. That will help." He jogs into the woods.

"It would be good for us to rest," I say, leaning against a tree.

"We can find you a new pair of boots when we get to the next town," Reed says.

"When's that going be?" Eve asks. Her voice is laced with irritation. "We've been climbing this mountain for weeks. We can't live off grass forever."

"We have to be close," I say, trying to quell Eve's rising hysteria.

"Close isn't going to matter if we all die first," Eve says.

Reed stands with his hands on his hips. His face is pale and placid. "I'm handling this. We'll get some food."

Eve gently places weight on her foot. She limps closer to Reed. "When? When are we going to get food? How do we know you didn't lead us up this mountain just to kill us?" Eve's voice rises. "You've been spinning a thread of lies since we left."

"That's not true," I say. "Reed's the one that's pushing us forward."

"All he's been doing is insulting all of us," Eve says.

Eve's blunt accusation brings an icy silence from Reed. His fists quivers.

I take a tentative step toward Eve. "Calm down. We're close. Just hold on a little longer."

Eve presses her lips together. She lifts a finger and points it at Reed. "If we hadn't taken this wretched road and you hadn't dropped the bag that had all the food in it, we wouldn't be in this position!"

"You better stop, woman," Reed says, staring Eve down.

Eve's eyes blaze. "Woman? I am your equal on this mission."

"He didn't mean it like that," I say.

A condescending laugh pours from Reed's lips. He then gathers himself and manages a straight face as he says, "You're hardly my equal in this or anything else."

Eve's face is red. Like a tea kettle, she's ready to boil over.

"Hey," I say, trying to catch Reed's eyes, but they're burrowing into Eve. "We're all just hungry."

My words fall into a void.

"You could never be the ruler of Elmyra," Eve spits.

Reed's veins pop from his neck. He looks at her through fiery eyes. I feel for my dagger. Reed raises his hand and slaps Eve across the cheek. She moans, grabbing her face in pain.

"Does hitting a woman make you feel like a strong ruler?" Eve shouts.

"Stop," I say, grabbing Reed's arm. He flings me off.

I fall onto my backside. Reed dives toward Eve. He grabs Eve's thin shoulder and holds it while he slaps her again. Blood appears under Eve's nose.

"Shut up, woman!" he yells while he shakes her body.

Eve screams as she scratches at Reed's face and eyes. My hand slips on the muddy snow as I struggle to stand. Eve's tiny legs kick and flail. She strikes his groin. Reed groans but keeps his hands on Eve. I jump to my feet and pull on Reed's arm. His grip is like an iron vise.

"Tuor!" I shout. "Tuor! Help!"

Reed slams his foot into Eve's foot. She screams in agony. Her body twists as she falls to the ground. Eve's face is white with horror. She grabs at her ankle. Like a vicious animal after its prey, Reed pounces. I throw my body in front of his brick-like chest.

"Tuor!" I scream again.

Tuor flies from the woods. He slams into Reed, and together, we tackle him to the ground. Tuor throws a punch to the side of Reed's head. Tuor's face contorts in rage as his wiry arms flail and hit Reed in the nose with an audible *crack*.

Reed's elbow swings and hits me in the eye. I'm knocked back on my heels. Reed attempts to hold Tuor off by wrapping his hands around Tuor's neck, but neither man relents. Tuor pummels Reed. Using both his arms, Reed flings Tuor off him, knocking him to the ground.

Tuor's shoulder lands on a sharp rock. He cries out in pain. Reed is unfazed. He rolls over and punches Tuor in the face once, twice, three times before I can get to him. It's so fast, I barely blink, and Tuor's face is bleeding. My blood boils. I link my arm through Reed's to stop the hitting, but he's driven by rage.

"Stop! Get off him!" I shout. "Get off of him!"

I wrap my hands around Reed's neck to choke him, but he doesn't notice. I clutch my dagger and press the cool blade to his neck.

"Stop or I'll slice you open," I growl.

CHAPTER EIGHT

REED'S ARMS STOP moving. His shoulders heave up and down with rapid breaths. I release my arm from around his neck but keep my dagger pointed at him.

"Get off my brother!" I bellow.

Reed moves slowly as he rolls off Tuor's body and sits awkwardly on the ground. The muscles in his face are tensed. His jaw is set and rigid. A purply bruise is forming around his left eye as the skin begins to puff.

I stand, keeping my arm outstretched. Eve moans. She flails in the snow while gripping her ankle. Tuor sits up. Blood oozes from between his fingers as he holds his nose. He wipes away the blood and crawls to Eve. Reed catches his breath, looking completely undisturbed.

My face contorts in confusion. "What is wrong with you?"

Reed stands suddenly and brushes dirt off his clothes. My dagger follows his every move. He rolls his jaw and wipes droplets of blood from his face. The fog of rage seems to drift away as his expression softens.

Reed lets out an uncomfortable laugh and says, "Just two men roughhousing. That's how we settle things. No need to point that dagger at me."

"Roughhousing? You beat them both to a pulp!"

"She provoked *me*!" Reed says, his voice rising.

"That's no reason to—"

"All I've been doing is trying to keep this mission together, and this little witch has been down my throat about every little move that she doesn't like. This is what I get?"

"You're a maniac. You need help!"

Reed flares his nostrils as he stares at me intently. "That's what everyone else says. It must be true." Reed speaks through gritted teeth. He glances at Eve and Tuor as if he's hoping one of them will defend him, but they're not paying him any attention. "We can't let this stop us. Everyone, just apologize, and let's get back on the road."

"I wouldn't apologize if I had to slice you in two," I say.

"No. Come on. We're bound to have disagreements, but we have to stick together," Reed says as he steps closer to me.

"Get away from me."

I hold my dagger with more resolve. Reed's body shakes with anger. It's like he's holding back a fireball of rage within his chest.

"Fine. This is how you want it to be? You need me. You won't get far on Thieves' Road without me. I hope the wildcats get you."

He curses under his breath before mounting his horse and riding down the mountain, out of sight. A sinking feeling fills my stomach. Reed Warwick, the future ruler of Elmyra, has now become our enemy.

***

Tuor calls my name for the third time. His voice pulls me from a swamp of dark thoughts. I realize I'm still standing with my dagger outstretched even though Reed has been gone for several minutes.

"Camilla!" Tuor shouts again. "I need your help."

I secure my dagger back on my belt, but I'm keenly aware of its presence in case Reed returns. I come to Eve's side. She's thrashing from side to side and moaning like a woman giving birth.

"It's her leg," Tuor says. His voice is shaky. He wipes more blood from his face.

"I have a towel in my bag. Go put it on your nose," I tell him.

I suddenly notice the stinging in my own eye where Reed elbowed me. Tuor obeys, and I'm left alone with Eve momentarily. Her face is flushed and sweaty. She won't let go of her ankle.

"Eve," I say calmly. "Let me look at your leg, okay?"

She continues to cry out as if she doesn't even know I'm there. I pull her hand away to reveal a round bulge protruding from her ankle. Already, the area around the bulge is swollen twice the size as her healthy ankle. Tuor returns, dropping to his knees and gasping at the sight of Eve.

"What's wrong with her ankle?" he whispers.

"I don't know," I admit.

I'm in over my head. If Mirabelle were here, she'd know what to do. I reach out and gently touch the part of her leg that's sticking out. Eve cries in pain. Tuor takes her hand and talks softly to her while I get a closer look.

It has to be her bone. It's hard and stiff. Eve may have a broken leg. I look up at her, feeling completely helpless. If she has a broken leg, she may never leave this mountain.

"Eve, take some deep breaths."

"It hurts so bad!" she croaks.

"I know. Let's sit her up," I tell Tuor.

The tan-colored cloth he's been holding to his nose is now soaked red. Tuor and I slide Eve backward and prop her against a tree. She flinches with every movement. Her body shivers as if she has a bad fever.

"Try and breathe," I say again. I remember Mirabelle saying this to me one time when I got hurt, and it seemed to help.

Eve takes a few long, shaky breaths before she begins to calm. "You should wrap my leg." Her voice is small and unsteady. Even in extreme pain, she still manages to give us commands. "I have a kit in my saddlebag with bandages."

Tuor runs immediately to Eve's horse and returns with a bag full of ointments and medicines. I look around the darkening woods.

"It's going to be sunset soon," I say to Tuor as I rummage through Eve's bag.

"We'll set up camp here," Tuor says.

Eve grabs his arm. "No." She takes a deep breath. "That monster could come back."

Tuor looks to me.

"She's right," I say. "I'll take care of Eve. You go look for a place that we can hide tonight."

Tuor hesitates, looking down at Eve. He squeezes her hand tightly between his.

"Do it," Eve groans.

Finally, Tuor concedes. He takes his horse and gallops into the woods. Eve and I are left in the solitude of the mountain. I take the long strips of bandages from her bag and begin wrapping them around her ankle. A sardonic laugh escapes Eve's lips. She lets her head roll back onto the tree trunk.

"Are you okay?" I ask, not sure how to react.

"It's just funny. I thought I was going starve to death on this mountain. Now, I know this leg will kill me before that happens." Eve's eyes dip closed. Her head sways back and forth.

"You're not going to die from either." I wrap another bandage snuggly around the bulging part of her ankle.

"This would be my luck: finding love again only for it to be cut short." Eve speaks through her delirium.

A breath catches in my throat. I tie the last bandage on her leg and sit back on my heels. "Love?"

This surprises me. Did she just say that she loves my brother? I knew there was something going on between them but . . . love?

"You barely know each other." The words tumble out of my mouth. It's all I can think to say.

"Love doesn't need a lot of time," Eve says.

"You should rest," I say, putting an end to this uncomfortable conversation.

Eve nods and lets her eyes close again. I stand and look for a task, but it's growing dark and there is nothing to do. I pace through the snow and pull my arms close to my body to keep me warm. I'm fidgety. Eve softly moans from her spot on the ground. Where is Tuor? Why isn't he back yet?

I decide to grab one of Eve's blankets and cover her. Her hands are cold and her face is pale. I sit next to her and mindlessly look through her medicines. I find a bottle of oregano oil. Mirabelle used this on me. It's a painkiller. I put a few drops into Eve's waterskin and urge her to sip it.

The oregano oil seems to work at least a little. Eve is restless, but she's not fussing as much. I squint as I scan the woods. It's now almost completely dark. I hear the thumping of a horse. I can't tell which direction it's coming from. I stand and pull my dagger. Tuor pulls his horse to a stop, and I breathe a sigh of relief.

"Tell me you found something," I whisper.

He nods, catching his breath. "There's a cave not too far from here."

"Can you find it again in the dark?"

"I'll find it. How is she?" Tuor asks as he dismounts. He kneels next to Eve and gently touches her cheek.

"She's okay, but it's getting cold. We need to get to shelter."

Tuor rises swiftly. "I could carry her, but it would take an hour to get there if we walked. You'll have to lift her up to me on my horse."

Tuor mounts his horse again. I scoop Eve up with both my arms. She's lighter than I imagined, but as I walk Eve over to Tuor, I feel a rush in my head and I'm suddenly lightheaded. One of my knees buckles, but I catch myself.

"You okay?" Tuor asks.

I shake my head. "Yeah . . ." But I'm not okay. I can feel my muscles weakening and the pain in my stomach is constant. We need food, but I can't say any of that to Tuor right now.

I struggle to lift Eve's body. Tuor takes Eve onto his horse and cradles her like a baby. He leads the way as I ride Shae and trail Eve's horse behind me. Hoofprints in the snow lead us. The temperature has dropped. My hands are icy as I grip hard to Shae's reins. A flurry of snowflakes starts to fall and land on my head.

The sickening howls of wolves split the air. I twist my head in all directions. There's a pack of them, and they sound close. My heart freezes in my chest. Another howl echoes up and down the mountainside.

"Tuor, are we almost there?" I whisper desperately.

"We're here," he says.

I jump off Shae, onto the crunchy snow. Tuor carefully hands Eve down from atop his horse. He leads me to a tiny cave shaped out of three big rocks smashed together. Tuor has to bend his tall frame nearly in half to take me through the entrance. Everything is black as I carry Eve inside and lay her on the ground. He works to build a fire while I secure the horses and carry our bags inside.

I brush snow from my hair as I enter the cave. A gap in the ceiling where the rocks don't connect allows the smoke from the small crackling fire to escape. I hang one of our blankets over the opening. The cave is narrow, with just enough space for the three of us.

"It's snowing harder now," I say. "At least it'll cover our tracks. Make it harder for Reed to find us."

"Do you think he'd come looking for us?"

I shake my head and gaze into the lapping flames. "Nothing would surprise me with him anymore."

The wind rushes over the hole in the ceiling. Eve moans, rousing awake. She breathes heavily and twists her legs in agony.

"What do you need?" Tuor asks as he takes Eve's hand, but she doesn't answer him.

Inspecting Eve's ankle, I notice that it's swollen even more. The bandages are tight. Her skin is hot to the touch and it's bursting between the wrappings.

"She's continuing to swell," I say.

"What helps with swelling?" Tuor asks urgently.

"When I used to get hit at the farm, Mirabelle would give me a cold cloth to hold on my cheek, and it always made it feel better. We could try putting some snow on her ankle."

"Her body is already so cold though," Tuor says.

"I know. We'll keep her close to the fire and just put the snow on her ankle."

Tuor presses his lips together and peers down at Eve sympathetically.

"We have to try," I say.

"Okay," he says with a nod.

Tuor ventures back out into the cold and brings me a bowl of fresh snow. I place a thin cloth over Eve's ankle and pack blobs of snow around her foot and leg. Eve flinches with my every touch. Her head rolls back and forth on the cave floor. She's delirious with pain. Tuor props a pillow under her neck, and I force her to drink more of the oregano oil. We tuck the rest of her body in tightly with blankets to keep her warm, and then we sit and wait.

Tuor strokes Eve's brow and quietly whispers into her ear. It seems to soothe her, but the lines on Tuor's face show his worry. A sudden pang hits my gut that has nothing to do with hunger. I've lost my big brother. He's infatuated with Eve. Perhaps in love with her.

"She'll be okay," I say, pulling Tuor's attention onto me.

"I will kill him, Camilla." Tuor's voice is hoarse. "I mean it. If she doesn't come off this mountain alive, I'll kill Reed."

"If it comes to that, I'll help you."

CHAPTER NINE

THE FIRE POPS, throwing sparks onto the damp cave floor. I pull my knees up to my chest, drawing as much warmth into my body as I can. The cold air seeps in through the holes in my ragged pants. I clutch my dirty hands together around my legs and consider how unprepared for this trip we were: no month-long food supply, no heavy winter jacket, and not even a pair of gloves. Never did I dream we'd be climbing a mountain, let alone camping in its snowy peaks.

"Look, she's sleeping," I tell Tuor.

Eve's chest rises and falls with her steady breathing. Tuor slides across the cave floor to her side. He touches her cheek, then inspects her ankle.

"The snow is helping." Tuor brushes stray hairs from Eve's forehead.

"I'll keep putting fresh snow on her ankle," I say. "You should try and sleep."

Tuor vehemently shakes his head. "I won't sleep tonight. I can't."

"You're exhausted."

Tuor rubs at the side of his head anxiously. "No, no. I won't. I have to make sure she's all right. Just stay awake with me for a while longer."

Tuor's nervous habits have been buried for the last few months. I assumed it was because the rebels had taken over Bear Gap and we'd been living in relative safety. The steady routines seemed to do him good. Now, I realize it was Eve that had kept him levelheaded. I watch Tuor from across the fire.

"So . . . how did things happen between you two anyway?" I ask, my voice awkward and stilted.

"I know you don't want to hear that story."

"I want to know," I say defensively. "Plus, we're stuck in this cave together. I welcome anything that distracts me."

Tuor chuckles despite the bleakness of our situations. Already some of the worry has left his face. He rests his head against the cave wall. "Well, it really started when we were hiding at Lindon Place earlier this year."

"What?" I whisper. "You two were getting together when we were planning our attack on the farm?"

"Not exactly. We talked here and there. I didn't even know she was interested in me. I thought she was just being friendly." Memories fill Tuor's eyes as he looks off into nothing and smiles. "After everything happened at the farm, we didn't talk for a while, but once our lives settled down, we started meeting up regularly."

"The first time was when I was standing guard at the front gate. She just walked right up to me, told me she wanted me to come over to the restaurant and try a new dish she'd made." Tuor runs his fingers through his curly hair. "Shows how much she knew me even then. I couldn't say no to food."

"I thought nothing of it. I walked over to Lindon Place that night. The next thing I knew, she and I were alone in the dining room. I'd just finished a delicious meal, and we were laughing over two mugs of cider."

I raise an eyebrow. "You were on a date and you didn't know it?"

Tuor rubs the back of his neck. "I haven't been on a lot of dates, not really any actually. When I was stationed in LilyAye, Lawrence was always treating some girl to dinner, but I've never been good with all of that. Women make me nervous, but with Eve . . . I never had a chance to be nervous."

I smirk as I think about how naive my brother was, but I was also blind. For months, I hadn't noticed anything between them. I was too busy keeping the rebellion alive, I suppose.

"Before I knew it, I was making that walk over to Lindon Place every chance I could get away. We'd talk for hours."

"You really love her, don't you?"

Tuor beams. He pokes the fire with a stick and says, "Yeah."

I've been so selfish when it comes to Tuor. He's *my* brother. He's *my* best friend. He's the reason I started the rebellion. Eve is always going to be the type of person that she is, uptight and annoying, but if Tuor loves her, then I'll have to accept that.

"Why don't you get some sleep and I'll stay up with her tonight," I try again. "If there's any change, I'll wake you. I promise."

Tuor hesitates, stroking Eve's hand.

"Come on," I urge.

Tuor leans over and kisses Eve on the cheek. He lays his body close to her and closes his eyes in sleep. Silence settles over the cave except for the sound of the wind as it twists through the creaking pine trees.

I feed the fire all night. Every hour, I repack Eve's ankle with fresh snow as the old snow melts away. In the early dawn, I notice that her swelling has gone down significantly, so I give her a break from the cold pack and cover her foot with her blanket.

I lay a snow-dusted log into the fire. It sizzles and bubbles as the flames lick up the wetness. I rest my head on my canvas bag and stare into the fire. My stomach aches. It doesn't even feel like a hunger pang anymore. It's just hallow and painful. My heavy eyelids close in sleep until Tuor's cries burst through my consciousness.

***

The wind has quieted. I wake with a start. Sunlight fills the cave. Tuor holds Eve as she lies on the ground, his soft whimper muffled by her golden hair. I scramble onto my hands and knees.

"What happened?" The words spill from my lips.

"Thank you," Tuor mumbles when he sees me crawling to Eve's side. "Thank you."

He lays Eve back onto her bed. Her eyes are open and bright. She manages a weak smile. The delirium is gone.

"She's okay," Tuor breathes.

"I still can't move it," Eve says with a wince.

I examine Eve's ankle by removing her bandages. The swelling is no worse than it was early this morning, but deep, purplish bruises have infested the entire area. I keep the concerned expression off my face.

"We should make a plan on how to get out of here," I say. "If we can get down the mountain to a town, we can find food and maybe even somebody to help with your ankle."

"How are we going to do that?" Eve asks, still struggling for breath.

"I'll carry you," Tuor says quickly. "I'll carry you the whole way if I have to."

"Let's just try and get her on a horse like we did last night," I say.

Tuor slips his arms underneath Eve. She sucks in air as he gently jostles her to get into position.

"Steady!" Eve warns. She clutches Tuor's shoulder.

He lifts her slowly off the ground. A scream escapes Eve's lips. "Stop! Stop! Put me down!"

Tuor lowers Eve back onto the ground. Tears pour from the corners of Eve's eyes.

"I'm sorry. I'm so sorry," Tuor says, immediately stroking Eve's hair.

"I can't do it," she says with a whimper. "It hurts too bad."

I rub my hands together vigorously to fight against the crisp morning air.

"Just him lifting you hurt that bad?" I ask.

Eve nods, squeezing her eyes shut. "It's excruciating."

"We have to give her time to heal," Tuor says.

My eyes settle on Eve's helpless body. Her cheeks are gaunt. Her skin is pasty and thin. I feel my own body shriveling. Even through my jacket, my hard ribs are ever present. We need food, or Eve's injury isn't going to be a concern anymore.

I clear my throat. "Tuor, will you help me gather more snow for Eve's ankle?"

"Why can't you—" Understanding fills Tuor's face. "Oh, sure." He squeezes Eve's hand. "I'll be right back," he tells her.

Tuor follows me to the cave door. I push aside the blanket to reveal a mountain transformed into a powdery white land. Globs of snow cover every branch and leaf. The sun sparkles off the crystalline surfaces.

"We can't stay in this cave forever," I say, turning to face Tuor.

He shivers then shoves his hands into his pockets. "Eve just needs more time."

"We don't have time." I lower my voice. "We've been without food for too long."

"I won't leave her behind."

"I know..." I pull the blankets off Shea's back, dumping the collected snow onto the ground. I rub her neck and scratch the spot between her eyes. "That's why I'm going out hunting while you stay here."

Tuor lets out a groan of disapproval as he nervously rubs at the side of his head. "Split up?"

"We're starving. Someone has to find some food," I say.

"Reed could still be looking for us. What if he finds you by yourself?"

"He might," I say matter-of-factly.

"All the more reason why we shouldn't split up," he says.

I take Tuor by the shoulders and squeeze them tightly like I used to when Tuor was in one of his panics.

"Eve can't move, and we don't have the strength to carry her through this snow and down the mountain even if she'd let us."

"I can carry her. Just give her a day, and she'll be ready to travel. Then we can all go together."

I give Tuor's body a jolt. "Listen. Unfortunately, we don't have time to let Eve heal." I speak with urgency. "We need food now."

"Yeah, but—"

I ignore Tuor's pleading for me to stay. It takes me mere minutes to saddle Shae, secure my dagger to my belt, and grab my bow and quiver.

"Please come back," Tuor begs.

"Keep fresh snow on Eve's ankle," I say, pulling myself into Shae's saddle. "I've been putting drops of oregano oil in her water. Make sure she drinks. I'll be back. I promise."

Tuor watches me with tired, glassy eyes. Shae kicks up the snow as we trot away from the cave. I go deeper into the woods, away from Thieves' Road, not wanting to take any chances of running into Reed.

What was muddled and confusing last night is now open and clear. I pull Shae to a slow walk through the bare trees. The sky is a pale blue. The cold is the only thing keeping me awake. My eyes close momentarily as Shae gallops. I shudder back to consciousness and grip the reins tighter. My body is on the brink of shutting down, but I force myself to keep going.

Heavy globs of snow collapse from the branches above me as the sun warms the treetops. I'll have no luck finding any onion grass now. My only chance for food is to find something to kill. I ride into a thick cropping of trees. The snow deadens the normal rustling sound of the woods, making it a peaceful sanctuary.

I pull on Shea's reins and scan my surroundings. Sliding from the saddle, my boots make a crunching noise as I step out onto the fresh snow. I tie up Shae to a nearby tree. My dry, cracking hand reaches for my dagger. Stalking through the woods, I search for movement.

Even after a short walk, I'm out of breath. I decide to find a place to sit completely still and watch the wildlife around me. Crouching next to a tree, I pull out my bow and set an arrow so it's ready. The wet snow permeates my body.

The brown flash of a squirrel's tail catches my eye. He runs down a branch toward the trunk of a tree, shaking chunks of snow onto the ground. I nock an arrow, and let it loose. It flies and hits the bark as the squirrel scurries up the tree. I groan at my missed hit, but stay put, hoping to see another one.

The woods grow vacant. Hours pass, and not a single insect crosses my path. As the afternoon wanes, I leave Shae tied up and continue on foot through the forest. A tightness grows in my chest from sucking in the cold air. I lift my eyes and standing gloriously at the other end of the thicket is a fallow-coated deer.

He's a stark contrast to the mounds of white around him. I shake as I raise my arm and carefully set an arrow. The tips of his ears twitch. I pull back on my bowstring and line up my shot. He turns sharply, noticing my movements.

The arrow releases. It whizzes through the air and strikes the deer in his hindquarters. He springs from his spot and bounds away. *No*, I breathe. I jog to the spot where the deer was standing. Splotches of red blood dot the snow. Perfectly round hoofprints lead away from the spot with drops of blood following.

I break into a sprint and run into the woods. The wind whips through my short, tangled hair. The thick snow grabs my feet and pulls me down farther into the earth. Every step makes a deafening, crunching sound.

I grab a nearby tree and stop to catch my breath. The patches of blood are bigger. The deer is slowing down. The woods darken as the sun begins its slow descent over the mountainside. An evening haze falls between the trees, and my cheeks turn icy despite my pounding heart.

The mountainside steepens as I start to run again. My feet slip on the ice-covered snow. I push myself faster and squint as it becomes harder to see. The air grows ever colder around me. My heavy breathing drowns out all other sounds. I skid to a stop and search the snow for blood. Then a familiar sound breaks through the silent woods like a crack of ice.

The piercing howls of a wolf pack send a shudder down my back. I have to get out of here. *Shae.* Where did I leave her? A yelp echoes down the mountainside. The thumping of their paws against the ground seems to be coming from all around me. I stagger backward, unsure of which direction to run. I turn in a circle.

The light of a lantern floats through the trees as another wolf howls into the night air. A towering figure treks toward me. The snow, now icy, causes me to slip. I fall backward. Their shadowy outline grows larger. I skitter across the ground on my hands.

A person wearing a broad-rimmed hat and an animal-skin trench coat approaches. Their face is dark despite the lantern they're holding. Reaching down, they grab me firmly by the arm and drag my nearly lifeless body deeper into the woods.

CHAPTER TEN

THE DEEP, LOW growl of the wolves pushes me and my captor swiftly through the trees. In the blue haze of the woods, an A-frame cabin comes into view. I'm thrust through the front door. My weak legs betray me, and I tumble onto the hard floor.

The figure, their face still shadowed by a large hat, bends and rips the bow and quiver from my hands and the dagger from my belt. My weapons are placed atop a tall bureau, out of reach.

"Warm yourself," comes the rich, silky voice of a woman.

I scramble to the stone hearth, where a fire softly crackles. Placing my hands up to the flames, I let my body slowly thaw. I glance furtively at the stranger. The one-room cabin is sparse with just a mattress on the floor, a black cauldron on the hearth, and a bench with various instruments and ointments. Boxes and bags line the wall next to the door as if she were either moving in or moving out.

The wolves snarl and yelp, sounding as if they were right outside the front door of the cabin.

"My horse, please," I beg. "She's out there. Let me go get her."

My captor snuffs out the lantern and hangs it on a curved hook on the wall, then turns to face me. She removes her snow-laden hat to reveal a face of smooth ebony skin. Her corkscrew curls are pulled back into a bulging low bun.

"I'm not risking my life again for your horse," she says. "Besides, the wolves are after that deer you shot, not your horse. And from the sound of it, they've already gotten to it."

"How did you find me?"

"You're on *my* land." The woman unbuttons her long deer-skinned coat and hangs it by the fire to dry.

"You live here alone?" I ask.

"I *was* alone until you wandered out here." The woman purses her full lips as if annoyed by me. She riffles through a crate on the floor and pulls out a parcel.

"I was just searching for food," I say.

She gracefully turns to face me. "I know. You nearly got yourself killed chasing that animal. Here."

The woman hands me the parcel. I unwrap the cloth and find a slab of flaky dark-orange meat sitting in my hand. I inhale it, taking no mind to its unfamiliarity or the fact that it's being fed to me by a mountain woman I don't know.

"What is it?" I ask through mouthfuls.

"Salmon. It's a fish from the river at the bottom of the mountain."

The woman crouches in front of me so we're eye level. Instinctively, I shudder backward.

"If I wanted to hurt you, I would have left you out there with the wolves," she chides.

I take another bite of the salmon as she lifts my chin and turns my face to inspect me. She then takes one of my hands and turns it over.

"What's your name?" she asks sternly.

"Camilla."

As soon as my name slips from my lips, I regret it. My mind is foggy with hunger. I'm not to tell anyone my name. The name Camilla is synonymous with governor killer and rebel, but the woman's face gives away no reaction.

"How long have you been out here?" she asks.

"A few weeks I think," I say, swallowing more salmon.

She stands suddenly.

"Don't I get to know your name?" I ask.

"My name is Roehana. What in all of Elmyra are you doing out here?"

"What are *you* doing out here?"

Roehana turns to her table of ointments and creams. The bottles rattle together as she searches through them. She bends in front of me again, this time a rag and a bottle in her hand.

"Someone in your position shouldn't be speaking with such confidence," Roehana says. Her face holds a youthful glow, yet the tiny wrinkles at the corners of her eyes make me think she's older than she appears. Roehana wipes a spot on my forehead with the wet rag, then dots cooling oil on the spot. I flinch, feeling a sharp sting.

"You're covered in cuts and bruises. Your face is sallow. You look sickly from head to toe. You've been drinking at least." She nods to my canteen of water.

"Are you some kind of healer?" I ask, taking the final bite of salmon.

"You could say that."

She continues her work over my exposed skin, even insisting that I remove my jacket so she can see my arms. I let her clean and treat every little scrape I've acquired since leaving Bear Gap.

Roehana screws the cap on her bottle of oil and peers down at me. She's amazingly tall with broad shoulders and thick forearms that explain how she can survive up here alone.

"Now, tell me how you find yourself half-dead atop this mountain."

Feeling some of my strength returning, I remove myself from the floor and sit on the toasty hearth, with the fire at my back. Fortunately, we had rehearsed a response to this question before we left Bear Gap.

"I'm a merchant. Just trying to find my way to LilyAye," I say.

"Going over this mountain is quite out of the way to get to LilyAye," Roehana says.

I swallow nervously. "The LilyAye Road has grown troublesome. I'm sure you've heard about the added security. I foolishly thought this route would be simpler. I should kick the tavern owner who told me that." I force a laugh.

"I haven't heard anything about the LilyAye road. I hear no news up here."

My eyebrows scrunch together curiously. "How long have you lived up here?"

Roehana pulls a blanket out of one of the crates and hands it to me.

"Nigh on ten years, I'd say. I do sometimes make it down to Wildenvalley in the winters, but it's been almost a year since I've seen another person."

A year . . . If Roehana is telling the truth, then she knows nothing of the takeover in Bear Gap. She'd know nothing of me or the rebels at all. I decide to keep Roehana blissfully ignorant. She takes a seat on her bed, clasping her hands in front of her.

"I consider myself lucky. Villagers can be troubling." Roehana gives me a scornful eye.

"Well, sorry about the inconvenience I caused you tonight. I guess I got turned around out there."

"This mountain is not friendly to travelers, in more ways than one," Roehana says.

"I don't want to bother you anymore," I say. Tuor will be wondering where I am. "If you'd return my hunting weapons, I'll leave you and continue my journey." I move to stand but find it difficult. "Perhaps I could have just a little more food for the road?"

"You can barely walk, and it's pitch-black outside now. How do you expect to travel at night like this?"

"I just don't want to bother you anymore," I say. Not true. I need to get back to Tuor, with food, and without this mystery woman knowing where we're hiding.

Roehana lets out a grunt. "Nearly being eaten by a wolf for your sake is bothersome enough already. You might as well continue to stack it up. You can sleep here tonight and rejoin your group in the morning."

"Group?" I ask, playing dumb.

"No one like you could survive on this mountain alone. By the looks of you, I'd guess you've lost at least one of your traveling companions to starvation by now."

She may be uninformed, but Roehana's not stupid. I can't risk her knowing about Eve and Tuor. She could be lying about everything, and if she plans to do something nefarious with me, at least they can have a chance to get away.

"No, just me," I say casually.

"Leave if you like," Roehana says with the wave of her hand. "But I won't save you from those wolves a second time."

I claw myself to my feet and stagger to the window facing out the front of the cabin. A deep blackness settles across the woods. Even the outline of the trees is barely visible. Trying to grope my way back to the cave at night might be the final event that does me in. Tuor will be worried, but I'm no use to Tuor and Eve if I freeze on this mountain.

"I'll spend the night and see my way out in the morning," I say, returning to the hearth.

"Whatever suits you," Roehana says.

She straightens a few things around her cabin before slipping under her covers and rolling over. I curl up next to the fire. I don't have my dagger by my side, but even if I did, I wouldn't have the strength to wield it.

***

I sleep heavily through the entire night. I wake refreshed, a feeling I haven't experienced since sleeping in my room at the Bear Gap House. Warm morning sun casts a golden glow inside the cabin. Despite my good sleep, my body aches and cracks as I rise from the floor. Tuor will be terrified by now. I have to get back to him.

"There's some more salmon for you," Roehana says. She stands over her ointment bench and places each bottle meticulously into a leather carrying case.

I gather that Roehana isn't one for chatter. Another parcel of smoked fish sits on the floor next to me. I nibble on the sweet meat.

"Thanks," I say, moving to join her at the bench. "What are you doing?"

"Every year about this time, I pack up and spend my winter in the town of Wildenvalley. The older I get, the harder the winters are on me. This year, winter is coming fast."

In the daylight, I notice how extensive Roehana's medicines are. Hundreds of bottles and tinctures and pots crowd the work bench. Dried herbs hang along the windowsill. Tweezers and splints and other devices that I don't recognize sit stacked in a box on the floor. It reminds me of Johnny's father's exam room. He's a doctor, a real one, and his collection isn't half what this is.

"So you are a healer?" I say, accusing.

"I'm well trained, yes, but a healer is someone who actually heals people. Since I've no contact with anyone, I don't have anyone to heal."

"Then why do you have all of this here?"

Roehana shrugs. "I like to research and test. These mountains are resplendent with herbs and roots."

I know little about doctoring, but it looks like Roehana has every tool and ointment enough to help everyone in Bear Gap. She would surely know how to fix Eve's ankle. I consider the consequences of telling her what's really going on. If I don't, we might die anyway.

"You have to help me," I blurt.

Roehana hurriedly fills her case with more bottles. She wipes her hands on the skirt of her dress, pulls the cover over the box, and clicks the latch closed. "I've helped you quite a bit already. You've eaten substantially from my salmon stores."

"Please," I turn, begging for her attention. "You were right. I'm not here alone. My brother and my friend are trapped in a cave a few miles from here. They're starved like me, and the woman, her ankle is severely injured. We can't even move her."

Roehana swiftly stands to cut down the dried herbs. "No, I cannot help you."

"Please, why not? You have every healing ointment I could imagine!"

Roehana hesitates. "I haven't worked on a real person in years. I'd probably make your friend worse."

"How could she be any worse? We're stuck here with no food and no way to travel."

"I'll send you with a little food, but that's the best I can do."

I search Roehana's dark eyes for a modicum of sympathy but find none. Grabbing her arm, I beg, "Please."

"I won't do it!" She flings my hand off. "I won't hurt another person."

Silence fills the small cabin. Roehana firmly presses her lips together.

"I'm a disgraced healer if you must know," she says through gritted teeth. "I used to deliver babies and perform surgeries. I'd mix the only medicinal concoctions that could heal mysterious diseases. I was worshiped as the best healer. One time I was careless." Roehana's voice rises. "That's all it took. My steady hand slipped, and—" Heartache surges through

Roehana's gaze as if she's living the very moment she's recalling. "Don't ask me for help. I'll only make things worse."

"I don't care about your past. We'll die up here if you don't help." I grip her arm again despite her attempt to get away from me. "You'll be just as responsible for our deaths if you walk away."

Roehana's nostrils flair as her eyes bore down on me.

"Please." My grip loosens around Roehana's arm. She whips it away from me.

"I think you should leave."

"If you don't help, our demise will be on your hands," I say.

Roehana exhales. "Fine. I will look at your friend, but that is it. If I'm to help you, then you must help me."

"What do you need help with?" I ask confused.

"Preparing for my departure."

"Agreed," I say quickly.

Together, Roehana and I pack up her meager belongings. She returns my weapons, and we secure her cabin for the winter. She loads down a small cart that trails behind her horse. In my weak state, she lets me ride her horse while she trudges through the snow beside me.

We meander through the woods while I try to recall which direction I came from. Roehana knows better than me.

"I watched you track that deer for quite a while. I could tell you were in trouble, so I waited to see what you'd do."

I call out for Shae and follow her whinnies until we find her still tied up to the tree where I left her. I slide from Roehana's horse and run to Shae, wrapping my arms around her neck. From there, we both ride. I follow Shae's prints from the day before all the way back to our cave shelter.

A fire crackles from behind the blanket that covers the opening to the cave. I pull it open and crawl inside. I find Tuor lying next to Eve, his thin, bony arm holding her.

"Tuor," I whisper, my voice cracking from breathing in the cold air.

I crawl to his side and call his name again. Eve's face is pale. She lies on her back. The snow pack around her ankle has melted into a puddle. Tuor's cheek is cold and dry. I snap my hand away. A surge of horror grips my heart.

"Tuor!" I shake Tuor's shoulder violently.

He sucks in a gasp of air. His eyes flutter open.

"Wake up," I say. "I have food."

Tuor wipes sleep from his eyes as he sits up. "Where were you last night?"

I unfold the bundle of food that Roehana gave me. A roasted turkey leg sits nestled next to a pile of boiled turnips. "I got lost, and it was too dark to find my way back."

Tuor grabs the turkey leg and starts devouring it.

"Go slow," I tell him.

"Where'd you find this?"

I sit back on my heels. "I found someone. Someone who can help us."

Tuor lifts his eyes and spots Roehana darkening the cave door. Worry shrouds Tuor's face. "Who's that?"

"This is Roehana. She's a healer."

Roehana bends to enter the cave.

"Is this the injured woman?" Roehana asks, a solemn look on her face as she peers down at Eve.

"Yes," I say nudging Eve awake. I prop her head on a rolled-up blanket.

Eve's droopy eyes blink open and her pasty skin is dotted with sweat despite the frigid air.

"Wait," Tuor says. "What are you going to do?"

"She's going to help Eve," I say.

Tuor holds the turkey leg mid-air. "We don't even know who she is!"

"Let her try," Eve says with a groan.

Without asking, Roehana kneels to inspect Eve's leg. I move behind Roehana to give her space.

"What are you doing?" Tuor asks again, leaning over Roehana's shoulder.

Roehana gingerly touches the outside of Eve's bandages. "What happened to her ankle?"

Tuor and I look at each other, wondering how to explain the fight to Roehana.

"Blasted Reed stepped on my ankle!" Eve spits out.

Roehana nods. "How long ago?"

"Two days."

"Hmm." Roehana begins unwrapping the crude bandages.

"Leave that on," Tuor protests. He's so concerned he tucks the turkey leg back in its parcel.

Roehana pauses. "Has she gotten any better with this treatment?"

"A little," Tuor says.

"No." Eve shakes her head. "It's worse today."

Roehana hesitates. Her touch is light. She presses her lips firmly together as she removes the bandages. Eve's ankle, enormously swollen, produces a cringe from Tuor. Using her fingertips, Roehana presses on

Eve's ankle, feeling every spot. Eve clutches the wool blanket and grits her teeth in pain. Roehana moves and works, uninhibited by Eve's cries.

"We were putting snow on it, and that was making it better." Still standing, I fold my arms over my chest and flinch as I watch Roehana press on Eve's bloated skin.

"A good attempt," Roehana says. "But that was only masking the real problem."

"So, what's wrong with her then?" I ask.

Roehana shifts so that the bottom of Eve's foot is facing her. She places both hands on either side of Eve's ankle. Muttering to herself, Roehana continues to touch and feel and press, drawing more painful moans from Eve. I hold a hand to my mouth. I find it more and more difficult to watch and wonder if I did the right thing by asking for Roehana's help.

"Be careful with her!" Tuor's voice is on the brink of hysteria.

Roehana ignores both of us. Her exploration stops. She holds her hands at specific spots on either side of Eve's ankle, then suddenly twists it with a violent shift. A pop echoes through the cave as Eve lets out a shriek of pain.

CHAPTER ELEVEN

"WHAT DID YOU do?" Tuor yells, ripping Roehana away from Eve.

Eve's head falls back onto the bed. Her breathing steadies, and her hands release their grasp on the blanket. Eve's ankle, although still purply and swollen, isn't bulging anymore. Roehana brushes off her shoulder, where Tuor grabbed her, and slowly backs away.

"Feel better?" Roehana asks.

Eve nods noiselessly. Her eyes dip closed. Tuor bends and furiously strokes Eve's cheek.

"Are you sure you're okay?" Tuor asks.

"Yes." Eve breathes deeply.

Roehana swiftly strides from the cave. I follow and find her standing tall, with her hands on her hips, staring down the mountain.

"Her ankle was dislocated," Roehana says, her back to me.

"What does that mean?"

"The part of the ankle bone that attaches to the leg bone separated."

"Her ankle was broken?" I ask.

Roehana sighs, turning to face me. "No. Your body isn't just made up of one solid bone. It has connectors at the ankles and the hips and your shoulders." Roehana adjusts the broad-rimmed hat she's wearing. "This girl's ankle came loose from its socket. All I did was put it back in. If I had seen it two days ago, it would have been a lot easier. The swelling should go down now."

"Thank you. My brother and I are truly grateful. You didn't have to help us."

Roehana chuckles. "Yes, I did. You didn't give me a choice. You must really care about that girl in there to risk your life hunting in those woods last night."

I shove my hands into my pockets. "She's growing on me. It's really my brother that I'd do anything for."

"You're lucky to have family like that." Roehana's big dark eyes peer down at me with tenderness, and the hint of a smile threatens at the corner of her mouth. "I should be going. I've lived on this mountain long enough to sense when another snowstorm will hit. I'd like to get below the frost line by tomorrow. You all should consider doing the same. I'll leave you with some more food."

"Wait. We're trying to get down the mountain too. Why don't we all travel together?"

Roehana takes a quick inhale, glancing around at our powdery white surroundings. "I'm not one for keeping company while I travel."

"It's Thieves' Road, isn't it? There's more safety in four than one."

"I have been ambushed once or twice in my years traveling this road, but I'm not sure taking an invalid with me counts as more safety."

"Tuor will look after Eve. He won't let anything happen to her." I gaze over my deplorable clothes. "I might not look it right now, but I'm a pretty skilled fighter."

Roehana eyes me. "Are merchants usually skilled fighters?" I press my lips together, regretting what I just said. "It's none of my business but I suppose anybody who can survive on this mountain is no coward."

"Then perhaps it's time you see what it's like to travel with someone besides yourself," I say with the raise of my eyebrow.

Roehana purses her lips. "All right. You have a deal. I'll see you to Wildenvalley. From there, we'll part ways."

I lift my chin and smirk. "Agreed."

***

"This will keep your ankle from moving about," Roehana tells Eve after splinting her leg with a device she had in her medical-supply box.

Eve looks at her leg apprehensively. "Can't we just camp out here for a couple of days? We have food now."

Roehana bends to Eve's level. "The snow is coming, the real snow. We should leave today unless you want to spend the whole winter up here."

"It'll be fine," Tuor croons.

"I'll lay you in the back of my cart. You won't have to move at all," Roehana says.

Eve nods reluctantly. Together, Tuor and I carefully lift Eve and carry her out of the cave. Roehana makes space for Eve among her bags and boxes. We tuck her comfortably into a spot just wide enough for her body. Laying her flat, we give Eve a pillow and cover her with blankets.

I stamp out the fire in the cave and gather our meager belongings. Although my full strength isn't back yet, Roehana's food has begun to return me to my old self. Shae shakes her head as I tighten the strap on her saddle. The sky is gray and cloudy. I fear that Roehana's prediction is right.

"Everyone ready?" I yell to our small company.

"Let's go," Roehana says, tugging on the reins of her horse.

I mount Shae and take a swig of water from my canteen. Clicking my tongue, I urge Shae forward into the woods. I'm elected to take the lead, with Roehana and her cart in the middle, and Tuor bringing up the rear. Eve's vacant horse rides behind him. It feels good to be back in the saddle and riding without the agonizing pangs of hunger.

"How far do we have to go to get to the bottom?" I ask as we turn onto Thieves' Road.

"It's about a three-day journey to the base of the mountain, then another half day or so to get to Wildenvalley," Rochana says.

"How much farther from there to LilyAye?" I ask.

"Another day," Roehana says.

Four days. That's it? Travel goes quicker when you're going downhill and not starving, I suppose. In four days, we could be in LilyAye. Of course, with everything that's happened with Reed, and then Eve's injury, we haven't even discussed whether we'll still go to LilyAye. Reed was our ticket inside the city walls. Now, I don't even know if I want to ever see him again.

Roehana pulls her cart down the snowy trail. Thieves' Road is still fairly steep for most of the day, but we're able to ride. The downward travel turns out to be far easier than coming up the mountain. By evening, the air has warmed, and the thick, clumping snow is now just a thin layer on the ground.

As dusk falls, we pull off the road. Roehana hops from her horse and tends to Eve. Roehana possesses an attentiveness that I imagine made her an excellent doctor at one time.

"We should be low enough to keep us out of the dangerous snowfall," Roehana says, scanning the tops of the trees. "We can make camp here."

I clear a spot to build a fire while Roehana and Tuor remove Eve from the back of the cart. They lay her gingerly on the ground. Roehana lifts the blanket to inspect Eve's injury.

"Very good," Roehana mutters as she carefully turns Eve's ankle side to side. "How does that feel?"

"It's okay," Eve says.

"The swelling is down, and you've regained some mobility. You're on your way."

That night, we sit around the fire and continue to eat from Roehana's food stores. Oddly, the more my body regains its strength, the more hungry I grow, but I continue to pace myself. We still have some travel ahead of us.

"Do Warwick soldiers ever pass through here?" I ask casually.

"I've never seen any," Roehana says, lifting a hunk of bread into her mouth. "That's part of why I like it up here. I can do whatever I want."

Tuor laughs. "I like you," he says, chewing with an open mouth.

The gentle sway of the leaves and branches above us adds to the eerie ambiance of the dark mountain.

"But, Roehana, you're a trained healer," Eve says. She lies on the ground, propped up by her elbow. "Why aren't you using your skills in LilyAye or another city?"

An awkward silence fills the space between us. Roehana glances over at me as the fire crackles softly. "I had a troubling experience with a patient many years ago. I felt at the time that it was a sign I needed to let this profession go."

"But you're so good," Tuor says.

Roehana gives Tuor a cheeky smile. "I'll admit, I have enjoyed having a patient."

"You should start taking care of people again," I say matter-of-factly. "You're too knowledgeable to just bury all that skill up in these mountains. People need you."

"I suppose I did just give up," Roehana says. Her big eyes watch me intently from across the fire. "It's the fear of making a mistake again that stops me."

"We all make mistakes," Tuor says.

"Yes, but my mistake was a deadly one."

Again, silence falls between us. A chilly breeze gusts through our camp, warning of the snowstorm higher up the mountain.

"I will see all of you in the morning," Roehana says, abruptly standing. "Good night."

Soon, the rest of us have turned in for the night too. We huddle around the fire to keep warm, even though the weather has returned to more of an autumn temperature. We wake to a dewy morning and a few patches of snow.

The next couple of days of travel are uneventful. The slushy, snowy trail morphs into one that's covered in dried leaves. Now that Eve's ankle is set right, she heals swiftly. Roehana spends an hour one evening digging a crutch out of her cart to give to Eve so she can hobble around.

This raises Eve's spirits exponentially. It's not long before I catch her and Tuor snuggled together, next to the fire, like two birds trying to stay warm. By the third day, we reach the foothills. Thieves' Road evens out. The temperature rises to that of a crisp fall day.

"We're close," Roehana says as we pull to a stop. "But we won't quite make it to Wildenvalley tonight. We should stop and rest up." She hops off her horse and brushes her hands on her riding pants. "By tomorrow, you'll be able to get some supplies in Wildenvalley and carry on to LilyAye."

"I'm going to miss traveling with you," Tuor says, unhooking his bed mat from his horse. "You travel with the best venison stew I've ever had."

"Happy to oblige," Roehana says.

"We'll repay you," I say. "For everything you've done."

"Why don't we settle up in Wildenvalley?" Roehana says.

"Fair enough."

Eve carries a bag from her horse over to the spot where we've decided to set up camp. She limps, barely using her crutch.

"Stop doing that," Tuor scolds, ripping the bag away from Eve. "Sit down and relax."

"I'm not useless."

"No, you're not, but right now you shouldn't be straining yourself."

"There's a particular berry that grows down here," Roehana says. "It's great for upset stomach. I'm going to see if I can find any."

"Okay," I say.

"Watch your backs," Roehana says, pulling her knife out of the inside pocket of her jacket. "The thieves are too lazy to climb very high. The closer we get to the bottom, the more dangerous it gets."

"Got it," I say as Roehana traipses into the trees.

I plop my bag next to Tuor, who has coaxed Eve to take a seat with him on a fallen tree trunk. Furtively I watch as Roehana walks out of earshot. I've been waiting for the chance to get Tuor and Eve alone.

"The three of us need to talk," I say in a hushed voice. "We have to figure out what we're doing once we get to the bottom of this mountain."

"I thought we were going to LilyAye," Eve says.

Tuor twists his face in confusion as he turns to Eve. "Not right away. We need to find a place to lie low and let you heal."

A cool breeze brushes a smattering of dried leaves off the ground and into the air like feathers.

"What about Reed?" I ask, crossing my arms over my chest.

"Don't say his name," Tuor growls. "He's gone. As far as I'm concerned, you're leading this mission now."

"We haven't seen him since he left us, and he didn't have any more food than we did. He could be dead." I'm surprised by the hint of sadness that fills my heart at that thought.

"He's not dead," Eve says.

"How do you know?" I ask.

Eve rubs at an ache on her leg. "We probably would have seen his body or his horse, and he's too

111

clever to die. He's survived years of Quinten trying to capture him, and still, he's found a way to elude the most powerful man in the country. All he wants is to kill his uncle. He'll do anything to stay alive to see that."

"Reed's a survivor." I nod in agreement. "But how do we carry on with Quinten's assassination if we're not on Reed's side anymore?"

"We can't," Tuor snaps. "We have to forget about him and move on with our lives. Let's get to Wildenvalley and—"

"Who says we're not on Reed's side?" Eve asks, scrunching her eyebrows together.

Stunned, I let my arms fall to my side. "Well . . ."

"He almost killed you!" Tuor shouts.

Eve adjusts her back to sit taller. "I'm not happy about what transpired between the two of us, but I can separate our dispute from the bigger mission at hand."

"Are you serious?" Tuor physically distances himself from Eve, his mouth agape.

I'm flabbergasted. Of the three of us to offer Reed forgiveness, Eve is the last I'd expect.

"I still want Quinten dead," she says in a low tone. "Don't you?"

"Yes, I do, but—"

"Reed is our best chance at making that happen," Eve says.

"But after what he did, do we even want Reed as the next Supreme Ruler?" I ask.

"I can't trust him to be ruler," Tuor says.

Eve lets out a long breath. She peers down at her fingernails, which she's somehow managed to keep clean on this trip.

"No," she says flatly. "My confidence in him as a ruler has disappeared, but we have no chance of murdering Quinten without Reed's help. One way or another, we have to join forces with him again." Eve swats a fly from her face. "We'll have to figure out the next Supreme Ruler along the way."

"What do you suggest?" I ask. "We keep traveling toward LilyAye and join Reed's rebels?"

"If he'll take us back, yes," Eve says.

"You can barely walk because of him," Tuor says.

"That should show you how dedicated I am to this mission," Eve says.

Tuor lets out an exasperated sigh as he stands and paces away from us. He rubs his face in tense, frustrated movements.

"We have to stay focused on Quinten and not let these distractions get in our way," Eve says. "Our month is almost up. According to our spy Quinten will be traveling soon. We have to get to LilyAye and find Reed."

"I can't believe what you're saying," Tuor says, turning to face us. "What do you think, Camilla?"

The heat of Tuor and Eve's disagreement creates an uncomfortable silence as they both stare at me, waiting for my opinion. I recall the night that Reed slapped Eve. I wanted to kill him. He betrayed me in more ways than one, but after coming out of this, onto the other side, I can't imagine going back to Bear Gap with Quinten still on the throne.

"Eve is right," I say in a small voice. "Reed's connections in LilyAye are our best chance at getting to Quinten. Let's at least give him the opportunity to apologize."

"We don't have to be friends with the man to get what we want," Eve says.

Tuor places both hands on his narrow hips. "So we're going to LilyAye, and we're going to search for the man that left us at the top of a mountain to die?"

I nod slowly. "Yes."

***

By the afternoon of the next day, the trail spills out onto level ground. Tension is thick between Eve and Tuor. The discussion about Reed has placed a wedge between them. As the trees open up, I feel a rush of excitement. I push Shae forward as I realize we've made it to the bottom of the mountain. The sound of rushing water assaults us.

"What is that?" I ask, shouting over the deep thrum.

"It's the Ebertier River," Roehana says. "We're in the great valley where LilyAye sits. Good place to take a break before we make that final jaunt to Wildenvalley."

I hop off Shae and raise my arms in the air, stretching my legs and back. I breathe in the cool mountain air.

"I'll go down to the river and fill up our canteens," I say, pulling my waterskin from my bag.

"We'll stay with the horses," Roehana says, handing me her canteen. "I'd like to take a look at Eve's ankle."

Tuor walks toward me in a sulk. "I'll come with you."

"You okay?" I ask, throwing the canteens over my shoulder.

He looks back at Eve and Roehana as we head toward the river. "I'm fine."

The Ebertier River rumbles as we walk through the thinning woods. The flat earth beneath our feet is something I thought I'd never feel again. Up ahead is the water's edge.

"Look, there," I say. The river crescendos to a roar, so loud it engulfs my voice.

A vast, raging body of water rushes past us in a riverbed wide enough to fit the width of the Bear Gap House. My mouth spreads open in awe as I survey its magnitude. Great buckets of water crash down from the peak of a waterfall that feeds the river.

Our faces are baptized in a spray of water. This is the gorge, I realize. The tiny river that seemed so far away from the top of the mountain now lies in front of us. Nothing like this exists in Bear Gap. The size of it would be unbelievable to me if I wasn't staring at it this very moment.

Tuor's mouth opens to form the word "wow". Amazed, he paces down the riverbank and takes in the panoramic vista. The edge is rough and rocky, lined with huge boulders. I find an opening between the rocks and carefully climb down to a beach-like embankment. Out of habit, I touch the dagger on my belt just to make sure it's still there.

The rushing sound of the river envelopes all my senses. I breathe in the dewy air. Bending to fill the waterskins, I pause when I spot movement in the corner of my eye. With the rush and tumble of the river, it's hard to be sure I saw anything at all.

"Tuor!" I call out to no response. "Tuor! I'm over here."

My body tenses and the only name that fills my mind is *Reed*. I stand suddenly and search up and down the coast.

"Tuor!"

An uneasy feeling fills my stomach. I peer over the tops of the rocks. As I start to crest the upper bank, I call out once again for Tuor. Movement flashes to my right. A pair of muddy boots faces me. A wooden club swings, knocking into the side of my head.

My grip on the rocks breaks loose, and I fall flat on my back, onto the wet gravel. The water rushes past my head. A moan pours from my lips as my attacker's blurry image approaches. I finger the handle of my dagger just before slipping into unconsciousness.

CHAPTER TWELVE

THE RUMBLE AND thud of wagon wheels rocks me back and forth. My head is slumped against rusty iron bars. The blistering sound of a baby crying fills my ears. I blink my eyes open to the piercing sun as I'm violently shaken from my slumber.

"Wake up."

Instinctually, I fling off the hand shaking me.

The putrid smell of feces and vomit floats to my nose. I grasp my face, covering my nose from the assault. A cough bursts from my chest. I lean forward and gag.

"Get off me," I groan. Someone is still grasping my arm.

"It's me." Tuor's familiar voice summons me into reality.

I struggle for air. Wiping my mouth, I find Tuor sitting next to me on the back of a caged wagon. Dread creeps up inside me.

"You're awake." Tuor breathes with relief. His eye has a purple ring around it.

We're sitting on the floor of a flatbed wagon with bars along the sides. Men, women, and children all huddle together like rats in a nest. I reach for the dagger on my belt, but it's not there.

"They've taken all our things," Tuor says, holding back a quivering voice.

My body shudders with panic. A woman sits across from me. Her skin is a deep shade of walnut. Tangled hair falls into her bruised face. She tries to console the baby in her lap by bouncing him up and down against her chest. An elderly man coughs violently on the other side of me. A little boy whimpers on his mother's lap.

I scramble to my feet, pushing the mob of people out of my way. We're squished inside so tightly there's barely space to move. I grip the iron bars. Three caged wagons barrel down a dusty road, across a vast grassland.

Hordes of people hang out the sides, as if their hands and arms were reaching for freedom. We're flanked on all sides by sheep-herding dogs and armed men on horseback. Dressed in scuffed leather jackets and high boots, they resemble a crude version of a Warwick soldier, but none of them bear the Warwick crest.

"Tuor, what's going on?"

He stands beside me. His eyes sag into a painful expression. "They're slave traders, the ones that Wilson warned us about."

The wagon thuds as it barrels over a hole in the road. Tuor squeezes a chunk of hair on the side of his head.

"They were lying in wait by the river for anyone coming off the mountain or traveling from

Wildenvalley," Tuor continues. "I screamed for you, Camilla, but the river was too loud."

Slavers . . . I was little more than a slave when I worked on the farm in Bear Gap. I won't go back to that life. My fingernails dig into the iron. I shake the bars and feel them rattle in their posts.

One of the guards rides up beside our wagon and yells at me to stop. He then hits my fingers with a club. I suck in air as I pull my hands into my chest.

"Careful," Tuor mutters, grabbing my shoulders and turning me around.

We sit again on the filthy floor. I moan as I inspect my fingers. Blood oozes from one of my nail beds. A dark bruise has started to form on my knuckles.

"You can't do that," Tuor scolds. "They'll beat you."

Tuor's voice is defeated. His eye is puffy, and I notice that he's holding his left arm.

Looking around the wagon I ask, "Where's Eve?"

"They didn't get her. She's still with Roehana as far as I know."

At least someone knows we've been taken. I glance out the side of the wagon, wondering . . . hoping that Eve can convince Roehana to help us. Tuor drops his face in his hands.

"I left her," he says with a muffled voice. "I was so mad at her that I left her there with the horses, and now I might never see her again."

I slide up closer to Tuor. "They'll find us."

The woman sitting across from us lets out a derisive scoff. Her baby's cry dulls to a fuss as she looks, dead eyed, at me, like I'm stupid.

"You think someone's going to rescue you?" she asks with a sick curve of her lip. Her eyebrows dip low.

"Once you been caught by Julian, there's no getting out. My mama warned me about the slavers when I left home, and they still got me."

"Who's Julian?" I ask, holding tight to my throbbing hand.

"Everybody's heard that name in Wildenvalley. He's the slaver that runs this area."

"What will he do with us?" I ask.

The woman shifts her baby so he's looking over the other side of her shoulder. She furiously pats his back.

"Sell us to some family with a lot of rings, I guess," she says.

"They can't just snatch people from the road."

"Hmph. They can now," the woman says, adjusting her baby again. "My name is Gracine by the way, and this is Dasante." Gracine sets her baby on her knee and proudly shows him off to us.

The idea of having to care for a baby in this filth sends shivers up my back. Gracine doesn't seem overly bothered. She glances around the wagon as if this were merely an inconvenience.

"I'm Camilla. This is my brother, Tuor."

"What do you mean? About the slavers being allowed to capture anyone now?" Tuor asks.

Hitting a rock, the wagon shifts its contents to one side. Tuor and I hold onto the bars until the wagon evens.

"You haven't heard? The Supreme Ruler's lifted all restrictions on the slave traders. They got a big need for slaves now in the cities, so he's letting 'em sell anyone they can find."

"Slavers been at each other's throats in competition with each other. They say there's a slave war goin' on." The woman leans back and rests her head on the bars. "I don't care about all of that. Wherever I end up will be better than where I came from."

"How?" I raise my eyebrow.

"My husband is nastier than them," she says.

I shake my head and look down at my lap. "It's worse than we thought," I whisper to Tuor. "Elmyra will crumble if Quinten enslaves half its citizens."

"Back where I come from, we call him the Dark Ruler," Gracine says.

I tilt my head. "Why?"

The woman leans forward and lowers her voice. "My mama told me it took blood magic to make him Supreme Ruler. Now, that magic is making him insane."

I let my face show surprise even though I know exactly what this poor woman is talking about. The blood magic came from my mother, Portia. She *is* the only reason he became Supreme Ruler, and now that she's not behind him anymore, and Reed is trying to take the throne, he's scrambling.

"I just pray that we'll be put in a nice home," Gracine says, bowing her head to kiss her baby's cheek.

We rock to and fro on the rough road like a small boat tossed on the river. The sun warms the back of my neck. To my dismay, my nose has already grown numb to the smell.

"Do you know where they're taking us?" I ask Gracine.

"Of course. Where else would they take us?" she asks with a snarky tone. "To the city."

She points ahead. I shimmy into a standing position again and peer through the cage, past the wagon driver. The road curves to reveal a thick city wall at the far end of the grasslands. My eyes widen at the sight. From the highest pinnacle, a long maroon flag flaps in the wind. It's emblazoned with the Warwick crest. Tuor comes to stand next to me. He stares in amazement at the massive city ahead.

"I guess we don't have to worry anymore about how we're going to get into LilyAye," he says.

***

We ride for several more hours across the expansive plain. Behind us, the great mountain range grows small. The Ebertier River continues along the edge of the grassland, snaking around the city walls. I furtively glance from side to side in the hopes that I'll see Roehana or Eve tracking us, but the only ones with their eyes on us are the slaver guards.

The stone walls of LilyAye tower over us like mountains. I crane my neck and peek my head through the bars to get a glimpse of the magnitude. Warwick soldiers march back and forth along the top of the wall. They appear like tiny bugs. White birds soar among the high towers. The Warwick flag is as big as a tent.

Our caravan comes to a halt behind a line of several other travelers. A massive arched gate is carved out of the side of the city wall with thick iron bars.

"Why are we stopped?" Tuor asks.

"It looks like there's a checkpoint at the gate," I say.

"This is the west gate," comes a voice from beside us. I turn around to find Gracine, with her baby, standing on the other side of the wagon. Someone shifts behind her, knocking her forward. I extend my hand to catch her.

"You okay?" I ask. She nods, then sidles up beside Tuor and me.

"They call it the slave gate," she continues, bobbing her baby up and down in her arms. "The front gate is far prettier I've heard, but no matter which gate you come through, you're searched, and you have to pay a toll."

"You have to pay a toll?" Tuor asks with raised eyebrows.

"You gotta pay if you want inside," Gracine says.

One of the Warwick soldiers guarding the slave gate pulls down on a lever. The iron gate opens with clanging chains. A merchant with a small wagon drives through. Our caravan moves forward by a few paces. It's our turn to cross through the checkpoint.

A man emerges from the front wagon. He's bald and dressed in black leather pants. His hands are also covered in leather gloves. A machete swings from his belt as he confidently strides toward the soldiers at the gate. Julian, I assume.

Julian opens his mouth to speak before the soldiers have a chance to say anything. The Warwick guards seem to shrink next to him. Julian puffs his chest and gestures wildly at his caravan of a hundred or more slaves.

The soldiers nod in agreement to whatever he is saying. Julian produces a bag of rings. He divides them among the five soldiers guarding the gate. He mockingly bows to the soldiers, then returns to his wagon with a smile. One of the soldiers steps forward and waves our caravan on as the gate slowly clicks open.

"No search?" I ask.

Gracine grunts. "Slavers own this city I guess."

The wagons rumble forward. We pass under the huge Warwick flag and through the city gates into LilyAye. My heart thrums in a quick, steady beat as the hustle of the city hits me in a big wave. A line of beggars clog the entryway. As our wagon crosses over the threshold, a dark, looming castle sits off in the distance, at the far end of the city.

The beggars swarm the slavers riding alongside our wagon. Dirty hands grapple at their saddlebags. Most are physically deformed, not even worthy to be captured and sold as slaves, I suppose. Julian's men kick them with their boots or prod them away with their wooden clubs.

Our wagon rolls down the dirt road into an open-air market. I clutch the bars of our cage, staring at the variety laid out before me. Tents and booths smash together along the street, looking like their own little village. Hundreds of people flood the market. Most of them are dressed in pristine white silken dresses with ornate collars around their necks. Other people mill about the market too. Women twirl through the booths, dressed in obscenely vibrant colors.

Workers unload wagons full of fresh produce. I recognize the wooden boxes as the ones that come from the Bear Gap farm. Bright green broccoli and brussels sprouts fill baskets and crates as servants pick through them, looking for the best food for their masters. Chickens squawk from bell-shaped woven cages.

Food isn't the only commodity in this market. Clothing, fabric, and jewelry all hang from the tops and corners of booths. Shoppers scoop out herbs and spices from burlap bags. Merchants shout about their wares. They yell over each other, trying to be louder than their competitors.

Kids screech and run across the road between Julian's horses. The wagon wheels kick up a cloud of dust as we continue through the west side of the city. Fences and cages hold cattle, horses, and pigs. The city is alive with chatter and business. The shops continue until we take a sharp left. As we curve around, I spot a wooden platform with a large fenced area behind it.

I turn to Gracine. "Is that for hangings?"

She squints and leans forward. "I think that's where we get sold."

Our caravan meanders down the dirt road as the noise of the market fades away. Houses line the street with modest lots behind them. They look like miniature farms with cages, fences, and watering troughs. I lean forward and press against the wagon bars. My eyes widen as understanding fills my mind. The cages aren't filled with animals. They're filled with people.

"Slaver's Row," the man next to me mumbles.

I turn to Tuor and say, "Whatever they do with us, we have to stay together."

Chills creep their way down my back as our caravan pulls up to Julian's compound. The property is surrounded by an eight-foot-tall fence. At the gate, a man sits perched high atop a wooden structure that resembles a hunting blind. He stands and waves to our driver as we approach, a crossbow poised in his left hand.

We bumble into the muddy yard. The gate closes ominously behind us. The driver leads our line of wagons around the back of the house. A pen of horses sits to our right. A bonfire rages next to another tall wooden structure with a guard stationed at the top. The yard is torn up with deep marks from the wagon wheels. Four massive cages take up most of the property. Our wagon jerks to a stop. Julian's men immediately jump from their horses. They unload our bags and luggage and begin rifling through our belongings.

"One at a time!" the men bark as they crack open the back door of our wagon.

The people around us start chattering fervently. They push and shove against us as they're ripped from the wagon. Gracine huddles close to me and Tuor. Our wagon slowly empties. The captives are directed into the cages. More guards stand at the ready, with knives in hand, a few yards back, just watching.

"Let's go. Let's go," the man barks at me.

I hesitate at the opening, scanning the yard. Like a factory, people are moved and sorted quickly. The guard yanks me, by my arm, from the back of the wagon. I fall to my knees, into a puddle.

"Camilla," Tuor calls.

I blink my eyes open. Tuor's pulled from the wagon. He helps me onto my feet. Then we're shoved through the yard, toward one of the cages. Gracine walks swiftly to my side. She's breathing heavily, clutching Dasante in her arms.

"Are you okay?" Tuor asks.

"Yeah." I wince with every step.

In front of us, a man breaks loose from the line and darts between the wagons. He shifts on his feet, searching for a direction to run. He pushes off and hurtles toward the front gate. Everyone in the yard stops and watches. The guards do nothing. They ignore the man, letting him run. Julian stands off to the side, observing. He cracks a smile and watches curiously.

My eyes dart to the watchman at the top of the tower. He lifts his crossbow, sets his sights, and lets an arrow fly. It careens through the air and strikes the man with great force in his lower back. He falls with the impact, twisting and moaning in pain. I struggle to breathe as I stand stunned and frozen.

"There's always one!" Julian yells across the yard. He sets his hands on his hips. "Let that be a sign to you. This is how we punish those that run."

A guard pokes me in the shoulder with the butt of his bat. "Keep moving!"

At the door of the cage, Tuor and I are prodded inside, but Gracine is stopped by the guard. He reaches down and rips the baby from Gracine's arms.

"No!" An agonizing shriek pours from her mouth.

"What's he doing?" Tuor asks.

"You can't do that!" I push my way back to the cage door. "That's her baby!"

Dasante wails as he's ferried across the lawn, toward Julian's house.

"Please, no. Don't take him from me! Please," Gracine begs.

The guard shoves Gracine inside. She runs immediately to the bars and cries out for Dasante. Anger bubbles like a cauldron of hot lava inside me.

"That's her baby," I yell again, standing toe-to-toe with the guard. "He needs his mother. You can't just take her baby like that."

The guard peers down at me as if I were an ant. "Get inside!"

"Camilla, come on," Tuor says, tugging on my shoulder.

I ignore him. "What are you doing to her baby?"

Red clouds my vision. Dasante's cries echo in my ears. I squeeze my fist and hurl a punch at the guard's face. He's taken aback, then looks down at me as his eyebrows dive into a deep V. The guard hurls the butt of his bat into my stomach. I fall back onto the sloppy cage floor.

He then lifts his hand. I raise my arm to block his blow, but he reaches over me and grabs Tuor by the neck. Tuor is dragged from the cage. I scramble to my feet and follow, screaming for them to let him go. The guard holds Tuor tightly in the crook of his elbow. He pulls a short knife from his belt. Another guard holds me back when I try to run to Tuor.

"It'd be a shame to kill this one," the guard growls, tightening his vise around Tuor's neck. "The men catch the most rings."

Tears burst at the corners of my eyes. I rip and tear at the slaver as I struggle to free myself. Everyone left in the yard stands unmoving.

The guard holds his knife to Tuor's neck. "This is how we deal with those that resist!"

I drop to my knees. "No!"

The guard presses the tip of his knife into Tuor's neck. A gurgle escapes Tuor's mouth. The guard holds my gaze with wide eyes.

"Please," I choke.

Julian stalks up to me, his hands still on his hips. He bends slightly and glares down at me with a condescending expression. "Are you going to give us any more trouble?"

Tears stream down my cheeks. Silently, I shake my head and decide, for once in my life, to shut up and obey.

CHAPTER THIRTEEN

"I THINK THAT'S enough," Julian says, patting the guard on the back. "Let's not damage the goods any more than we have to."

The guard returns his knife to his belt. A thin line of blood oozes down Tuor's throat. We're thrown back into the cage along with the remaining slaves. The door is bolted shut. Mud is smeared on the cage floor, and it reeks of urine. A long trough of water sits against the cage wall. People bend and scoop their dirty hands into it as they sip desperately.

"Let me look at it," I say to Tuor, still wiping tears from my face.

Tuor holds a hand to his neck. I urge his hand down. A nick in his skin reveals a red and bloody wound.

"It's fine," Tuor says, brushing me away. His voice is small and quiet.

Gracine is huddled in the corner of the cage. I clutch at the side of my stomach as Tuor and I scrunch down next to her. Gracine's face twists in agony. Tears bubble from her eyes.

"I'm sorry . . . " I say.

"They'll sell him to a good family, right?" Her words are hiccups between sobs.

I nod and search for a way to comfort Gracine, but think of nothing that seems sufficient. So I reach an arm around her shoulders and pull her tight. Gracine weeps as she rests her head on my shoulder. Tuor is quiet for the rest of the day. We're gifted with a bucket of slop that's dropped in through the bars of our cage: dinner. Then Tuor, Gracine, and I fall asleep, huddled together in the corner.

***

"Up, up, up!" the guards bark.

They run their wooden clubs across the bars of our cages, rattling us awake. I suck in a mouthful of rancid air. My back aches where I spent the night pressed against the hard iron. Gracine's body lays slumped over my shoulder as she slept the whole night by my side.

"Everyone on their feet!"

"Wake up," I say, nudging Gracine. Tuor stirs next to me.

I pull myself to standing. A deep throb pulses on the side of my stomach where I was hit with the guard's club. The cage door cracks open. A battalion of men stand outside, knives in hand. They pull us from the cage one by one. We're shoved out into the yard and lined up for processing. The guards dump buckets of freezing water over our heads. We're told to wash, and then we're thrown dirty rags and towels to dry ourselves. The nippy fall air bites at my wet skin and hair.

We stand in a crowd with a hundred other shivering slaves. A thudding *clunk* draws my attention to the front. I bob my head between a group of girls to get a look. A guard ratchets an iron collar onto one of the slave's necks. That collar is attached by a short chain to another collar, which he uses on the next person, and then on Gracine, until it's my turn. He sets the cool metal against the back of my neck and clamps the front closed over my throat. Instinctively, I claw at the vise as he uses a wrench to tighten the bolt that holds the cuff closed.

Breathe, I tell myself. *Don't let the panic overtake you.*

Tuor is attached to me, on the next collar. In groups of ten, we're nudged to the next station, where one of the slavers paints a symbol on each of our arms. I look down to see a black X inside a circle. I can't make out the meaning of it, but it reminds me of the ravaged Warwick brand on the inside of my wrist.

We're led away from the processing area and forced to walk onto the road that leads out of the compound. The heavy cuff digs into my shoulders. I rub the base of my neck, where, already, I can feel it bruising. Gracine whimpers, her tears glistening in the sun.

The men circle us as more groupings are added. I shift on my feet and take in my surroundings, but every move I make rattles the chain on either side of my neck and pulls at Tuor's and Gracine's collars, so I stay put. Everyone stands anxiously. A man hops into the driver's seat of a wagon that holds all of our confiscated belongings. Julian appears from the back of his house. His bald head gleams in the sunlight.

"Suit up, gentlemen," he shouts as the last of the captives are directed into our line up. His men mount their horses as if they're preparing for battle, weapons in hand and ready for a fight. Julian walks up and down the herd of captives. He inspects his product the way a jeweler views a fine gem.

"Looks good. This is a nice crop," he muses to one of his men. "Have they all been tagged?"

"Yes, sir. Everyone's been cleaned up and we're ready to go."

"All right then," Julian says with a smile.

He slaps the guard on the shoulder. The head slaver mounts a horse of his own. He rides to the front of our caravan, and the other men encircle us.

"Move!" one of the guards yells.

Julian leads the way as we walk forward and exit the front gate on foot. My boots kick up dust. The chains around our necks *clang* as we shuffle forward. Slowly, we walk past the other slaver compounds. Through the fences, I catch glimpses of other men and women being prepped for the auction block.

The market bustles louder than yesterday. The tall auction platform looms. Rich buyers sit poised in the audience while the less fortunate stare from a distance. How bizarre, I think to myself. Hordes of chained humans in the middle of the road doesn't seem to be a strange sight to anyone except me.

We're funneled into a large fenced area, behind the auction platform, like cattle. We're pushed in so tight there's no room to sit down. Bodies press up against me on all sides. I stumble, feeling the pull of the neck cuff as Tuor and Gracine are jostled around too.

I feel like I'm choking. I grip hard onto the cuff as I start to cough. More caravans arrive, and their slaves are dumped into the same fenced area as us. I suck in air, struggling to breathe as we're shifted and pushed about. We're pressed up against one side of the fence, and soon, we're packed so tight that no one can move.

The confined space and the constraint of the collar transports me back to Karla's bedroom. My whole body tenses. I squeeze my eyes closed and brace for the sting of her knife. My breathing quickens. My heart trips and tumbles over itself.

"Not again . . ." I mutter to myself, feeling my old demons returning.

"It's okay," Tuor says.

His calm voice surprises me. I open my eyes and remember that I'm not in Karla's bedroom.

"This will be over soon," he says.

I nod, steadying my body and forcing myself to take even breaths.

"I will find you," I tell Tuor, my voice strained from the collar. "Whatever happens to us today, I will find you."

Tuor's curly, scraggily hair falls over his dark eyes. "I love you."

"I love you too."

Tears burn at the corner of my eyes. I grab Tuor's hand, and he squeezes mine in response. Tuor, Gracine, and I stand behind the auction platform. In front of me is a sea of slaves, many with the black X and circle on their arm, but some have different shapes painted on their bodies. Our symbols identify us with the slaver that caught us, I realize.

Beyond the crowd is a tall wooden staircase that leads to the auction platform. A man walks across the stage to a podium, his back toward us. He faces the audience of potential buyers.

"We will begin the auction," he shouts. "Ready your tickets for bidding. All sales are final. Rings must be paid to the clerk before taking your merchandise. Remember your numbers. Thank you." The auctioneer turns to look down the steps. He waves to one of the guards in the pen to bring up the first person.

The guard grabs the person closest to the steps and unscrews the latch on his neck cuff. He marches a middle-aged man up to the auction block.

The auctioneer begins. "Number one on the block this morning: man, tall, able bodied. Let's start the bidding at fifteen rings."

A flag pops up from the crowd on the other side of the platform. "Fifteen rings," the buyer calls.

Another flag signals. "Sixteen."

The first buyer bids again.

The auctioneer points to the audience. "Seventeen rings. Is there another?"

A third bidder enters the competition.

"Eighteen," says the auctioneer. "Nineteen, anyone?"

The original bidder calls again.

The auctioneer responds. "Twenty! Anyone else?"

He scans the audience. "Anyone for twenty-one rings? Good price for a solid field worker or stable hand."

No one else calls. The auctioneer slams the head of a gavel onto his podium.

"Twenty rings for number one on the block today."

The man is quickly ushered off the auction block and another person is brought up. This time it's a woman. She's crying softly as she reaches her hands up to wipe the tears from her eyes.

"Item number two for sale this morning: woman, older, but appears sturdy. We will begin at eight rings."

My mind twists as I try to comprehend this kind of debauchery. Working at the farm, I always felt like a slave. I called myself a slave. I fought to stop that form of slavery. But *this*, this is different. Working at the farm became a necessity for people, but they ultimately made the decision to walk to the farm and take a job. That's a far cry from these people who were plucked from their homes and will soon become the property of some wealthy LilyAye family.

"Sold!" the auctioneer calls out.

The woman goes for thirteen rings. Another person is brought up to the platform, then another and another. The auctioneer and his men work swiftly, pushing slaves across the platform as if this were a butcher shop. One man gets sold for a whopping 110 rings. Some of the children sell for as low as three. Slowly, the crowd thins. Tuor, Gracine, and I inch our way closer to the platform. The morning wanes. The slaves all start to look the same.

"Sold!" shouts the auctioneer.

Seventeen rings for a teenage boy. He's ushered off the stage by two men. We're nudged to the bottom of the stairs. Gracine is next. She swiftly turns and faces me as the guard removes her collar.

"Thank you," she says. "Thank you for trying to save my son."

The guard pushes her up the steps before I have a chance to respond. He holds the chain taut so I'm pressed against him. I grip tight to Tuor's hand, knowing that our goodbye is fast approaching. Gracine sells for nine rings, a figure I've learned is a deal at this slave auction.

"Next up!" calls the auctioneer as Gracine is removed from the platform.

The guard unscrews my collar.

"Let's go," he says in a gruff voice.

He grabs me by the arm and shoves me up the steps. My hand slips from Tuor's. My chest tightens as I take the wooden steps. With every rise of the stairs, I regret my decision to come to LilyAye more and more. I've sacrificed my brother, and even my own life, for nothing. I could have been free in Bear Gap, but instead, I'll be a slave in LilyAye.

Trying is never a failure. The phrase enters my mind unprovoked. Knox said it to me once. Why am I thinking about him right now? Maybe it's because he's right. Despite my hatred for Knox, he was right. We tried. Eve, Tuor, and I tried. I guess that's all that matters.

At the top, the guard tosses me onto the stage. I stumble toward the auctioneer. The sun bursts into my eyes. Blocking the glare with my hand, I scan the audience of buyers. I feel exposed and embarrassed. They stare up at me as if they were critiquing a crude painting.

"Next up, number seventy-six on the block today." The auctioneer positions his glasses on his nose and scans my body. "Young female, sturdy build."

My eyebrows pinch forward into a scowl at the auctioneer's description of my body. Awkwardly, I wrap my arms around my middle.

"Let's start the bidding at ten rings."

"Ten," a bidder shouts.

"Twelve."

"Great, is there another?" the auctioneer asks.

A third flag goes up. "Fourteen rings."

That voice . . . it's familiar.

"Sixteen," calls the original bidder.

"Eighteen rings." Comes the familiar voice again. It's clear and somber, not spirited like the other bidders. I search the crowd. My eyes settle on a man dressed in a blue button-up suit. His silky black hair is combed to the side. He lifts his chin. My heart pounds in my chest. Those dark eyes, that smooth, olive skin . . . it's Lawrence.

CHAPTER FOURTEEN

"SOLD!" THE AUCTIONEER shouts as he slams his gavel into the podium.

My body jolts in response.

"Sold for eighteen rings to the fellow in the back."

I'm swiftly ushered off the stage as Tuor is brought up to be auctioned off. Dazed, I walk down the steps on the other side of the wooden platform. Halfway down, I pause and peer out across the crowd of buyers. Lawrence's lips are pressed tightly together in a scowl. A rush of excitement fills me. Lawrence is here. I don't know how he knew we'd be at the slave auction today, but he's going to buy Tuor and me and save us.

"Let's go!" A guard at the bottom of the steps yells at me. He grabs my wrist and pulls me down the last few steps. He then takes a piece of fabric and ties it tightly around my arm. The same family crest that was on Lawrence's bidding flag is stamped at the end of the fabric.

I'm pushed into another holding area where the recently purchased slaves wait to be picked up by their new masters. It's a bustling crowd of nervous people. Gracine stands with two other girls and her buyer at the clerk's desk. Immediately, he affixes them with wrist restraints. The buyer pays the clerk and then loads them into a flatbed wagon.

"Next up is number seventy-seven," the auctioneer says.

I back away from the platform to get a view of Tuor. The auctioneer scans Tuor up and down.

"Young man, able bodied, tall frame. Let's start the bid at twenty-five."

"Twenty-five." A shout rings out from the crowd.

"Twenty-seven," Lawrence bids.

A third person enters the competition. "Thirty-two!"

Flags pop through the crowd like kids eagerly raising their hands for a piece of candy.

"Thirty-seven rings."

"Forty!"

"Forty-two," Lawrence says sternly.

"We have forty-two," the auctioneer announces. "Anybody for forty-four?"

One of the bidders lowers his flag. Tuor is too expensive for him.

"Fifty rings," shouts the original bidder.

Lawrence raises his flag. "Fifty-two."

"Fifty-five!"

Two flags stand at attention. I crane my neck to get a look at the other man fighting for Tuor. He's a small, slender man with greasy shoulder-length hair. Lawrence pauses.

"How about fifty-seven?" The auctioneer prods Lawrence.

His face is a stone. *Bid fifty-seven*, I scream in my head, but Lawrence slowly lets his flag dip, resigning the sale to the other man.

The auctioneer slams his gavel. "Sold! Fifty-five rings."

"What!" I mutter. "What is he doing?"

Lawrence stands quickly and excuses himself as he slinks down the row of buyers. Tuor takes the steps off the platform. I run to him as the guard ties a piece of fabric around his arm.

"Lawrence is here," I say into Tuor's ear.

"I saw," Tuor says through gritted teeth.

"We'll get you out. Wherever they take you, we'll find you."

Lawrence's familiar voice hollers across the holding area. "That one right there."

Lawrence stands at the gate and points at me. The guard manning the gate stalks in our direction.

I turn to Tuor and grab both of his hands. "I'll come for you. I promise."

The guard hooks his hand under my arm and pulls me away.

"Is this all you got?" the guard asks Lawrence.

"That's it for today," he says.

Lawrence doesn't meet my eyes. I'm dragged over to the clerk's table.

"Number seventy-six . . ." says the clerk as he peers down at his ledger book. "That's eighteen rings, Sir. Thatius."

Lawrence smiles coolly as he reaches into the breast of his jacket pocket and pulls out eighteen Catahli rings. The clerk carefully counts them before giving him a nod of approval. I furtively glance over at Tuor as he stands alone in the fence.

"Will we see you next week?" the clerk asks.

Lawrence bows his head. "I hope not," he says with a chuckle. "I should think we've got enough servants to keep three houses running."

The clerk grins. "Have a good day, Sir. Thatius."

"You as well. I've got her." He addresses the guard, who's still tightly gripping my upper arm.

"Are you sure?" the guard asks.

"I think I can handle one servant."

"Yes, sir," the guard says before releasing my arm and lumbering back to the holding fence.

"Come," Lawrence says.

"What about Tuor?" I ask in a hushed tone.

Lawrence ignores me and places a hand on the small of my back. He nudges me through the bustling crowd. People crisscross in front of and behind us. I stop short and look one last time over at Tuor. He hangs on the edge of the fence and watches me.

"Wait," I say.

"Keep walking," Lawrence murmurs into my ear.

"But it's Tuor," I protest.

Lawrence doesn't seem to notice Tuor. He pushes me forward, more forcefully now, toward a black horse-drawn carriage.

"That's my brother. We can't just leave him here," I say, twisting against Lawrence's prodding. Passersby stop and stare. Lawrence grabs me by the arms from behind and pushes me into the carriage. Quickly, he slides into the seat across from me, latches the door closed, and pulls a curtain across the window. He leans forward and taps on a glass partition between us and the driver. The driver snaps his reins against the horse's back, and our carriage lurches forward.

"We have to get Tuor!" I say.

Lawrence sits on a plum-colored velvet bench. He straightens the jacket of his suit. "How many times am I going to have to rescue you, Camilla?" His words escape his lips in a terse, annoyed fashion.

I furrow my brows. "Rescue *me*?"

"I'm risking a lot right now to save you."

"Oh, well, I'm sorry for inconveniencing you. I risked a lot when I begged Ralf not to torture you when we were overthrowing Bear Gap. Guess I shouldn't have gone through the trouble!"

Our carriage rumbles down the road. Lawrence's mouth forms a hard line.

"Why save me and not Tuor? He used to be your friend."

"I tried. I was outbid. I didn't have enough rings."

"Oh . . ." I lean back on the seat and take in the contrast of the ornate carriage next to my dirty, tattered clothes. Lawrence is dressed in a sharp blue suit with a short collar. The buttons of the suit go all the way to his neck. It's an odd look. LilyAye style, I suppose.

"Who bought him?" I ask.

Lawrence sighs. "Gregor Creighton. He owns almost all the iron-mining pits around LilyAye. He's contracted by Warwick, so he's got more rings than some of the wealthiest in the city. He makes it a point to come to all of the auctions and buy up the able-bodied men to work in his mines." Finally, Lawrence raises his head to meet my eyes. "I tried to save him, Camilla, you have to believe me."

"I believe you."

Lawrence puts his face in his hands. "Why can't you ever just stay put?"

"You don't seem pleased to see me."

Lawrence purses his lips. "Of course I'm happy to see you." The sparkle that I remember returns to Lawrence's eyes. "I just wish it wasn't like this. I almost didn't recognize you with your hair like that."

I finger my short, boyish hair, which, over the last month of travel, has grown down over my ears. The carriage bumps gently as the wheels roll over the cobblestone street.

"So that's how it works in this city? You gotta be rich if you want to buy people?"

"You have to have a family crest, which is appointed by Quinten himself. If you have a family crest, then you're allowed to bid at the slave auction."

I look at the piece of fabric tied to my arm. "This is your family crest?"

"Not exactly."

I brace myself against the window as we take a turn into a peaceful neighborhood. Grand estates are lined with iron fences. The houses are all made of a beautiful variety of white and pink Catahli. Servants dot the lawns in their white robes. Warwick flags are staked into the ground or hung over balcony railings.

"These houses are made of Catahli?" I ask in awe as we pull onto a winding driveway that leads up to the house.

Lawrence nods, unimpressed. "Get used to it. Everything in LilyAye is made of Catahli."

My mouth hangs open. Our horse clip-clops up a smooth white road, toward a house that's almost as big as the governor's mansion in Bear Gap. I lean out the window. Bright bursts of freshly trimmed grass create a sea of green. The house's towering Catahli walls are swirled with light blue.

The mansion glows in the sunlight. Tall columns line the front of the house. Palm trees flank either side of the entrance. The road circles around to the front door, but we drive past that and pull around to the back of the house, in front of a set of stables. The driver jumps from his seat and begins tending to the horse.

"This is where you live?" I ask as I observe a gazebo in the backyard with flowers snaking their way up the posts and rails.

"No," Lawrence says. He leans forward to face me. "Not yet, at least. Listen, Camilla, I bought you, but I don't personally own you. It's a little more complicated than that."

"What do you mean?"

"This isn't just anyone's house. I know this family well. I'm very . . ." Lawrence clicks his fingers together as he searches for the right words.

"What?"

"I'm intimately connected with these people. I'm placing you here to be their servant for a while. Don't worry. They're kind. They'll treat you well."

I shake my head. "I'm not going to be anyone's servant. Why can't you just tell them you didn't buy anybody today?"

"Because," Lawrence growls. "I used their rings to buy you. In order to make this whole thing work, I had to arrange the purchase of a new servant for the woman of the house. Fortunately for you, she was in need of a new lady's maid, so you're going to have to pretend you know how to tend to a lady."

"Wait, how long do I have to stay here?"

"I'm not exactly sure. But long enough so that there's no suspicion." Lawrence furtively glances out the carriage window. "Look at me." Our eyes connect.

"You and I don't know each other. We've never met. Do you understand?"

I nod.

"Okay. Just follow my lead." Lawrence knocks on the carriage door frame. "Hobbes!" he calls.

"Hold on." I grab his arm. "I don't understand how you pulled this off. How did Eve find you so quickly?" My mind spins with how she managed to get to LilyAye on her gimp leg and then find Lawrence and have the idea to have him buy back Tuor and me.

Lawrence cocks his head to the side. "Eve? I haven't seen Eve."

"Then how did you know we'd been picked up by slavers?"

The driver swings open the carriage door. Lawrence straightens his back and immediately exits.

"Wait," I whisper.

"Come now," he commands me.

I follow Lawrence as he strides through the yard. It's a utopia of funny-looking trees and vibrant-colored flowers. We walk down a narrow path that leads to the back door. I want to tug on Lawrence's arm and ask him again how he knew about Tuor and me, but Hobbes is within earshot, and a stern-looking woman stands at the back door, her hands behind her back.

"Sir Thatius," the middle-aged woman says as she holds the door open for Lawrence.

She's dressed in the long white silken gown that all the other servants are wearing, and her gray hair is pulled tightly into a low bun. I follow Lawrence inside the house. We stand in a round vestibule with a table in the middle that's topped with a magnificent vase of flowers. Clattering dishes echo from down the hall.

"I see your mission was . . . successful," she says, scrunching her nose as she looks down at me.

My ears perk at the word *mission*. A plump, long-haired white cat saunters into the room and rubs against my leg.

"Yes," Lawrence says. "I hope the lady will be pleased."

They're talking about me, I realize. The mission was to go and purchase me . . .

The woman speaks. "I'll take her from here."

"Very well." Lawrence nods and marches down the hallway without even a backward glance at me.

CHAPTER FIFTEEN

"MY NAME IS Ronda," the woman announces, clasping her hands together. "I'm the head maid, which means I run this household. I set the rules for the servants. I expect obedience and a respectful spirit. Do you understand?"

"Uh, yes," I say, stunned. I peer down the hallway, hoping that Lawrence will return and rescue me from Ronda.

"What is your name?" she asks.

Such a simple question, yet I'm surprised by it. The furry creature at my feet begs to be petted. She purrs, sending buzzy vibrations up my leg.

"Kat," I blurt, knowing I can't use my real name.

"Kat?" Ronda questions with the raise of an eyebrow.

"With a *K*," I add.

"Hmm," she muses, pursing her lips. "All right, Kat, let's go."

Ronda drags me, by my wrist, out of the vestibule and into the hallway. Her tight grip instantly brings shivers to my body.

"First rule," Ronda proclaims. "The master doesn't tolerate dirty, shabby-looking servants. You will wash every day and comb that ratty hair."

Ronda gives my head a disgusted look as she continues to pull me through another hallway and past the kitchen, where I notice several servants scrubbing dishes. Ronda peeks in the kitchen door and snaps her fingers at one of the kitchen maids.

"You can bring that hot water now."

"Who's the master?" I ask.

"You'll meet him soon enough."

Ronda carries on with her swift walk. We pause at the top of a set of steps that look like they lead into a dark room. A flickering torch provides the only light.

"At the bottom of these stairs is the servant's dining room. We meet down there for meals. Come. This way."

We continue into the far corner of the house. There, we stop at a line of four or five archways, each with a curtain over the opening. The kitchen maid scurries past us, carrying a large pot of steaming water. She slips through one of the curtains. Ronda releases my hand and turns up her nose as she looks me up and down.

"This one is for you, set up as the lady requested," Ronda says, pointing to the curtain that the kitchen maid just passed through. "Get yourself cleaned up, and I'll be in to see you shortly."

Ronda turns on her heels.

"Hardly worthy . . ." she mutters under her breath.

"Excuse me?" I ask, unable to keep the snark from my voice. "What do you mean, *hardly worthy*?"

Ronda spins back to face me and clasps her hands in front of her.

"Look at yourself, a girl straight off the auction block, and now you're a lady's maid to one of the richest women in LilyAye. You're hardly worthy of Fairalisa."

"I have experience," I say, remembering what Lawrence said.

Ronda laughs. "You have no more experience as a lady's maid than a pig has being clean. I don't know what kind of ruse you're playing, or how you wiggled your way into this house, but since Sir Thatius bought you, I'll do as I'm told."

I cock my head to the side. "Why do you have to obey him? He's not your master."

"Not yet, but seeing as he'll someday inherit this house, I think it best that I treat him as such." Ronda leans in close and points a finger at me. "Just know that when you make a fool of yourself as a lady's maid, I'll be the first one to suggest we ship you off to the iron mines and find a real lady's maid."

Fine. The iron mines is where Tuor has been taken, and somehow they sound better than being someone's slave in LilyAye. Regardless, I decide to play the game, for now. I turn my eyes downward, feigning humbleness.

"I'll do my best to please you and the lady," I say.

"We'll see." Ronda grunts before stalking away.

I look around the stark yet peaceful hallway. A breeze ripples the soft, sheer curtains that cover the line of archways. I slip past the curtain and into a washroom. Half of the room has a roof over it, with white, fluffy towels and a clean set of clothes laid out for me, while the other half is open to the sky.

My eyes widen at the sight of a large porcelain tub, sitting on a bed of pebbles, in the outdoor area. The kitchen maid dips her fingers into the tub water while now holding an empty pot in the other hand.

"Should be warm enough for you now," the girl says demurely before slipping from the room.

Bright green bushes surround the outdoor area, creating a privacy wall. Large lengths of canvas drape either side of the bushes like giant curtains. I study them and try to understand. A portable roof, in case it rains, I reason. A stove whirs away, keeping the room a toasty temperature despite the chilly fall air. Seems a waste of wood to heat a room that's open to the outdoors. LilyAye wealth...

I step back into the room and catch a glimpse of myself on the wall to my left. I stop. An oval-shaped mirror with curved silver designs around the edge hangs on the wall.

Who is that person staring back at me? I approach the water basin sitting under the mirror. I look horrendous. My hair falls just below my ears in a poofy, straggly mess. My face is sallow and nicked with tiny cuts under my eye. I disrobe, untying the fabric band from my arm, and tossing my filthy clothes into the corner of the room. A big purply bruise stretches across my middle, along my rib cage, where I was hit by the slaver's bat.

The tub is filled with hot, steamy water. When I step into it, a soft, silky substance covers my skin. It's soapy and smooth. My muscles relax as I sink my shoulders into the tub water. The sky above me is a light blue and spotted with white clouds. It's quiet aside from the chattering robins in the trees surrounding the washroom. Maybe being a servant in LilyAye isn't so bad.

Sliding to the bottom of the tub, I let my head dip below the surface. Warmth engulfs my whole body. Beneath the water, I feel utterly alone, like I could shut the whole world out and cease to exist. Part of me wants to stay here.

Finally, I come to the surface, sucking in a great gulp of air. A bottle of liquid soap sits on a gold tray next to me. I squirt a blob of it into my hand and wonder how the magicians in LilyAye managed to make soap like this. I scrub away a month of filth from my scalp down to my toenails. Not surprisingly, the shower I received at Julian's compound didn't do much to actually clean me.

I step out of the tub and rinse myself on the cobblestone with a vase of clear water and then wrap myself in a towel that's warm from sitting next to the stove. A long white silken dress lies on a plush bench against the wall. My slave outfit even comes with a set of fresh undergarments and flat, slipper-like shoes. I dress in the long sleeved, ankle length dress and comb my hair at the mirror.

Lying next to the wash basin is a hair clip shaped into a white flower with big green leaves. I finger the clip. It's made of real silver. A note next to the accessory says, "For you. Hope to be friends soon. Love, Fairalisa." I can't help but roll my eyes. This will sell for quite a few Catahli when I finally get out of here.

I towel my hair dry and secure the clip onto the side my head. It does little to calm my dark curls. I step back and take in my new appearance. Although still visible, the cuts on my face don't look as bad. Even my hair, which I lamented when I had to cut it, has grown into almost a cute style now that it's washed.

I creep over to the bushes surrounding the tub. They're dense enough that I can't see through them, but I bend onto a knee and pull aside a set of branches. The green lawn stretches all the way to a black iron fence that surrounds the property. Voices from the gardeners waft in my direction as I watch them trim trees in the yard. I wonder for a moment if I could squeeze myself through these bushes and hop over the fence, but I know that beyond that fence is just another mansion owned by a Warwick dignitary.

Footsteps echo in the hallway outside the washroom. I jump to my feet just as Ronda walks in. She looks around at the mess I made washing myself and lets out a disgruntled groan.

"Come," she says, waving me toward her. She holds a set of chains in her hands.

I furrow my brows as she directs me to take a seat on the bench. Ronda places a delicate silver collar around my neck. I grasp the smooth edge and tug it away. It's tight against my skin and comes to a triangle point on my clavicle. The only similarity it bares with the one the slaver put on me is that Ronda uses a key to attach it in the back. Aside from that, the collar resembles a thick necklace.

Ronda then bends and lifts the hem of my skirt. She clasps cool silver cuffs, which are attached by a thin chain, around each of my ankles. I wriggle my legs and feel the tension of the chains. Immediately, panic creeps up my spine at the feeling of being trapped. My momentary joy at cleaning myself in this luxury has melted away.

I want out of this place.

"Why aren't you wearing any shackles?" I ask Ronda.

"I've been head maid here for thirty years. The family trusts me. As someone with experience, surly you know that nearly every servant in LilyAye wears some kind of binding to protect the master's investment." Ronda gives me a mocking smirk. "Once you've been a lady's maid for thirty years, then we'll talk about having your chains removed. How does that sound?"

I glare at Ronda under heavy eyelids. She sets me on my feet and takes a good look at me.

"Better," she says, squinting her critical eyes. "We go now to meet the master. Try your best to look presentable and not ask so many questions."

Ronda leads me through an archway at the end of the hall. We take a sharp left down a short set of stairs, then curve into another hallway. We pass another servant, robed in a long white dress. She turns her eyes downward at the sight of Ronda.

We curve through a Catahli tunnel until we empty out of another archway, into a seating area. The floor, the walls, everything in this room is made of Catahli. I can barely believe it. I've never seen so much Catahli in my life.

The ceiling opens up and reveals two levels of balconies behind me. A pond is inlaid in the middle of the floor. It's been carved into an abstract geometric shape. Bright-orange-and-blue fish swirl around.

"This way," Ronda says.

She leads me away from the sitting room and up a flight of four steps, through another hallway, and down another set of steps, into a long room lined with books.

I can't hide the awe on my face. It's a library, just like Mirabelle's house, but this room is like a great hall. The books are meticulously stacked together on mahogany shelves. A servant stands on a ladder and dusts the surfaces.

Ronda directs me with her hand. "Over here."

We walk all the way to the end of the library. Our footsteps echo across the Catahli floor. An elderly man dressed in a pinstriped suit sits in a plush chair by a fireplace. A woman stands behind him, her hand on the back of the chair. She faces the fire as if she's mesmerized by its flames. In a chair, next to the elderly man, sits Lawrence, his legs crossed and a cigar between his lips.

"Master," Ronda says with a bow. "May I introduce the new lady's maid?"

"Lawrence, my boy," the elderly man says with a chuckle. "You do amaze me. When you set your mind to something, you go after it with all you've got."

Lawrence grins demurely. "I was lucky is all."

The woman turns to face me. Her soft rosy cheeks curve into a broad smile. She shyly touches the back of her head, where her black curls have been twisted into a comb. I scrunch my eyebrows together in surprise. She's young, very young, perhaps no older than me.

"Would you introduce us?" the old man asks. "I'm sure Fairalisa is anxious to meet her new lady's maid."

"Of course," Ronda says. "Let me introduce Kat."

Lawrence lets a puff of smoke out of his mouth and taps the ashes off the end of his cigar.

"What an adorable name," Fairalisa says with glee.

"Yes," Lawrence agrees.

"Kat," Ronda continues. "This is Master Anthond Hewe Balley, owner of this estate. He also serves on the Supreme Ruler's council."

"I still do that? Maybe it's time I retire," Anthond says with a chuckle.

"And this is Fairalisa," Ronda continues. "Master Anthond's daughter and lady of the house."

"So nice to meet you," Fairalisa says in a mousy voice.

"Uh uh! She's not just my daughter," Anthond says with a wink. "She's also Lawrence's fiancée!"

CHAPTER SIXTEEN

FIANCÉE?

My head jolts in Lawrence's direction. Fairalisa gives Lawrence a flirtatious wink as she fiddles with a long pearl necklace on her chest. He licks his lips nervously and forces a smile as he gazes at Fairalisa.

"We have quite a big affair coming up soon, so we couldn't have gotten a new lady's maid fast enough." Anthond leans forward in his chair and picks up a smoking cigar from the gold cart sitting between him and Lawrence. "I will warn you, Kat, you will have your hands full with my daughter," Anthond says lightheartedly.

He takes a long puff on his cigar. The thick smell of tobacco and cedar rests in a fog around us.

"Daddy!" Fairalisa says bringing a hand to her heart.

"Oh, it's true dear. We had to sell off your last lady's maid because she couldn't keep up with you!"

Fairalisa pouts. "Henrietta was just old."

"I'm old!" Anthond announces, his voice booming through the library.

His joke garners laughter from Lawrence and the other servants standing in the wings.

"I'm always appreciative of your service to this family, Lawrence." Taking another puff of his cigar, Anthond waves at Ronda. "I think it's time we get Kat started on her duties. I'm tired of hearing my daughter gripe about getting a new lady's maid."

"Daddy . . ." Fairalisa scowls, placing her hands on her hips.

"Yes, sir," Ronda says with a bow. "Come. Come."

Ronda nudges me to turn around. My shackles echo across the hall as I take baby steps.

"So your father's doing well?" I hear Anthond ask as we walk the length of the library.

"As well as could be expected," Lawrence says.

"He was absent from the last council meeting. Would you tell him I asked after him?"

"He isn't home much these days, always being sent out on some duty. I don't see him very often," Lawrence says.

"Always being sent away," Anthond muses. "Like father, like son."

Lawrence's father: the man who chased Tuor all the way to Bear Gap just to make sure he was executed for a crime he didn't commit, and the reason that Lawrence was brought back to his life in LilyAye. I hadn't considered that I'd hear the name Captain Ridley Thatius in LilyAye. Ronda and I exit the library and head down a dark hallway.

This will all be Lawrence's, I think to myself: a grand house and a young, beautiful bride on top of it. I guess his little rebellious streak in Bear Gap was all he needed to get it out of his system. I always felt bad for Lawrence being dragged back home, but it looks like he's settled quite well into LilyAye life.

"We eat dinner now so that we're able to serve the master during his dinner," Ronda explains. "You aren't a part of the kitchen staff, so you don't have to worry about that as much, but you'll still have duties to perform while Fairalisa eats."

Ronda waves me downstairs to the servant's dining room. I nearly fall as I struggle to take the stairs with my new chains. We walk into a warm dining room filled with candlelight. The room is ornately decorated with gold-plated picture frames surrounding colorful tapestries. A long cherry-colored wooden table sits in the middle with candlesticks resting in brass holders.

This is the *servant's* dining room?

A gaggle of servants already seated around the table chat raucously while two other women carry over bowls of food from the kitchen and place them in the middle of the table. The smell of fragrant rice and stewed fish hits my nose. My stomach growls in response. I haven't had a proper meal since we were with Roehana.

"Oooo, look, a new girl." The voice comes from a teenage boy. The girls sitting next to him giggle and huddle together as if they are part of their own club. He smirks as he takes the folded cloth napkin from his plate and sets it daintily on his lap.

"Everybody, this is Kat," Ronda announces. Servants continue to bustle into the room and find their seats at the table. "She is our new lady's maid." Ronda can't hide the lack of enthusiasm in her voice.

The boy who called me out a moment ago meows and makes a hissing sound, which draws more gleeful laughs from his friends.

"Jaunty, that's enough," Ronda scolds. She then turns to me as she takes a seat at the head of the table. "Find a seat."

I shuffle down the table, awkwardly searching for an open seat, but the table fills quickly as servants continue to pour into the room. A woman nudges my shoulder as she eases up next to me.

"There's always room at the very end of the table for the people who aren't trying to suck up to ruddy Ronda."

I chuckle, but the woman just gives me an ironic, flat grin.

"I'm Pip," she says.

"Kat."

"Pip and Kat. We could start our own theater act with those names."

Again, I laugh softly, but Pip manages to keep a deadpan face. We find seats at the end of the table. A big bowl of sautéed zucchini is placed next to the rice and fish, along with several carafes of red wine. Glass goblets sit at every place setting, which consist of white porcelain plates and real silverware. I pick up the wine glass and stare in awe as the candle's flame bursts through the glass, perfectly clear.

"This is all for us?" I ask Pip.

She pours herself a glass of wine and leans over to pour some into my glass. "Anthond is very generous. Kat, that's Sindle and Teddy." Pip points across the table at an elderly woman and a copper-skinned man who appears to be in his thirties. Teddy has grass-stain blotches on his white garb.

Sindle waves. "Welcome. Where do you come from?"

"Bear Gap," I say hesitantly. "This is my first time in LilyAye."

"What sort of work did you do before coming here?" Sindle asks.

Farmer? Fighter? Rebel?

"Um, I was a lady's maid to the governor's wife in Bear Gap."

"Impressive," Pip says, popping a zucchini in her mouth. "No wonder you got picked for this job."

"You forgot to introduce me," says the girl sitting on the other side of me. "My name is Trixie."

Trixie, a tiny woman with short blonde hair, lurches around me to give Pip a glare.

"Oh, hey, Trix. Didn't see you over there," Pip says sarcastically.

Trixie scowls. "She loves me," Trixie whispers into my ears.

She has a book open in front of her that she reads between jabs at Pip. We pass the bowls of food around the table. The bounty is astonishing. I scoop heaps of food onto my plate and shove it into my mouth, unashamed. Immediately, I feel guilty when I think of Tuor. I wonder where he is and what kind of meal he's eating, if he's eating at all. It can't be as good as this, wherever he is.

"Are all masters this generous in LilyAye?" I ask as I pass a bowl to Pip.

"Not everyone, but most are," Trixie says. "It's considered shameful if your servants look ill-treated."

"But some *are* mistreated?"

"Well . . ." Trixie twists uncomfortably in her seat. She closes the cover on her book. "Of course, you hear stories about a cruel master, but that is very rare."

"Don't listen to her," Pip says, taking a gulp of wine. "Trixie loves weaving stories. Truth is, we're all massively lucky that we got placed in this house. Worst part about working here is having to deal with Ronda the Righteous."

Teddy speaks. "I grew up in a house where my mother was a maid, and we didn't get treated this good."

"But we're still all slaves," I say, wiping my face with the napkin.

Silence falls between the five of us.

"Uh oh," Pip groans.

"What?" I ask.

"No, no," Trixie says. "We don't use that word."

"What word?" I ask.

"We're not slaves, we're *servants*," Trixie corrects, a spark in her tone.

Teddy shakes his head and scrapes a bite of fish from his plate.

"That's just a choice of words, though. In reality, you—*we* are slaves," I say.

"Well, not exactly. The household masters need us as much as we need them," Trixie says. "That makes this more of a give and take."

"It sounds like you enjoy being here," I say, passing Pip the platter of fish.

Trixie strokes her hair against her neck. "I believe it's the life I was called to."

My stomach drops. Did I hear her right?

"Stop trying to indoctrinate the new girl," Pip calls over my shoulder. "Trixie doesn't know anything. For heaven's sake, Trix volunteered for this gig."

I turn back to Trixie. "You volunteered?"

"I didn't volunteer exactly." Trixie's petite lips curl into a stern expression.

"Then how'd you end up here?"

She holds a finger up to me. "I grew up in LilyAye, was born here, but my family struggled to make enough money to feed me and all my siblings. I'm the oldest out of my brothers and sisters, so I told my parents that I would work and take the burden off their household.

"At that time, someone told them Master Anthond was looking for a female servant. My parents brought me to this house, and he took a liking to me. He paid my father a healthy sum of money, and now I live here, fully fed and taken care of. I don't have to be a burden to my family anymore. They know I'm safe, and I can rest easy knowing they can live off the money I was sold for. It was an honor."

I furtively glance around the table to catch the reactions of everyone else. Pip slowly shakes her head while Teddy says nothing.

"That was a very kind thing you did for your family," Sindle says in a sweet, grandmotherly way.

"So you have no problems with being a . . . servant?" I ask, trying to keep the shock from my voice.

"No," Trixie says confidently. "Of course, I wish I were rich. Everybody does, but this was my only way to help my family and myself. The system that the Supreme Ruler set up works, and I'm living proof of that."

"This isn't about what's right or wrong," Teddy says. "Some people are just born wealthy and privileged, and others aren't."

"Accept your place," Trixie agrees.

"See what we have to deal with?" Pip whispers into my ear. "Ms. Perfect over there."

Trixie straightens her back as she diligently reads her book. I scrape the last bit of food from my plate and consider what I'll say next. I haven't yet learned what's taboo to say in LilyAye, and I'm not about to risk a fate similar to my time with the slavers.

"Don't mind her," Pip continues. "She's more idealistic than the Warwicks themselves."

"What are everyone's duties here?" I ask, figuring that's a safe enough question.

"Trix helps with the laundry," Pip says. "Sindle is on the cleaning crew. Teddy works in the garden, and I'm food supply. That fish you're eating"—Pip points to my plate—"I'm the one who haggled with the fishmonger for a per-fish price reduction if I bought three whole carp. Sometimes it feels odd trying to save the master a few rings when he's one of the wealthiest in the city, but that's my job." Pip shrugs her shoulders. "Of course, now that produce is hard to come by since the incident in Bear Gap, it makes what I do so much harder."

I press my lips tightly together and hope that no one asks me any questions about Bear Gap and the *incident*.

"I'm at the market almost every day, so if you ever need anything, just let me know," Pip continues.

"Thanks." I nod. "They let you go to the market by yourself?"

"It's like we're capable adults," Pip says, raising an eyebrow.

I laugh. Pip is funny, and I haven't laughed in so long. Ronda slides her chair back and abruptly announces the end of dinner. Pip swings her leg over the bench to stand. I notice that, although she wears a collar, she doesn't have a set of shackles around her ankles, like Ronda. I pinch my eyebrows together, finding that curious. I decide to be extra cautious about what I say around Pip.

"Come on. I'll show you where we put our dirty dishes," Pip says.

The kitchen crew begins carting away the crates filled with our dirty plates and sweeping the floor.

"Let's get going on the master's dinner," Ronda shouts as the kitchen crew hustles around the room. She approaches me and Pip. "You, come with me. It's time I show you to your duties."

"Have fun," Pip calls.

The servants disperse throughout the house as Ronda takes me back upstairs.

"The master and the lady are being seated for their dinner now," Ronda explains as she takes me toward the front of the house, where the sitting room is.

A set of steps carved out of Catahli leads to the upstairs. Although the staircase is tall, there's no railing to catch a misstep. Heights don't normally scare me, but taking these steep steps in my tight shackles makes me nervous. At the top, Ronda leads me down the hall. We stop in front of an ornate mahogany door.

"This is the lady's bedroom. You will spend much of your time in here, helping her wash and dress, but of course, you already know that since you're so experienced."

I ignore Ronda's cutting remark. She leads me a few paces down the hall to another door, equally ornate but not as big. Ronda turns the knob and swings the door open with a click, directing me to enter. "And this is your room."

"Whoa," I mumble under my breath.

My whole room is bigger than the shack I lived in with Malcolm. A bed rests against the wall in a simple four-poster frame with a downy bedspread. A porcelain washbasin and chamber pot sit in the corner. Across from the bedroom door is a set of glass doors that open onto a balcony. Long draping curtains hang on either side of the doors.

"Where's the wood to light the fire?" I ask, noticing the empty fireplace.

"One of the boys will come do that for you."

"I don't have to start my own fire?"

Ronda narrows her eyes at me. She says, "Surely you know that a lady's maid doesn't dirty herself with the soot of lighting a fire."

"Oh, right. I was just making sure."

They have servants for the servants, I realize.

"You'll tend to the lady by accessing her bedroom through here," Ronda continues.

To our right is another door. It connects my room to Fairalisa's room through a closet. The closet is a room unto itself with curved walls and hundreds of dresses hanging around me in a big circle.

Shoes line shelves underneath the dresses, and an array of hatboxes fills every ledge and corner. The floor is cluttered with clothes, dirty hosiery, and ribbons.

"As you can see, Fairalisa is in dire need of a lady's maid. I've been cleaning up this room every morning, and by the evening it looks like this."

How can one person change their outfit this often in a day? Ronda leads me out of the closet and into Fairalisa's bedroom. Fairalisa's bed is wide enough to sleep five people and sits atop a platform with three steps on either side. Opposite the bed is a fireplace, encased in gold and stone. A massive oil painting of yellow-and-red-tipped tulips hangs above the mantel.

"This room is gorgeous," I say, unable to keep my awe hidden.

I turn slowly in a circle as I admire the feathery carved molding along the ceiling and the shimmering floral designs on the wall.

"It's an absolute mess, is what it is," Ronda says.

Blouses and socks hang on the arm of a plush chair in the corner of the room. The bedcovers are twisted, and a pillow lies on the stairs. We walk around the bed to Fairalisa's own balcony. The glass doors look out over the grounds at the rear of the house. The door is cracked open, and a light breeze fills the room.

In front of the window is a mahogany vanity with a tall mirror. Little silver pots of rouge and white powder are strewn about the surface of the vanity, along with brushes and dirty powder pads. A glass cabinet, filled with necklaces, bracelets, and earrings all dripping with silver, gold, Catahli, and an array of precious gems, sits next to the vanity.

"We have a maid that cleans the lady's room once a day, but you'll be responsible for delivering her dirty clothing and sheets to be laundered, and you'll need to keep the room straightened." Ronda walks slowly toward the bedroom door as she speaks. "Along with keeping her clothing and jewelry organized and her washbasin filled with warm water."

Ronda turns to face me. "If it were up to me, I'd have you set to work this instant, but the lady has insisted that I allow you to rest this evening after your long and arduous journey to LilyAye. So I suppose we'll just leave this place a disaster for the night."

Ronda lets out a huff, unable to keep her dissatisfaction hidden.

"Well, good night then," I say.

"Good night."

Ronda grumbles under her breath before leaving through Fairalisa's bedroom door. Finally alone, I warm myself by Fairalisa's fire and run my hand along the smooth wood mantle. No Catahli here. Held over direct flame, Catahli crumbles and turns to sand. That's a testament to how cocky the people of LilyAye are, building their whole city out of it.

Fairalisa's mantle is filled with useless decorative trinkets: a porcelain statue of a horse, a rag doll, and a vase of fresh flowers. There's more riches in one inch of this bedroom than I've seen in my entire life.

I scoff at the exorbitance of it all. It feels so pointless. My job is to tend to a person who's perfectly capable of washing and dressing themself? I don't get it.

Tuor is probably shivering right now, without even a coat to keep him warm, yet this very room I'm standing in has enough blankets and fabric to warm all those beggars at the gate. It's painful to think about Tuor and what he's going through right now, stuck at some iron-mining pit. I also wonder about Gracine and where she ended up today. I feel sickeningly guilty.

I tear out of Fairalisa's bedroom and into my own, unable to stand the meaninglessness of her life. Everything around me feels strange and foreign. I find a pair of white fuzzy slippers by my bed. The sight of them infuriates me. Just last night I was sleeping in one of Julian's crude cages, my feet damp and freezing, and my stomach rolling with hunger.

Now, I'm supposed to be a meek servant? I pick up the slippers and hurl them across the room. I let out a groan, not caring who hears me. I march to my bed and chuck the decorative pillows off. My chains tug on my ankles, reminding me that I'm bound and unable to run.

The collar around my neck presses against my skin. It feels like it's growing tighter. I wrap my fingers around it and try to rip it apart. I squeeze my eyes closed. Visions of Karla assault my mind. The panic returns, and I beg it to go away. *Let me go. Let me go!* This house is just a new kind of cage, and I want out of it.

I pace my bedroom, willing my breathing to steady. Finally I sit on the cool floor, pull my knees up to my chin, and wrap my arms around my legs. Closing my eyes, I rest my head on the tops of my knees. I'm not sure how long I sit like this, but the balcony curtains fall dark as the sun dips behind the horizon.

A gentle knock comes at the door breaking me from my reverie. My eyes pop open. The tapping comes again. I stand swiftly and realize someone's on my balcony.

CHAPTER SEVENTEEN

THE RAPPING ON the glass doors continues. I pull aside the curtain and reach for my dagger, but again, I'm frustrated to find it's not there. The city lights just barely outline a dark hooded figure on my balcony. My heartbeat tumbles. The tall frame, the cloak, the late-night visit are all hallmarks of my mother.

I turn the knob on the balcony door and step into the cool night. The sky is clear. The bright moon casts a peaceful blue haze across the city. Hands reach to draw back the cloak's black woolen hood. That shadowy face and those icy blue eyes are unmistakable.

I cast a look of disgust at the sight of Reed. "It was you that told Lawrence?"

"Thank all Elmyra this is the right balcony." Reed breathes deeply, ignoring my question. "How are you? Are you injured?"

"I'm fine."

"Where's Tuor?" Reed asks.

"He's not here. He got bought by someone else at the auction."

"We'll get him back." Reed leans forward and takes my hands in his. "I was so worried about you."

His voice is soft and quiet, a tone I've never heard him take before. I wriggle my hands from his grip.

"You're the one who told Lawrence?" I ask again.

Reed reluctantly accepts my rejection. "Yes. I did what I had to, to save you."

I shake my head, nauseated by Reed's words. "Don't talk to me like you care about me. You abandoned us on that mountain to starve!"

Reed hangs his head. "I know."

"That's all you have to say?"

"What do you want me to say? It's obviously not how I wanted things to happen."

"How did you even find out what had happened to us?"

Reed exhales as he walks to the edge of the balcony and rests his hands on the railing. I gaze out over the darkening city. Lights pop up in windows as people begin lighting their candles.

"After we parted ways, I made it all the way to Wildenvalley before I knew I needed to return and put our group back together. I realized the damage I'd caused. I couldn't stand being parted from you."

I cross my arms over my chest and fight the urge to roll my eyes.

"I returned to the river," Reed continues, "and decided to wait for you there, assuming you'd be passing through shortly. By the time I got there, I saw that you'd been captured by the slavers. I was going to fight them off, but they already had you in the back of the wagon and there were just too many of them. They had twenty men running their operation."

I ease up behind Reed and join him at the railing. Crickets sing in the cool backyard. Reed turns and looks at me with a steely gaze.

"So I decided to rescue you in LilyAye. I knew I couldn't buy you off the auction block myself. I couldn't risk anyone recognizing me. That's when I thought of Lawrence. I know a lot of wealthy families in LilyAye, but none of them could I trust to purchase you without raising any alarms to my uncle."

"How'd you get through the city gate?"

"I came in right behind you. I pretended to be one of the slaver's men. They never questioned me. I went immediately to the Thatius estate and waited for Lawrence to arrive home. I begged him to rescue you." Reed slides his hand across the railing and places his slender fingers on my hand. "I risked my life to save you, Camilla, but it was worth it. I need you back."

My arms relax slightly. I study Reed's face and search for truth. There's something disingenuous about his story, and the image of Reed attacking Eve is still burned into my mind.

"You nearly crippled Eve."

Reed removes his hand from mine and drops his head in what I can only assume is shame.

"How is she?" he asks, meeting my eyes again.

"I haven't seen Eve since we were captured." I shift on my feet. "But she was better when I last saw her, no thanks to you."

"I never wanted any of that to happen," Reed says.

In the yard below, Hobbes emerges from the stables. Reed and I slink back against the wall of the house, our bodies now closer than before. Hobbes whistles as he walks down the path and inside the house.

I wait for the door to close and then say, "I have to agree with Eve. You showed yourself a poor leader."

My words bite. Reed's mouth sets in a hard line. I ready myself for another rage-induced outbreak from him.

"You're right. I didn't want our mission to sour in that way, but you can't blame me now for wanting to make it right. I haven't lost sight of our plan. Have you?"

Truthfully, I haven't thought much of killing Quinten since we've been captured, and now with Eve and Tuor somewhere else . . .

"Quinten is the reason you were captured by those slavers," Reed says urgently. "He has allowed this slave trade to take over the country. I'm not giving up on assassinating my uncle, and neither should you."

"I haven't given up," I say, my voice firm. "I want to get Tuor back and rejoin the rebels, even if that means still being in your company."

"Don't hate me, Camilla." Reed is nearly begging. "I need you as much as the rebellion needs you."

Reed's sharp crystal gaze softens. The naturally dark circles under his eyes look as if they could actually be from stress and lack of sleep.

"I want to be with the rebels," I admit. "But I want Tuor back, and I want to find Eve too."

"We'll get them," Reed agrees.

The cool night air chills my bare arms. I rub my hands over my skin to generate some heat. Reed removes his cloak and places it over my shoulders. Holding onto the edge of the cloak, he tugs me close and wraps his arms around me. My breath shudders. I haven't officially forgiven Reed, and I'm definitely not ready to be this close to him, but I don't fight his embrace. In this house of odd styles and weird routines, it's nice to hold something familiar, something from home.

"That's better," Reed muses, pressing my head against his chest.

We stay like this, clutching each other in the shadows, listening to the chatter of the city beyond.

"Where are you staying?" I ask, pulling away.

"There's a rebel safe house in the northern part of the city, in the slums," Reed says, pointing past Anthond's estate. "It's barely a house, more like a shack, but for now Quinten doesn't know about it."

"Take me there. Get me away from this place."

Reed straightens, and he lets go of my arms. "No, we need to keep you here."

"Why?" I protest.

"It's far too dangerous to try and sneak you through the city. Being in this house, under this disguise, is the safest place for you right now."

Fairalisa's bedroom door squeaks open and then clicks closed. The light emanating from her balcony door glows brighter, signaling that she's lighting her candles.

"I can't stay here," I say, fighting the urge to raise my voice. "I need to find Tuor."

Reed's businesslike form returns. "You'll stay here. I'll come for you when the time is right."

Reed swiftly bends and presses his lips against mine. I push him away, but it happens so fast, he barely registers my disapproval.

"Be a lady's maid. Keep a watch on Anthond. He's the oldest advisor to my uncle. That's the best you can do for the rebellion right now."

Reed removes the cloak from my shoulders and dons it himself. He pulls up the hood to cover his face and swings his legs over the balcony railing. I watch as Reed scales the side of the house, placing his foot on the Catahli crevices and hopping onto the ground. He skirts to the edge of the yard and jogs into the back alley and out of sight.

Quietly, I close the balcony door and draw the curtains. I lie back on my bed, letting my arms hang at my side. *Be a lady's maid.* This has to be the trickiest rebel assignment I've ever been given, and the one I'm the least prepared for.

I kick off my shoes and carefully set my hair clip on the nightstand. I slip between the soft sheets and exhale as I rest my head on my pillow. I can't think of a time that I've ever laid on a bed so soft. Rolling onto my stomach, I splay out my arms and stretch as far as I can, never feeling the edge of the bed.

***

"Experience!" Ronda proclaims, barreling into my room and ripping open the curtains. "Where's this experience you claim to have? I knew you didn't know anything. You should already be dressed and fetching warm water for the lady's wash basin at this time."

I rub the side of my head. The sharp, blaring sun pours into my room. I groan, feeling every ache on my body.

Ronda comes to stand next to my bed. "Wake. Up!"

"Okay, okay," I mumble.

"Her breakfast is waiting for her downstairs. Her undergarments need pressed, and I shudder to think what the state of her room is in."

I roll out of bed as a knock comes on my closet door. "Great," I mutter. The last thing I need is for the lady to see that I'm just now waking.

"Has anyone seen my blue cardigan? It's chilly this morning," Fairalisa asks, rubbing sleep from her eyes.

"I'll get it," I say quickly.

Ronda scoffs. "You are not fit for this job." The words fly from her mouth like arrows.

Fairalisa moans loudly like a mewing cat. "Please leave!"

Ronda presses her lips together and stares at me as she plants her fists on her hips. Fairalisa sleepily rubs at the side of her head.

"I'm sorry, my lady," I say quickly, remembering Reed's assignment to stay in the house. "I can be better."

"Kat?" Fairalisa says, confused.

"I thought—"

"I want Ronda gone!" Fairalisa stomps her foot like a toddler.

"My-my lady," Ronda stutters. "I only wish the best for you."

"Ugh, be gone!" Fairalisa says, turning around and walking, half-asleep, back into her bedroom.

Ronda takes a shaky breath. She puffs out her chest and walks silently from the room. I sneak into Fairalisa's bedroom, finding, on the way, her blue cardigan on the closet floor. Fairalisa has flopped onto her plush chair. Her eyes are closed, and her head is resting on her hand.

"My lady?" I ask with an awkward bow.

Her eyes flutter open as I hand her the blue cardigan.

"You don't have to address me like that. Just call me Fairalisa. When Lawrence is master here, I will have him ship Ronda off. She's dreadful," Fairalisa says, taking the cardigan and wrapping it around her shoulders.

"I am sorry I was late to rise," I say.

"It is of no import. I don't fault you. You're still exhausted, I'm sure, but could you fetch my breakfast? I take black tea with lots of cream and sugar in the morning."

I take a deep breath. "Yes, of course. I'll tend to that now."

Slipping back into my bedroom, I quickly change my dress. I run my fingers through my hair and splash my face with cold water. Breakfast and tea have to be in the kitchen, right? Scurrying down the steps, I pass Trixie on her way up with a stack of linens in her hands.

The house is peaceful. Only the gurgling of the fishpond drifts through the front hall, but once I dip inside the kitchen, I'm hit with shouts and a sizzling griddle. Steam rises from a pot on the stove. A maid chops an onion furiously with a thick butcher knife. Jaunty, wearing a pious look, carries stacks of dishes to a nearby cabinet and places them with a *clang* on the shelf.

"And who are you?" asks a burly man standing over a cast-iron skillet.

"I'm Kat. I'm the new lady's maid."

"Good morning, kitty-Kat," Jaunty mocks as he saunters to the sink.

I give Jaunty a look on par with a death threat. What did I ever do to him? The man grunts as he pours water onto the skillet and begins scrubbing it with a metal brush. He's so tall his back is arched severely as he bends to clean the skillet. Steam fills his face, reddening his skin and dampening his wild black hair and thick sideburns.

"You're late," he says gruffly. "Breakfast has been over for an hour. Her plate is there."

The chef points to a gold tray sitting on an island countertop in the middle of the kitchen. I peek under the dainty pink napkin that covers the plate. Two boiled eggs sit in fluted porcelain egg cups. Fresh melons have been sliced into fancy designs and fanned out onto the plate along with a biscuit and a sprig of mint. Tiny gold salt-and-pepper shakers also adorn the tray.

"Um, what about her tea?" I ask.

The chef points to a shelf behind me with a line of tea tins.

"Okay," I say, rushing to the tea shelf. I move my hands, unsure of what to grab first. Mug, I need a mug, I think to myself. I hustle toward the cabinet and nearly bump into Jaunty as he places another stack of clean plates on the shelf.

"Sorry," I mumble.

"Those are the servant's dishes," the chef calls, keeping his head down while he continues to scrub.

I press my lips together in a hard line. "Where are the dishes for the lady?" I ask, not hiding my annoyance.

The chef points to another cabinet on the opposite side of the kitchen. I pull open the glass doors to find shelves and shelves of delicate, intricately painted dishes.

"Those are one-of-kind," Jaunty says in a warning tone. "Painted with the Balley seal. If you break anything in that cabinet, Ronda will have your head."

I stand on my tiptoes and take down a single teacup and saucer from the top shelf. Carefully, I close the cabinet doors and hurry back to the tea tins. Even though they're each painted with a different design, they're not labeled. I pick up the first one in the line, open the lid, and sniff the leaves. Is it black tea? I have no idea. I don't remember having different types of tea in Bear Gap. We drank whatever we could get.

I close the lid on that tin and pick up the next one, sniffing its contents to look like I know what I'm doing. It smells the same as the last one. Perhaps I should just pick a tea and hope that Fairalisa doesn't notice. How important is this tea anyway?

Behind me, the chef continues to scrub his skillet. Jaunty and the other kitchen maid bustle back and forth with their work, stopping for a moment to whisper to each other. My pride won't allow me to ask for help from people who have been so rude to me. Why is this so hard? I single-handedly started a rebellion in Bear Gap and overthrew the local government, but now I can't even make a simple cup of tea.

The door to the kitchen opens, and Pip walks through, a notepad under her arm and a pencil in her ear. I'm flooded with relief.

"Hey, Kat." Pip pauses and eyes me. "Looks like you need help," she says, coming to my side.

"Yes, please," I say under my breath. I glance over at the chef.

"Oh, Benji isn't being very helpful? Surprise, surprise," she says loudly.

Benji stares at us under thick black eyebrows as he wipes soot onto his apron. Pip sets her notepad onto the countertop and leans in close.

"He and Ronda are like this." Pip twists her first two fingers together and holds them up for me to see. "They're not, like, in love or anything, they just both enjoy bossing us underlings around."

Pip smirks. "So, what kind of tea does the lady want?"

"Black tea with cream and sugar."

Pip lifts up the tea tins and tilts them to look underneath. On the bottom of each of the tea tins is painted its name. I smack my forehead. I'm an idiot. Pip shuffles through all the teas until we find the one labeled "black tea."

"Okay, so you need to use a strainer," Pip says.

From a drawer below the tea tins, Pip pulls out a little strainer with a handle just big enough to sit inside the teacup. She places a spoonful of the tea leaves into the strainer.

Ignoring Benji, Pip walks to the stove and shows me a large tea kettle that's kept hot on the stove all day. She fills a smaller tea pot, which matches the teacup, with hot water. She also shows me the matching sugar pot and cream pitcher and where to find the cream and sugar to fill them.

Once we're done with that, we load the tray up with the tea. I carry the tray while Pip grabs a plate sitting next to it.

"This is your breakfast," she tells me as we slip out of the kitchen. "Benji might be a pain, but he has to make you breakfast too. I'd suggest getting down here early and eating before putting the lady's tray together."

"Got it," I say as we shuffle up the stairs.

The dishes clatter on the tray as I try to hold them steady. Pip and I enter my bedroom. I head straight for the closet door to deliver Fairalisa's breakfast.

"Wait," Pip says in a whisper. "Eat first, or you won't get another chance for a while."

I hesitate, then set Fairalisa's breakfast tray on my dresser and shovel in a nearly identical breakfast to Fairalisa's.

"She's cranky if she doesn't eat, but you'll be miserable too," Pip says, handing me a napkin. "I need to get back downstairs. Good luck with your first day."

I nod at Pip with a mouth full of food as she leaves. I swallow hard before taking up the gold tray again and quietly padding into Fairalisa's bedroom. She's lying on her bed, half-covered by blankets and buried tightly in a sweater.

"Here you are," I say, setting the tray next to her on the bed. "I'm sorry it took so long."

Fairalisa immediately grabs the spoon and scoops heaps of sugar into the cup of tea and begins guzzling it down. "That's okay," she says, taking a big bite of the biscuit.

She lets out a satisfied sigh as her stomach fills. I busy myself by picking up stray articles of clothing that have somehow appeared on the floor through the night.

With an armful of clothes, I face Fairalisa and ask, "Um, shall I help you find a dress for the day?" I look at her expectantly, hoping this is something a lady's maid would ask.

"Yes, but first, tell me what you think of this."

Fairalisa leaps from her bed, downing the last bite of biscuit. From her closet, she pulls out a shimmering white veil. She places a pearly crown on her head and lets the veil cascade down her back and pool in a pile on the floor.

"What do you think?" she asks, beaming.

I lay the pile of clothes on Fairalisa's bed and take a seat on the corner of the mattress. "It's beautiful. Are you going to wear that . . . today?"

Fairalisa lets out a carefree laugh. "No, silly. It's for the big day."

I raise my eyebrows.

"It's for the wedding!" she clarifies.

"Oh, right."

Fairalisa removes the veil. "This is the third one I've had made. It's fancy enough, but I don't know if it's *the one*."

"It looks pretty to me."

"I don't want it to be just pretty. I want it to be perfect."

I squirm on the bed, feeling the weight of Fairalisa's extravagant world. Her life on its own could be simple, but it seems intentionally complicated by all of the . . . stuff.

Fairalisa sighs as she places the veil back in its box. "We'll see. I'm so glad you're here to help me now. We have a very busy day ahead of us."

Fairalisa climbs back onto her bed as I deliver my armful of clothes to her closet. A busy day for a girl like Fairalisa, I think to myself. She'll probably spend the day being painted with rouge and eating cakes in the parlor.

"So, what do we have to do?" I call from the closet as I hang up her clothes.

Fairalisa appears at the closet door. An impish smile forms on her face.

"Wedding planning!" Fairalisa squeals.

CHAPTER EIGHTEEN

IT TAKES LESS than half a day for me to realize I'm severely lacking the patience needed to be a lady's maid. Fairalisa waved away six dresses that I showed her as an option for the day's clothing. We took out and redid her hair three times, and tried on so many different pairs of earrings, I lost count.

For having a lot of things to accomplish, Fairalisa took no shortcuts in perfecting her appearance. What irks me the most is she savors every moment of the delays. She seems to drink up the attention and revel in the glory of being a doll who can be dressed up.

Later that morning, we sit in the front room, a trolley of tea and candies laid out for us, with a man who is the top weaver in the city. He shows Fairalisa boxes filled with hundreds of different fabric swatches.

"What do you think of this one, Kat?" Fairalisa asks as she shows me a light-green fabric.

I anxiously tap my foot against the hard Catahli floor. "It's lovely."

This has become my rote answer for everything.

"But do you think it will work with my overall color scheme?" Fairalisa presses.

What in all of Elmyra is a color scheme?

I clear my throat. The weaver watches me carefully for my opinion. We've already been in this meeting for two hours. He has to be exhausted too. I consider for a moment if tedious wedding planning is worse than being stuck on the mountain.

"What is this one for again?" I ask.

"This is the accent color for the bunting that will go around the family table, remember? And this is the color we're using for the tablecloths."

Fairalisa holds up a plain white fabric swatch. I know absolutely nothing about matching or accent colors, and I definitely have no idea what bunting is.

"Well," I say awkwardly, "if the tablecloths are to be white, then green bunting should match just fine, right?"

I look to the weaver who nods in agreement. Fairalisa lets out an exaggerated huff.

"This isn't white!" she nearly shouts. "This is cream, which means it has tones of yellow, which means we need something that will bring out the yellow undertones, like green."

"Well, great," I say. "Green, it is."

"I hate the color green!" Fairalisa says, exasperated.

The weaver leans back in his chair and gives me a wide-eyed look.

"What about this pink?" I suggest, digging a swatch out of the box. "I know you like pink."

"I do." Fairalisa gazes at the small square fabric. "But this isn't a sophisticated color for a lady's wedding to a very high-ranking and important man like Lawrence."

Fairalisa rises to her feet and marches to the other end of the room. She crosses her arms and peers out the front window, onto the street below. The weaver looks to me as if I'm supposed to know how to handle a temper tantrum. I rub my forehead in frustration. I never thought I'd be in LilyAye babysitting. I let out a breath of air and decide it's up to me to fix this.

I come to my feet. "Fairalisa," I say sternly.

She turns around to face me. Tears stream down her cheeks.

"I think we need to take a break. I'm sure Mr. Phillips can set aside the swatches that you liked."

The weaver nods. "Yes, of course. I agree with your lady's maid. Perhaps we could reschedule for another day to make your final decisions?"

We both look at Fairalisa hopefully. Her bottom lip sticks out ever so slightly.

Mr. Phillips says, "The wedding is not for another three weeks. We have a little bit of time."

"Three weeks?" I blurt before I have a chance to stop myself. "Your wedding is in only three weeks?"

"It's my father," Fairalisa says with a sniffle. She takes a few steps closer to me. "His health is failing, Kat, and we just can't wait any longer."

"Why don't I come back tomorrow, and we can continue to tackle this decision?" Mr. Phillips says.

Fairalisa silently nods.

"Thank you," I say.

I help Mr. Phillips box up his swatches before he bows to Fairalisa and calls for his driver to bring the carriage round.

"I just don't know about this," Fairalisa says, taking a seat on the couch. "It's moving so fast, and I'm excited, you know? I want to be married, but it's a lot of decisions to be made all at once. Were you ever married?"

I take a seat next to Fairalisa.

"No," I say quickly. "I doubt I'll ever be married."

"Oh, well, I'll allow you to get married." Fairalisa straightens her back. "Some masters don't, but I would let my lady's maid get married."

I smile. "That's sweet. I probably won't ever get married though."

"That's a horrid thought." A deep crease forms between Fairalisa's eyebrows as her expression grows serious.

"It's okay." I chuckle, shaking my head. "Truthfully, men are a lot of trouble."

"Not Lawrence," Fairalisa says with a serious tone. "He's so sweet, and he always buys me a gift when he travels."

"Fairalisa, how old are you?" I tilt my head curiously.

"I turned sixteen two months ago!" One of Fairalisa's curls bounces as she speaks.

"And you're already set to be married?" I ask, surprised.

"In LilyAye, sixteen isn't too young to marry, plus Lawrence and I have been betrothed our entire lives. Our houses have planned to be joined in marriage for many years. We were destined to be together before I was even born."

Realization washes over me. It's an arranged marriage.

I understand now. Lawrence doesn't have a choice. No wonder he fled to Bear Gap last year. He wanted to know what it felt like to live like the rest of Elmyra. I suppose he decided a grand house and a pretty wife was what he wanted in life.

Fairalisa giggles as she takes my hands in hers. "I can't wait to marry Lawrence." Her dreamy expression makes me realize how truly naive and innocent she is.

"Kat?"

"Yeah?"

"Thanks for helping me," Fairalisa says, pulling me into a tight side hug.

"Oh, you're welcome."

Fairalisa jumps to her feet, wiping the remaining tears from her cheeks. "Tomorrow, we meet with the baker to taste some cakes, and that is one job I know won't make me cry."

***

The next morning I'm up before Fairalisa. I dress, make sure her fire has been tended to, and fetch warm water for her wash basin before it's fully light outside. I pull aside her curtains then scurry downstairs to retrieve her breakfast. Although I'm convinced that wedding planning is its own kind of torture, if being stuck in this house is the best I can do for the rebellion right now, I might as well be good at my job.

Benji eyes me as I enter the kitchen. Jaunty and two other maids are working around him, cracking eggs and slicing bread. He doesn't look up when I walk in, but I notice that Fairalisa's tray is waiting for me. I fetch Fairalisa's tea cup from the cabinet, but when I get to the tea shelf, something's off.

The tins are shuffled about and all askew. I turn them over and search for Fairalisa's favorite tea. The black tea is gone. Flustered, I look through the teas again. Behind me, Benji lets out a throaty guffaw. Jaunty snickers. I turn around and shoot daggers at Benji with my eyes.

"Where is it?" I growl.

Benji ignores me, his shoulders bobbing up and down as he scrapes his spatula against the cast-iron griddle. I scan the kitchen and start pulling open every drawer and cabinet, searching for the tea. I get in the way of one of the kitchen maids, and she barks at me to get out of their kitchen.

"Where is it?" I yell.

"Uh oh, kitty-Kat is going to scratch someone," Jaunty hisses.

The griddle sizzles and pops.

"The lady's breakfast is getting cold," Benji says.

"I'll tell her it's your fault when she doesn't get her tea," I say.

"It's not my fault you're too short to reach it."

I squint in confusion. Jaunty ruefully points to the ceiling. Sitting on one of the wooden rafters that runs the length of the kitchen is the small silver tea tin. Benji continues to laugh as realization settles around me. Putting the tin up there was no problem for Benji's tall frame. With these shackles around my ankles, getting it myself won't be easy.

I grab a stool from the corner. The chain on my shackles is just long enough to let me step onto the stool. I reach for the tin, but it's a foot and a half higher than I can reach. I angrily kick the stool away. One of the kitchen maids lets out a surprised yelp. I grasp hard onto the side of the countertop and lift myself up with my arms. I strain as I pull myself onto my knees.

"Are you crazy, woman?" Benji asks.

"Whoa, apparently she can pounce…" Jaunty says.

It's my turn to ignore them. With a burst of energy, I push myself up with my arms and swing my legs underneath so I'm on my feet. I walk to the edge of the countertop.

"Watch the dishes!" Benji shouts.

I get as close to the rafter as I can, but the tea tin is still far out from the countertop. I stretch my arm. I'm still too short. Finally, I use my right hand to hold on to the rafter. I let my feet curl around the edge of the counter as I lean forward and reach. The tin is mere inches away. My body lowers farther, and the gap between my hand and the tea tin closes.

I wrap my fingers around the tin and pull it close. I moan as I let my feet slip off the countertop and swing down. After momentarily hanging off the rafter, I let go and land on the floor. Jaunty, wide eyed, stares at me.

I lift my chin. "I've worked with worse people than you lot," I say, breathing heavily.

"It's just meaningless teasing," Benji says as if to absolve himself of any guilt.

After fixing Fairalisa's tea, I snugly shove the tin under my arm and take it with me. If somebody else wants black tea in this house, too bad. Benji and Jaunty say nothing, but when I pick up the tray of food, I notice that my breakfast is a pile of rotten fruit and burnt toast. I turn to leave the kitchen but stop. Jaunty jolts as I drop the tray back onto the counter. I pick up a soft, brown glob off my plate that was once a strawberry and shove it whole into my mouth while keeping my eyes pinned on Benji. I chew and swallow. Jaunty's mouth falls open.

"I've eaten worse than this," I spit.

***

"I had such an odd dream last night," Fairalisa says, gazing past me with a faraway stare.

She sits across from me at a small round marble table in the parlor. Above us hangs a sparkling chandelier, dripping in crystal.

"What was it about?" I ask.

"I dreamed that Lawrence and I were married, and we had a grand dinner in our dining room, with Lawrence's parents. My mother and father were there too." Fairalisa lets out a soft giggle as she leans back on her sapphire-blue velvet chair. "Which is silly because Lawrence won't be head of the house until my father dies, and my mother has been gone for ages."

A fire softly crackles, gently warming this quiet corner of the house.

"What happened to your mother?" I ask.

Fairalisa purses her lips. "She died of a fever when I was little. My father stayed by her side for days. Isn't that such a romantic way to die?"

"I can't imagine death being romantic in any way."

"Come on, Kat. Haven't you ever thought of how you'd like to die?"

"No." I cinch up my face in disgust. "I don't want to think about that. I just know someone will get me someday."

"Someone?" Fairalisa questions.

I catch myself. "*Something*," I correct.

A plump man pushing a silver-trimmed cart enters through the wide archway. It's filled with decadent-looking tiered cakes. My eyes widen at the tall four-layered cake and the one that's been somehow painted with red roses.

"Yay!" Fairalisa claps furiously as the baker parks the cart in front of us. He clasps his hands over his large belly and beams at us.

"My lady," the baker says, bowing deeply for Fairalisa. "To start, I have made you a tea-infused cake with a delicate buttercream frosting."

I can't help but watch intently as the man cuts into one of his cakes and plops a thin slice onto a porcelain plate. He slides the plate and a fork in front of Fairalisa, then brings a second slice to me.

"I would be honored to know what you think," the baker says with a smile.

I cut off a hunk and shove it into my mouth. I'm eager to get the taste of rotten strawberry out of my mouth. The soft cake and the creamy frosting melt on my tongue with a symphony of flavors I've never tasted.

"Oh my . . ." The words bubble from my mouth before I have a chance to catch myself.

Fairalisa smirks.

"That's amazing," I say, taking another bite.

"It is quite delicious," Fairalisa says with a sophistication that I simply can't muster right now.

"Thank you," the baker says demurely, taking a step away from our table while we eat.

A thudding cane echoes against the Catahli floor, through the high ceilings of the parlor. Anthond rounds the corner, into the room, his manservant just a pace behind him.

"I'm devastated to have to interrupt this feast." Anthond's voice is breathy. He teeters in, gripping hard to his cane, then eases into the couch across from the fireplace.

"Daddy!" Fairalisa jumps to her feet and wraps her arms around Anthond's neck.

The baker nods at the master of the house and slinks back against the wall. He's silent and nearly unseen, just like Anthond's manservant, and just how I'm supposed to be, I guess.

"How are things getting on between you two?" Anthond asks.

"Marvelous," Fairalisa says, returning to her seat across the table from me. "Kat's the best. She's really fun to be with."

Anthond is bent forward, leaning on his cane. "Good. I'm glad to hear that. I won't bother you ladies. I know you have a lot to do in preparation for the wedding, but I have just received an invitation that I thought would interest you." Anthond waves a creamy piece of parchment in the air.

Fairalisa gasps gleefully. She jumps from her seat again and snatches the letter from her father. She stands, moving her lips as she reads.

"Oh, Daddy," Fairalisa says, laying a hand on her chest as if she might faint. "We have so much to do to get ready."

Anthond chuckles. I glance furtively around the room, unsure of my etiquette in this situation.

"We have to get to work immediately." Fairalisa begins to pace.

"Don't be such a Drama Darling," Anthond says lightheartedly.

"If ever there was a time!" Fairalisa turns to me. "We have been invited for dinner at the home of Captain Thatius."

"Lawrence's father?" I ask nervously.

"Yes! It's just like my dream, Kat."

"How strange," I mutter, my mind spinning. The only other person in LilyAye besides Reed and Lawrence who knows my identity is Captain Ridley Thatius, right hand to the Supreme Ruler, and apparently the man Fairalisa is to dine with tonight.

CHAPTER NINETEEN

ANTHOND GRINS AT his daughter as he pulls himself to standing. "Sounds like you ladies have a lot to do. I think it's time I take my leave."

"Thank you, Daddy . . ." Fairalisa says, staring at the floor, her normally empty head now seemingly full of thoughts.

"Kat, you must cancel all of our prearranged appointments for the day! I can't be distracted with wedding things right now. We need to put all of our focus on this dinner."

"What about the cake tasting?" I ask, the one wedding-planning activity I'm enjoying.

"Cancel it. The cake doesn't matter right now."

The baker lets out a squeak of disapproval.

"Are you sure?" I ask, desperately scraping up the last crumbs from my plate.

"There is no time for that, Kat." Fairalisa runs to my side and pushes my fork down, causing it to clatter against the plate. "Come on."

I give a half-hearted apology to the baker as Fairalisa takes my hand and pulls me from the parlor. We scurry through the hallways and up the steps.

"What am I going to wear tonight?" Fairalisa barrels into her bedroom and summons me to her closet. Her eyes dart over the carousel of dresses.

"Why are you so nervous? Surely you've had dinner with these people before."

"Rarely have I been present for a dinner with the captain," Fairalisa says, her eyes wide and her tone serious. "He's a very important man, Kat. He's always traveling, and when he is home, his schedule does not allow for social visits. Although I had hoped a dinner like this would happen prior to the wedding, this is still quite an extraordinary event."

"I'm sure it will be fine," I say, taking down a purple dress from the rack and showing it to Fairalisa.

She shakes her head, waving the dress away.

"Lawrence's father is a rather critical man." Fairalisa lowers her voice. "I'm nervous to measure up to his standards."

"What about this one?" I ask, showing off a white dress with gold sashes.

"Ugh, no. No. No. No!" Fairalisa throws each dress onto the floor as she rejects them.

"Okay, listen. You have to calm down."

Fairalisa fans herself with her hand.

"I have been in far more stressful situations, and they always work out."

"You've been to more important dinners than one where you have to impress your future father-in-law?" Fairalisa asks innocently.

"Yeah . . . kind of."

Fairalisa groans.

"Just trust me. This will be all right. Why don't we start on your hair, and then maybe once your hair is done, you'll know what dress you want to wear."

"Okay, yes. You are right." Fairalisa takes a deep breath and nods.

I place Fairalisa at her vanity. She gazes into the oval mirror and lifts her chin slightly. Her long chestnut-brown hair cascades down her left shoulder. An hour later, after I manage to fiddle with her hair and pretend like I know what I'm doing, Fairalisa is back to her normal, carefree self.

"So you like this shade of rouge better?" Fairalisa asks me as she holds up two pots of pink powder.

"Oh yes, definitely the one on the right," I say with confidence.

They look identical to me.

Fairalisa nods as she dips her feathery brush into the powder and gently spreads it across her cheeks. When she's done, she leans back in her vanity chair and tilts her head side to side to inspect her work.

"Looks good. What a mad day it's been." She screws on the rouge lid and lets out a long sigh. "I can't believe I'll be dining with the captain tonight. What will we talk about?"

"The weather?" I suggest.

"I can't just talk about the weather with Captain Thatius. I need to appear intelligent and well read."

I smirk at the prospect of Fairalisa appearing intelligent and well read.

Fairalisa twists in her chair to face me. "You're from Bear Gap, right, Kat?"

"Yeah."

"I know the captain has traveled there before. We could talk about that."

My heart seizes at the thought of Bear Gap coming up at the dinner table tonight.

"Bear Gap is kind of boring," I say casually. "Why don't you talk to him about a place that you've been before?"

Fairalisa's gaze falls to the floor. "I've barely been outside the city gates. Daddy won't let me travel anywhere."

"Oh..."

"You're the only hope I have, Kat. What's it like in Bear Gap?"

"Um, okay, well, Bear Gap is . . ." I struggle for the appropriate words to describe my home territory. I sink into a chair next to the window. "It's very different from here, very . . . The farm is in Bear Gap, so most people only know how to farm. It's our livelihood, especially the people who live in Rande, which is the town that I was born in."

"Most people? Did you work at the farm too?"

I open my mouth to speak but hesitate. I'm supposed to have lady's maid experience. "Yes, I worked at the farm until I was seventeen, and then I worked for Governor Leo as his wife's lady's maid." It's a half-truth, which are the ones that sound the most convincing.

"Karla Warwick!"

I flinch at the sound of Karla's name.

"You were lady's maid to Karla Warwick? How exciting!" Fairalisa places a hand on mine. "She's to be a guest at the wedding!"

My throat goes dries. "*Your* wedding?" I ask, hopeful that I've misunderstood.

"Of course I'm speaking of my wedding!"

Karla will be at Fairalisa's wedding. My stomach twists. Fairalisa turns back to her mirror and strokes her long tendrils.

"What about the riots?" Fairalisa whispers.

"You mean the rebels?"

Fairalisa shushes me. "Daddy has very strong opinions about the rebels. I don't want to get him going."

I lean in close to Fairalisa. "I saw the rebels firsthand."

So did Lawrence, I think to myself, remembering how we held Lawrence and his father at knifepoint, but I guess Fairalisa doesn't know about that.

"Did they really storm the governor's house?"

"Yup. I was there when it happened."

Fairalisa's mouth hangs agape as I speak.

"The rebels overthrew the governor's house. They took Karla captive and held her ransom until the Supreme Ruler himself rode to Bear Gap and begged for Karla to be set free."

I talk excitedly as if I'm telling a fairy tale to a child. Fairalisa laps it up in the same way.

"How horrid." Fairalisa's face scrunches in disgust. "After all the Supreme Ruler has done for those people and that's how they treat him?"

My jaw clenches and suddenly telling this story isn't fun anymore. White-hot rage simmers just beneath the surface. She's just a rich, senseless LilyAye girl, I remind myself.

"That is terrible," Fairalisa says again as she turns back to her mirror. "I'm glad you survived it all right."

"Yeah . . . but we were being oppressed," I blurt out, unable to stop myself from defending the rebels.

Fairalisa purses her lips and looks at me thoughtfully. "How?"

"If you're born in Bear Gap, then you grow up with no other choice but to work on the farm to survive. There is no other way to make money, and the wages are barely livable."

"Well, yes," Fairalisa says. "That's why the Supreme Ruler created a system for people like you to be able to work and have the ability to make a living for yourself."

People like me?

"But we were treated horribly on the farm," I say. "I had to work when I was only ten. I was beaten and whipped and worked nearly to death."

Fairalisa's eyes widen. They glisten as if she's about to cry. I wait expectantly for her to show me the same sympathy that she shows for Quinten.

She shakes her head. "Think about how much worse your life would have been if the Supreme Ruler hadn't given you these opportunities. Look at yourself now. You're in LilyAye, living in a fine house. That would have never been possible without the system that he put into place."

Fairalisa smiles at me as if she's just delivered the best news I could ever hear. She twists the end of her hair around her finger. I'm dumbfounded.

"You're right. I'm so blessed." I force the words out of my mouth.

Of course, Fairalisa would believe that any good thing that comes to people like me is from the benevolence of people like her.

"That is great information, Kat," Fairalisa says excitedly. "I should have plenty to say about Bear Gap to impress the captain."

The clock on Fairalisa's mantel strikes the hour with a piercing chime.

"We have to hurry!" Fairalisa announces. "The carriage will be here soon to pick us up."

Us. The word doesn't go unnoticed by me. If I go to the dinner tonight and Lawrence's father recognizes me, he will know that more rebels have moved into LilyAye. I'll be arrested, and Quinten will have me hanged.

Being a servant in this house is getting too tricky. First the dinner with Captain Thatius and now Karla. I need to find a way out of here. I help Fairalisa slip into her dress. She has finally chosen a poofy white chiffon gown with pink ribbon accents. I only know it's chiffon because Fairalisa told me all about how she picked out the fabric herself.

"Do you wish me to come along for dinner?" I ask, tying up the back of Fairalisa's dress. "Karla always preferred we stay outside the dining room when she ate with guests. So, if you—"

"Of course you will come!" Fairalisa twists to face me and gives me a scowl. "I need you by my side the entire night."

Panic sets in as I tie the dress's ribbons into a tight bow.

"You can't leave me for a moment," Fairalisa says, turning around and taking my hands. The skirt of her dress makes a *swooshing* noise as she moves. "You're the only reason I got through this day without losing my mind."

I nod slowly, knowing that I can't say no to my master, even if it means coming face-to-face with Lawrence's father.

"All right. I'll be there," I say twisting my hands together nervously.

Maybe Captain Thatius won't recognize me. I'm not dressed in my usual rebel outfit. I've cut my hair, and he'd never expect to see me in LilyAye, right?

Fairalisa hurries around the room looking for her handbag. When she finds it, we meet Anthond in the front hall. The three of us, along with Anthond's manservant, load into the carriage and clip-clop down the driveway, to the street.

My hands tremble in my lap as we ride through LilyAye. The cobblestone streets are neatly trimmed with bright green bushes. Boys climb ladders to light the street lamps as the sun begins to set. We pass one magnificent house after another, until just a short drive later, we pull up to a black-iron-fenced estate.

A man emerges and pushes open the wide wings of the gate, allowing us to enter. The Thatius home is stiff and tall, just like Ridley, with straight lines, and a row of perfectly rectangular windows along each story of the home, of which there are many. It's a looming spire with statues of creatures perched on the ledges. The white gleam of the house is unmistakable in the low evening light. It's built out of Catahli, just like all the others.

Fairalisa squeezes my knee excitedly as our carriage pulls around to the front of the house. Lawrence stands at the door, waiting for us, a dazzling, flawless smile on his lips. He turns the knob on the carriage door before our driver has a chance to dismount.

"My lady," Lawrence says with a slight bow.

Fairalisa giggles as she takes Lawrence's hand and steps down from the carriage.

"Lawrence, my boy!" Anthond's voice is strained as his manservant helps him from the carriage.

"Master Anthond," Lawrence says, shaking the old man's hand. "My parents are waiting for us in the dining hall. Will you join me?"

"Sounds wonderful," Anthond says jovially, hobbling toward the solid-oak front door.

I peer up at the facade of the Thatius home. It towers over me like a scolding mother. Lawrence stiffly bends his elbow to allow Fairalisa to link arms with him, and the two stroll inside. A soaring narrow staircase leads up to an impossibly high second story. A fishpond is inlaid into the floor of the front hall, just like at Anthond's house. It must be a LilyAye thing. We stride past it and enter a dark hallway.

"We're overjoyed to have you for dinner," Lawrence says.

"He's an awfully busy man, your father," Anthond says. "It's been far too long since we've had a meal together!"

Warm candlelight emanates from a wide archway at the end of the hallway. Two figures darken its threshold. I swallow hard. Captain Thatius and his wife stand waiting to greet their guests in the dining hall.

"Oh." Lawrence stops suddenly in his tracks.

"What is it?" Fairalisa asks with a worried gaze.

"My apologies," Lawrence says. He presses his lips together in a hard line. "I forgot to tell your driver that we've had a flood in the stables from that last storm. We've moved all the horses up to a new building on the eastern bank while we do repairs." Lawrence looks at me. "Could you hurry and tell your driver before he tends his horse?"

I hesitate, glancing over at Fairalisa.

"Would that be all right?" Lawrence turns and asks Fairalisa.

"Of course. Hurry along," Fairalisa says.

Slightly stunned, I turn around and walk back down the hallway. In front of the house, I catch Hobbes tightening the reins on the horse.

"I'm to tell you that the stables have flooded," I say. "You're supposed to use—"

"I know," Hobbes says, standing and placing his hands on his hips. "The eastern building. Sir Lawrence told me that the last time I was here."

The driver steps up into his seat. "Thanks," he says before snapping his reins and pulling away.

I stagger backward, allowing the carriage to pass. The wheels grind against the driveway. I furrow my brows. Was this an oversight on Lawrence's part? Did he forget that he'd already told our driver the news? I walk slowly down the hallway, taking in the beautiful paintings that hang from the walls.

One of those paintings is of a young, black haired girl. I pause and gently stroke the canvas. Lawrence's mother perhaps? Understanding floods my mind. It must be Lawrence's sister. I recall the story he told of her. She was born crippled, never lived much of a life, and then died far too young. And in her short life she must have felt the intense pressure of the captain's high standards. My mood falls. I miss that Lawrence, I muse to myself, the man who tenderly opened his heart to me. I force myself to turn from the image and the memory of the old Lawrence.

Light piano music drifts from the dining hall. Two servants hurry inside, carrying silver-domed trays. I take a deep breath before slipping into the room.

Ridley sits at the head of a long oak table. His dark hair slicked back, and his sharp gaze pinned to Anthond.

My heart hammers in my chest. I retreat to the shadowed edge of the room where Anthond's servant stands. My entrance goes unnoticed, and I realize that Lawrence's ruse was to keep me out of his father's line of sight.

"Lawrence will be your problem soon enough," Ridley tells Anthond just before taking a drink from his glass of wine. Ridley wears a suit decorated with militia pins and badges.

"Anybody who's willing to look after my daughter is a saint in my eyes," Anthond says with a chuckle.

Lawrence's mother *tsks* at the men. "I'm not ready for my baby to move out." Ridley's wife has deep olive skin and wears her long black hair in a crystal clip.

"You'll see him plenty, I'm sure, Ohbolina," Anthond says.

Ohbolina takes a bite of bright green asparagus. "It's not the same," she pouts.

"When do you plan to move in?" Anthond asks.

"Hopefully in a few days. I'm afraid I'm being called out again on militia business later this week. I'd like to be settled before that."

"You're going away again?" Fairalisa asks.

"I only got the news this morning, which is why we arranged this dinner so quickly," Lawrence says.

Fairalisa stares at her plate. "That's so close to the wedding."

A servant comes round and fills Ridley's wine glass.

"I know," Lawrence says firmly. "It's the way it has to be."

Lawrence places his hands neatly on his lap. He's so poised and controlled. He seems to have lost all of the boyish mannerisms he had when I knew him in Bear Gap.

"Fairalisa, darling, are all of your arrangements for the wedding set?" Ohbolina asks.

Fairalisa straightens her back. "Most things are set, just a few more details to work out."

Lawrence's mother nods. The dining room falls into silence as their first course ends and servants collect the dinner plates.

"Captain," Fairalisa says, clearing her throat. "Lawrence has told me about your trips to Bear Gap. My lady's maid is from there, and she's told me much about that interesting territory."

My body freezes.

Ridley cocks his head and stares intently at Fairalisa. "Is that so?"

"Yes, she's told me about the magnificent farm and the economy there."

Ridley's eyes flick from Fairalisa to me. I bow my head and concentrate on the floor.

Please don't recognize me.

"Hmph!" Anthond exclaims. "Did she tell you about those deranged rebels who are taking over down there?"

"Daddy, calm down."

A line of servants returns to the room, carrying the next course. Each holds a silver plate, which is then set before the guests, the lids pulled off to reveal a puff of steam.

"That's a sheer mess down there if you ask me," Anthond says.

Ridley's jaw is set as he takes in a measured breath. "Bear Gap is a complicated situation."

"They've taken over the farm," Anthond continues, taking a forkful of chicken into his mouth. "Disrupted our food supply, and made the Supreme Ruler to look a fool!"

"I can hardly argue with your latter point," Ridley says.

Anthond hits the palm of his hand against the arm of his chair. "He needs to send the militia down there and take that territory back, or soon it'll be the start of the end for Elmyra as we know it."

"It's not quite that simple," Ridley says.

What about Quinten's supposed trip in a few weeks? Wouldn't these men know of his plan to travel to Bear Gap?

"The farm is still functional even under rebel control," Lawrence says.

"Don't tell me you support those miscreants?" Anthond's voice rises.

"Of course not. I only mean, there is no crisis. An unplanned attack would affect the food supply more severely."

"My son is correct," Ridley says. He snaps at a nearby servant girl to remove the plate of food he's barely touched. "Since they've begun providing wages, the farm doesn't produce as much. We have to handle the Bear Gap situation with some delicacy lest the whole country starve."

"Hmph." The old man waves his hand at Ridley. "You can't have delicate negotiations with rabble-rousers like that! The Supreme Ruler must go in with a strong arm, and that's exactly what I keep telling him."

"How you men accomplish anything for Elmyra amazes me," Ohbolina says.

"Our disagreements are what make being on the council together so invigorating," Ridley says with a wry smile.

Ridley seems supportive of Quinten's soft handling of Bear Gap, which surprises me. The memory of Ridley standing in Johnny's cabin after Governor Leo's death floods my mind. He'd come there to take his son back home. He'd said, "I serve a *different* ruler."

Anthond's wrinkly face softens, and he allows a gruff laugh to pass over his lips. "The council is growing weak."

"Must we always talk Warwick business?" Ohbolina asks. "This is supposed to be a celebration of Lawrence and Fairalisa."

"You are right, my darling," Ridley says silkily. "Why don't we move into the parlor for our dessert?"

"Yes, yes," Anthond says. "The captain will do anything to change the subject from his political stance."

"Daddy . . ." Fairalisa scolds.

Lawrence rises and helps Fairalisa from her chair.

"It's all right," Ridley says. "Your father and I are used to arguing this way. Right through there, ladies and gentlemen," Ridley says, motioning toward the archway.

Anthond's manservant brings him his cane and helps him from his chair. Fairalisa and Lawrence, arm in arm, nearly skip from the dining hall. Still holding his glass of wine, Ridley approaches me. I keep my head down, staring at the intricately woven rug beneath my feet.

"Fairalisa tells me you're from Bear Gap?" Ridley says, trying to catch my eyes.

"Yes, sir." I speak in a mousy tone.

"I know a few people from there."

I say nothing, clasping my hands behind my back. Ohbolina assists Anthond out of the hall.

"What are their names?" he muses to himself. "Ah yes, the Crim siblings." My heart seizes and I freeze in place. Ridley bends in closer. "It is good to see you, Camilla. Would you tell your brother I asked after him?"

CHAPTER TWENTY

"RIDLEY, DEAR!" OHBOLINA calls from the other room.

I keep my lips glued shut, and my face pointed to the floor.

"Coming!" Ridley calls to his wife as he takes one final look at me before striding from the dining hall.

I steady my breathing by forcing myself to watch the servants methodically clear the table. He hasn't ordered that I be arrested this moment. Is it his loyalty to Anthond that has caused him to wait? Maybe he wants to handle this with Lawrence. He's toying with me, but why?

I feel the pulsing in my heart as I realize I might not have a lot of time. Ridley knows who I am. He knows I'm in LilyAye, and he's rightfully assumed that Tuor is here too. Whatever his reason for not calling for my arrest, I'm not waiting around to find out. I've toiled with this family long enough. I have to get out of here, and I have to find Reed.

"Do you want me to take you to your lady?" a small servant girl asks when she sees me still standing awkwardly in the dining hall.

I clear my throat. "Yes, thank you."

I'm led to the dimly lit parlor, where Fairalisa and Ohbolina sit across from each other in chairs draped in black bear skins. Fairalisa chatters expressively. Like a good servant, I step into the room and demurely slink into the corner. Anthond leans back on a wooden chair while Ridley stands in front of him, puffing on a pipe.

"You'll never convince me that your weak diplomacy works!" Anthond jeers.

"You just enjoy the old ways of war," Ridley says, sucking in a puff of smoke.

Lawrence sits next to Anthond. He swirls a glass of dark liquid in his hand. I shoot my gaze directly at Lawrence and catch his eyes. I press my lips together and try to communicate my concern without saying a word.

"Excuse me gentlemen," Lawrence says, setting down his glass and rising.

Fairalisa looks up from her future mother-in-law as Lawrence crosses the room to her. He bends slightly and asks, "Would you mind if I stole away your lady's maid for a bit? I have a little surprise I'd like to discuss with her."

Fairalisa twists in delight. Her shiny lips spread in a smile. "Of course," she says, composing herself.

Lawrence waves at me to exit the parlor. His boots click across the Catahli floor. The chain on my shackles rattles as I struggle to keep up with Lawrence's long strides. I follow reverently as he leads me down the hall, toward the back of the house, and out into the courtyard.

The cool night air hits my bare arms. Long torches dot the yard, and candles hang from curved posts in the ground. It's a quiet, peaceful garden with only the sound of crickets and distant voices from the city. Lawrence pulls me behind a line of bushes, under the cover of a drooping willow tree. He glances across the lawn and peeks over the hedge of bushes to make sure no one can see us.

"We should be quick," Lawrence says, scanning me up and down. His voice is low and hushed. "Your appearance is much improved. You looked like you'd been fed to the dogs when I picked you up a few days ago."

"It's amazing what regular meals will do for your complexion," I say dryly.

"I'm sorry we couldn't talk much the other day. I wanted to tell you about Reed finding me and asking me to buy you and Tuor from the auction."

"Yeah, I figured that out. Listen, I—"

"How's everything going in the house?"

I purse my lips. "I'm a lady's maid, Lawrence. I'm fixing her hair, tying bows, and emptying her chamber pot. How do you think it's going? I want to get out of here."

Lawrence chuckles. "Fairalisa can be a handful."

"Your father knows I'm here. He just called me by name."

Lawrence throws his head back and runs his hand through his smooth hair.

"I was hoping he wouldn't recognize you," he says.

"Well, he did. What is he going to do?"

"I'm not sure," Lawrence admits. "My father likes to play chess. He may just sit on this information until it's convenient for him to use it."

"I can't sit around anymore," I say urgently. "Reed says it's safer for me to stay here, but I don't think that's true anymore. You have to get me to the rebels before your father decides to play his hand." I hug my arms close to my body. "*We* have to get with the rebels."

"We?" Lawrence cocks his head in confusion.

"Yes. *We*," I snap back. "You are a part of this rebellion whether you like it or not."

Lawrence leans away from me. "How do you figure?"

"You rescued me, and you're keeping me alive and safe so that I can continue my mission in LilyAye."

"I only saved you because you're my friend. I don't want any harm to come to you, but I'm going to make one thing clear: I don't want anything to do with the rebellion."

I cross my arms over my chest. "You haven't changed at all. Look at you. You've finally taken the job your father always wanted you to. You look very LilyAye, and you even have a brainless fiancée on your arm."

Lawrence peers down at me under heavy eyebrows. "Don't be like that, Camilla. I've already told you I won't turn my back on my family."

I grab Lawrence's arm and squeeze it tightly. "Reed and the rebels are waiting for us."

"They will keep waiting."

"You've gone through all of this to save me, but you still won't aid the rebellion?" I don't hide the disgust from my voice.

Lawrence turns from me. "You know I can't. I'm dedicated to my life here in LilyAye."

"Why? Forget about this high-society job!"

Lawrence shakes his head as if he himself doesn't even know the answer. "I don't expect you to understand what it's like to live a life of duty. I don't agree with everything Warwick does or stands for, but I have a duty to the crown. That's more important than how I feel, or what I want."

I narrow my eyes at Lawrence. "That's not what you said to me when we sat in Mirabelle's library."

My words seem to cut Lawrence. He falls silent for a moment. "I was foolish in my ideals back then."

"Do you even know why we came to LilyAye?"

"I don't want to know," Lawrence says, his jaw set. "I get what you're trying to do in Bear Gap, but you have no business being in LilyAye. This city is different. You will just get killed here. If you really want me to help you and the rebels, then take my advice. When I can get you out of here, go back to your territory, hold the lines in Bear Gap, and be happy that you have the freedom there that you want."

I shake my head. "I just lived through the horrors of LilyAye's slave trade. I can't just move along and do nothing about it. Oppression in LilyAye means oppression everywhere. Besides, we won't be able to maintain our freedom in Bear Gap as long as Quinten is ruler."

Lawrence backs away and holds up a hand to stop me from talking. "Silence. The rebellion has been a strain on LilyAye. People here are starving because of the lack of food supply. You're in over your head, Camilla."

"Don't be so naive! Bear Gap is an hourglass. Soon, the sand is going to run out, and we'll be under siege again." I implore Lawrence with my eyes. "Please.

We need you. You work for the Warwick Militia. You can give us information."

"I'm a glorified errand boy for my father. That's it. My position with the militia is not glamorous. That's not what this is about. My family is everything to me. If I join the rebellion, then everyone I love is lost to me."

"You're hanging on for the sake of your father? He's a monster."

"Keep your voice down," Lawrence scolds. He peers through the long tendrils of the willow tree.

The distant sound of the city floats into the backyard.

I point an accusing finger at Lawrence. "He hunted down Tuor and accused him of murder. Tuor almost died, or have you forgotten about your friend?"

"I was there for Tuor when that happened."

"Yet now, you continue to do nothing to help him! Your words are empty."

"I already told you, we can't go get Tuor right now. I have too many eyes on me, especially with the wedding. And this isn't just about my father. I would lose everything. That includes Fairalisa."

"Who cares about that trifle of a LilyAye girl?"

Lawrence looks at me, confused. "I care. I love Fairalisa."

My mouth hangs agape. I struggle for words. How can he love her when their marriage was arranged?

"This is the life I want," Lawrence says firmly.

"Fine." I shake my head. "Have your glittery life, but you won't stop me, and you won't stop the rebellion. I should warn you, there won't be a crown for you to be loyal to for much longer."

"Don't. I don't want to have a reason to keep you here." Lawrence's words have a sinister ring to them.

"What do you mean?"

"Don't say it. Don't spell it out for me. If I know what you're planning, then I can't let you go."

Is Lawrence so devoted to Quinten that he would keep me as a slave here if he knew I was going to take part in Quinten's assassination?

"We need to get back before they start looking for us," Lawrence says. He slips his hand into his suit jacket. "Here. I was going to give this to Fairalisa tonight, but since we need to come up with a surprise, would you place this on her pillow?"

From the pocket of his jacket, Lawrence produces a square velvet box. He sets it gingerly in my hand. I pop open the lid to reveal a gold-chained bracelet. Big boat-shaped diamonds dangle from the chain like jangling charms. It's stunning. Even I'm mesmerized by it. I finger the sparkling jewelry.

"I feel bad leaving her again in a few days. I wanted to get her something nice that would make her think of me."

"She won't have any trouble remembering to think about you." I glance up at Lawrence. The anger I felt a moment ago drips away.

"You really want to marry her?"

"Yes," Lawrence says without hesitation. "I want nothing more than to call her my wife."

Slowly, I close the jewelry box.

"Come on," he says, tugging me back inside.

***

Fairalisa rests her head on my shoulder as we drive through the dark streets of LilyAye, toward home. I feel for the jewelry in my pocket just to make sure it's still there. I look down at Fairalisa and envy her peaceful countenance. My mind is racing.

I always knew Lawrence struggled between his life in LilyAye and the freedom he craved, but I hadn't expected him to be so resolute about his decision. Sadly, I can't fully trust him anymore. Lawrence is far more loyal to Quinten than I ever imagined. He leaves in a few days for some trip: Warwick business. The hardest reality to accept about Lawrence is that he doesn't seem to want to help me get out of my position as a lady's maid, which means I'll have to do it myself.

Our carriage bumps gently as we turn onto the driveway that leads to Anthond's estate. Lanterns line the drive, leading us all the way to the back of the house, near the stables. Anthond yawns loudly as the carriage comes to a jerking stop.

"That was a lovely dinner, but I'm exhausted," Anthond says. "You might just need to carry me to my bed chamber!"

Anthond's manservant helps him from the carriage. I rouse Fairalisa, and she holds my hand as we climb the stairs to her bedroom.

"I acted okay over there, right?" Fairalisa asks as I open the bedroom door for her.

"Yeah. You did great," I say.

Fairalisa turns around, and I begin untying her dress.

"But do you think the captain was impressed by me?"

"Definitely." I nod, willing to say anything to get Fairalisa to bed quicker.

She steps out of her dress, and I hang it up in her closet before pulling back the covers of her bed. I check to make sure Fairalisa isn't looking and then place the small velvet box on her pillow. Fairalisa sits at her vanity, in her nightgown, waiting for me. There, I tie her hair loosely with a ribbon. I catch a glimpse of her downturned face in the mirror.

"What's wrong?" I ask.

"I don't know." Fairalisa waves me off.

I watch Fairalisa curiously, tilting my head. Is she actually insecure about her dinner with Lawrence's family?

"It's just . . . did you hear the question his mother asked about the wedding preparations?"

"Yeah?"

Fairalisa turns in her vanity chair to face me. "As if I can't handle putting together my own wedding!" She stands and marches across the room. "And then, when we were in the parlor, she leaned over to me and asked if I wanted any advice for the wedding night." Fairalisa twists her face in disgust. "How horrible of her to ask me something so crass."

I raise my eyebrows. I'm genuinely curious for the first time during one of Fairalisa's story. "How did you respond?"

"I politely declined any conversation related to my and Lawrence's wedding night. It's none of her business!" Fairalisa puts her face in her hands and walks the length of her bed. "This whole affair is so tedious and stressful. Sometimes I wish I could just ride away with Lawrence to somewhere outside of LilyAye and away from both of our parents."

Fairalisa's eyes fall to the box on her pillow. She pauses, confused for a moment, and then lets out a squeal of delight.

"Is this the surprise?" she squeaks, holding the box.

Fairalisa pops open the box and lets out an over-the-top gasp. Lips spread and hand on her chest, tears fill the corners of her eyes.

"See, tonight wasn't that terrible, was it?" I ask.

Fairalisa silently shakes her head. I help her clasp the bracelet which she insists on wearing now, then tuck her into bed before blowing out her candles. Quietly, I slip into my room. I click the closet door closed and lean against it. My head falls back against the dark mahogany wood. A sigh escapes my lips. I can't spend one more insipid day inside this house, with this family.

From my bureau, I pull out a white shawl, one of my few possessions, and tuck Fairalisa's hair clip into my pocket, hoping to barter with it later. I wrap the shawl tightly around my shoulders and waist and move to the balcony doors. A part of me feels bad for leaving Fairalisa before her wedding. She seems genuinely encouraged by my friendship, but at the end of the day, I couldn't care less about her. Ridley knows exactly where I am, and Lawrence is completely useless in getting me out of here.

I gingerly turn the handle on the balcony door and slip into the cold night air. The lawn is still and peaceful. Only one lantern remains lit at the back door. Beyond Anthond's estate, the lights of the city sparkle like tiny diamonds. A distant shout and horse whinny echoes into the quiet yard.

Grasping the edge of the balcony railing, I tug on my shackles, feeling the tight restraint. Normally, an escape like this would be easy for me, but I can hardly move my legs. Using the palms of my hands, I clench the balcony railing. I lift my legs high as one and swing them over the ledge. My dress rips as my feet land on the outer edge of the balcony.

I steady myself then peer down the side of the house, looking for the same footholds that Reed used. I stretch my leg to set it on a jutting Catahli brick, but my shackles are too close together. Shuffling along the outside of the balcony, I get as close to the brick as I can. I stick out my foot and strain, willing my leg to reach. With my right foot midair, my left foot slips off the edge of the balcony, and I fall into a crumple on the soft grass.

A groan threatens to escape my throat. I roll over and bite my lip to keep quiet. I sit up, rubbing my backside, and scan the yard to check if I've been spotted. It's quiet aside from the chirping crickets. A sharp pain hits my knee as I pull myself to standing. My white dress is streaked green. I pause to steady my breathing, then hobble across the yard, to the fence. I grapple for the handle on the back gate and spill into the alley.

Glancing up and down the alley, I pull my shawl tightly around my shoulders and scurry toward the main street. My gait is an awkward shuffle. At the end of the alley, I look behind me and see only a dark gravel road. I turn left onto the sidewalk, in the direction that Reed said the rebels were hiding.

My heart races while I limp down the street. Bright green lawns border the sidewalk on either side. To my left, a hill leads up to a towering mansion. A tall black fence encompasses the whole property. A street lamp illuminates a guard milling around the gate, a long sword hanging from his belt. I duck behind a tree and watch him intently.

I'll be in a bad way if I have to run. I can't risk that until I get these cuffs off my ankles. Doubling back, I reach the alley behind Anthond's house and cross the road there. I keep going straight, slipping between the yards of two more estates. I take advantage of the lavish trees and bushes to hide myself.

Finally, I empty onto a road on the outskirts of Anthond's neighborhood. The grand estates dwindle and are replaced with a line of row homes. I sneak around the corner of the block and hide in the alley behind the houses. Soft candlelight fills the frosted windows of the row homes. Orange and red leaves drift onto the ground. Pressing my back against the wall, I peer across the street. It's peaceful, not a soldier in sight.

Although subtle, there's a change in appearance from the well-maintained homes behind me and the less-than-spotless sidewalk on the other side of the street. The squat homes across the road are made of brick instead of Catahli, and the Warwick crest isn't plastered on every surface. I must be getting close to the slums, where Reed said the rebels are hiding.

I creep to the road's edge and cautiously peer in all directions. I'm nearly to safety. I can feel it. If I can get to the alley across the road without being seen, I think it's just a short walk to the slums. I take a deep breath, then break from the sidewalk and shuffle across the street, my gaze locked on the shadowy alley ahead.

"Kat, no!"

In the middle of the road, I twist to find Pip standing on the sidewalk behind me, waving me down. She's followed me here. I can't go back. I've already made my move.

"Kat!" Pip screams. "Stop!"

I turn and pump my legs, nearly tripping on my shackles. My foot crests the curb. I reach for the safety of the dark alley. A *whooshing* sound zooms toward me.

A sharp stab hits me in my lower back. A shriek bursts from my lips as I search for my breath. Hot sensations spider up my back and down my arms. I stumble into the alley. A thousand pinpricks run down my legs. My muscles weaken. I struggle to stand.

I grapple for the source of the pain and pull a short arrow from my back. An oily substance drips from the silvery tip. My eyes grow heavy. The arrow slips from my hands. My knees falter, and I tumble like a rag doll to the ground.

CHAPTER TWENTY-ONE

THE COLD, DAMP ground seeps through my thin dress and chills my body. A figure stands at the entrance of the alley. The street lamp behind him creates an ominous outline of a tall, broad-shouldered man. He steps toward me, a crossbow still gripped in his hand. His thick boots come to rest in a puddle near my head.

"You're coming with me," he says.

The street lamp illuminates the Warwick crest on his armor. He's a soldier. I've been caught, but how did they know I was out here?

"Sir! Sir, please!" Pip shouts.

I strain my neck and try to move, but the tingling in my body is sharp as a knife. Pip runs into the alley and kneels by my side. The film in front of my eyes drizzles away, and Pip's worried expression comes into view.

"Who are you?" the soldier bellows.

"Look what you've done to her," Pip says as she peers down at me.

She cups her hand under my neck and wipes sweat from my brow. It's then that I realize my whole body is convulsing as if I were having a fit.

The soldier pushes Pip away from me. "What do you think you're doing? I'll take you in too!"

Pip presses her lips together firmly, then comes to her feet. "Forgive me, sir." She bows. I notice she's still anxiously observing me with her downcast gaze. "My name is Pip. Anthond Balley is my master. I come from his home, where both of us are servants. She didn't mean to break the law."

I groan and try to roll onto my side.

"She stepped outside the district," the soldier says matter-of-factly.

He grips my arm firmly and pulls me up. I search for my breath as every move sends shooting pains up and down my limbs. My chest heaves in and out.

"She didn't mean to," Pip says. She collects my shawl from the ground. Its pristine white fabric is now splotched with dirty water. "She just got lost."

"Right," the soldier chuckles. He drags me out of the alley and onto the sidewalk.

"Wait!" Pip yells, running after us.

A tall wooden structure stands in front of one of the houses. It's not so different from the guard towers at Julian's compound. My head rolls on my neck as I stare up at it and understand that the soldier had been lying in wait for someone to cross his path.

"Go home." The soldier's deep voice echoes down the street. "Before I throw you in the dungeons too."

"She doesn't know about the district. She's a new servant, just purchased at the auction the other day. Please. Listen to me!"

The soldier stops in his tracks and spins around to face Pip. Even in my delirium, I catch the scowl on his face. His eyes dart to Pip's ankles, and he seems to notice her lack of shackles.

"I sent her out to pick up a book that Master Balley requested from Master Pennington, just down the road from us. I watched her walk down the drive and noticed she turned in the wrong direction, so I came after her to stop her."

"It looked to me like she was trying to run away."

"No." Pip breathes heavily. "She just misunderstood my directions."

The soldier, still gripping my arm, turns to face Pip more fully. His eyebrows scrunch together.

"Your master requested a book at this hour?" the soldier questions.

"He's an avid researcher. He often requests books late at night. Normally, I fetch them myself, but I had other things I wanted to do tonight."

Their voices clang around in my ears, making my head ache.

The soldier sucks on his teeth. "Why would you send a brand-new servant out into the night when you know she doesn't understand the district yet?"

Pip's mouth opens to speak, but she hesitates. "I forgot. We are in the midst of preparing for the lady's wedding, and it has spread us all very thin. In the chaos, I simply forgot that Kat was new to LilyAye and hadn't yet been shown the boundaries." Pip looks at me sympathetically. "She's never even been to the market yet."

"Whose house did you say you're in?" the soldier asks in a clipped tone.

"Master Anthond Balley."

223

The soldier lets out a derisive sigh. He shakes his head. "They're bringin' in new ones every single day. It's hard to keep 'em all in line."

Pip nods, swallowing hard. "She just got lost. I'm sure she's learned her lesson now."

"Fine," the soldier says, tossing me over to Pip. "Get her out of here. Make sure she knows how this city works. Some of the guards shoot to kill."

"Yes. Of course. Thank you," Pip says, bowing.

Pip slips an arm around my waist and helps me limp across the road. "Are you okay?"

I nod, leaning on Pip for strength. We connect with the sidewalk on the other side and head toward Anthond's house.

"Go slow," Pip says. "It's a small dose, but it's still poison."

Poison. I hold a hand to my throat. The hot sensation in my back cools to a dull ache. We pause in front of the row homes, looking left and right before crossing the street.

"What was he talking about?" I whisper. "The district?" A dry cough bursts from my throat.

"The Servant's District," Pip says. "There are only certain parts of the city that we're allowed to go by ourselves. We can walk freely throughout those parts, but if we venture even an inch past the border, well . . . You saw what happens."

"I'm guessing the borders aren't very big," I croak.

"You can't go past this neighborhood, but we can take the main road through the city square and into the market. It's an invisible wall. Soldiers tightly guard the perimeter."

Pip half carries me into the alley behind Anthond's house. We sneak down the lawn.

"There's no getting past it, Kat, unless your master is with you," she says as we stand in the glow of the lantern that hangs above the back door.

"How are we going to get inside without Ronda seeing me like this?" I ask, my silken white dress stained with grass and mud.

Pip raises her eyebrows. "Fortunately for you, she's in bed."

Nearly all of the candles have been blown out in the house. The distant hum of the city drifts through the open windows. The white, fluffy cat follows us as Pip helps me upstairs and into my bedroom. I crumple onto my bed and curl into the fetal position.

The cat meows, sniffing my nose and rubbing her face against my twitching hand. I moan as the tingling in my body turns into a feverish ache. Pip quietly rushes around my room, carrying my wash basin to my bedside.

"Lift your arms," she says in a low voice.

Without asking, Pip pulls my dress up and slips it over my head. My bare skin exposed, I shiver and reach for the blankets. Pip removes the gifted hairclip from the pocket then tosses my slave dress into the fireplace. She stokes it with the fire poker as it ignites in a bright burst.

"What are you doing?" I ask, peeking over the edge of the covers.

Pip sets the hair clip on the mantle then comes to my side and dips a cloth into the wash basin. "If Trixie saw that hole and the blood on the back of your dress while laundering it, she would be suspicious and show it to Ronda."

Pip helps me lie on my side and pulls the covers down to expose my back. I flinch as she dabs my skin with cold water. A tingle runs down my body. I feel sick all over, like the time I missed work at the farm for a week.

"So this is what Warwick does?" I ask, my voice small. "He cages in the slaves with this invisible wall, and poisons them if they step out of line?"

Pip rinses the cloth in the water and continues wiping the blood from my wound.

"Yes," she says solemnly. "Slavery has been in LilyAye for a long time. They've pretty well perfected the system."

I exhale, feeling nauseated that I'm back inside this house.

"I know what you were trying to do, Kat. And no one in this house can find out."

"Why did you lie for me?"

Pip dips the cloth in the wash basin. She sighs as she takes a seat at the end of my bed.

"I've seen it before. A new person comes to the house. They don't want to be here. They've never been anyone's servant before. So the first chance they get, they head for the city gates. Sometimes it happens when they're out at the market for the first time. Sometimes people stay here for months, concocting a plan, only to find that they can't make it past the soldiers. I've seen too many servants come and go from this place. I just wanted to save you."

"And if you're caught?" I ask.

"The official story is you're taken to the dungeons, but people just seem to disappear from the city. There's no trial or chance for redemption. You'll never be bought as a servant again. That's for sure. Nobody wants a servant who could run any minute." Pip's shoulders slump. "After watching it so many times, I have my own theories. I think they get sent to one of Warwick's work camps, but there's no way to know for sure."

Pip stands and inspects the spot on my back where the arrow hit me. "The only reason I've survived here as long as I have is because I've obeyed."

"Is that why you don't have to wear shackles?"

"Master Anthond trusts me," Pip says, pressing lightly on my lower back. "Look, I got torn away from my family too. I know what it's like, but you have to promise me you won't try and run again." Pip leans forward and catches my eyes.

I nod to appease Pip. She bends to get a closer look at my back. I sense her pause. She reaches for the candlestick on my nightstand and holds it up to my bare back. A subtle gasp escapes her mouth.

"Kat, are these whipping scars?"

"We had slavery in Bear Gap too," I say.

Pip awkwardly clears her throat. She sets down the candle then retrieves a silky camisole from my bureau and rangles it onto my body. Urging me to lie still, Pip helps me to get under all the covers and tucks me in tightly. After placing a cup of water on my nightstand, Pip stands over my bed.

"I know this is hard. You don't want to be here, but I can tell, by those scars on your back, that you were once taught how to comply." Pip leans in close. Her eyebrows knit together. "Please stay. Learn to be okay with your life here. If you don't, you'll just be taken away, and I kind of like having you around."

Despite my shaking chills, I force a smile. I'd always thought these scars were what urged me to rebel, but maybe I just wasn't getting the message.

"Promise me you'll obey," Pip says.

"I promise."

***

I wake a few hours later with intense cramping. My stomach roils like a turbulent sea. I throw off the covers, run to my chamber pot, and vomit violently. I wipe the sick from my mouth and gasp for air. The poison marches through my body like an army. I take a sip of water and curl back into bed only to be awoken a short time later to vomit again.

The sun blinds me as I find myself sprawled on the cold floor of my bedroom. I roll over and feel the nausea overtake me. The door of my closet opens.

"Kat?" Fairalisa calls.

She glances at me and lets out a scream.

"Are—are you okay?" she asks, taking two steps into the room before retreating back inside the closet. "I'll get you help!" she yells through the door.

I grip the sides of the chamber pot and empty my stomach once again. Exhausted, I lay back. Time eludes me. Ronda visits and mumbles that my illness is a grave inconvenience and asks if I know where the black tea tin is. Pip is there too. I hear her tell Ronda that I must have picked up something from Slaver's Row. At some point, I'm placed back in my bed, because I wake up sweaty, with my blankets tangled around my legs, and the cat still curled up next to me.

A tray of food sits untouched on my nightstand. It's dark outside. I sit up and try to drink. I'm feverish and chilled. My skin is tender to the touch. Pip returns in the night to check on me. She forces me to drink and promises that the poison will leave my body soon. With nothing left in my stomach, I hunch over and dry heave uncontrollably. The days melt by. I lose track of how many times Fairalisa and Pip check on me, and I can't remember the last time I felt normal.

My door clicks open and the sound of clanking dishes stirs me to waking. Through my balcony doors, I can see the sun setting behind the trees. Pip carries a tray of bottles into the room and sets them on my dresser. She pours a combination of the bottles' contents into a glass cup and brings it to me.

"You're awake," she says with surprise. She presses the back of her hand to my forehead. "How are you feeling?"

"Better," I mumble.

"I think your fever broke. Here, drink this."

Without question, I suck down the syrupy liquid. My face twists as the bitterness lingers on my tongue.

"That'll help," Pip says, taking the empty cup from my hand.

"How long have I been in bed?"

"Three days," she says with a pained look. "I never thought the poison would hit you this bad. I'm glad to have you back." She smiles.

I eat a small bit of food that evening, but I have to force it down. I still have no appetite. I sleep through the night, uninterrupted for the first time since I was shot with the poison. I'm up early, and by morning, I'm feeling more like myself. My muscles are weak, and when I look at myself in the mirror, the outline of my ribs is more pronounced.

After bathing, I slip on a new white dress and comb my hair. I wear the hair clip that Fairalisa gifted me upon my arrival at this house and even adjust the silver collar around my neck. Downstairs, I push open the kitchen door. A cloud of steam bathes Benji's face.

He clears his throat when I enter. "I heard you were out of bed. I fixed you a light breakfast this morning. You know, to settle your stomach."

Something about Benji's demeanor is odd. I give him a suspicious look and peek under the tea towel covering my breakfast. A bowl of warm porridge sits on the tray. It smells faintly of apple and walnut. Benji sets down his spatula and awkwardly wipes his hands on his white linen apron.

"I feel bad about what you went through, being sick and all," Benji says. "Pip was pretty worried about you, and Pip doesn't get worried about much so . . . anyway, I hope you feel better."

Is this Benji's way of making amends, through food?

"Thanks," I say, picking up the trays.

"Jaunty, you know, he's kind of a bad influence."

Benji gives me a toothy grin before returning to his griddle. I expertly balance the trays as I take the steps to Fairalisa's bedroom. Ronda stands, stiff backed, at the top of the steps.

"So you're back to your duties?" Ronda asks.

I steady Fairalisa's tray in the crook of my elbow. "Yes, I'm back. You don't need to cover for me anymore. I'll handle all of the lady's needs from here on out."

"Hmph." Ronda purses her lips and looks me up and down. "We'll see." She turns toward the stairs.

"I should tell you"—she pauses on the top step— "I know you don't like me, but I'm committed to serving the lady and this house."

Ronda lifts her chin and eyes me. "Well, I'm glad to see a change in your countenance."

Change, yes. I have certainly changed.

Fairalisa is still sleeping when I enter with her breakfast. I hurriedly eat my porridge, then dig the tin of black tea that I confiscated out of my dresser drawer and run back downstairs to make Fairalisa a cup. When I return to Fairalisa's bedroom, I open her curtains and allow the bright autumn sun to warm the Catahli floor. I stoke the fire, bringing it to life, and warm the water in her wash basin. I even tidy the room and start picking out a dress I think she might like for the day.

"Kat!" Fairalisa squeals as she stretches her arms over her head.

"Good morning," I say brightly.

"You're back." Fairalisa climbs down from her bed and pulls me into a tight hug. She buries her face in my neck. "Oh, I've missed you so much."

"I missed you too. Did anything exciting happen while I was sick?"

Fairalisa pulls out of our hug and returns to her covers. "Ugh, I had to deal with Ronda as my lady's maid, which was terrible!"

Fairalisa gasps when she sees the teacup.

"I haven't had tea for days!"

"Yeah, sorry about that," I say, closing the lid on one of Fairalisa's hat boxes.

"I sent word to the weaver to tell him I've chosen the emerald-green table runners and, don't be mad, but I finished the cake tasting without you." Fairalisa opens the dome lid on her breakfast plate.

"That's okay. I'm not all that interested in food right now anyway."

"Oh, good! I was so afraid you'd be upset. Don't worry because tomorrow will be such an exciting day." Fairalisa giggles. "We're actually going to visit the place where the wedding will be held."

"Uh huh," I say from the closet.

"It is gorgeous, Kat. You won't believe it." Fairalisa comes to the closet door, holding a biscuit in her hand.

"Where is it?"

Fairalisa wears a mischievous smile. "It's the old palace where Supreme Ruler Bradac lived when he reigned. It's magnificent! And only special people can have access to it, but because of my daddy . . ." Fairalisa takes a bite of her biscuit. "Technically, Warwick built a new castle for himself because this one was too small, but still, it's fit for a king."

Fairalisa gasps. "I almost forgot the most important news of all. Lawrence moved into the house while you were indisposed." A satisfied sigh escapes Fairalisa's lips. "It's been dreamy having him around, but don't have any inappropriate thoughts. We have our own bedrooms until we're married. He leaves tomorrow for his trip, which means tonight will be my last dinner with him until he's back. Oh, Kat, we have so much to do!"

I help Fairalisa dress, and we spend most of the day preparing for Lawrence's last dinner. Fairalisa talks with Benji about the evening's meal. She picks out a special bottle of wine, and even asks Pip to make her famous honey cake.

"I didn't know you could cook," I say to Pip as we gather in the servant's dining room for dinner.

"I try to stay out of Benji's way, but I can make a thing or two. Baking is kind of my specialty," Pip says, settling into her seat.

"It's good to see you back," Sindle says from across the table.

A few other servants chime in and agree with Sindle. I didn't know I was so missed. Even Trixie gives me a side hug and tells me she's happy I'm feeling better. Jaunty ignores me from the other end of the table which is the kindest thing he could do. Later that evening, Pip walks with me upstairs. We stop in front of my bedroom.

"So do you think you'll stick around for a while?" Pip asks, her voice low.

I lean against the door frame. Lawrence strides past us down the hall. We bow our heads until he's out of sight.

"It's not so bad here," I say.

"Good." Pip exhales in relief. "Get some sleep. You'll need your strength for these next few weeks."

I chuckle. "Goodnight, Pip."

Alone in my bedroom, I walk to the balcony doors. Darkness blankets the city. I look beyond Anthond's estate to the city wall. A shiver runs up my back at the thought of what lies beyond the Servant's District. I swing the latch to secure the doors and snap my curtains closed.

The act is a symbol. I don't want to relive the last few days again. I don't want to be punished by a Warwick soldier. I don't ever want to try to escape again. My body shakes as those haunting memories from Karla's bedroom invade my thoughts. The heartache I've experienced, it's too much. I can't take it anymore. I back away from the balcony just as a note is slipped under my bedroom door.

CHAPTER TWENTY-TWO

THE FOLDED-UP parchment sits inconspicuously on my floor. I open it cautiously and read.

Meet me in the gazebo tonight when it's clear.

~Lawrence

For a moment, I consider if he meant to give this note to Fairalisa. It's the word *clear* that convinces me; the note was intended for my eyes. There's no real danger in Fairalisa and Lawrence slipping out together at night, but if I were caught out of the house after sunset, there would be questions to answer.

"Kat! I'm back from dinner!" Fairalisa calls through the closet door.

I toss the letter into the fire before answering Fairalisa's summons. I help her out of her dinner dress and into a nightgown and wish her good night before she has a chance to tell me how much she's going to miss Lawrence when he's gone. Little does Fairalisa know, I have a meeting with him to get to. I pace around my bedroom for a bit in case Fairalisa needs me, but when I crack open her bedroom door, her gentle snoring floats into my room.

I slip downstairs into the dark front hall. The cat leaps from her spot on the couch, begging me to pet her. Tiptoeing across the cool Catahli floor, I quietly click open the back door and dip outside. The leaves of the trees rustle as a breeze floats through the yard. A carriage rides past Anthond's house, the jingling of the reins mixing with the hum of the city.

The gazebo sits in a dark corner of the lawn. Deep-green vines twist and curve around every post and railing.

"Camilla?"

Lawrence emerges from the shadows of the gazebo. The faint candle glow from the windows illuminates his face. I take the wooden steps and join him.

"Thank you for meeting me," he says. Lawrence holds his back straight and tall. "I heard about your illness. Are you recovered?"

"Yeah. Just something I picked up from Slaver's Row," I say, not wanting Lawrence to suspect I tried to run. "Why did you want to meet?"

"I wanted to apologize," Lawrence holds his bent arm tightly against his waist like a true Warwick dignitary. "Our last conversation was... disappointing." Lawrence paces the length of the gazebo, his face sullenly turned to the floor. "I want you to know, I'm grateful for our friendship and the different life you showed me when I was in Bear Gap." I lean against the gazebo railing, watching Lawrence carefully. "I just don't want to see harm come to you."

"I was probably being a little stubborn," I say.

Lawrence faces me and raises one of his eyebrows. "A little?"

I chuckle, holding my arms close to my body.

"I want to offer you a deal." Lawrence's voice shifts to a serious tone. "I know you think people like Anthond are the enemy, but in this world, a home like the one he's built is the best life for these servants. They're being fed better here than they would if they were with their families."

"What are you getting at?"

Lawrence steps toward me. "I don't know what my father is up to, but stay here. Choose to stay in this house. When Anthond dies, I become the master, and I can protect you even better."

I twist my face in disgust. "You want me to be your slave?"

"Not my slave, a servant in my house. It would be for your safety."

I turn swiftly from Lawrence, shocked by his proposal.

"You are a wanted fugitive, Camilla," Lawrence says, following after me. "There's nowhere for you to go that you won't be hunted down by Warwick. Even Bear Gap isn't safe. You said that yourself."

I peer out the side of the gazebo at the manicured lawn and the well-placed foliage.

"No one would ever suspect you here," Lawrence continues, easing up behind me. "You and Tuor could find solace in my house." He places a hand on my elbow, and I snatch it away. "With your master being a close friend."

"My friend is my master?" I practically spit the words as I spin around to face Lawrence. "That doesn't make any sense."

"I could protect you and Tuor, really protect you. You could live here comfortably, without threat of imprisonment or death."

My resolve dims as I allow my eyes to fall to my fingernails. I pick at them absentmindedly. When I merely think on my escape attempt from a few days ago, the burning sensation returns to the wound on my back where the arrow struck me. I shudder. A life of safety . . . I've been on the run so much the last year, I can hardly imagine what that would feel like.

"That would mean giving up on the rebellion," I say. "And my freedom."

Lawrence nods solemnly.

"I can't do that," I say.

"Are you really willing to sacrifice everything for this fruitless rebellion? I know you, Camilla. You're stubborn enough to give up your own life for something you believe in, but what about Tuor? Are you willing to sacrifice his life?"

Lawrence's words are a hit to my chest. They're sharp and swift but painfully true.

"All I ever wanted was a safe place for Tuor and me," I admit. Staring into the darkness, I shake my head slowly.

"I can give you that. When the wedding is over, and the attention is off me, I'll find Tuor and bring him back here, I promise."

"After the wedding? Why can't you get him now?"

"I leave tomorrow on a mission. Plus, we have no need for another servant right now, and Anthond knows that. If I bring in someone new, I fear he'll question my ability to run this house, and I don't want to jeopardize my union with Fairalisa."

I gnaw on my lower lip nervously.

"We'll get him," Lawrence says, grabbing my shoulders as if to shake sense into me.

His firm touch sends jolts of terror up my neck. The panic I'd managed to bury for the last week comes flooding back all at once. I shake Lawrence off and stumble backward on the gazebo's wooden floor.

"Are you all right?" Lawrence asks.

"I'm fine."

Lawrence reaches out a hand to me. "Camilla—"

"Stop. I'm fine, just . . . bring me Tuor, and we'll talk about your offer."

I stumble down the gazebo steps and hurry inside. Racing up the stairs, I close my bedroom door and grapple for something to steady myself with. My breath is heavy in my chest. I gasp, my lungs begging for air. Holding tight to my bedpost, I shake away the bad thoughts: Karla, Slaver's Row, the poison.

Lawrence's words roll around in my head. Is a life of peace really possible for me? Everywhere I go, the stigma of Camilla Crim follows me. What if I could have a new life as Kat, a girl who never started a rebellion or challenged the Supreme Ruler?

My breathing steadies. I take a seat on the end of my bed and bury my face in my hands. No matter where I go, my demons are still close on my heels. Lawrence's proposed arrangement is ludicrous and insulting. And yet... I'm surprised to find that I'm actually considering taking it.

***

"Bye, Daddy!" Fairalisa says cheerfully. She crosses the front hall and bends to give Anthond a kiss on the cheek.

He holds a long piece of parchment in his hand, the daily news of LilyAye. Anthond looks from me to Fairalisa, to the driver, Hobbes, who's standing at the front door, waiting for us.

"And where are you going?" Anthond asks.

"I told you. Today's the day we visit the Bradac palace."

"Ah yes, already?"

Fairalisa secures the button on her cloak. "Yes, Daddy. The wedding is less than a fortnight away!"

"Goodness," Anthond huffs. "Well, be careful out there." Anthond brings the parchment back to his face. "You wouldn't believe the things I read about in here."

"Don't tell me. I don't want to know." Fairalisa turns on her heels and calls to me. "Come, come!"

Hobbes holds open the front door for us as the crisp fall air hits our cheeks. Fairalisa giggles and scuttles her feet against the carriage floor as we ride down the driveway.

"This is so exciting, Kat! It feels like today could be my wedding day." Fairalisa pulls a pocket mirror from her purse and examines her lipstick. "It's just the thing I need to distract me from Lawrence's absence. He was already gone before breakfast this morning."

Hobbes pulls the carriage onto the cobblestone road. I can't help but think of my conversation with Lawrence last night. Could I really turn my back on the rebellion? How could I betray everyone back at Bear Gap? Even if some of the old rebel members, like Mirabelle and Johnny, don't seem to care anymore.

Another carriage passes in front of us before Hobbes turns right. The sidewalks are filled with passersby. Horses clip-clop past us. I look out the carriage window and notice the Warwick soldiers patrolling the street.

"What's that?" I ask, pointing ahead.

"Oh, that's the city square," Fairalisa says excitedly. "Isn't it beautiful?"

Hobbes takes the carriage around a circular marble fountain. I tilt my head to look at the height of it. A spray of water tumbles from the top.

"Down there is the front gate of the city, so gorgeous," Fairalisa says.

We ride past the intersection that leads out the front of the city and turn onto a wide road, which stretches out in front of us. Stately homes line the street, but what really catches my attention is the dark castle sitting at the end of the road. It's not the Bradac castle; it's Quinten's castle.

I spread my lips in awe as I take in the Warwick castle. Always a shadowy presence at the edge of the city, it takes on a new aura as it towers over me. Made of marbled black-and-gray Catahli, Warwick's home is accented with flags of his signature maroon crest. Tall towers grow and branch out from the thick round base, which reminds me of a gnarled pine tree. A bridge leads to a gated door that looks like a wide mouth with long metal teeth.

Fairalisa gasps, shaking my arm. "There it is, Kat!"

I'd been so distracted by the fabled Warwick castle that I hadn't noticed the grounds leading up to the old Bradac estate. A stone wall encompasses the property. Our carriage turns right onto a long driveway that takes us to a comparatively small brick castle. The facade is a warm earthen tone, a stark contract from the shiny Catahli covering the rest of the city. Looking at this building, I can imagine an older LilyAye, before Catahli was plenteous and Quinten Warwick was sitting on the throne.

"Yay!" Fairalisa claps as we reach the front door.

A thin man with a curled white mustache stands at the ready. He approaches our carriage as Hobbes dismounts and opens the door. Fairalisa bursts out, smiling sweetly at the man.

"Good morning, my lady," the man says, taking Fairalisa's hand and giving her a bow.

I turn to admire the battlements lining every edge of the castle walls. A bird swoops past one of the lofty turrets.

"It is wonderful to see you, Willip," Fairalisa replies. She appears so excited that she might pass out. Fairalisa turns to me. "Willip is the caretaker of this property."

"A duty that I consider an honor," Willip says in a posh, lilting voice. "We have everything set up for you as it will be on your wedding day aside from a few precise decorations."

"Excellent," Fairalisa says.

Willip folds his scrawny hands together. "Why don't we begin in the courtyard where your ceremony will take place, and then we'll move inside? This way you'll be able to experience your wedding as your guests will."

"I love that idea!" Fairalisa says.

Willip leads us alongside the Bradac castle, down a quaint, winding path. A bird with a long neck and a giant feathered emerald-green backside struts around the grass. The courtyard is hugged on all sides by bushes and trees. A blooming rose garden sits at the back of the courtyard, behind rows of pristine white chairs lined up with a wide aisle between them.

"You'll exit from the back of the castle"—Willip gestures with his skinny arms—"and then you'll walk down the aisle, to the arbor."

"Oh, it's beautiful!" Fairalisa says, putting a hand to her cheek. She twirls as she practically skips down the aisle in mock matrimony. She clasps the side of the flower-laden arbor and spins around to face us.

"I can truly picture it," Fairalisa says, stretching her arms to the audience that isn't there.

"Would you like to see how we have it set up inside?" Willip asks.

"Yes!" Fairalisa scurries down the aisle toward us.

We enter with the clunking sound of the castle door being opened. Willip leads us through a maze of dark hallways and into the castle's grand dining room.

Fairalisa turns and tells me, "Supreme Ruler Bradac used to host incredible feasts in this very room."

Her voice echoes through the cathedral ceiling. I pause, staring at the grandeur in awe. The curved brick walls meet with a balcony railing that runs around the whole perimeter of the room. A wide fireplace sits at the front.

"Your guests will be seated here," Willip says, pointing to the tables that run nearly the length of the room. Gold candelabras with deep-green leafy garlands twisted around the stems are the centerpieces. Tall milky-white candles flicker in the cave-like shadows.

"You and Sir Lawrence, will sit here." Willip points to a table at the front of the hall running perpendicular to the guests' tables. "And your special guests will be over here."

Willip takes Fairalisa to an ornate table sitting catty-corner to the head table. Fairalisa's face scrunches into a worried expression as she rushes to the spot.

"No, no." She shakes her head. "This won't do."

"Why not, my lady?"

Fairalisa lifts her hand as if feeling the air. "There's a draft in this corner. They need to be closer to the fire. We cannot risk the Supreme Ruler catching a chill at my wedding!"

My ears perk up. The tedious droning of wedding details suddenly melts to reveal something important.

I turn to Fairalisa and ask with great urgency, "The Supreme Ruler will be at your wedding?"

CHAPTER TWENTY-THREE

MY EYES WIDEN as I wait for Fairalisa to answer.

"Mind yourself, servant!" Willip says to me in a warning tone.

Fairalisa flinches, putting a hand over her lips.

"I wasn't supposed to say that." She rushes to my side. "It's quite confidential. Only a few people are privy to this, you know, for the Supreme Ruler's safety."

"He's going to be *here*?" I ask.

"My lady, I must protest this conversation," Willip says.

"It's fine! Kat is a very reliable lady's maid with immense discretion. Right?" Fairalisa raises her eyebrows at me.

"I won't tell anyone," I say, feeling that these are the words required of me.

"See, everything is fine," Fairalisa says. She links her arm into mine and turns me about so we're facing the guest tables. "This is the view he'll have during dinner. It needs to be perfect, absolutely perfect."

Fairalisa takes a deep, calming breath. "I'm so nervous, Kat. The Supreme Ruler will be at *my* wedding."

"Willip!" Fairalisa calls. "I want more of the greenery along that archway, and . . ." Fairalisa turns me around to face the fireplace. "Switch my table with the Supreme Ruler and his wife's."

"But you are the bride and groom," Willip says. "You should be—"

"I will not diminish the Supreme Ruler! Even on my wedding day. He should have the best, most prominent table. I want him closest to the fire and up on a platform for all to see."

Willip gestures with his hand. "I'm not sure we'll have time to construct something that elaborate, my lady."

"You will find a way," Fairalisa says, waving him off.

The rest of the tour drags on as Willip takes us to Fairalisa's bridal suite. The upstairs room is adorned with everything a princess would need to dress for her wedding day. After a lengthy conversation about how Fairalisa will get downstairs with her wide-hooped dress and long train, Willip finally sees us off.

***

"He has been my father's friend for years," Fairalisa says as we ride home from the Bradac castle. "Certainly, it was difficult to arrange. The Supreme Ruler rarely emerges for public appearances, but in light of my father's lengthy tenure on his council and the fact that I'm marrying into Ridley Thatius's family, who is another important member of the council, the Supreme Ruler finally agreed to attend."

Fairalisa crosses her legs as the carriage bounces down the road. "It is such a relief to finally tell you,

Kat," Fairalisa says, patting my knee. "I've been holding in this amazing news for so long! Now, I can tell you this too. I've had an idea. I want to present the Supreme Ruler with a special gift at the dinner feast. I'm just not sure what to get him . . ."

Fairalisa's droning voice fades into the jingling sound of the horse's reins as my mind drifts. Quinten is not traveling to Bear Gap as Reed had told me. That story got twisted, or perhaps intentionally spread to confuse anybody who wants to bring him harm, someone like me. Quinten will be at Fairalisa's wedding. He'll be guarded, I'm sure, but he'll be right there, sitting at a table, eating roasted pheasant with all the other wedding guests.

An opportunity to kill Quinten has fallen right in my lap. My mind twists and tumbles with murderous ideas. I could shoot Quinten with an arrow from the balcony in the dining hall. As a servant I could offer my assistance, get close, and slip a knife into his stomach. If I had to, I could trap Quinten and start a fire. I've done it before. My eyes fall to my quivering hands in my lap. But can I get past my panic to focus on killing the Supreme Ruler again?

I lean my head back as we pass the fountain in LilyAye Square. I couldn't turn my back on the rebellion, as Lawrence advised, even if I wanted to. But if I kill Quinten at the wedding, surely that will negate any offer of safety from Lawrence, and maybe jeopardize Tuor's return. That life of safety that I'd briefly pictured falls away. I pinch the bridge of my nose, feeling a headache coming on.

"My father tells me the Supreme Ruler fancies pear pudding," Fairalisa continues. "So perhaps I could have a dish made up especially for him and present it during dinner. What do you think, Kat?"

Hobbes pulls the carriage around to the front of Balley Estate.

"Yeah, pear pudding, that sounds lovely," I say.

"It's not like I can just go to the market and buy something for the Supreme Ruler," Fairalisa says as she climbs out of the carriage. "He's the wealthiest man in Elmyra. What could I possibly buy for him? My only choice is to make something meaningful or sentimental."

We enter the front hall and take the Catahli steps upstairs.

"I could have a signet ring made," Fairalisa muses as we enter her bedroom. "No, no, I'm sure the Supreme Ruler has many signet rings."

Fairalisa unbuttons her cloak and tosses it on her bed, then takes a seat at the vanity. "I think I'll rest this afternoon, Kat. Would you let my hair down for me?"

I move like a ghost around the room, slow and dazed. My mind is somewhere else as I hang up Fairalisa's cloak in the closet and come to undo her hair. How would I even manage to kill Quinten when my panic is so bad? The thought of approaching the border of the Servant's District terrifies me. Even just a touch on the shoulder from Lawrence sent me down a frenzied spiral.

"I miss him already," Fairalisa says, fiddling with a bottle of lip paint. "There are only so many wedding things to distract me before I start to think about him again."

"Mm hmm." I pull a pin from Fairalisa's hair, letting a thick tendril fall to her shoulder.

"And truthfully, Kat, I'm beginning to tire of the wedding preparations. It was fun when I started, but now it's just all detail and logistics." Fairalisa gazes at herself in the mirror. "You've been very quiet since we left the Bradac castle."

I force my mind to leave its spinning thoughts. She's noticed that I'm distracted.

"Oh no, I'm fine," I say quickly, searching for something to change the topic. "It's just, I sympathize with you. A party of this magnitude would frustrate the best of us. Plus, it's hard to be separated from someone you love."

"Yes. It's dreadful."

"I have family that I haven't seen for a while." I wonder vaguely if empty-headed Fairalisa could possibly miss Lawrence as much as I miss Tuor.

"Have you ever been in love, Kat?"

"What?" The word bubbles from my mouth.

"I know you said you were never married, but maybe you were in love once?"

I hesitate, my hands hovering over Fairalisa's hair. It's been a while since I've thought of *him*. "Yes, I've been in love."

"Really?" Fairalisa half turns around to look at me. "Who was it?"

"His name was Johnny," I say with a smirk. "We used to get along really well."

"Like Lawrence and me."

"Yeah, but Johnny was . . . fiery. He brought out this passion in me I didn't know I had."

"Oh!" Fairalisa says, excitement painted on her face.

I suddenly feel as though I've betrayed Reed for talking about Johnny in this way. Why didn't I immediately think of him when Fairalisa asked if I'd ever been in love? Have I ever actually felt love for Reed?

He terrified me, the way he acted on the mountain, but he's been a steady hand throughout the rebellion, and he expressed regret for what he did to Eve. Reed is actually here in LilyAye. Who knows if I'll ever see Johnny again?

"What happened to this Johnny?" Fairalisa asks.

"Nothing." I shrug my shoulders as I pull another pin from Fairalisa's hair. "He's still in Bear Gap."

"Is he married to someone else?" Fairalisa asks solemnly.

I scrunch my forehead. "No." It's then that I remember the girl I saw in his cabin the night I spied on him. "I don't think so . . ."

"Then why didn't you stay together? Would Karla not let the two of you marry?" Fairalisa folds her arms across her chest. "I hate it when I hear about masters who are so cruel."

I debate for a moment on how to answer Fairalisa. Of course, I never actually worked for Karla, but if I had, there's no way she would have been kind enough to let me marry while being her lady's maid.

"No, she wouldn't allow us to marry," I say, letting my voice drop to a sorrowful tone. "Karla liked her girls to live with her full time and not have husbands and children of their own."

Fairalisa scoffs. "That's just terrible!"

I can't help but notice the irony in Fairalisa's thinking. She has no problem procuring a lady's maid from beastly slavers who auction people like cattle, yet not allowing two people to marry is abhorrent to her.

"I've just had an incredible thought!" Fairalisa shouts, grabbing my arm. Her curls bounce wildly.

I gather all the pins I'd just removed from Fairalisa's hair and place them in a silver box on her vanity.

"We can bring Johnny here, and I'll allow the two of you to be married!"

"Oh no. That's kind, but I don't—"

"No, please, you must let me do it! I can't let true love sit and rot in Bear Gap when the two of you could have a beautiful life here."

Instinctually, I back away.

"It'll be perfect. I'll send a courier to Bear Gap. You can send a letter along with the courier so you can explain to Johnny the good news. He'll travel to LilyAye. He can live right here in the house with us. Then after Lawrence and I are wed, and we're back from our honeymoon, we'll arrange your wedding."

"Fairalisa, please, I beg of you, this is too much."

"It'll be so fun!"

I kneel in front of Fairalisa so that I'm eye level with her. It seems like the only way I can get her attention. "I don't—"

"It's no trouble," Fairalisa interrupts.

"No, it's not that." I search for the right words. "I don't *want* a wedding." Confused, Fairalisa looks at me. "Things are complicated between Johnny and me."

"You don't love him?"

I turn my gaze to my squirming hands. "No, I definitely love him, but trust me when I tell you, he doesn't want to hear from me."

"I see . . ." Fairalisa deflates.

"We don't hate each other, but—"

"Was he cross with you?" Fairalisa asks with wide eyes.

"No, I think he might have found someone new."

"But if you still love each other . . . ?" Fairalisa lays her hands out as if she were begging for Johnny and me to be together.

"Love isn't as simple for other people as it is for you and Lawrence," I say.

Fairalisa nods. She seems to finally concede that there won't be a winter wedding with Johnny and me.

"Thanks though," I say, standing. "No one has ever been so intent on finding me a husband." I return to my spot behind Fairalisa and begin brushing out her curls.

"Of course I would want you to be as happy as Lawrence and I are," Fairalisa says, her bright smile reflecting in her vanity mirror.

"You have your own wedding to plan, anyway. I couldn't take your time away from that."

Just then, my mind rushes back to Fairalisa's wedding and the decision I must make.

Fairalisa picks at her fingernails. "Ugh, I'm very ready to be married and not have to fuss with all of this anymore."

"You seemed to enjoy yourself at the Bradac castle today."

"Yes," Fairalisa sighs. "But now that I've seen it all decorated, I'm ready to be done with all the planning and just be married."

I lay Fairalisa's hair out on her back so it flows over the vanity chair. After combing it, I fold it into a loose braid. Fairalisa yawns as she saunters over to her bed. I draw her curtains to block out the midday sun. It's then that I realize, if Fairalisa is willing to retrieve my old lover and throw me a wedding, what else is she willing to do?

"Perhaps there's something else you can do for me," I blurt out, turning swiftly to face Fairalisa. "Something that would still reunite me with someone I love."

She shifts into a seated position under her covers and cocks her head. "There's another man you're in love with?"

"Can you purchase my brother?"

I stiffen my body as I wait for Fairalisa's response. Lawrence didn't want me to tell anyone about Tuor. He was going to handle it himself, but I'm tired of waiting.

"You never told me you had a brother!"

"He traveled to LilyAye with me and was bought by a miner. We got separated at the auction block." The words I've been holding back pour from my lips.

Fairalisa's face morphs into a pout. Her eyes glisten. "That's so sad," she says, resting a hand on her chest.

"I haven't seen him or heard from him since then. I don't even know if he's still alive." My throat tightens.

"Oh, Kat." Fairalisa reaches out her arms, summoning me to her side. I sit on the bed next to her as she wraps her arms around my trembling shoulders. "I didn't know you carried this pain. All this time I thought you were secretly pining for a lost love, but here it is." Fairalisa pulls me out of our hug and looks me in the eyes. "It's your brother you've been missing."

Fairalisa leans forward so our noses are almost touching. "Of course I'll help you get your brother. I can't have my lady's maid in a state like this."

"Really?" I ask, feeling tears at the corner of my eyes.

"It's done!" she says cheerfully. "We'll find him, and we'll buy him back. It'll be easy."

"What about your father?"

Fairalisa waves a hand at me.

"Even if he doesn't like it, Daddy can't stay mad at me," Fairalisa says with an innocent smile. "Worry not, Kat. We'll find him.

She pulls the covers up tight around her neck before I slip out into the hallway to let her sleep. Fairalisa's words repeat in my head. They're like sweet honey. *We'll find him.*

CHAPTER TWENTY-FOUR

I TAKE IN a deep breath and try to temper my excitement. I don't want to get my hopes up. Fairalisa may be a well-meaning girl, but she's also impossibly vain and very preoccupied with planning her wedding. Can she actually bring back my brother?

I make my way downstairs to the servant's dining room to have lunch while Fairalisa rests. A new energy surges through me at the thought of seeing Tuor. I slip into the table and sit across from Pip and Trixie. I scoop spoonfuls of fluffy rice and eggplant from the platters.

"Tell that story again!" Pip says, holding back laugher. "Kat hasn't heard it yet."

Trixie narrows her eyes and smirks. "Fine . . ."

"What story?" I ask.

"I was laundering the sheets one day outside. It was the summer, and this bee wouldn't leave me alone," Trixie says. "I swatted it away, and it kept coming back!"

Pip stifles her laughter, holding a hand over her mouth.

"So finally, I jumped up to run away, but I—"

Trixie is interrupted when Pip bursts out laughing.

"Sorry, sorry," Pip says. "Continue."

I listen with rapt attention.

"I stood up, tripped as I tried to get away, stuck my foot in one of the buckets, and fell backward on the lawn," Trixie says, folding her arms across her chest. "It wasn't funny. I had a bruised backside for a week!"

"You left out the best part!" Pip says.

Trixie rolls her eyes. "While I was lying on the ground, *suffering*"—Trixie looks at Pip as she punctuates that word—"the bee stung me on the lip, and I had a fat lip for days."

Pip rolls with laughter.

"That's terrible," I say, unable to hold back a chuckle.

"It's a little funny, you have to admit," Pip says.

Trixie purses her lips as she returns to her plate of food. She glances over at Pip. The two connect eyes, then simultaneously burst into laughter. I watch them: safe and happy. Being a servant isn't all that bad. I wonder if that could be Tuor and me.

***

I sit alone at a small table in the parlor. The cat lies on the couch, licking her fluffy white fur. The fire behind me crackles softly. A basket of tiny dried flower buds mocks me as my stubby fingers struggle to tie their short stems together. I gather a miniature bundle of baby's breath and petite roses. Using an emerald green ribbon, I wrap the stems together and tie a crude bow at the front.

Leaning back in the chair, I examine my latest creation. The ribbon is lopsided and uneven, certainly not the perfect bow that Fairalisa requested. Frustrated, I tear the knot open and try again. I groan audibly. Binding these delicate stems together is annoyingly tedious.

Days have passed since Fairalisa asked me endless questions about the brother she didn't know existed. She asked me simple things like what his personality is, and what he looks like, and then she asked me about the auction block, and the name of the man who bought him. Fairalisa swiftly set up a meeting with a neighbor down the street who she says sits on Quinten's council and handles all of the crown's outside contractors, like the miners.

"What are you working on?" Pip asks, standing in the parlor doorway.

I don't answer but simply let out a groan. Pip saunters into the room. She leans her hip against the back of the couch and crosses her arms over her chest.

"That fun, huh?" she asks.

"The lady asked me to make these little flower bouquets." I hold up one of my better-looking ones. I scrunch my face, not hiding the fact that I don't get why anyone would spend their time doing this.

"What for?" Pip asks, squinting her eyes.

"They're gifts for each of the wedding guests. It seems pointless to me. We never did anything like this in Bear Gap."

Pip chuckles as she comes to stand next to the table. "Where is the lady at this hour?"

"Tea," I say. "With one of the neighbors."

I keep my eyes focused on the flowers. I try to sound casual, but I'm feeling anything but relaxed. My hands are slightly damp as I wonder about what is being said of Tuor or me.

"The master is away too," Pip says. "And I think Ronda's made a trip to the market."

I grunt in response. Pip throws her hand in front of my work.

"Stop it," I protest.

"I think you need a break."

"I should get these done before the lady returns," I say.

"How about this," Pip says, crossing her arms again. "Come take a break with me, and I'll help you finish these up later."

I look up at Pip under heavy eyelids.

"You look so tightly wound that you might dissolve into a puddle on the floor," Pip says.

"Fine." I let the flower drop from my hands.

Pip stops by the kitchen and picks up a basket covered with a tea towel, telling me I'm not allowed to peek at what's inside. We take the steps to the upstairs hallway. Pip clicks open one of the bedroom doors.

"Have you ever been in here before?" she asks.

I shake my head as we enter a neatly kept bedroom with a blue coverlet on the bed. It's simply decorated, with no personal effects on the dresser and a cold fireplace.

"It's one of the guest bedrooms," Pip says. "It'll actually get used for once when the family starts arriving for the wedding, but I like to come up here and sit on the balcony."

Pip pulls the curtains across the rod and swings open the glass balcony doors. A crisp breeze envelops us. I pull tightly on the white shawl I've begun to wear just about every day.

"Can't beat this view," Pip says, plopping onto one of the white wicker chairs.

Leaning against the wrought-iron railing, I peer across LilyAye. We face out the front of the house. The long driveway empties onto the road. The square of LilyAye buzzes with flamboyantly dressed women and men in their trimmed suits. They look like mere colorful dots from where I'm standing.

The water from the fountain sparkles in the sunlight. Horse-drawn carriages click along the cobblestone road. Past the streets lined with Catahli homes is the front gate of the city. It's gold-flecked designs glimmer like one of Fairalisa's necklaces. Off in the distance stands the dark, imposing Warwick castle.

"Why doesn't anyone use this bedroom?" I ask, dropping into the other chair.

"Street noise makes it hard for Master Anthond to sleep at night," Pip says, pulling back the tea towel. "So he hulled up in one of the bedrooms at the back of the house years ago."

Pip reveals a basket full of lightly browned rolls. The yeasty aroma brings me back to Mirabelle's kitchen.

"These are for the master and the lady's dinner tonight, but I made a few extra," Pip whispers as she hands me one of the soft, warm rolls. "This wedding is a bit draining, isn't it?" She bites into the bread's crusty shell.

"Yeah," I chuckle. "Everything is linens and china and tiny flower bouquets."

"How are you holding up?"

Pip's poignant question takes me off guard. I tear off a chunk of the roll and pop it into my mouth. "I'm fine."

"Come on, Kat. You don't expect me to believe that." She lowers her voice. "It wasn't that long ago that you were poisoned. Before that you were at the auction. There's no way you're *fine*."

I squirm in my seat, suddenly feeling the pressure of Pip's inquiry, and understanding why she brought me out here.

"I'll be okay," I say.

Pip peers over the balcony railing. "You know, I didn't tell you this before, but when Master Anthond first bought me, I tried to run away."

Thin clouds move across the pale sky as an autumn wind blows through my shawl.

"I wasn't shot like you. But I was just a little girl, and the soldiers terrified me. They drug me back to the house and asked if Master Anthond wanted me thrown in the dungeons. Fortunately, he was kind enough to tell them that he'd handle me, but I never forgot that day. Just seeing that Warwick uniform, even today, brings tightness to my chest."

Looking down at my lap, I wonder if Pip could actually understand what I'm going through. I've never really had a friend like her, a woman I could talk to. Mirabelle was always more like a mother to me. She'd scold me if I told her half the things I did. My fingers tremble as I cup the half-eaten roll.

"I'm terrified," I admit in a small voice. I keep my eyes pinned to my lap. "Everything I do scares me."

"That's what they want. That's how they keep us in line. You can't let it get to you."

"It's not just the soldiers. It's everything. It feels like every time I scramble to my feet someone knocks me down."

Pip nods slowly. "This life will do that to you. I had to learn to be content in this place, make friends. I don't like all the rules, but I've learned to live with them."

"How can I carry on when fear grips me at every turn?" I look imploringly at Pip.

"You have to find your strength."

I sigh and lean my head back. I'd be better if Tuor were here. Maybe he's my strength? I tear another piece off the roll and savor its salty bite.

"Friends help too. If you need to talk, I'm here," Pip says with the raise of her eyebrow. She turns her gaze back to the city.

"The bread doesn't hurt either."

Pip guffaws. "You're right."

"Kat!" a voice calls from down below.

I hurry to the railing's edge. Down on the lawn, I find Teddy standing with a rake in his hand. The sun glistens off his deeply tanned skin.

"Kat?"

"What is it?" I ask.

"I've been looking all over for you. There's a man at the delivery door waiting for you."

"Who is it?"

"How should I know?" Teddy shrugs. "He said he has something for the lady of the house."

"Thanks," I call as Teddy walks away.

I give Pip a curious look before shoving the rest of the roll in my mouth and leaving the balcony. Who would be here to see me? Fairalisa didn't mention any delivery, but she's been so crazy with the wedding preparations, I'm sure she just forgot.

I make my way down the steps, into the dimly lit servant's dining room. It's the odd, quiet time of the day after lunch but before the dinner rush. A maid carries down a basin filled with clean dishes. She sets them on the long table and begins folding a pile of freshly laundered napkins. Another young girl sweeps the crumbs from under the table. Besides that, the dining room is empty.

I walk the length of the table to the back door. It's used for deliveries, usually food deliveries, but the servants will use this door for anything that's too unsightly for the upstairs. I turn the knob and pull open the heavy door. A man waits. He's dressed in riding pants and black boots and wears a cloak over his head.

"Are you the lady's maid?" he asks.

"Yes," I say with trepidation. "My name is Kat."

The gentle rustling of leaves fills up the moment of silence while I peer under the cloak to get a look at the man's face.

"Kat, you say?" He steps over the threshold into the shadowy room.

"Yes."

The man slowly lowers his hood. A pair of crystal-blue eyes peers out at me from under a head of black hair.

"Reed," I sigh.

He clears his throat and glances at the two maids. The one girl finishes her sweeping and props her broom up before heading upstairs. I pull Reed into the corner and turn his back to the other girl who absentmindedly folds the napkins.

"You're going by the name Kat? That's smart. I've heard your real name around the city. There are rumors that you left Bear Gap."

"Yeah." I awkwardly push a chunk of my hair behind my ear. "Uh, how have you been?"

"Great. We have him, Camilla," Reed whispers, leaning in close. "Listen, I have to be fast. My uncle isn't traveling; he's attending a wedding. The wedding of your lady." Reed's eyes widen with excitement.

"I know. I found out the other day."

Reed lets out a careful chuckle as he clenches his hand into a fist. "This is perfect. The rumor of his traveling was just a cover. We couldn't have planned this if we tried."

I force a laugh.

"I'm working on a plan to get inside the wedding, but you already have a ticket in. You're the bride's lady's maid so you'll be there to help her dress that day, right?"

"I think so."

"Okay, so we just have to make a plan to get you close to Quinten. Nobody would suspect the lady's maid."

"I can't do it," I blurt.

Reed's eyebrows form into a deep V.

"What do you mean?" he booms.

The maid looks up from her work.

"Those colors won't do," I say, clearing my throat. "The lady demands everything to be in emerald green."

The maid returns to her work, finishing with the last napkin. She then scoops out the clean plates and sets them on the buffet. She takes the basin and returns upstairs.

"Camilla," Reed growls, squeezing tighter on my arm. "You have to do this."

"I won't do it, not now." I back away from Reed.

"What has changed with you?"

I swallow hard, feeling the lump of panic at the back of my throat. "They're going to find out it's me. I'll be arrested and—"

My chance at safety will be gone. That's what I want to say, but I bite my tongue.

"I'll take care of you once I'm Supreme Ruler," Reed says. "It doesn't matter if they know you killed him at that point. The rebels will rise up."

"Tuor is trapped at some mining camp outside the city, and Fairalisa says she can help me get him back. I'm not risking my identity until I know he's safe."

"Once Quinten is dead, we'll go get your brother!"

"No," I say defiantly. "Maybe after the wedding and—"

"This is our only opportunity!" Reed's clenched hand now begins to quiver. "This is what we traveled here for. Please. You have to do this for me." His voice suddenly grows tender.

I give Reed an indignant scowl. His selfishness is so obvious. He's using me to fulfill a personal vendetta against Quinten.

"I care more about Tuor than the rebellion," I say.

Something about actually saying those words out loud settles it in my mind. At the end of the day, I choose Tuor over the rebellion.

"I can't risk my own identity by going out to some mine and negotiating a slave purchase, but in just a few days, Quinten will be present at this wedding and that will be our chance. Have sense!" Reed grabs my wrist and shakes me. My shackles make a clanging noise.

"Stop it," I groan as I try to loosen Reed's grip from my wrist.

"Please!" he begs, his eyes wild.

I press my lips firmly together and snap free of Reed's grasp.

"Leave," I demand.

Reed bares his teeth at me. He throws the hood back over his head and slams the door on his way out. I stand in the servant's dining room, shivering. *What have I done?* Have I turned my back on the rebellion, just like Lawrence wanted?

A sick feeling fills my stomach as I stare at the door Reed just walked through. I hold the ticket to murder Quinten Warwick, and I'm choosing not to use it. I've been waiting for this opportunity for so long. I draw in a shaky breath and smooth my silken dress before turning to face the dining room. Tuor is more important, I tell myself.

Trixie takes the last few steps into the dining room, carrying a neatly folded stack of tablecloths. She hums lightly, somehow walking with a spring in her step despite the shackles.

"Hey, Kat," Trixie says as she places the linens on the table. "You okay?"

"Yeah." I shake my head to pull myself out of my thoughts.

"Who was at the door?"

"Salesman. Turns out everyone in this city has heard about the wedding and is trying to make a ring off it."

"Hmmm." Trixie purses her lips and scrunches her face in confusion. "That's awfully bold, just showing up at the delivery door."

I casually skirt around Trixie and head for the steps. "I know. They're so pushy. I have to get upstairs. I'll see you later at dinner," I call as I hustle up the steps.

I pause in the hallway to catch my breath. What if Fairalisa can't get Tuor, or worse, her inquiry shines too bright a light on our identity? I might have thrown away my chance with the LilyAye rebels on account of what Fairalisa can do for me. I suddenly feel like vomiting.

CHAPTER TWENTY-FIVE

THE *CREAKING* OF the front door echoes through the hallway. *Fairalisa's home.* She enters the front hall, removing a velvet hat. Her hair is blown back from the windy day.

"My lady." I rush to help her remove her cloak. "How was your tea?"

Fairalisa's cheeks are flushed pink, and she wears her signature mischievous smile. "I have found your brother!" She grabs my hands. Her face beams.

My breath catches in my throat. "You have?" The words are barely a whisper. "Where?"

"Turns out this man, Gregor Creighton, owns mining pits all over Elmyra." Fairalisa flails her hands excitedly as she steps further into the front hall. "Finding out who Mr. Creighton's identity was easy enough, but finding out where he'd taken your brother was another thing altogether. Unsurprisingly, these miners do not keep good records."

"So how did you find him?"

"Well, turns out we don't need those hapless records. Sir Benson told me that even though Gregor owns lots of mines, only one of those mines is yielding wagons full of iron ore right now." Fairalisa stands proudly, a finger raised in the air as she speaks. "He said that Gregor moved all of his workforce to this one mine, so chances are good we'll find your brother there." Fairalisa lifts her chin, and a satisfied look spreads across her face.

"Do you know where this mine is?" I ask.

"An hour's carriage ride outside the city."

"Fairalisa, I . . ." I search for words. "Thank you."

"It was nothing," Fairalisa waves a hand at me. She takes a poised seat on the couch. "It was quite fun plying our neighbor with samples of the wedding cake to get him to divulge the information about Mr. Creighton." Fairalisa giggles, straightening her back. "We'll leave first thing tomorrow morning to get your brother."

"Tomorrow?" My heart surges. "I'll be ready," I tell Fairalisa.

***

Sleep eludes me. Far too excited to see Tuor, I toss and turn and stare out at the sparkling city. I'll have Tuor here with me *tomorrow*. It's as if there's no life after tomorrow. I have no plans beyond getting my brother out of that mining pit.

I wake before sunrise, dress in a hurry, and fetch Fairalisa's breakfast. I even steal a spoonful of Fairalisa's beloved black tea to make a cup for myself. I'll need the strength.

In the kitchen, Trixie tells me that the annoying salesman is back at the delivery door, asking for me again. I can't deal with Reed right now. I have to get

Tuor. That's all that matters. After telling Trixie to send him away, I help Fairalisa dress, and we prepare to leave.

"Will you tell my father I'll be back for dinner this evening?" Fairalisa asks Ronda as she slips on a pair of leather gloves in the front hall.

"My lady, may I ask where you'll be *all* day? I'm sure your father would want to know your whereabouts."

"Kat and I are off to the market for a few last-minute wedding items," Fairalisa says, swiftly walking to the front door. "And then I'll be paying my aunt a visit. You know, the one who lives outside the city."

Ronda opens the door for us. "Surely one of the maids can go to the market on your behalf."

"No, no," Fairalisa waves her off. "I'm looking for something quite particular."

Fairalisa strides through the door before Ronda has a chance to question her again. I follow, the morning air cold and damp.

"I've asked Hobbes to fetch the plain carriage," Fairalisa whispers to me as we walk. "I don't want anyone recognizing our family seal."

A crooked smile plays at my lips. I'm stunned, but also pleased by Fairalisa's deceptive thinking. She's serious about this ruse. Hobbes is waiting for us at the carriage. We slip inside, and he clicks the carriage door closed behind us. Fairalisa brushes her hair back over her shoulder as Hobbes climbs into the driver's seat and kicks off the horse.

"Hobbes is the only one in the house who knows what we're up to," Fairalisa says.

"How exactly are we going to get my brother?" I ask as we roll down the driveway.

Fairalisa gives me a wry smile. "Our wits, of course. We are two intelligent, beautiful women. I think we'll be able to charm our way through."

Our charm?

How in all of Elmyra is our charm going to get my brother back? I feel my heart sink at the thought of using our charm to retrieve Tuor. Hobbes takes a right turn onto the road in front of the house. We clip-clop down the cobblestone.

"It won't hurt that I have a bag of rings to convince him," Fairalisa says, holding up a velvet drawstring bag.

Without thinking, I snatch the bag from Fairalisa. Pulling open the string, I stare at a pile of smooth Catahli rings.

"How did you get this?" I ask in awe.

Fairalisa shrugs. "Daddy gave it to me for the wedding. I have plenty more."

I'm at a loss for words. Fairalisa is willing to spend her wedding money to save my brother? I've only known her for a few weeks. A pang of guilt hits me as I remember it wasn't so long ago that I tried to escape to get away from this girl.

Hobbes snaps the reins, urging the horse forward, down the stretch of road leading to the city gate. The gleaming gold panels that flank the thick wooden gate reflect the low-hanging sun. We reach the checkpoint. The armor-clad Warwick soldier approaches our carriage. He taps on the window and then opens the door.

"Good morning," Fairalisa greets him.

"Whose house are you from?" the soldier asks.

"Master Pennington," Fairalisa says without hesitation. She smiles sweetly at the man. I keep my head pointed at my hands in my lap.

"Where are you off to today?" the soldier asks.

"Visiting my aunt."

The soldier quickly searches the carriage, looking under the benches and asking Hobbes to jump down while he checks behind the driver's seat. He then waves us forward. It takes four men to pull the city gate open. A low rumble emanates from its hinges as we ride through.

The LilyAye Road doesn't stop at LilyAye. It continues north into a territory I know little of and have definitely never been to. We ride through a smattering of small villages and towns until we veer off onto a bumpy dirt road. Fairalisa grabs my hand and squeezes it, excitement glowing on her face. The carriage dips and barrels over rocks. After far too long on that road, we finally turn off onto a dirt trail that leads through a wooded area.

"We're approaching, my lady," Hobbes calls from his driver's seat.

"How do I look?" Fairalisa asks turning to me.

"Good," I say, not sure how else to respond.

"This is important. For this to work, I need to look my best."

"You look beautiful," I say finally.

"Thanks!" The word bubbles from Fairalisa's lips.

I peer out the window as our carriage pulls up on a vast landscape. The trees have all been felled, and before us is a massive pit. The pit slopes down, level by level, as if into the depths of hell. As we draw closer, my eyes widen at the sight of hundreds of men moving across the layers like ants.

They chip away at the iron with chisels, hammers, and pitchforks. A steady drumming emanates from the pit. Other workers fill baskets or wheelbarrows with the iron and push or carry them up the hill, out of the pit. All the workers wear shackles similar to mine. They're half-naked and covered in whipping stripes.

Our carriage comes to a stop in the shadow of a tall wooden platform. Atop the platform is a man in a canvas jacket, the sleeves rolled up to his elbows. His long, greasy hair lies over his collar. He angrily paces back and forth across the wooden planks, a riding crop gripped in his hand and a length of coiled-up rope hanging from his belt.

"I think we're here," I mumble. My heartbeat pounds in my ears. I ball my hand into a fist and remember Pip's words.

Find your strength.

Worry flickers on Fairalisa's face as she scans the mining pit. The man spots our carriage. He squints at us before barreling down the crudely built steps.

"Come, Kat," Fairalisa says, squeezing my hand. "Now is the time."

Hobbes jumps down and opens the carriage door for Fairalisa and me. She lifts her chin and steps out of the carriage as if she were a princess. When my feet hit the rocky earth, my shackles jingle. The man, balding in the front, grasps the hilt of his sword as he approaches. His face is a snarl. Fairalisa folds her hands in front of her demurely.

"I think you're lost," the man barks.

"I don't believe I am," Fairalisa says.

The man leers at Fairalisa. His sunbaked, leathery skin is plagued with jagged wrinkles. Hobbes sidles up behind Fairalisa.

"What do you want?" the man snaps.

One of the workers in the pit screams. It draws the attention of everyone except for the man standing before us. I peer past the legs of the platform and spot a whip flying through the air and striking a bare back. I feel like I've returned to Slaver's Row. My fist tightens. I shift around Fairalisa and search the pit for Tuor. Fairalisa lets out a light laugh and bats her eyelashes at the gray-haired man in front of us.

"Well, my name is Fairalisa," she says sweetly, drawing out the *ee* sound. "And I just think you have a marvelous operation here. I find mining so interesting, and—"

"You better tell me quick what you've come here for."

"Right," Fairalisa says, clearing her throat. "I seek a one Gregor Creighton."

"What for?"

Fairalisa holds the bag of rings behind her folded hands. It's not completely hidden. The bottom sticks out as she casually shakes the rings. The man scrunches his face. Finally, he spots what she's holding.

"I may have a business proposition for him," Fairalisa adds. "Perhaps you could take me to Mr. Creighton?"

The man sucks on his teeth and digs out a stray piece of food with his fingernail.

"I'm Gregor." He rests his hand on his sword. "And if you want to buy one of my men, you can just move along. They ain't for sale."

Gregor shifts toward the platform. I shoot Fairalisa a worried a look.

"Uh, please, sir!" Fairalisa calls. She scurries up to him and places a hand on Gregor's hairy forearm.

He looks at her hand as if he's about to chop it off with a machete.

"I would be so pleased if you'd help me," Fairalisa says in a sickly sweet tone. "You should know, I have quite a lot of rings to negotiate with."

Undeterred by Fairalisa's feminine manner, Gregor shakes off her hand and says, "Unless you're the Supreme Ruler himself, you don't got enough rings for me to blink at. Do you think you're the first rich folk that's come looking to buy one of my men? The slavers can't catch enough of them for me. The men in that pit down there make me more rings every hour than what you got in that bag."

Fairalisa's confidence wavers. She purses her lips as if searching for the next piece she can play in this negotiation, but she falls silent.

"Now, get off my property before I sic the dogs on you and your pathetic escorts," Gregor barks. "I have work to do." He moves toward the platform steps.

"I beg of you," Fairalisa cries, her voice dropping. "The truth is, the brother of my lady's maid is one of your workers, and she's despondent without him. She's terribly worried and just wishes to be reunited."

Gregor turns his head to the sky as he lets out a cackle. "Everyone in that pit is someone's brother or father! If I bent every time I heard that, I wouldn't have any workers left."

"Have you no heart?" Fairalisa asks. Her true innocence shines as she looks up at Gregor with glassy eyes.

"Ha! I lost that a long time ago." Gregor chuckles to himself as he starts to climb the stairs to the platform, his back bent like an old man. He presses the tip of the riding crop onto the steps and uses it like a cane.

"I'm so sorry, Kat," Fairalisa says with sympathetic eyes.

Her words wash over me.

"My lady, I fear for our safety," Hobbes says urgently.

Blood rushes through my body like a galloping horse. My temples pound. Tuor is close, somewhere just beyond, in this wretched pit. I march toward the platform, my shackles pulling with every step. I take the stairs. Gregor pauses when he hears me.

I swipe his riding crop out from under him. He wobbles. I grab the end of the crop and slam the bar into the back of Gregor's knees. He cries out as he tumbles backward down the steps. I crouch, narrowly dodging his flailing body.

Fairalisa screams. "Kat!"

Gregor groans, his face smashed into the ground. I run to him, planting my foot on his back and snatching his sword from behind. Breathing heavily, I toss the riding crop behind me and hold the tip of the sword at Gregor's face. He rolls onto his back, dirt pressed into his face.

"What have you done?" Fairalisa shrieks.

I bark a command at Hobbes. "Grab the rope from his belt."

"What? No!" Hobbes shudders.

"Do it now," I growl.

"What do you think you're going to do, you skinny mite?" Gregor moans. "My men are all over!" he laughs.

I furtively scan the edge of the pit. A few guards pace, whips in hand, along the other side of the pit, but for now, we're shielded by the platform.

"Hobbes!" I yell. He nervously approaches Gregor, reaching out for the rope as if it were a snake. "Fairalisa, give me that bag."

"What for?" she asks with a shaky voice.

Gregor yelps. "They'll come looking for me!"

"Just give me the bag!" I say.

Fairalisa hands me the velvet bag filled with Catahli rings. Still holding the sword to Gregor's neck, I turn the bag over, dumping all the rings onto the dusty ground. Gregor bares his teeth. He lurches forward and grabs at my hand. I swipe smoothly, cutting a gash in his forearm. He grunts as bright red blood drips onto the brown earth. The sword skills I learned from Johnny return without a pause.

Taking the empty bag, I shove it into Gregor's mouth and demand he roll over onto his stomach. I hold my ground while instructing Hobbes to remove Gregor's jacket and to hog-tie his wrists and ankles together. I then take off my white shawl and wrap it around Gregor's mouth so he can't spit out the bag.

"What do we do now?" Fairalisa asks, terrified.

"Now, I go get my brother," I say, donning Gregor's jacket.

He screams from behind his gag, but it's muffled. I drag Gregor's body underneath the steps, then take his long sword and awkwardly chop at my shackles. I can't rescue Tuor with these on.

"No! You can't do that," Fairalisa says.

With every *clang* of the sword against my chains, Fairalisa gasps. Taking a deep breath, I whack at my restraints, feeling a tug on my ankles as the sword collides. One of the links breaks. I pull my legs apart. I'm free. I hack off the loose chains so that all that remains are the cuffs around my ankles.

"Oh dear," Fairalisa moans, burying her face in her hands.

I notice that Gregor has grown quiet. When I check on him, he's reaching for something on his thigh. Wrapped around his leg is an inconspicuous strap with a sheathed knife attached to it. I grab it before Gregor has a chance to make his escape. I go to attach the knife to my belt, then remember I'm wearing a stupid dress.

"Here, you take this," I say, holding the handle of the sword up for Fairalisa.

"I'm not touching that!" she says.

"Then you take it, Hobbes. I can't carry it into the pit. It's too obvious, and you need a way to protect yourselves."

"You're going down *there*?" Fairalisa asks. She holds a delicate hand to her forehead.

"Yes," I say.

Hobbes hesitantly takes the heavy sword from me.

"Wait for me here," I say. "Turn the carriage around so you're ready to go. I'm going in to get Tuor."

"This isn't right!" Fairalisa begs. "We can't go about it like this!"

"The only way I'm getting my brother out of here is by fighting for him. Keep a watch on Gregor. I'll be back," I say, slipping Gregor's knife into his jacket, which hangs baggy off my body. I grab the riding crop and grip it tightly in my hand.

"Kat, no! You'll be killed," Fairalisa cries.

I ignore her, sneaking past the platform and creeping to the edge of the pit. Past the wide opening, barren hills roll for miles. A cluster of straw huts sits on the northern side of the mining site. A wooden tripod structure hoists baskets of iron from down below. Each layer of the pit is crawling with emaciated slaves. My eyes dart from man to man, inspecting them for Tuor's lanky frame and messy black hair, but I can't find him. There are just too many people.

A massive rock pile sits above a ramp leading out of the pit. Workers emerge, dump the iron rock, and head back down into the pit to gather more. A thick-muscled guard on the other side of the rock pile supervises the men as they come and go. A whip is poised between his sausage sized fingers.

Hacking and coughing mixes with the tinny sound of metal on metal. A thin dust cloud rises from the bottom of the pit. I try to stay unassuming. I search for Tuor, but the pit seems to go on for eternity. I wait until the ramp is clear of workers and furtively run and duck behind the pile of rocks, just out of view of the guard.

His back is to me. Profanity spits from his mouth. The guard is a behemoth of a man, with a thick neck and broad shoulders. A worker comes up the ramp and dumps a wheelbarrow of stones onto the pile. The guard watches, shaking his whip as if it were a reminder. Taking the riding crop, I hold it firmly in both hands at each end. I wait for the worker to leave.

As soon as there's an opening, I creep up behind the guard. I lurch forward, throwing the riding crop over his head and pressing the bar into his throat. He drops the whip and grapples for my hands. I hang on the ends of the crop and squeeze with all the strength I have. A grunt escapes my lips as I hold on tight.

The guard collapses to his knees, pulling me forward onto his back. I flail as he tries to shake me off. Jamming my knee into his back, I create leverage and hold the crop even tighter against his neck. The guard gurgles and chokes. He drops his hands and falls face down on the dusty earth, finally losing consciousness.

I remove the crop and let his body crumple. My arms are weak and rubbery. I nudge him with my foot. He doesn't move, but his chest still rises and falls with breath. My heart pounds against my ribs. Lightning courses through my body and into the tips of my fingers.

I feel alive.
I feel in control.
I feel like myself again.

Glancing left and right, I toss the riding crop and squeeze my fist around the handle of Gregor's dagger before diving into the pit.

CHAPTER TWENTY-SIX

THE TEMPERARURE DROPS as I run down the ramp, into the pit. Despite the swirling dust cloud, I stick out among the hordes of men. I pull Gregor's jacket tighter over my white dress. Giant earthen steps lead to the bottom of the pit. Workers move up and down the levels like a colony of ants. Shouts echo through the pit. Guards bark at the men to work faster.

I scramble off the ramp and wait, praying that none of the guards saw me. A man hobbles toward me. He's so weary that he doesn't even notice me at first.

I grab his arm, jolting him out of his thoughts. "Tuor Crim. Do you know where Tuor Crim is?"

"Who?" The man's face contorts in confusion.

"Tuor Crim," my voice rises.

He shakes his head slowly. I let out a frustrated groan, then jump down the giant step onto the next level.

"Tuor Crim," I say to the next man I find. "Do you know anyone named Tuor Crim?"

He ignores me, continuing toward the ramp. I scurry away, walking the length of the step. I glance toward the top of the pit and scan for guards. I grab another man. His body shakes as I touch his bony arm.

"Please," I say. "Do you know anyone here called Tuor Crim?" To my surprise, the man gives me a half smile. "He's my brother," I add, hoping this will help.

"No one down here has names," he says, turning and walking away. "Some days I forget my own name . . ."

How am I going to find him?

I twist, searching the endless layers of this dismal hole. Yelling draws my attention to the end of the row. A guard berates one of the men.

"Drop that off at the top, and get yourself back down here, and do it before the sun sets!"

I shrink behind one of the steps to hide myself and contemplate how impossible this is. Tuor could be anywhere. The squeaky moan of a wheelbarrow approaches. I turn around as a worker pushes a wheelbarrow full of iron toward the ramp. He stops when he sees me. I grip the knife but hesitate to pull it out. The man, thin with a scraggly gray beard, bends toward me.

"You're looking for your brother?" he asks.

I nod.

"Don't know who he is, but they make the young boys work down below."

I give him a quizzical look.

"Deeper in the pit." The old man points to the bottom of the pit. It's so far down that it's just a blurry haze.

"Thank you," I whisper

I search my surroundings before scooting onto the next step and shuffling down the ramp. A guard stands to my left with his back to me, a coiled-up whip in his hand. I retreat to the right. When he's not looking, I break off the ramp and run in the other direction, down the step. I find a ladder and descend to the next level.

Scanning for Tuor, I study each sallow, dirty face, but none of them are my brother. I keep moving, scurrying away every time I see a guard. The pit grows dark and cold. Flaming braziers dot the lower levels, but it's still easy to hide in the shadows. I pray that Fairalisa and Hobbes haven't left, or worse, untied Gregor in a moment of weakness.

My descent continues. I'm nearly at the bottom. I stop at the edge of one of the big steps and catch my breath. I shift away from the firelight. From the shadows, I watch the men work. The dull *clang* of pickaxes hitting iron thuds in my head. Voices echo and reverberate off the walls. A thick cloud of dust slowly rises.

A man on the step below me coughs. It sounds familiar. I peer down onto the top of his head. Dark curly hair grows like a mop. He wields a pickaxe, driving it over and over again into the hard rock.

"Tuor?" I whisper cautiously. He pauses but then returns to his work. "Tuor!" Desperate for him to hear me, I come to my knees so I'm closer to his head. "Tuor!"

He stops swinging his axe but continues to stare at the rock wall in front of him. He then lifts his head and slowly meets my eyes. His face is black with soot. The bones of his cheeks protrude.

"It's me," I say, tears welling in my eyes at the sight of him.

"Camilla?" he says in a quiet voice. He walks over to the edge of the step where I'm kneeling.

"Stay there," I say. "I'm coming down."

A guard stands near the ramp, just a few yards away from where Tuor is working. I wait for him to look away, then scoot to the edge of the step and leap down. My feet hit the hard ground. I grab Tuor and pull him into a hug. He drops his pickaxe onto the ground. His body is scrawny. There's nothing to him.

"I'm getting you out of here," I say with a smile.

Tuor doesn't smile back. He shakes his head. "You can't."

"Yes, come on. I have someone who can drive you away. We just have to get out of this pit and go," I whisper.

Tuor looks left and right in a flurry. Terror fills his face. He pushes me up against the wall so I'm out of the guard's sight line.

"Get down," he insists. "You don't understand, if they catch us trying to escape, they will kill us both."

"If you stay here, you'll die!"

"I can't, Camilla. Just go." Tuor's voice is low but urgent. "I don't know how you got down here, but you need to go."

"I'm not leaving you," I say in a shaky voice.

Tuor takes my arms in his hands. "I love you, and that's why I can't risk knowing you died for me. You need to go. Save yourself."

My eyes grow wide and wild. "You're leaving with me! I didn't come all the way here, track you down, risk everything to—"

"Camilla." Tuor squeezes my arm. His jaw clenches.

A commotion erupts from behind Tuor. I look past his shoulders. The other workers are ducking out of the way as a guard looks in our direction. He squints through the darkness and the dust. Tuor twists me around so that his body is shielding me from the guard's line of sight. My heartbeat picks up its pace.

"We have to go now!" I say, tugging on Tuor's arms.

Tuor shakes his head furiously. "We won't make it."

I bounce on my feet, peering over Tuor's shoulder to the guard. He marches toward us.

"Hey," I say, grabbing Tuor's shoulders. "Remember when I came and found you in the dungeons underneath the Justice House?"

Tuor nods.

"You thought it was impossible for me to get out of there, but I did it, right?"

I shake Tuor. He nods again.

"I'm going to get us both out of here, but we have to go *now*."

I stare at Tuor, waiting for him to wake up and care again. The spark in his eyes returns. He's coming back to me. He glances up at the pit opening.

"Let's go," he breathes.

"This way." I grab Tuor's hand. The guard sees me now and shouts. We jog the length of the step but Tuor is encumbered by shackles. We come to a ladder.

"Stop!" the guard shouts.

"Go! Go!" I say, pushing Tuor up the ladder. I follow. Tuor reaches the top. He extends a hand to help me crest the next level. The guard runs up the

283

ramp, keeping pace with us. We'll never get out of here this way.

"Is there another ramp like that one?" I ask quickly.

"On the other side of the pit," Tuor breathes. "This way."

He takes my hand, and we hobble along the step, dodging workers as we go. The guard abandons the ramp and runs along the step. Behind us, he trips over a wheelbarrow. We curve around the giant circular pit. The shadows shift, allowing the sun to light our way. Another guard spots us.

"Halt!" he bellows as he pulls a whip from his belt.

I see the other ramp up ahead. I burst into a sprint. Tuor stumbles over his chains and falls. He pulls me down with him. We skid onto the dusty earth. I cough as I suck dirt into my throat. Pulling myself up onto my knees, I grope for Tuor.

"Camilla?" he croaks.

A hand wraps around my upper arm. I shout, my throat dry with dust. I claw at my captor. My eyes blink open. A guard pulls me up. Another guard has Tuor pinned to the ground with his foot on Tuor's neck. All the air escapes my lungs.

"Where did you come from?" one of the guards asks me as he notices the white dress under Gregor's jacket.

"We'll take 'em both to the top and show 'em to the boss," the other guard says.

Tuor and I are hauled up the big ramp, out of the pit. The workers stare solemnly as we're marched past them. My hatred for the shackles grows to an explosive point. We could have gotten away if it weren't for them. I struggle against the guard's grip and try to throw a punch, but he pushes me up the ramp by my neck.

The crest of the pit comes into view. I squint at the bright sun. I feign a stumble and fall to my knees. Slipping my hand into Gregor's jacket, I wrap my fingers around the handle of his dagger. The guard bends to pick me up. I twist and drive the knife into the guard's stomach.

"You—what?" he mumbles.

Blood drips onto my jacket. I pull out the knife and stab him again quickly. He grabs my shoulders. I shove the knife again into his side. He falls back onto his heels, holding a hand to his wounds. I kick the guard's face so he tumbles backward down the ramp. The other guard's expression contorts into confusion. He holds Tuor by his wrists. I run at him.

He releases Tuor and reaches for his own weapon. He pulls a machete from his belt and swings high. I narrowly block his blow with the short blade of Gregor's knife. The workers shout and cheer around us. Tuor grabs the whip from the guard's belt and wraps it around his neck. The guard swings his machete wildly. I duck and bend to miss his blows.

Swinging my leg, I knock the machete from his hand. It lands with a thud onto the ramp. A whoop of excitement bursts from the hapless slaves. The guard grapples at the whip around his neck. His massive biceps manage to tear the vise away and knock Tuor's skinny body to the ground.

The guard pounces on me. I fall backward onto the ramp. He squeezes my wrist and wrangles the knife from my hand.

"Tuor!" I scream, squealing underneath the guard. I scratch at his tough skin. I try to jerk my knee at his groin, but his heavy body pins me to the ramp.

He raises his arm, dagger in hand. The guard's teeth seethe with spittle. A gray-haired slave comes up behind him and grabs his arm. The guard swipes for my face. I flinch. I roll and barely miss the blade. The slave wrestles with the guard's bulging arm. Another mine worker rushes to my aid carrying the dropped machete. He swings the wide blade, chopping the guard's knife wielding arm so that a wide gash opens and gushes blood.

The guard's body convulses on top of me. He screams hysterically. The arm barely hangs on. Blood spurts onto Gregor's jacket. My face twists at the sight. The two slaves tug on the guard's body as I push from underneath. Together, we roll his colossal frame off me.

Jubilant cheers echo through the pit. The workers clap and yell as I stand. The bloody machete lies at the feet of my two rescuers.

"Thank you," I breathe. My chests heaves for air.

"You best run," one of the slaves tells me. "They're coming."

Above the pit, by the straw huts, a group of guards barrel toward the commotion.

"Tuor!" I shout.

Still lying on the ground, Tuor rubs at the back of his head, dazed. I grab his hand and pull him to standing. We run the rest of the way up the ramp. The warmer air blows past my cheeks as we sprint around the edge of the pit. My thighs burn, feeling the hard earth with every step.

"Get them!" a guard from behind us shouts.

I spot the wooden platform. It's empty except for Gregor who's still tied up underneath. I pump my legs, glancing behind me to make sure Tuor is keeping pace. The black carriage comes into view. Fairalisa and Hobbes stand frozen, huddled together.

"Fairalisa!" I scream. "Get inside!"

She looks up, then glances behind me at our pursuers.

"Get in the carriage!" I yell.

Fairalisa jolts. Hobbes nervously drops the sword onto the ground and hustles Fairalisa to the door of the carriage. I focus on them as I run. My lungs burn. Fairalisa's head pops out. She waves at me to hurry, holding the door open. Hobbes climbs into the driver's seat. Dust kicks up at my feet. Tuor's chains jangle behind me. I fly through the door of the carriage and slide onto the seat. Tuor tears in after me. Three guards barrel toward us. Tuor pulls the door closed with a click.

"Drive!" Fairalisa shouts as she bangs on the window that separates us from the driver. Hobbes cracks the whip on the back of the horse. The carriage lurches forward with a jerk. The wheels screech down the dusty road, pulling us away from the dreadful pit.

CHAPTER TWENTY-SEVEN

THE GUARDS STAGGER to a stop and stand helplessly on the road as we drive away. Hobbes pushes the horse into a full-speed gallop down the dirt trail. We turn off Gregor's property, onto a road lined on both sides with trees. I look behind the carriage, waiting for Gregor's men to catch up to us on horseback, but we're alone.

I exhale, easing into the velvet-lined seat. Tuor sits across from me. His sallow, dirty face stares back at me in a look of utter astonishment. I lean over and touch his hand. Tears threaten at the corners of my eyes.

He's here.

I squeeze his hand. In a daze, Tuor looks to my touch as if he's not sure what he's seeing is real. He then slips his hand from mine and bends forward to wrap his arms around me in a tight hug.

"Camilla," Tuor mumbles into my shoulder.

A sob escapes my lips. I close my eyes tightly as hot tears pour down my cheeks. The carriage rumbles over the bumpy road as Hobbes keeps up the speedy pace.

Fairalisa places a quavering hand on my back. I peel myself away from Tuor and wipe wet drops from my face.

Fairalisa scans my blood-splotched clothing, a look of horror on her face. "So this is your brother?" she asks, her brow crinkled in pity.

"This is Tuor," I say.

"My name is Fairalisa." She says it slowly as if Tuor were a child. Her hands squirm in her lap.

"I'm Fairalisa's lady maid," I tell Tuor with an awkward smile. He nods in understanding.

Fairalisa clears her throat and asks Tuor, "Are—are you hurt?"

Besides Tuor's overall gaunt appearance, he's filthy. He also has a swelling eye, and his hands and arms are covered in cuts, some scabbed over, some pink and puckered, and others completely raw and bloody. His bare chest shows the defined ridges of his ribs, and thin wounds run down his back from the whip.

"I'll be okay," he says in a quiet voice.

"We're taking you home," I say.

"I can't take you back there looking like that," Fairalisa says, horror painted on her face.

I look down at myself, still wearing Gregor's jacket. Hobbes slows the carriage into a small village. We pass a blacksmith's shop and a bakery before Fairalisa instructs him to pull over. Hobbes stops the carriage next to a stone building with a watermill sitting overtop a narrow creek. We tuck ourselves out of the way from the main road.

The creek babbles over the smooth river rocks as the wheel of the watermill groans with each revolution. A bucket-sized amount of water dumps into the creek with every turn. I toss off Gregor's jacket, burying it under a nearby haystack. I brush the red dirt from my dress as best I can and wash my hands and feet.

There's not much to be done with Tuor. Fairalisa and I wash off some of the dirt, but eventually we agree that perhaps the worse he looks, the more sympathy we'll garner from Anthond. Tuor takes his weak and tired body back into the carriage while I finish up.

"Here, let me help you," Fairalisa says. She dabs the sleeve of her dress in the water and wipes droplets of blood from my face. I notice her anxious expression.

"I'm sorry if I scared you back there," I say, shaking my head.

"What happened in the pit?" Fairalisa asks nervously.

"I did what I had to do to get Tuor. All I was thinking about was my brother."

Fairalisa nods. "Here. Wear this," she says, removing her long cloak. "It'll cover up the blood."

I button the cloak at my neck and pull the flaps over so that my body is almost completely covered. Fairalisa steps back to take a look at me and nods in approval.

"Hey," I say, interrupting what looks like a torrent of worrisome thoughts. "Thank you for bringing us back together. I wouldn't have my brother if it weren't for you."

"It is quite amazing seeing you two together," she says, her eyes turning glassy with tears. Fairalisa draws a shuddering breath. "But I'm afraid they'll come for us. Those men, they were so horrible. I just—what if they track us down? And my father . . ."

"It'll be okay," I say, grabbing Fairalisa's shoulders. I force her to look at me. The gentle splashing of water from the mill seems to calm her. "They have no idea who we are. All they know is your first name. Right?"

"Yes." Her voice is quiet.

"Hundreds of wealthy families live in LilyAye and I'd bet there are many women that go by the name Fairalisa."

"What if they find out it was *me*?" Fairalisa asks. "My father sits on the Supreme Ruler's council. Do you understand how this could ruin our family?"

"Of course," I say, feeling a twinge of guilt. "But they won't find out who you are, and if by some miracle they do, you'll deny it. Deny it to your grave. They have no way of proving it. Gregor won't remember Tuor's name or what he looked like. It's your word against that... that disgusting man's."

Fairalisa bites her lip and nods in agreement.

"I'm forever indebted to you, Fairalisa."

She clears her throat and steadies her composure before we crawl back into the carriage. The three of us sit in silence for the remainder of the ride. Fairalisa rests her head on my shoulder and periodically looks out the window to see if we're being followed. It's not until we pull onto the quiet street of Fairalisa's house that she finally sits up and smoothes her dress.

"What are we going to tell your father?" I ask.

"We'll tell him the truth," Fairalisa says confidently. "I have no good reason for purchasing another servant. My father would never believe that I'd go to the auction. I hate it there. We'll tell him the truth, that Tuor is your brother and that you were distraught without him here."

Hobbes turns the carriage onto the driveway. Tuor gazes in awe at the house as we approach.

Fairalisa continues. "And we'll tell him that we purchased him from another master. We just won't tell him that it was Gregor Creighton." Fairalisa shivers at the mention of his name. "And we definitely won't tell my father that we left the city to get Tuor, or that we all nearly died . . ."

"So who did we buy him from then?" I ask.

"I don't know. I-I'll think of someone . . ." Fairalisa rubs at her forehead.

Hobbes pulls the carriage around the half-circle driveway to the front of the house. Two gardeners trim the bright green bushes flanking the front door.

"Best we get this over with quickly," Fairalisa says as Hobbes helps her from the carriage.

She nervously waits for Tuor and me to emerge. "You'll never speak of what happened today," Fairalisa tells Hobbes. "Do you understand?"

"Yes, my lady."

"Now get this carriage back to the stables and scrub it of any evidence that it was ever at that mining site," Fairalisa commands. "I don't want to see a speck of dirt on it."

"Yes, my lady." Hobbes bows.

Fairalisa stands tall as we enter the home of Anthond Balley. Unsurprisingly, Ronda is close on our trail. She enters the front hall nearly the moment the door clicks closed.

"Stay behind me, Kat," Fairalisa tells me.

I cinch my feet together to hide the missing chain from my shackles, but Fairalisa's cloak does a good job of covering my ankles.

"Who is this?" Ronda asks, furrowing her brows at Tuor's visage. He gawks at the house's interior.

Ronda's face contorts in shock. "And why is your lady's maid wearing your clothing?"

"I needn't tell you that," Fairalisa says. "Where is my father?"

Ronda purses her lips. "The parlor."

Fairalisa strides past Ronda and brings Tuor and me to the parlor, where her father is sipping a cup of tea and poring over a stack of documents that bear the Warwick crest. The fire warms the room.

"Father? May we speak?" Fairalisa asks.

Tuor and I keep our distance as Fairalisa bends to kiss her father on the cheek.

"Yes, dear," Anthond says, lowering the parchment. His eyes fall on me and then Tuor. "Oh, I'm sorry." Anthond straightens his back. "I didn't realize we had a guest."

Anthond eyes his daughter curiously.

"This is what I came to talk to you about, Daddy. I'd like to introduce you to Tuor."

"It's a pleasure," Anthond says slowly. His politeness comforts me, but it's obviously forced. "This boy doesn't look to be in a healthy state."

"No, he's not," Fairalisa says.

She takes a seat next to her father, on the soft, plush couch, and links her arm through his.

"What's going on, dear?" Anthond asks. "You have the same look in your eye that you had when we found that kitten in the alley."

"I'm glad you brought that up," Fairalisa says, sitting up straight and plastering a perky smile on her face. "Remember when we found Pearly and you didn't want to keep her?"

"Yes," Anthond says in a low voice.

"And now she's a very adored cat in this house. I've even seen you pet her from time to time."

Anthond lets out an exasperated sigh. "Okay, enough of this." He coughs harshly into his handkerchief. "Tell me why there is someone else's servant standing in my parlor."

Fairalisa's face grows serious. Her lips fall into a hard line. "Tuor is Kat's brother."

"And what is he doing here, might I ask?"

"Tuor and Kat are very close, Father. It's how I imagined I would be if I had a sibling."

Anthond lets out a hearty chuckle. "You were enough for your mother and me to handle."

"Master Anthond," I say. Fairalisa looks at me with wide eyes. "I came to your daughter and told her how miserable I was without my brother. I knew he was in a very bad place, not being treated well, and as much as I wanted to serve your daughter well, I couldn't focus on anything, knowing that my brother might be in danger." I take a step closer to Anthond and Fairalisa. "Your sweet, sweet daughter did something amazing for me. You should be proud of her."

Fairalisa's lips spread into a pleasant smile.

"And what is this *amazing* thing that my daughter did?" Anthond asks.

"She went and got my brother for me so we could be together." I shake my head, still in awe over the kindness. "And I'll be forever grateful for what she did."

Anthond leans away from his daughter. "You purchased this servant from another house?"

"Yes, Daddy," Fairalisa says. She puffs her chest in pride.

"Fairalisa Balley," Anthond scolds. "You should have spoken to me about this before you went out and did this behind my back. I don't care for you to leave this house without my knowledge, let alone go about negotiating the purchase of a servant. That is dangerous work and should be left for the men. Why do you think I've been sending Lawrence to handle these things?"

"Because he's to be the master of this house someday?" Fairalisa asks.

"Yes, but also because it's dangerous." Anthond raises a finger at Fairalisa. "Now, who's house did you buy this boy from?"

As Anthond's voice rises, I shrink away from the couch and come to stand next to Tuor. I grab his hand. I won't let this old man take Tuor away from me again.

"The Perelies," Fairalisa says, holding a finger to her chin in thought. "It's not anyone that we know personally."

Anthond strains as he comes to his feet. A nearby manservant brings Anthond's cane to him. "Well, young lady, you're going to take me back to that house, and we're going to set this straight."

"But they wanted to sell him," Fairalisa says, shooting up straight on her feet. "We did it all legitimately."

"That's not the point. A girl like you has no knowledge of servant trade, and you were surely taken advantage of. How much did you pay for the boy?"

Fairalisa bites her lower lip. "I'm not sure of the exact amount," she says absentmindedly. I remember Fairalisa's bag of rings that I dumped on the ground.

"Was it more than thirty rings?"

Fairalisa nods hesitantly.

"Well then, there you go," Anthond says. "The going rate right now for male servants is thirty rings. The only time you'd pay any more than that is for someone with special skills. Does this boy know masonry work, or perhaps how to medically attend to the horses?"

"No," Fairalisa says. "But I think he is good with horses, and he's very strong."

Anthond looks Tuor up and down. "My dear, he looks rather skinny to me. I'm afraid these people sold you a less-than-skilled servant for an exorbitant price. Now, I will go down and talk to these people, and we will set this right." Anthond snaps his fingers at his manservant. He starts to hobble from the parlor, but Fairalisa grabs his arm.

"Daddy, you don't understand. They were beating him badly. Don't you see all those cuts and bruises on him?"

Anthond presses his lips into a hard line as he scans Tuor's face. He shakes his head. "You know I believe in treating servants humanely, but it is not our business to interfere with another household and how they handle their staff. This boy could be troublesome. All the more reason to return him." Anthond turns again from his daughter.

"Daddy . . ." Fairalisa's voice cracks. Tears threaten in her eyes. "Please, Daddy."

Anthond takes a deep breath as he looks sympathetically at his daughter. She comes to his side and wraps his frail arm in a hug while laying her head on his shoulder.

"I used the rings you gave me for the wedding to pay for him."

"The rings are not the point," Anthond says, his voice softer now. "The city is dangerous, and you didn't tell me what you were doing."

"I know. I'm sorry." Fairalisa tilts her head to look up at her father with watery eyes.

I shudder to think how Anthond would react if he knew the truth about where we had to go, and what we had to do, to get Tuor back. The distant sound of knocking on the front door wafts into the parlor. My chest tightens. Have Gregor's men followed us back here? Anthond scrunches his nose in annoyance.

"Is this one of your wedding people coming to interrupt us?" Anthond asks. "All day long this house is like a shipping port."

"I'm not expecting anyone," Fairalisa says.

"Hmph." Anthond rubs at his chin. He then pats Fairalisa on the head and says, "I need to think about all of this. I'm upset that you went behind my back, and we don't need any servants right now. Where would we even put him?"

Fairalisa releases her father's arm and stands up straight. "I thought we could put him in the stables with Hobbes. Tuor said he knows horses, and you know, Hobbes is getting older. I'm sure he could use some help."

"Be careful with all that *old* talk. Hobbes is younger than me. I'm sure he's got plenty of good years left in him."

"Of course, Daddy."

Ronda enters the parlor, drawing all of our attention to the door.

"Master," Ronda says with a slight bow.

Anthond continues his shuffle across the parlor floor. "Yes. Who's at the door?"

"Lawrence has returned, sir."

CHAPTER TWENTY-EIGHT

"OH, THANK ALL Elmyra you've returned," Anthond says as he shuffles back to the couch. "Come, take a seat. I'm sure you're tired from your travels."

Dressed in a sharp suit, Lawrence steps into the parlor like a dignitary. His hair is combed, and his hands are clasped neatly behind his back. Fairalisa is quiet. She gives Lawrence a weak smile, but she seems distracted by Tuor's sallow appearance.

"How was your ride in?" Anthond asks.

"Just fine," Lawrence says. Clearing his throat, he takes a seat near the fire and straightens his jacket. Lawrence furrows his brows as his gaze falls to Tuor. He eyes his old friend curiously.

"You don't know how thrilled I am that you'll soon be here full time to help me run this house," Anthond says, pointing a bony finger at Lawrence. "Fairalisa has just purchased this servant boy without my consent." Anthond gestures in our direction. "I wish you a sharp mind and a lot of patience as you handle this woman's misadventures," Anthond says with a laugh.

Understanding floods Lawrence's face as he looks again at Tuor. A worried crease forms on his forehead.

"I'm inclined to have him returned to the home he came from," Anthond continues. "I'm not sure we have a place for him here."

"I told you, Daddy, the stables, with Hobbes."

Lawrence stares at Tuor and me. "Yes," he says, straightening his back. "Fairalisa is right. I think Hobbes could use a helper. Especially when we have guests. The purchase has already been made. No need to agonize over it any longer."

"You think I should keep the boy?" Anthond asks in surprise.

"Well, you did say I had an opinion on the running of the house," Lawrence says ruefully. "I think we should keep him. Our family will soon be growing, and we'll need more servants."

Lawrence's comment garners a grin from Fairalisa.

"Well, all right then," Anthond says. He turns to his daughter. "I just wish you'd come to me before you make any more impulsive decisions."

"I will, Daddy. I promise," Fairalisa says, giving her father a side hug.

"Okay, okay," Anthond says, playfully waving off Fairalisa. "Eh, Ronda? Is she still around?"

"Yes, sir?" Ronda asks from the archway of the parlor.

"Take the boy and get him cleaned up. We'll get him started with Hobbes first thing in the morning," Anthond says.

I feel a hiccup in my chest as I watch Tuor being led away by Ronda. *He's safe*, I remind myself. He'll be safe in this house.

"How was your journey?" Anthond asks Lawrence.

"Exhausting if I'm going to be truthful," Lawrence says, coming to his feet. "In fact, I'd like to get unpacked now if my urgency doesn't offend you?"

"Of course not," Anthond says. "Make use of the new servant boy if you so desire."

Lawrence bows to his future father-in-law. "Thank you," he says before striding from the room.

"Kat and I should go too, Daddy, lots to do before the wedding."

"Fine, fine. Everybody wants to leave me," Anthond says.

Fairalisa gives her father a kiss on the cheek and then leads me toward the parlor archway.

"Darling!" Anthond calls.

"Yes?" Fairalisa asks.

Anthond shakes his finger at me. "What happened to your maid's chains?"

Looking down at my feet, I curse under my breath. I was afraid of Ronda noticing. I never considered this old man would be so vigilant.

"They broke," Fairalisa blurts.

"Impossible!" Anthond barks.

"It was a weak link, Daddy," Fairalisa says taking a few paces closer to her father. She gently urges him back into his seat. "I think it was just a bad set from the blacksmith."

"Hmph. Have Ronda get a new set on her immediately."

"I will take care of it, Daddy."

Upstairs in her bedroom, Fairalisa turns the key on my broken shackles. I sit on the edge of her bed as she removes the cuffs from my ankles and latches on a new pair. The tension that I'd grown used to returns. A bolt of panic runs up my body. Standing, Fairalisa clutches the key to her chest and averts her eyes.

"What's wrong?" I ask.

"Oh, Kat . . ." Fairalisa eases onto the bed next to me. "I didn't know it was like that out there." She looks up at me with wide eyes. They're wet and glossy. Fairalisa then shivers, pulling her arms in on herself. "That place," she croaks. "All those men . . . It—it was horrendous."

"I know," I mumble, hearing the crack of the guard's whip in my head.

Fairalisa's lip curls in disgust. "Is that how other servants are treated? The way your brother was?"

She asks the question as if she doesn't want to know the real answer. I squint at Fairalisa. Understanding etches her smooth, delicate features. Is she growing a heart for the slaves?

"I'm afraid so," I say.

Fairalisa's innocence seems to melt away before my eyes. "I knew that some houses weren't as nice as us, but . . . I didn't know it was like that."

"In my experience, most servants in Elmyra are treated little better than animals," I say matter-of-factly.

"That can't be true!" Fairalisa protests. She looks helplessly at her hands. "I—I don't want to believe that."

I shift, Fairalisa's mattress squeaking as I move.

"When I lived in Bear Gap, I used to work on the farm. I wasn't treated much better than what Gregor was doing at the mine. The only difference was the beatings were coming from Warwick soldiers."

"But the farm is supposed to be a great thing! Daddy is furious that the rebels have taken it over. He said the people that work there will be treated terribly without the Warwick Militia."

"I've seen it firsthand," I say, scrunching up my eyebrows. "Bear Gap is a better place since Quinten pulled his men out of there."

Fairalisa tilts her head. "Did you call him *Quinten*?" She hops off the bed. "How dare you speak so disrespectfully of our Supreme Ruler!"

"I wasn't thinking," I say quickly, feeling my fake identity slip away.

"How did you do all those things at the mining pit?" Fairalisa's tone is accusing. Her eyes flash, and she presses her lips together. "I saw how you handled that sword and pounced on Mr. Creighton. How did you learn to do all of that just by serving as Karla Warwick's lady's maid?"

I open my mouth, searching for an excuse. I wasn't in my right mind at the pit. My whole focus was on getting Tuor.

"That's why your brother called you Camilla in the carriage," Fairalisa says. She backs away from me as if I were a fuzzy spider, a glimmer of fear in her eyes. "Who really are you?"

"Fairalisa, I . . ."

I stand slowly, trying not to frighten her more.

"Are you the Camilla everyone is speaking about?" Her voice is a whisper.

"No."

"You are! Aren't you?" Fairalisa's voice hits a fever pitch. Her eyes are wet with tears.

"Kat is just a nickname. It's true that my real name is Camilla, but I couldn't go around LilyAye having people call me that or they'd be suspicious. You understand, right?"

"Then how did you know how to fight like that?"

"It was just excitement of the moment. I was desperate to get my brother back." I hold my tongue, hoping that Fairalisa will believe my lie. She slowly shakes her head.

"You came from Bear Gap. You admit you worked on the farm and lived in the governor's house, and now you tell me your name is Camilla." Fairalisa scrambles backward to the door. "Do you think I'm stupid?"

"Fairalisa, listen to me."

She turns the knob on her bedroom door, her eyes never leaving me.

"Daddy?" Fairalisa yells into the hallway. Her eyebrows are pinched in worry. "Daddy!"

I purse my lips together. Charging toward Fairalisa, I slam the door shut before she has a chance to call out again. Fairalisa squeals as I push her back to the bed and force her to sit.

"Please don't hurt me!" she cries.

"Shhh, I'm not going to hurt you. Just listen to me. Give me a chance to explain."

Fairalisa backs up against her pillows and pulls her legs to her chest. I pace the room, trying to collect my thoughts.

"You must understand," I tell Fairalisa urgently. "You can't allow people to become property and then not expect that some of them are going to be abused. I know you have a good, kind heart. I know you care for people...all people. You must believe that no person can be someone's property."

"You speak of kindness but you killed Governor Leo! What about that?"

"He was trying to kill Tuor. He forced all of his villagers into slavery."

"But you murdered him and killed many others." Tears stream down Fairalisa's face as she whimpers.

"Okay, fine. What about this. What if it was your brother at that mining pit?"

Fairalisa sniffles, running her sleeve under her nose. "If I had a brother, he'd be the son of a Warwick council member, so he'd never have to live a life like that."

"But what if he did?" I press, walking to the end of the bed.

"It would never happen," Fairalisa says, raising her voice. "My family has served the Supreme Ruler loyally. We don't need to be servants."

"Then what if Quinten was overthrown by another ruler, and this new ruler didn't recognize your family as important anymore? What if he stripped your family name of its title, took away your father's salary, home, and all your possessions, and you were forced into slavery? Then what would you think?"

Fairalisa's forehead creases into a horrified expression. Her gaze settles on her embroidered bedspread and she whispers, "That would be... distressing."

I walk around the bed and take a seat next to Fairalisa. She shudders, shifting away from me.

"I am a rebel. Some of what you've heard about me is true, but you should understand why I did the things I did." I turn away from Fairalisa. Pulling down the strap of my silken dress, I let it fall open to reveal the tops of the long, bumpy scars on my back. Fairalisa gasps.

"What is that?" she croaks.

"It's from working at the farm. Everyone there was whipped."

Fairalisa's breath comes quickly. "Cover it up."

I pull up my strap and turn to face her again. "I was only ten years old when I began being beaten at the farm."

Tears bubble from Fairalisa's eyes. "Stop, please."

"You should see this too." I roll up my sleeve and expose the inside of my left arm and the marred Warwick brand. The *W* is distinguished by the raised, discolored skin. A scar from the soldier's knife runs down the middle, splitting the *W* in half.

"This is how we were marked to work on the farm," I say. "Like animals."

I remember Lawrence has a similar brand that he keeps hidden with his long-sleeved jackets. Someday, he'll have to tell his bride the truth. Fairalisa bends forward and inspects the brand, a twisted look on her face.

"I can't… I can't think about this," Fairalisa says as she scurries off her bed. "It's too much!"

I slowly come to my feet and watch Fairalisa from across the room. Her lower lip quivers as she hugs her body. She knows who I truly am. My only hope now is to draw this privileged, LilyAye girl to the rebel side.

"The truth is, I came to LilyAye to end slavery." My eyes fall to the tasseled rug on the floor. "Recently I'd turned my back on that goal, resigning myself to this servant life. It's not so bad being your lady's maid." My eyes meet Fairalisa's as I take a step toward her. "But many slaves out there still suffer every day. They're beaten and separated from their families. They die never tasting true freedom. But after today…" I shake my head. "I must do what's right. I can't just rescue my brother and forget about all the others."

It's in this moment that I realize I've been just as foolish and selfish as Fairalisa by refusing to kill Quinten at the wedding. I stand in silence, waiting for Fairalisa to speak. She sniffles then paces to the balcony doors, gazing out onto the back lawn.

"Daddy says the rebels are vicious, violent people. If he knew about you…"

"Please, Fairalisa. You can't tell anyone my true identity. Quinten will have me hanged."

Bowing her head, Fairalisa whispers, "Leave me." Her voice is unsteady. "I will ready myself for dinner tonight. I'm sorry, Kat, but I must contemplate this alone."

I stare at Fairalisa's back, begging for her to turn around and accept me for who I am, but she won't meet my eyes. Nodding, I quietly slip from the room and wonder if my time as a lady's maid has come to an end.

***

In my own bedroom, I use my nervous energy to clean myself from the events at the pit. The red dirt seems to stain every crevice. Splashing cold water on my face, I run a cloth over my neck, chest, and limbs. Blood speckles the hem of my dress so I burn it, just like Pip did when I was shot with the poison. I scrub my feet, then put on a fresh dress and brush out my hair.

Downstairs, I spot Tuor emerging from the washrooms in his new shackles and servant garb. I want to call out to him, but Ronda has begun her explanation of the house rules and duties to him. He's safe, I remind myself once again, but for how long? I try not to think on the fact that I may have brought

Tuor to this house only to turn around and have us both arrested.

Desperate for Fairalisa to keep my identity hidden, I decide that maybe a cup of tea will make her feel better. The kitchen is quiet. Dinner preparations haven't begun yet, but I find Pip standing over the stove.

"Why didn't you tell me they were buying your brother?" Pip says when she sees me.

"Oh, you know about that?"

"Word spreads quick around here."

I sidle up beside Pip. She's intently watching a simmering pot. I smile, pushing myself to act normal. "I'm excited for you to meet him."

Pip glances around the empty kitchen. "Is that why you tried . . . to run away?" she whispers. "To find your brother?"

I nod.

"You could have told me that," Pip says.

"I didn't know who I could trust."

"You can trust me." Pip says as if it's ludicrous I would be so skeptical.

"What are you making?" I ask.

Pip lets out a long sigh. "It's kind of a secret but I'm making pear pudding. I'm practicing for the wedding. Fairalisa asked me to make a special portion for the Supreme Ruler." She takes a fork and pokes at the softening pears in the pot.

"That's right," I say, remembering what Fairalisa had said at the Bradac castle.

"She asked me a while ago, but I've been too busy securing a vineyard to provide enough wine, and of course, she wants scallops at the wedding dinner, so I had to find a fishmonger who could get me some." Pip shakes her head. "The coast of the Rose Sea isn't far, but it's not like I can just snap my fingers and have enough scallops for four hundred guests."

"Well, the pears smell good at least."

"Thanks. It's a little nerve-racking making food for the Supreme Ruler. I hope I don't make him ill."

Pip lets out a sardonic laugh as she scoops out one of the poached pears and lays it in a bowl of custard.

"That would be unfortunate," I say.

"Unfortunate indeed. Here, try it. Tell me what you think." Pip cuts off a piece of the pear and scoops it with some of the custard. I savor the sweet, creamy bite on my tongue. It's perhaps even more delectable than the wedding cake. For a moment I forget about my troubles with Fairalisa.

"You're making this just for the Supreme Ruler?" I ask, swallowing.

"Specially made, just for him," Pip says.

This perfectly portioned dessert will be presented to Quinten as a gift from Fairalisa, a gift that he wouldn't refuse. Quinten's life seems to have been laid out for me in the delicately painted china bowl that the pear pudding sits in. A satisfied smile fills Pip's face as she takes a bite of her own, and I suddenly realize how I'm going to kill the Supreme Ruler.

CHAPTER TWENTY-NINE

THE KITCHEN DOOR swings open.

"There you are," Ronda says, standing at the threshold.

"I was getting the lady some tea."

Ronda clasps her hands in front of her and gives me a sour look. "It doesn't take two girls to make one cup of tea, now does it?"

I drop the spoon and move to the tea kettle.

"That'll have to wait," Ronda says tersely. "I've just finished up with your brother and now Sir Lawrence asked me to summon you. He wishes to see you this moment."

Ronda seems pleased, as if she's sending me to slaughter.

"Okay," I say, waving to Pip.

"He's waiting for you in the piano room."

Ronda holds the door open as I leave. I'm not surprised Lawrence wants to see me. He'll be furious about what happened today. I walk the long hallway, past the dining room and the parlor, and stop in front of a paneled oak door. I turn the brass knob and enter, letting the door click behind me.

Lawrence stands in front of a wide picture window. Deep blue velvet curtains hang on either side. His hands folded behind his back, Lawrence stares out the magnificent window at the front lawn foliage and the street below. A grand piano sits in the corner, poised atop a polished floor.

"You wanted to see me?" I ask, not sure if I should speak to Lawrence as a friend or as his servant.

"I want to thank you," Lawrence says in a clipped voice. "For looking after my fiancée these past few weeks."

He's being sarcastic, trying to make me feel bad.

"It's not like I've had a choice in the matter. You're the one who made me a slave in this house."

"Anthond said that Fairalisa bought Tuor from some other family in LilyAye," Lawrence says while still looking intently out the window. "But here's the thing. I know who bought Tuor at the auction. It was Gregor Creighton, the miner."

Lawrence turns swiftly on his heels to face me. His jaw is set. "You took Fairalisa out to that mining site, didn't you?"

"I wanted my brother back, and you weren't helping. I did what I had to do."

"You intentionally planned this while I was absent." Lawrence angrily presses his fingertips to his chest.

"Yeah, I knew you'd never let us go."

Lawrence marches across the wood floor toward me. "Why don't you ever just do what I tell you to? I told you we'd go get Tuor once the wedding was over."

"Unlike you, I wasn't fine with him slowly dying in that pit!"

"You two could have been killed out there. How did you even find him?"

I cross my arms over my chest. "Fairalisa figured it out. She was more helpful than you, and she didn't even know Tuor. It's like he was never your friend."

"If Fairalisa had been hurt, so help me, Camilla, I'd . . ." Lawrence seethes. His face is snarled like a protective dog's.

"She's fine. The only thing different about her is that she sees the horrors of this society you're trying so hard to protect."

"Don't you dare indoctrinate her," Lawrence says.

"She's figuring it out on her own! You can't keep turning away from this."

"Camilla, I'm trying to help you. I placed you in this house, under Anthond's care, to protect you from Quinten."

"And I'm grateful for that," I say, the words tasting bitter in my mouth.

"You've gotten what you want. Tuor is here. Are you ready to take my offer?"

The offer: safety, protection, and anonymity, all in this beautiful house, with my brother by my side. The only thing I have to give up is my freedom.

Lawrence takes a calming breath and unbuttons the top button of his suit jacket. "You can live here, but you have to actually obey for once."

"What if I say no?" I scrunch up my face in disgust.

Lawrence's jaw quivers as he stares at me. "I'll make you stay."

"LilyAye has turned you into a power-hungry monster the likes of Quinten Warwick!"

"You do not talk to me like that. Soon, I'll be your master whether you like it or not."

Fire blazes in my eyes as I stare at Lawrence.

Master.

Did he really just use that word? A slew of curses flit across my mind, but Lawrence is too far gone and not worth the breath to speak them.

"I'll never call you that." I press my lips firmly together and stalk across the floor of the piano room, toward the door.

"I won't let you leave this house!" Lawrence yells as I storm from the room.

Unfortunately for Lawrence, I don't have to leave this house to plan Quinten's assassination. I need only for Fairalisa to stay silent about my true identity until I can kill Quinten and get out of here. I march down to the servant's dining room and find Trixie folding the napkins for dinner.

"Hey, Trix," I say, breathless. "Remember that salesman from this morning?"

"Yeah," she says, neatly lining up the edges of the napkin.

"If he stops by again, come and get me immediately, okay? The lady has decided to buy what he's selling."

***

That evening I attempt to deliver a cup of tea to Fairalisa but she turns me away. She practically banishes me from her room, dressing herself for dinner and getting into bed without my assistance.

I nervously pace my bedroom floor. It's not just the delicacy of this situation that has me on edge. It's the lack of tasks for me to do. I can't force Fairalisa to keep my secret and I have no way of contacting Reed

313

to tell him I'm ready to help kill Quinten. I'm forced to do nothing but wait.

By morning, I'm actively reminding myself to stay calm. Since Fairalisa has locked her doors, it's easy for me to take a break from my duties and go visit Tuor. At first light, I scamper across the lawn, toward the stables. We've barely seen each other since his arrival at the house yesterday.

"Hey," I call from the stable door. I glance up at the hazy gray sky.

The tangy smell of manure hits my nose. Tuor rakes out one of the horse stalls. He leans on the wooden handle. Sweat pours down his face despite the chilly fall air.

"How is it out here?" I ask.

"It's better than where I was." Tuor comes to the end of the stall to stand in front of me. "How'd you manage to get away from the house?"

I shrug my shoulders casually, not wanting Tuor to know about the rift between Fairalisa and me. "They're not very strict here."

Tuor's black curls sit on his head like a mop. He's dressed in the same uniform as the rest of the male servants: a loose white cotton shirt with light-blue embroidery down the front, a matching pair of white pants, and a silver collar around his neck. Even though Tuor works in the stables, he's only allowed a pair of tan sandals, which leave enough room for the shackles hanging from his ankles.

"Where's Hobbes?" I ask.

Tuor wipes his forehead. "He's outside, shoeing one of the horses."

"You okay?"

"I'm alive," he says, his eyes pointed toward the hay-strewn floor. "Thanks to you." Tuor clears his throat awkwardly. "I didn't think I'd ever get out of there. It felt like I was in that pit for years."

Horse hooves shuffle against the planked floor. A breeze pushes through the slats in the walls. I pull my shawl tight over my shoulders.

"We're safe, for now."

"I can't stay here for long, Camilla. I have to find Eve."

"She may never have made it into the city."

"Then I'll go back to Wildenvalley to look for her."

"You're not going anywhere without me," I scold.

Tuor peers down at me, a determined look in his eyes. "I have to find her."

"We will," I say.

Dried leaves flutter across the lawn.

"Why is Lawrence holding us here?" Tuor's voice drops.

"He says he's protecting us, but he's really trying to keep us from the rebellion."

"When we pass in the hallway, he doesn't even look at me. It's like he doesn't know me."

"We can't trust him anymore," I say.

"Does he know what we came to LilyAye for?"

One of the horses at the end of the stable whinnies.

"Not fully." I sidle up closer to Tuor. "He knows we came here on rebel business, but I don't think he knows our exact plan."

"What is our plan?" Tuor asks. "I didn't travel all this way to muck out a horse stable."

I take a deep breath. It's a fair question that I haven't been able to fully explain to Tuor yet. I inch closer to Tuor. "Quinten will be at Lawrence's wedding. My plan is to poison him at the dinner."

"Can you do it without being seen?"

"I think so. The problem is, I have no way of getting poison while we're stuck in this house. I need to ask Reed to fetch me some, but he hasn't been by in a while."

"Reed?" Tuor spits his name.

"Be careful," I whisper, scanning the stables. "Yes, Reed. He's the reason Lawrence knew to buy me from the auction."

Tuor anxiously rubs the side of his head. "I thought we were rid of him?"

"We need him, not just to kill Quinten, but to get out here. Lawrence has said he'll keep us here."

"We're conceding to the man who beat a woman!"

"We have to stay reconciled with Reed. What other choice do we have?"

Tuor lets out a frustrated groan as he forces his hand away from his head.

"Fine. But this wedding is happening soon," Tuor says. "How are we going to get the poison in time?"

"One thing I know about Reed, he wants Quinten dead more than any of us. This wedding is his best chance at making that happen. He'll need our help to do it, so he'll be back. Trust me."

I say those words more to encourage myself than Tuor. Reed will come back, right?

"Isn't there another way to find poison in this city?" Tuor asks.

"We're trapped here," I tell Tuor firmly, remembering my attempt to escape the Servant's District. "He'll come."

"What about Eve?"

"I'm sure she's safe. She's probably holding up in Wildenvalley with Roehana. There's nothing we can do until we get out of this house and we can't get out of this house until Quinten is dead. We'll find her after this is all done."

He doesn't like my answer, but he nods in agreement. Whistling draws my attention to the other end of the stable. Hobbes leads a brown mare into her stall.

"I better go," I say quickly. "We stick together, remember?"

"We stick together," Tuor agrees.

I slip out of the barn before Hobbes can spot me. Throwing my shawl around my shoulders, I run back to the house, the dewy grass tickling my ankles.

***

I spend the rest of the day begging for jobs from Pip, anything to keep my mind busy. She puts me to task on cleaning dishes since apparently nobody in the house enjoys doing that. I move my hands furiously in the soapy water, fearful that if I stop I'll dwell on the delicate nature of Fairalisa and I's relationship. Don't think about the fact that she can have you hauled in front of the Supreme Ruler any moment, I tell myself.

"Whoa, whoa, kitty-Kat. Take it easy on those plates," Jaunty says as he dries the stack I just finished washing. "You're going to scrub those painted flowers right off."

"You're speaking to me again?" I ask in a clipped tone, handing Jaunty the next clean plate.

"I only left you alone because I felt kind of bad about you being sick for so long, but now that you're better…"

I roll my eyes. Behind us, the griddle steams as Benji scrapes the cast iron. Jaunty watches me as he carefully stacks the plates.

"Look, I only tease people I like," Jaunty continues.

"You have an odd way of showing friendship."

Jaunty shrugs his bony shoulders. "Yeah, but it gets boring around here, especially when there's nothing to gossip about. How about a truce?"

I pause and let my wet, soapy hands hang over the edge of the wash basin. The last thing on my list of concerns is my status with Jaunty, but it wouldn't hurt to have another person in the house on my side.

"Truce."

"Great!" he says excitedly. "Now I can tell you about the gossip."

"There's gossip?"

Jaunty leans in close as I scrub out a bowl.

"News is, there was an uprising at some mining site outside the city. The workers turned on the guards, even killed the master."

I freeze. My mouth goes dry. The bowl slips from my fingers and sinks beneath the soapy water.

Gregor.

Jaunty continues. "Apparently Master Anthond was reading about it at breakfast this morning. One of the kitchen maids overhead him telling Sir Lawrence not to tell us about the uprising because it could put ideas in our heads."

With a satisfied look on his face, Jaunty revels in the delicious gossip. He leans back and waits for my reaction.

"That's… interesting," is all I can manage to mutter.

An uprising. I never thought that rescuing Tuor would cause the slaves to revolt, but the death of Gregor Creighton is certainly deserved. He was the only one at the mine that day that knew Fairalisa's name which means, as long as Anthond never connects Tuor to the mine, we're in the clear.

***

Once dinner has ended, I can't beg a job from anyone in the house. There's nothing left to do. Since Fairalisa still hasn't spoken to me, I mosey up to my bedroom. I listen for her through the closet door as she returns from dinner and readies herself for bed. I know Fairalisa. She can't go long without a maid's help. Surely she'll call out for me any moment.

She doesn't. Soon her room is quiet and the only thing I can do is go to sleep too, but sleep doesn't come. I lie in bed wide awake well past sunset. With my arms outstretched, I wonder if Fairalisa can ever face me again. I start to suspect that the shunning isn't just about my involvement with the rebels. If she was truly afraid, she would have called for my arrest that very moment. Fairalisa saw me as a friend and I lied to her about who I was.

The closet door creaks open. I shoot up in bed, my defense instincts kicking in. The ghostlike silhouette of Fairalisa steps quietly toward my bed.

"Are you all right?" I whisper, wondering if she's sleep walking.

Fairalisa crawls onto my bed and nestles up next to me. Unsure of what to do, I awkwardly wrap my arm around her shoulder.

"They won't go away." Fairalisa's voice is tiny.

"What won't go away?"

"The nightmares."

The stream of moonlight through the window glimmers off Fairalisa's tears as they slowly roll down her cheeks.

"Ever since we escaped that pit, I can't stop thinking about those poor men," she says. "When I close my eyes, images burn in my mind. When I try to sleep, they haunt me."

I stroke Fairalisa's soft hair. "I know."

She sniffles and tilts her head to look at me.

"How do we make it stop?"

"The nightmares?"

Fairalisa shakes her head vehemently. "The pit. Slavery. All of it. All the suffering!" She buries her face into my shoulder and weeps. "I can't stand to think about the men who are still in that pit right now!"

I open my mouth to speak but stop myself. I'm not sure what to say. Is Fairalisa just being her normal, dramatic self? Or does she mean what she's saying? More darkly, I wonder if this is some kind of trap.

"Is that what you really want?" I ask.

"What I saw was…disgusting. It was reprehensible!"

Fairalisa pulls out of our embrace. Her concerned eyes, tear-soaked cheeks, and twisted mouth are such an unusual expression for Fairalisa that she barely looks like herself.

"Slavery doesn't have to exist in Elmyra," I say.

Fairalisa's demeanor steels. "It must be ended." She's nearly begging. "It must."

Little does Fairalisa know that the pit has changed me too. Seeing firsthand the devastation of Quinten's slave-infested country has galvanized me to action. I am once again plotting the murder of the Supreme

Ruler. Unfortunately for Fairalisa, I'm planning to use her wedding to do that very thing.

***

Despite the frantic wedding planning and icy glares from Lawrence, life has been somewhat peaceful in Anthond's home the last couple of days. Fairalisa has officially reinstated me as her lady's maid and promised to keep my identity a secret. I'm doubtful Fairalisa has any real comprehension of how her life would drastically change if slavery suddenly ended, like she asked, but I have noticed a difference in her countenance. She's more serious, less giddy.

We test taste the scallop dish in near silence, and even with Lawrence now living in the house, I can't get much of a smile out of her. But true to her word, Fairalisa tells no one that I'm the infamous Camilla Crim from Bear Gap. I'm finding her to be a more reliable person than I ever thought possible.

Tuor and I hardly get any time alone, but we do eat dinner together every night. He scarfs down the food like it's his last meal. His body fills out to its normal thin-but-not-scrawny form. I introduce him to Pip and Trixie and the others, and soon remember the allure I initially felt at taking Lawrence's offer and staying under the safety of this roof. It's true that I'm not eager to throw Tuor back into danger after rescuing him from the pit, but conceding to Lawrence's offer of servanthood is not an option anymore. Fairalisa is right for once, we can't sit in this house while people are out there suffering.

Late one morning, I sit on Fairalisa's bed and watch as her seamstress adjusts the bodice on her wedding gown. Fairalisa stands in front of the balcony doors, her lacy powder-blue dress cascading into a pool on the floor. She'd be a perfect vision if it weren't for the rain pattering against the glass.

"What do you think?" the seamstress asks.

Fairalisa stares at herself in her vanity mirror. Storm clouds fill her eyes more than they do the sky outside. She sullenly soothes the fabric over her waist.

"It's lovely," Fairalisa says, forcing a smile.

The seamstress, a tall women with spectacles, uses a straight pin to gather the train of the dress. She stands and tugs on the ribbon that holds the dress together in the back.

"I could put more of the pearl embroidery on the straps if you like?" she asks.

"That's not necessary," Fairalisa says, turning from the mirror.

"Is the length comfortable to walk in?" the seamstress asks.

Fairalisa's gaze looks as if it were territories away. "It will do."

The seamstress pulls up a fold in Fairalisa's dress and sets another pin. She gives me a curious look.

"Please tell me if you're not pleased, my lady," the seamstress says, coming to her feet. "I'll do what I must to make it right."

"No, no, I'm quite pleased," Fairalisa says. "Would you wait out in the hallway until I'm ready for you?"

The seamstress nervously twitters her fingers together, then slips from the room. Fairalisa exhales slowly as she grabs tightly to the poster of her bed and gazes out into the storm. Her eyes dip closed. When they open, tears glide down Fairalisa's flawless skin.

"What's wrong?" I ask.

"How can I carry on with all of this frivolity when I know people are suffering?"

My eyes fall to Fairalisa's intricately stitched wedding gown. I don't have a good answer for her, but Lawrence and Fairalisa must get married or I won't have a chance to poison Quinten.

"You can use your status in the city to help them."

Fairalisa nods, dabbing the tears from the corner of her eyes. "Once we're married, I will talk with Lawrence. Things will be different in this house, and I will convince the people of LilyAye to treat their servants better."

Fairalisa eases onto the bed next to me. "I'm not sure I can take much more of this. The wedding and the people and the food. It's . . . too much."

"It'll be over soon."

Fairalisa turns her glistening eyes to me and says, "And I don't know anymore if I should call you Kat or Camilla. It's all so confusing." She buries her face in her hands.

"Call me Kat," I say quickly. "It's safer."

"I've been pondering this thought. If you're one of the rebels from Bear Gap, then what are you doing here in LilyAye?" Fairalisa whispers.

I spread my lips to answer but pause. I can't tell Fairalisa the truth and risk ruining our plan. She's begged for slavery to end, but I don't think she knows how messy that will be or that it involves murdering Quinten Warwick. So I lie to Fairalisa.

"I'm in hiding. Even some people in Bear Gap didn't like what I've done, so my brother and I decided to flee. We figured the best disguise was to be servants. We just never thought we'd get separated."

"I see." Fairalisa's gaze falls to her hands. "Kat, could you do something for me?"

I shift on the bed. "Sure."

"I've been so caught up in my own troubles, I've forgotten where I came from." Fairalisa rises and paces to the balcony doors. She rests her hand on the frame and gazes through the glass as if it might tell her future.

"I've forgotten about my mother. She and Daddy had the most beautiful life together before she died, and I always promised I'd honor her at my wedding, but . . . all I've been fussing over is pear pudding and scallops."

"What do you want me to do?" I come to stand behind Fairalisa. The rain falls in sheets against the balcony floor. The trees sway with the hard gusts of wind.

"My mother's favorite flowers were verbena. They're these adorable little purple flowers."

The first genuine smile I've seen in days spreads across Fairalisa's face. "Daddy says they look like a weed to him, but my mother loved them. Sadly, not a lot of them grow around LilyAye, but I want a bouquet at the wedding." Fairalisa turns from the doors to face me. "Could you arrange a florist to bring me some?"

"I'll try," I say sympathetically. "But your wedding is only a few days away."

"I know. Do what you can," Fairalisa pleads.

Staring past Fairalisa, I spot a figure trudging through the backyard. He passes the stables and heads in the direction of the delivery door. Dressed in a long black trench coat, he pulls the hood of his jacket up against the raging storm.

Reed.

CHAPTER THIRTY

"IF YOU COULD find these flowers, I think I could be happy again," Fairalisa says.

"Of course. Yes." I grab Fairalisa by her elbows. "Why don't you finish up with the seamstress, and I'll get started on this right away?"

Fairalisa's eyes brighten. "Thank you."

After telling the seamstress she can go back into Fairalisa's room, I hustle downstairs, trying to keep my pace steady. Rain still taps gently against the windows in the front hall. My adrenaline soars. I was right.

He's back.

I nearly run into Trixie in the hallway next to the kitchen.

"Oh, hey, that salesman is back again," Trixie says.

"Yeah, thanks," I say, breezing past Trixie.

I take the stairs to the servant's dining room. A few maids collect the dirty dishes from breakfast. Reed stands just inside the delivery door. He's a dark tower in the dimly lit room. My heart skips a beat. I force my feet to walk at a normal pace. Smoothing my hair, I approach Reed. His icy blue eyes follow me.

"Kind of you to finally see me again," Reed says, glancing furtively at the maids.

"I'd like to speak with you on behalf of the lady of the house." I speak loud enough for the maids to hear me. "Will you come with me?"

Reed eyes me suspiciously, then says, "Lead the way."

I take Reed through the dining room and down a hallway, into the servants' quarters. This is where all the other servants sleep, including Tuor. It's quiet. Everyone is about the house, doing their duties. Reed follows me to an alcove where the stone wall is carved out and a torch hangs. I glance down the hallway. A line of doors sits on the other side of the hall, which leads to the servant's bedrooms.

"We're alone," I whisper.

"Tell me you've finally come to your senses."

I take a deep breath, already put off by Reed's attitude. "I told you I needed to get Tuor back first."

"Is he safe?" Reed asks.

"He's here. Working in the stables."

"I don't appreciate being ignored for days." Reed's eyes dart from side to side. His Warwick privilege is showing already, and for a moment, I wonder if I'm talking to Lawrence.

"What do you want me to say? I'm sorry?" I snap.

"We just need to get to work."

"I have a plan. But I need your help."

Reed cocks his head. Water rolls down his jacket sleeves and falls onto the stone floor. "I'm listening."

"They're presenting a special dessert for Quinten, which they're giving to him at the wedding dinner. I know the person who's making it. I could easily have access to it. All I need is poison."

A sly smile spreads across Reed's face.

"What?" I ask.

"I'd prefer to just cut his throat, but I suppose your plan has more finesse."

"It's simple and discreet."

"He'll have his taster there," Reed says. "The trick will be getting an odorless and slow-acting poison."

"What do you mean?"

The torchlight flickers across Reed's face. "His taster will be trained in identifying poisons by smell and taste. If he detects any of the common poisons, he'll refuse the dish and Quinten won't get anywhere near it. Even if we find a poison that's undetectable by smell and taste, if it kills the taster instantly, Quinten will know better than to take a bite."

"What about something that doesn't kill right away?" I ask, realizing my plan isn't as simple as I thought. "Quinten would eat the dessert and then die later that night or the next day. It could never be traced back to me."

Reed nods as he rubs the bottom of his chin. "I guess that will be for me to figure out."

"The wedding's in three days. Can you find it in time?"

"I have nothing else on my agenda other than working on a way to kill my uncle," Reed says, tilting his head down to meet my eyes. "I've just about worked out my disguise to get into the wedding."

"You'll be there? I thought you were trying to distance yourself from his murder."

"I can't miss this," he says in a low voice. "I want to see his demise."

A sense of relief floods over me at the prospect of Reed being there. I suddenly notice the space between us. It's wide and cold. Reed's hands are shoved into his pants pockets. The flirtatious looks we once shared have disappeared. I clear my throat, brushing away the thoughts.

"Stay here and act normal for now," Reed says, buttoning up his jacket. "I'll return with what you need."

I peer one more time down the hallway before leading Reed back to the delivery door. The kitchen is empty now.

"Oh, one more thing," I say, as Reed clicks open the door. Rain peppers the lawn outside. "I need some flowers, too, for the wedding. Verbena. Could you get me a bouquet?"

Reed throws his hood up over his head. "Am I your errand boy now?"

I search for a hint of playfulness on Reed's face, but find none. "Fairalisa asked for them. Please?"

"I'll see what I can do." Reed slips through the door without another word. He's no longer angry at me, at least now that I've agreed to do what he's asked.

***

Fairalisa and Lawrence's wedding day has arrived in a similar fashion to that of the Warwick Militia at the Bear Gap House gates: swift and terrifying. I nervously finger the clip in my hair that Fairalisa gave me the day I arrived in LilyAye.

The impending excitement and doom of the day hangs heavy in the air. Quinten will be on this very property in mere hours, and I have yet to see Reed. I have no poison, no weapon, and no way of killing the

Supreme Ruler, even though he'll be within shouting distance of me.

From the second story of the Bradac castle, I peer through the stained-glass window that looks down upon the front courtyard. Every tree or passing carriage that crosses my gaze is crystalized and painted an unnatural color by the cut glass. The lanterns lining the driveway are being decorated with silk bunting. Servants bustle through the hallway behind me. Shouts from the chefs in the kitchen wind their way through the many rooms and corridors of this mansion.

At the end of the hallway, the door to Fairalisa's bridal suite cracks open.

"Fetch the white one!" the seamstress barks at an apron-clad maid.

The young girl scurries down the hall, past me, quicker than a bunny darting across the lawn. When I arrived this morning with Fairalisa, the seamstress and her gaggle of helpers took over Fairalisa's room. So much so that I slipped out a while ago to keep watch for Reed, and no one has noticed yet. The decorators in the front yard step back to admire their work as another carriage flies up the driveway. I wait, watching as a man emerges. He carries a crate of wine bottles into the house. It's not Reed. A sigh escapes my lips as I force myself to turn from the window.

I walk through the marble hallway lined with bedrooms on all sides, then take a set of steps downstairs. I pass a Warwick soldier. The house is teeming with them. Fairalisa told me that Lawrence ordered even more security for the event a couple of days ago. He has the authority to do such things with his father's military position. Lawrence isn't stupid. Although he has me and Tuor in captivity, he knows the rebels could attempt something today. It's obvious he's trying to protect Quinten.

The kitchen bursts with barking commands as I pass by the door. I cross into the grand dining hall and walk under a man, atop a ladder, hanging a garland of greenery over the doorway. A sinister breeze blows through the skirt of my dress as I step out into the backyard.

Days of thunderstorms have left this outdoor marriage ceremony questionable. I squint at the sky. It's not raining now, but a swirl of gray clouds threatens. As I walk across the lawn, the maid who ran from Fairalisa's bridal suite a moment ago sprints past, carrying a white sewing basket.

Past the rose garden, at the edge of the property, I find Tuor busy with the horses. A row of unhitched carriages sits in the muddy tracks in front of the stables. I wave to Hobbes, who's brushing the horse that will lead away Fairalisa and Lawrence's carriage at the end of the day.

"Have you seen him?" I whisper, pulling Tuor inside.

Two long rows of horse stalls face each other inside the massive Bradac stables.

"No. I don't see much from in here. What are we going to do if he doesn't show up?" Tuor asks.

"I don't know . . ." I glance down at the floor. The horses poke their long faces out of the stalls. One of them shakes their head, sending a spray of flies into the air.

"There's gotta be another way to kill him," Tuor says.

"If I could just get my hands on a bow and arrow…" I lean against the wooden door frame and cross my arms over my chest. Tuor musses his shaggy hair.

"This needs to be over," Tuor says, desperation in his eyes. "I have to find Eve. I'm getting out of this place tonight whether Quinten is dead or not."

My eyes widen. I kick off the wall and grab Tuor's elbow. "Staying in Anthond's house might be the only way to get close to Quinten again."

"When?" Tuor snaps. "In a month? In a year, maybe?"

"I can't answer that," I say.

"I'm not waiting around for that. *We* can't wait around that long."

"Fine. Whatever happens tonight, we meet out here in the stables and make a run for it."

Tuor nods, already appearing calmer. Ronda marches down the yard, toward us. I scurry out of her line of sight, inside the stable.

"Blast!"

"What's wrong?" Tuor asks.

"Take me to the getaway carriage."

"Why?"

"Just do it!" I bark.

Tuor leads me to the end of the stables and out a sliding barn door, to a black carriage trimmed in gold. I glance furtively to my right as Ronda approaches. I unlatch one of the luggage chests in the back and start riffling through it, pretending not to notice Ronda.

"Thank you, Tuor. That's all I needed," I say brightly as Tuor slinks away.

"Kat," Ronda says, pursing her lips.

"Yes?"

"I need you to come with me."

"The lady asked me to check that her pink nightgown was packed for the honeymoon. She was very insistent that I assure her it's here, and I don't know . . ." I trail off as I dig through Fairalisa's meticulously packed luggage.

"Well, she's quite forgotten about that. The lady needs you by her side now."

I pause. Ronda's saggy, wrinkled face doesn't wear its usual sour expression. She looks . . . concerned.

"Come now, Kat," Ronda urges.

I slam the chest lid closed and follow Ronda back inside the Bradac castle. Ronda marches swiftly through the dining hall and upstairs.

"What's the matter with her?" I ask as we approach the door of Fairalisa's room.

Wailing mixed with blubbering hiccups bursts through the door.

"I'm not exactly sure. We've all tried to calm her down, but she just keeps asking for you." Ronda twists her hands together. "Poor thing never had a mother or a sister growing up. Never liked any of her lady's maids until she met you. The ceremony is to begin in an hour. You've got to calm her down."

The sliver trimmed double doors leading into Fairalisa's bridal suite seem to tower over me ominously. What is it about this day that's so *unnerving*? I try to give Ronda a reassuring look before turning the crystal knob. My palms are sweaty. As the door swings open, Fairalisa's cries pierce my ears.

"Get out! GET OUT!" Fairalisa screams at the seamstress.

"But your dress, you'll rip it if you keep—"

"I don't care about this ridiculous dress!" Fairalisa cries. "Just get out!"

The seamstress spots me at the open door. She slams the spool of thread she's holding into her sewing basket, tucks the basket under her arm, and marches past me in a flurry.

"Good luck," she mumbles, leaving Fairalisa and me alone in the room.

Fairalisa tosses her head into her hands as she continues to weep. The bridal suite is a magnificent room with massive windows looking out at a duck pond. A white-and-gold encrusted fireplace sits beneath an old oil painting of Supreme Ruler Bradac. Everything in this room sparkles and shines except for Fairalisa. I push the doors closed. The latching sound draws Fairalisa's attention to me.

"Kat?"

Fairalisa's breath quivers. I rush to her side. Her eyes, wet and red rimmed, no longer beam with innocence. I help Fairalisa onto a cushioned bench at the end of the canopy bed. She crumples into me as if she's lost all of her strength.

"What's going on?" I ask.

"Oh, Kat. I don't think I can go through with this."

My brows cinch together.

"With what?" I ask nervously.

"The wedding."

I bury Fairalisa's face into my neck so that she can't see my concerned expression. This wedding has to happen. If Fairalisa calls off the wedding, I'll lose my chance to kill Quinten.

"I can't marry Lawrence," Fairalisa cries.

"But you love him."

Fairalisa sits up and dabs her tears with a blush pink handkerchief. "If I marry Lawrence, I will live the same life I've always lived: beautiful dresses, important council meetings, tea with the ladies on my street, and a gorgeous house full of servants and Catahli."

"I thought that's what you wanted."

"Not anymore." Fairalisa shakes her head and sighs. "I don't want any of this anymore."

Fairalisa stares at the lines and swirls of embroidery on the billowy skirt of her wedding dress.

"What do you want?" I ask.

"I'm not sure," she admits with a sniffle. "I love Lawrence, with all my heart, but it wouldn't feel honest to marry him when my desires have changed."

"Well, that's not exactly true," I say.

"It's not?"

"People who are married change their minds and decide to do new and different things. The point is that you do them together. You grow together. You just don't change your mind about each other."

"But how do I know that Lawrence wants what I want?" Fairalisa asks.

Lawrence.

I look into Fairalisa's hopeful, begging eyes. What can I honestly tell her about Lawrence that would make her still want to marry him? He's lost his way. There's no doubt about that. He's turned into his father: greedy and controlling. But I remember the Lawrence I met in Bear Gap.

"You should marry Lawrence. And I'm going to tell you why."

"Okay . . ."

"I've known Lawrence a little longer than you think."

Fairalisa straightens her back and crinkles her forehead. "What do you mean?"

I hold up a finger to Fairalisa's mouth. "Let me get through this before I lose my nerve. You deserve to know. Remember how you told me Lawrence spent some time in Bear Gap?"

Fairalisa nods slowly.

"I met him during that time. Lawrence and my brother were in the militia together and were once very good friends. He and I even grew to be good friends. You see, Lawrence was very briefly on the rebel side."

Fairalisa's mouth drops open, and her face twists in confusion.

"But he left and came back here because he always puts his family first. He put *you* first. He chose his life with you over anything else."

"He lied to me," Fairalisa says.

"Yes, but he did it to protect you. He knew that, if anyone found out what he'd done during his time in Bear Gap, he wouldn't be able to marry you, and he'd probably be arrested."

"When he brought you home from the auction, he . . ." Fairalisa's brows furrow. "He already knew you?"

"He saved my life that day, like he had many other times." I look down at my hands. It's as if I'm having this pep talk with myself. "I think, at his core, Lawrence is a good man who wants to see Elmyra bettered. But most of all"—I lift my eyes to look at Fairalisa straight on—"most of all, I know he loves you."

"How do you know?" Fairalisa chokes.

I tilt my head and think of Johnny. "Because I've seen what true love looks like."

"You think I should marry Lawrence?"

"I don't think you should turn your back on marrying the man you love."

Fairalisa draws in a deep, shaky breath. She wipes a stray tear from her eye. "All right."

Relief floods my heart. Fairalisa leans across the space between us and pulls me into a hug.

"You're a true friend," Fairalisa says.

I chuckle, feeling like I've been the worst friend. "How do you figure?"

"You've always been there for me, and you told me the truth even when it was hard. I've never had a friend like you before."

"I've never had a friend like you either," I smirk.

Fairalisa's lips spread into a smile. "I have something for you. It's a gift."

Fairalisa pops off the bench and walks to an open chest in front of the fireplace. She pulls out a small velvet bag. I join Fairalisa in front of the fireplace, watching her curiously.

"It's a necklace," Fairalisa says, pulling a thin silver chain from the bag.

She holds up the necklace and lets the pendant drop with a clunk to the bottom of the chain. Touching the pendant with the tips of my fingers, I realize it's not a gem or a pearl.

It's a key.

Fairalisa giggles, her lively spirit returning.

"What does it open?" I ask, confused.

Fairalisa says nothing as she closes her lips together mischievously. I glance down at my shackles and suddenly understand. My face falls to a serious expression.

"They're for your chains," Fairalisa says. "And that collar around your neck too."

"But why?" is all I can manage to utter.

"You showed me what happens when you chain other humans. I know I can't let every servant in LilyAye free, but I can let you go."

Fairalisa drops the necklace in my palm and squeezes my hands around it.

"I'm giving you a choice," Fairalisa says. "Stay as my lady's maid, without your chains or… leave. I want you to stay, but I won't make you. I don't ever want to keep someone here against their will ever again."

"Fairalisa, I—"

A knock comes at the bridal suite door. "May I come in?"

"Daddy?" Fairalisa calls.

Fairalisa strides to the door, lifting the heavy skirt of her dress. I throw the necklace over my head and tuck the key inconspicuously down my top. Anthond hobbles through the door, a bouquet of flowers in his hand and his cane in the other.

Anthond speaks. "Sweetie, I heard you were having a rough morning, but look at what the delivery man just dropped off."

Fairalisa gasps. "Kat, you did it!"

"Did what?" I ask, walking to the center of the room.

Fairalisa grabs the bouquet of flowers from her father. She turns to face me and exclaims, "You found the verbena!"

No, I think to myself. Reed found the verbena, which means he's here.

CHAPTER THIRTY-ONE

"OH, KAT! THANK you so much!" Fairalisa squeals.

Verbena, the flowers I asked Reed to find for me. I'd almost forgotten about them.

"Looks like the florist came through after all," I say, working to sound casual.

The bouquet sits in a thatched basket. Fairalisa carries it tucked into the crook of her elbow as she hugs me with her free arm.

"Thank you for everything," she whispers into my ear.

I don't quite have the mental wherewithal to tell Fairalisa that I'm the one who's thankful. Not just for the key that's around my neck, but for her friendship. We're alike in that way, I realize. Neither of us has had a close female friend until I came to the Balley Estate.

"What a lovely thought, dear," Anthond says as he eases his tired legs onto a cushioned high-back chair. "Your mother would be so pleased."

Fairalisa carries the flowers to the light of the window. She buries her face into the petals, breathing in their floral scent. I watch the basket of flowers intently. If Reed delivered those, then surely there's something more tucked into that basket than just verbena stems.

"Kat, leave us. I'd like to have a moment alone with my daughter before the ceremony," Anthond croaks, leaning his cane against a side table.

"Of course. You know what, why don't I take those flowers and get them set up in the dining hall for everyone to see?"

Fairalisa fiddles with the delicate purple petals. "Yes, you're right." She places the basket in my open hands.

"Will you be okay?" I ask, meeting Fairalisa's eyes. She knows what I'm really asking is, *will I see her at the altar in a few moments?*

"I've never felt more like myself," she says, giving me one of those true, genuinely happy smiles that I rarely see in this world.

I give Anthond a quick bow before ducking from the room. Instantly, my energy pulses. The bouquet feels like hot lava in my hands, and I fear that if I drop it, it will burst into flames. I scurry down the steps. The dining hall is flooded with servants placing creamy white plates at each table setting. A maid carefully sets the long candlesticks in each of the golden holders. Leafy green garland runs all along the balcony railing that encompasses the hall.

"Where do you think you're going with that?" Willip asks me, his eyebrows forming a deep *V*.

"The bride would like these displayed. They're in honor of her mother."

Willip's mouth twists in disgust.

"Verbena? She couldn't have chosen something a little more formal…" Willip mumbles under his breath.

"I thought I'd put them on the bride-and-groom table."

"Absolutely not. There's already a floral centerpiece there. You can stick them on the mantle."

Willip waves me away as he runs after a girl tying an uneven bow around the back of one of the chairs. I hear him scold her as I sneak over to the table where Fairalisa and Lawrence will eat their dinner and rest the basket there. Nearby, I spot Quinten's table. It's thick and marble topped, with the face of a lion carved into each of the legs.

Scanning the room, I make sure no one's watching me before digging into the basket. I pull out the bouquet and find the stems have been tied together, a wet rag wrapped around the ends to keep the flowers fresh. Some soggy leaves and loose petals speckle the bottom of the thatched brown basket. I scrunch up my eyebrows in confusion.

Where is it?

Running my hand along the corners and crevices of the basket, my fingers finally touch something hard and smooth. Expecting to find a vile of poison, instead, a wet silver ring sits in my hand.

"This is a mess!" Willip's voice echoes around the cathedral ceiling of the dining hall. He marches down the aisle, between the tables. "That's not how I showed you to do it!"

I shove the flowers back into the basket. Placing the verbena on the fireplace mantel, I slip the ring on my finger and stride from the dining hall. I find a quiet spot in the hallway outside the kitchen. Holding my hand up to a flickering torch, I inspect the ring. It's gaudy with an oval-shaped silver center. There's no gem, just a flat top that looks like it's been pressed with the Warwick brand seal. I run my fingernail along the curly *W*.

A tiny latch sits on the side. *The ring opens*, I realize suddenly, like a locket. Carefully, I flick open the latch and swing the top over. A bowl is poised on my finger with a shimmering clear liquid inside. It reminds me of the consistency of the alcohol my father used to drink. I sniff it and smell nothing. Invisible . . . Odorless . . . Undetectable . . . Reed has delivered on Quinten's poison.

"The Supreme Ruler is here!" one of the maid's shouts from the dining hall.

Quickly, I close the lid on the ring. Pip exits the kitchen, wiping her hands on her smudged apron.

"Want to go watch with me?" she asks.

"I wouldn't miss it," I say.

Pip and I join the commotion in the dining hall. Maids and manservants stand in a huddle by the windows that run alongside the castle wall. Pip bobs her head, trying to get a glimpse of Quinten Warwick. A flush of nerves hits me. Of all the times I've spoken of this man and vowed to kill him, I've never been face-to-face with him before. How can someone who's ruined my life be so excluded from it?

Walking along the path that leads to the back courtyard, an entourage of Warwick soldiers and servants walk together in a mob. They bend around a curve in the path. Past the neatly trimmed bushes, in the midst of the crowd, I spot Quinten's face.

His dry lips are pressed together tightly. Wrinkles crack at the corners of his eyes. What once must have been midnight-black hair is now a stringy mop of gray that starts halfway back on his balding head and covers his neck. The broad shoulders of the infamous battle warrior are shrouded in a fur-trimmed cloak.

"He's not as tall as he looks in the portraits," Pip says.

"The pictures lie," I say.

A young blonde-haired woman hangs on Quinten's arm: Queen Dina, his third wife. I imagine my mother and him once tangled in a torrid affair. Two wretched people playing this country for their own selfish desires. I'd say they deserve each other if it weren't for the terror they'd reign together. Quinten and his soldiers sweep past the windows and disappear into the courtyard.

"Come now! We have work to do!" Willip yells.

The servants groan as they move away from the window.

"Have you finished the pear pudding?" I ask, clutching the ring on my finger.

"Yeah," Pip says. "But it's madness in the kitchen. The Supreme Ruler sent his own chefs over this morning to *help* with the meal." Pip rolls her eyes.

"They're not helping?"

"More like watching our every move. There's even a couple soldiers back there," Pip whispers. "They picked up every jar and spice like it was their kitchen. I went to use the stove and had to work around one of the soldiers. He questioned every single ingredient I put inside that pear pudding."

Pip shakes her head in disbelief. Quinten is vigilant if nothing else. Is he always this way, or is expecting an attack at the wedding?

"I better get back in the kitchen," she says.

"You're not going to watch the ceremony?"

"I wish I could." Pip shrugs her shoulders. "Unfortunately, all these people want to eat. Hey, make sure you come say goodbye to me before you leave with the lady on her honeymoon." Pip then leans toward me and whispers. "I want all the gossip from that trip when you get back."

"Yeah. Okay," I say with a chuckle.

I try to smile back at Pip, but I can't. I won't be here after the wedding. One way or another, I'll be gone. As Pip rushes back to the kitchen, it dawns on me that I may never see her after tonight.

***

A line of ornate carriages parades through the circular driveway. The wedding guests, dressed in suits and gowns fit for a ball, wander into the courtyard and take their seats. I stand with the other servants just outside the castle doors, at the back of the courtyard waiting for the ceremony to begin.

An arbor, nearly overtaken by vines and flowers, is the altar where Fairalisa and Lawrence will exchange their vows. A cleric stands waiting. The guests, their backs to us, patiently sit in their colorful garb. Quinten has the front-row seat. Warwick soldiers flank all sides of the courtyard, their long swords hanging from their belts in warning. I fiddle with the ring on my finger, the shiny silver flashing in the first bit of pure sunlight we've seen in days.

The back doors of the Bradac castle groan as two men pull them open. Ridley and Ohbolina, Lawrence's parents, stand tall at the threshold. In LilyAye tradition, they walk the aisle first, followed by Lawrence, who waits at the arbor for his bride. His hair, smooth and slick, is perfectly combed back, and he wears a deep blue suit, a perfect complement to Fairalisa's dress.

Anthond is next to hobble down the aisle. He takes a seat across the row from the Thatius family.

The musicians pause their soft melody. Silence falls over the audience. My heart seizes. I glance, like everyone else, to the empty space at the castle doorway. It's a dark, shadowed hole. Maybe I misunderstood Fairalisa when I asked if she was okay. Maybe she's not coming. Then, a carol of gasps and exclamations fills the courtyard as Fairalisa emerges from the castle.

Her dainty feet take careful, measured steps as the orchestra plays a romantic tune. Her lace-and-pearl-coated dress is a vision against the bright green lawn and opaque flowers. Her train, so long that three maids spread it out, feathers over the silk runner.

Fairalisa looks like a queen. Her hair is perfectly pinned. The giggle on her lips is one of true happiness. The long vibrato notes of the violin strike something deep within me. My throat tightens. Fairalisa takes Lawrence's hand when she reaches the arbor, and the cleric breaks into his charge.

A wave of emotion washes over me, and I find myself brushing a stray tear from my cheek. *What's the matter with me?* It feels like my best friend is being married off, or perhaps the sister I never had.

The cleric speaks of commitment and trust, love and acceptance. I'm supposed to be murdering the Supreme Ruler within the hour, and all I can think of is Johnny and how much I wish it were he and I standing at that arbor. The thought surprises me, and I'm glad it's contained to my own head.

I'm gripped from head to toe by thoughts of marriage, family, and my future. It's not until Fairalisa and Lawrence are pronounced married and petals are thrown at them as they walk down the aisle together that I finally regain my composure. In a flash, everyone's countenance becomes jubilant.

As the crowd of wedding guests are guided inside, a man catches my attention. He's smartly dressed with soft, blond hair. His eyes light on me. My heart skips a beat. He looks an awful lot like Johnny. The man sweeps inside the castle speedily. I twist my head to follow him as he walks away.

It is Johnny.

Or perhaps it's not him. Is it my sentimental mind playing tricks on me? I shake my head and force myself to focus on the task at hand. The mood shifts from sentimental to celebratory as the musicians play a slew of jolly songs. Quinten is seated atop his platform in the dining hall. The candles are lit. The fire crackles, transforming the naturally cold and hollow room into a warm party.

I stand in the wings, just off to the side from Fairalisa and Lawrence and search for the man who looks like Johnny. After the scallop appetizer, platters of goose, pig, and pheasant are carried out from the kitchen by white-gloved servers. The popping of wine corks mixes with the boisterous conversation. But there's no sign of Johnny.

My chest tightens as my eyes fall to Karla who's sitting at a table with other members of the extended Warwick family. Her stringy hair falls over her bare shoulders. She laughs as she swirls a glass of wine and bobs her foot up and down to the beat of the music. My breath quickens, but I determine to ignore her. I watch the newlyweds *clink* their wine glasses together. I watch the feast unfold, course after course. Most of all, I watch Quinten.

His taster, who sits in his own spot below Quinten, meticulously sniffs and shuffles his food. He picks off pieces of every item on the plate before rolling it around in his mouth and swallowing. Quinten is thorough. He waits a few moments after each tasting, even allowing his food to grow cold, before ingesting it himself.

Warwick soldiers stand in a semicircle behind Quinten and his wife. Many more pace up and down the outskirts of the dining hall, dutifully watching every guest's movements. I glance out the window and see that even more soldiers guard the castle's outer perimeter.

"I'd like to offer a toast," Anthond shouts, tapping his cane against the wooden table. "To the joining of our two families." Anthond raises his glass with a shaky hand.

"Kat!" Fairalisa whispers. She leans toward me, trying to grab my attention. I scurry to her and Lawrence's table as Ridley stands to follow Anthond's toast. Lawrence never looks at me, keeping his eyes pinned to the speakers.

"I'd like to present the pudding next," Fairalisa says.

My heart instantly beats faster. I nod swiftly and discreetly rush through the dining hall. The kitchen, easily three times the size of the one at Anthond's house, is filled to capacity with servants. A burst of heat hits me in the face. Steam and smoke billow from the stove. White-shrouded men and women hustle in and out of the swinging kitchen doors.

The head chef shouts for more onions. A grand six-tiered cake sits in the corner. A man with a handkerchief wrapped around his neck carefully decorates the cake with flowers. Pip carries stacks of dirty dishes over to the wash basin, where three maids scrub and dry.

"It's time for the pear pudding," I tell Pip.

She exhales, wiping sweat from her brow. "Good. I'm ready for this dinner to be over."

Pip takes me to an icebox, where she pulls out a petite gold-trimmed bowl. She removes the tea towel that covers it, revealing a perfectly poached pear sitting atop a pool of creamy custard.

"Here goes nothing," Pip says, handing the bowl to me. "I hope he likes it."

"He'll love it," I say with a smirk.

I place the bowl on a golden tray and carefully ferry it from the kitchen. I duck into the hallway and pause just inside the light of a torch. A maid breezes past me, carrying a goose carcass that's been picked clean. A soldier stands at the end of the hall. He watches me carefully.

Shifting the tray onto my right arm, I pretend to be fixing the hem of my dress but instead click open the ring's latch and tilt my left hand backward into the pudding. The soldier eyes me, but it's too late. The poison already trickles down the pear, mingling inconspicuously with the custard. I slip off the ring and toss it into a nearby potted plant.

In mere seconds, I exit the corridor into the dining hall. I stare down the row of long tables and realize that to deliver this pudding to Quinten, I will have to walk right past Karla. A hot sensation settles on my neck. The tiny markings all over my skin burn. It's not the revelation of my identity that I'm worried about. I doubt Karla could recognize me now. I'm not sure I have the strength to face the woman who's left me scarred in more ways than one.

The tray rattles. I begin to feel dizzy. At the other end of the hall, Fairalisa summons me. I'm reminded of Pip's admonition: *Find your strength.* I step into the row. A juggler stands at the front, entertaining the wedding guests. My hands are sweaty. I fear I'll drop the tray. Raucous applause breaks out as the juggler bows. It causes me to jolt.

Karla lifts her head as I near the end of the row. Our eyes connect. I freeze in place. Instantly I'm zapped back to her bedroom in the Bear Gap House. She's cackling at me, a pointy knife in her hand. Suddenly every cut and poke on my body stings. Then Pip's voice breaks in through the clatter.

Find your strength.

I'm back in the dining hall. Chatter and laughter echoes through the high ceiling. Karla has turned from me. She's now engrossed in a conversation with someone else. I exhale and lower my head as I take the final steps toward Quinten. I set the tray on the taster's table then bow and duck away.

"Thanks, Kat," Fairalisa mouths to me as I slink back against the wall.

I stare directly at Karla, but feel nothing. Relief floods my body. The panic, it's gone. My joy is short lived as I remember that I'm about to poison Quinten Warwick. My instinct is to run from this room as fast as I can, but any movement will look suspicious. It's a slow-acting poison, I remind myself. He won't die for hours. By the time any blame or suspicion is cast, I'll be far from this place. I bob my head to search the back of the hall for Johnny.

Fairalisa stands. "I would like to say something," she says, trying to project her childlike voice. She clears her throat and smooths her wedding dress. She steps out from her table so she's standing in front of everyone.

"When I was a little girl, my daddy always talked about his friend." She smiles as she tilts her head toward Quinten. "I didn't understand at the time, but my daddy's friend was the Supreme Ruler."

Light laughter wafts through the hall.

"Daddy said his friend loved pear pudding and that he would often request it after dinner, or even nibble on it during their council meetings."

This revelation draws a chuckle from Quinten.

"I remember thinking, I really like a person who prioritizes his desserts." Fairalisa giggles as she turns to face Quinten straight on. "So I wanted to thank you sincerely for attending this most important day for Lawrence and me." Fairalisa holds a hand to her heart. "Will you accept this special gift of pear pudding?"

A flood of *awws* spills from the audience. The wedding guests clap as Quinten nods graciously. I clutch my hands together. Fairalisa stands and waits. The taster sniffs the pudding, then takes a spoon and cuts off a hunk of the pear. He chews and swallows. Scooping a mound of custard onto the spoon, the taster holds it up to his mouth but pauses.

He clutches his throat. I freeze. The taster drops the spoon with a clatter against the table. His face burns red. The chair scrapes across the floor with a screech as he struggles to stand. Fairalisa gasps. She looks back at Lawrence in horror. He's on his feet. The soldier next to me draws his sword.

The taster spews vomit onto the nearest table. The

guests cry out, scrambling from their chairs. I shudder back against the wall. The taster falls to his hands and knees, coughing violently. His eyes bulge. He drops to the floor as a convulsion rocks his body. The taster falls still, his eyes bulged open in terror.

CHAPTER THIRTY-TWO

THE TASTER LIES dead in the midst of the wedding feast. Quinten is on his feet. Queen Dina screams as Quinten flips their table forward, tossing hunks of meat and bread pudding onto the floor. The plates shatter into a thousand shards. Lawrence pulls Fairalisa away from the fray.

"You planned this!" Quinten rages, pointing a finger at Anthond. "You planned this whole affair to kill me."

"I did no such thing!" Anthond protests.

"Get him!" Quinten commands.

Anthond stands and staggers toward Quinten's table. "I wouldn't—"

Two soldiers grab each of Anthond's arms. His cane is knocked from his hand.

"Daddy!" Fairalisa cries.

Quinten steps down from his platform and yells, "His daughter too and the chef that made it. I want them all arrested!"

A barrage of soldiers march to the kitchen. The soldier next to me rips Fairalisa from Lawrence's grasp. *Anthond. Fairalisa. Pip.* No . . . My heart pounds faster than a racing horse. This wasn't supposed to happen.

"I had nothing to do with this!" Anthond says defiantly.

Fairalisa screams against the soldier's grasp.

"Let her go!" Lawrence demands.

The wedding guests shuffle and scramble. Chairs scrape across the floor and tip over. A few couples disappear out the back of the hall.

"I've heard what you've been saying about me!" Quinten bellows, approaching a restrained Anthond. He stands toe-to-toe with the old man. "Telling people I don't know how to handle Bear Gap. That I don't know how to handle my own country!"

"Nothing I haven't said to your face," Anthond says. "As your advisor!"

"Take them away!" Quinten yells.

"Not my daughter. Please," Anthond begs.

Quinten returns to his wife, his fur-lined cape trailing behind him. They're encased in the protection of the guards. Anthond yells as he's dragged between the long tables.

"Search the castle!" Quinten commands as he's ushered from the building.

Pandemonium breaks loose. The wedding guests flee as soldiers barrel through the hallways. They swing open doors and turn over tables. Pip is escorted from the kitchen by two soldiers.

"Fairalisa," I croak as she's carried away, flailing.

Lawrence runs after his bride. I follow, searching for a way to help. My hand trembles. It begs for a weapon. The pointed heels of Fairalisa's shoes tear at the lace of her wedding gown as she kicks against her captor. Fairalisa screams as she's hauled out the door.

I tumble into the side lawn after Lawrence. He grapples for Fairalisa. Another soldier approaches and holds Lawrence back. Fairalisa's wails are absorbed into the cool night air. The lamps stationed along the walkway illuminate her being bound and taken away.

I peer through the window, into the dining hall. The servants are corralled together into the middle of the room. Trixie is forced onto her knees. Ronda tries to be in charge, but even she is instructed to kneel.

If I go now, I might be able to make it to the stables without being seen. I stumble backward, distancing myself from Lawrence.

"Tell them to let her go!" Lawrence shouts. He swings around and punches the soldier in the face. They break into a brawl. Lawrence is knocked onto his back. He jumps to his feet and attacks the soldier like a tiger. The soldier draws his sword. In a flash, I recall all the times that Lawrence has saved my life. The soldier raises the sword.

Lawrence is going to get run through.

I dart across the grass, toward the fight, my shackles pulling and tugging at my ankles. I grab the soldier's wrist from behind. He yelps as I twist and pull his arm backward in one swift movement. The sword falls from his hand. I snatch it up just as the soldier turns to me. Lawrence throws another punch at the distracted soldier.

He staggers backward. I lift his sword. It gleams in the flicker of the lamps. Lawrence hits him again. He falls onto the ground. I lunge and drive the sword through the soldier's black, leather vest and into his belly. Slipping the sword from the wound, the blood pools into a black puddle under the dark sky.

Breathing heavily, Lawrence sneers at me. "You did this. It was *you* that tried to poison him, wasn't it?"

I say nothing. Lawrence's face falls into the shadows, and his sinister expression sends chills through my body.

He takes a step toward me. "You're the reason they arrested her!"

"I didn't want her to get hurt. Please believe that."

The gallop of horses draws my attention behind me. More soldiers ride up from the direction of the stables. I drop the sword, tossing it in Lawrence's direction, and decide to take my chances inside.

"You'll pay for this!" Lawrence shouts as I scurry through the door.

The wedding guests have cleared. Servants are still being gathered up. Soldiers march through the halls. I run for the kitchen, hoping to hide there. As I swing open the kitchen door, I bump into a man in a black trench coat.

"Camilla." It's Reed, disguised with a fake mustache and a black hat.

"There's another door," he says, grabbing my wrist.

We run down the corridor and turn left into the library. Our footsteps pad across the rugs that line the long room. Reed pulls me through another silver door. We empty into a dark hallway, which leads to a sitting room. Reed stops suddenly. His hand quavers at his side. A door nearby slams shut.

"How do we get out of here?" I ask urgently.

Reed turns in a circle. "I thought there was an exit over here."

"We have to get to the stables to get Tuor," I say.

Reed stops and stares at the floor. Squeezing his eyes shut, he concentrates.

"Hurry!" I moan.

Reed's eyes flash open. "Why didn't it work?"

"I don't know. You're the one that found it!" I practically shout.

"It wasn't supposed to work that fast," Reed says, biting his lower lip. "He should have taken the poison!"

Two soldiers march through the door we just passed through.

"Come on!" I scream.

We tumble through a door at the end of the sitting room. It leads to a set of steps that we take upstairs. We twist and wind from one dark hallway to another. Reed's hat flies off his head, narrowly missing my face. We lose the soldiers behind us, at least for now. Reed runs the length of a corridor. I struggle to keep up, my shackles rubbing against my ankles.

"Wait," I croak.

Reed barrels ahead. He turns a corner. I pause, leaning my back against the wall. My breath comes quick in my chest. A commotion breaks out at the end of the hallway where Reed just ran. A deep shout echoes in my direction.

"Stop!" one of the men yells.

Reed comes running back toward me, the same two soldiers on his heels. My eyes dart around the hallway. I open one of the doors. Reed and I spill into a bedroom. I slam the door closed. Together, we shove a dresser in front of the door, momentarily barricading the soldiers on the other side.

Reed frantically runs to the window. He flips the latch over and pushes open the glass pane. A burst of cold air floods the room. The soldiers bang on the door. Reed swings his leg over the sill.

"We're twenty feet up," I say. "That's too far to jump."

"Then we climb down," Reed says, frustrated.

How am I going to climb down with these shackles? The dresser skids across the floor as the soldiers manage to push it open slightly.

"Come now!" Reed yells at me as he shifts his other leg out the window.

I reach into my dress to pull out the key to my shackles. The soldiers bang on the door. The dresser moves farther out. I fiddle with the lock on my shackles, struggling to get the key in the hole.

Reed hoists his whole body through the window, dropping himself onto another windowsill, the next story down. My hands shake as I try to get the key in the lock at the back of my ankle. I peer out the window as Reed scales down the side of the wall, onto the ground.

He's leaving without me.

"Camilla!" Reed shouts from the bottom.

The soldiers burst through the barricade. I moan, clutching the key in my hand. I scramble out the window. Wind gusts at my dress. I search for a footing but find none. The soldiers charge after me. I jump, falling like a sack of flour.

My knee buckles as I collide with the ground. I crumple onto my side, twisting in agony. I suck in air. The same knee I injured when I jumped out of my bedroom window now pulses and burns. Reed runs to me. He bares his teeth and glances up at the window. Frustration bubbles at the back of his icy blue eyes.

"We have to go *now!*" he says.

I reach out for Reed, the pain spidering down my leg.

"Come on, Camilla!" Reed growls, tugging on my arm.

"Wait," I mumble, struggling to sit up.

A soldier in the window above us yells instructions to his comrades. Barking echoes into the courtyard where I lay. Soldiers round the corner of the castle. The light beaming from the castle windows forms their shadows on the damp grass.

Reed clutches at my arm as he twists his head back and forth, scanning the yard. He moves to stand.

"Don't leave me!" I cry.

His face floods with agony. "I can't be arrested," he says, shaking his head. "I can't."

Reed stumbles backward. He looks to his right. Soldiers jog toward us. Reed darts through the lawn and disappears into the inky blackness of the night.

"He went that way!" the soldier at the window yells.

The soldiers on the ground chase after Reed. I scuttle backward, out of the light of the window, and hide behind a bush. Anger pulses in my head, but I push the thoughts away. My hand still grips the key to my shackles. I force a steady breath as I painfully shift my feet and push the key into the lock.

Turning the key, the shackles around my ankles pop and release. I tear them off. The skin on my legs is raw and bloody. I shove the key into the lock on the back of my slave collar and rip it off, tossing the silver piece on the ground. I roll my head, reveling in the freedom, and return the key around my neck.

The window above me has grown quiet, but another soldier now searches the courtyard where I'm hiding. My leg throbs. I force myself to my feet, shifting to hide behind a tall, neatly trimmed bush. Scanning the courtyard, I search for an escape. The soldier, sword drawn, inspects every crevice of the courtyard. I can't outrun him, not the way my knee feels.

He draws closer, using his sword to rattle the vegetation. Reaching for the only weapon I have, I take up the shackles in my hands. I grip each end tightly. The soldier's boots squish against the soft earth. My heart pounds. He's inches from me.

His head tilts up. He spots me. Creasing his brows, he raises his sword. I lift the shackles, blocking his blow with the chains. I cry out, pulling his sword down as I twist the chains around the blade. His grip on the hilt is firm.

The soldier slips his sword from the chains with a *clang.* I stumble backward, out into the grassy lawn, needles pricking at my injured knee. The soldier strikes again. I dodge his attack. My knee falters. I dip and almost fall but catch myself. The sword hisses as it swipes through the air. I duck, blocking the blow again with the chains.

I yank on the vise I have around his blade. He grunts, holding tighter to the sword's handle. I lunge toward him. The chain shrieks across the blade until it collides with the hilt. I twist. The soldier grabs my hair with his free hand. Fairalisa's clip shakes loose from my head. I step on the tip of the sword. It falls to the ground.

The soldier jostles me by my hair. I scream out and butt my head into his face. His grip loosens. I drop the chains and snatch the sword. Blood oozes from the soldier's nose. I swing the sword swiftly through the air. The soldier jumps back. I swing again, slicing across his breastplate. I swipe the sword at his leg this time and manage to nick a gash in his thigh.

He falls backward onto the ground. I approach his crumpled body. Power seems to pulse from the sword and course through my arms. My white silk slave dress is now streaked with mud and grass. The soldier clutches the wound on his thigh and twists his face at me in utter confusion.

"Who are *you*?" he asks as I stand over him.

"I'm Camilla," I say before driving the sword through the soldier.

***

The barreling of carriage wheels over the cobblestone street drifts into the courtyard. I scan the grassy plot and find that I'm alone. Shouting still echoes from inside the castle. I snatch my hair clip from ground and pin it back into my tousled locks. Gripping the sword tightly, I tuck it close to my body. I hobble, with a limp, into the backyard. Skirting along the edge of the Bradac property, I furtively glance right and left.

The remnants of the ceremony sit near the castle's flower gardens. The arbor stands in a dark shadow. The flowers that bloomed beautifully a few hours ago are now closed and hiding. Deep voices catch my attention. A line of soldiers guards the castle's back entrance. I duck behind a tree. I still need to get across the yard and down the hill, to the stables, to get to Tuor. My knee is hot and swollen. It throbs as I stand.

I turn around and press my back against the tree. The pain ripples down my leg. I draw a shaky breath and squeeze my eyes closed.

Is it worth it? I'm rattled that the thought has entered my mind, but Anthond, Fairalisa, and Pip have been arrested. Lawrence hates me, and Reed has run away. What is left of this rebellion?

Taking a deep breath, I steady myself. Tuor is waiting. I won't give up on him. A noise rustles in the bushes nearby. My eyes pop open. I gasp as a hand reaches out and grabs me.

CHAPTER THIRTY-THREE

"STAY BACK," A husky voice says.

I'm tugged into a set of warm arms and pulled deeper into the darkness of the decorative trees.

"Get off," I growl, tightening the grip on my sword.

"Shh! Camilla, it's me."

The moonlight casts a glowing beam on a set of broad shoulders and a square jaw that I know well. *My mind wasn't playing tricks on me.* Johnny holds firmly to my upper arms, pressing me close to his chest. He's clean shaven and dressed in a finely trimmed suit. I stare at him, my mouth agape.

"How—?"

"We have to get out of here." Johnny urgently scans the yard. "I saw you limping. I'll carry you." He bends to scoop me up at the knees.

"Hold on. We have to get Tuor," I say.

"I know. He's waiting for us in the stables. Drop the sword. It'll make it easier."

I hesitate, then decide to trust Johnny. I lay the sword on the grass. Johnny picks me up, lifting me into his arms like a baby. The pressure on my knee is instantly relieved. I wrap my hands around Johnny's neck as he swiftly carries me through the trees.

He pauses at the tree line's edge and looks in all directions. Johnny then darts through the intricate rose gardens. He winds noiselessly through the narrow brick paths. Curving around flower beds and bushes, Johnny makes it to the edge of the garden. He bends onto one knee, holding me tighter against his body. His chest heaves in and out, heavy with breath. The stables sit just down the hill from us.

"There could be soldiers down there," I warn.

"They've already searched the stables. Now, they're halting all carriages from leaving through the gate. Hang tight."

Johnny waits until it's clear, then pushes down the hill. The cool air whips past my face. I huddle against the warmth of Johnny's arm. A smattering of abandoned carriages sits outside the stables. Johnny's boots pad onto the wood floor. He moves slowly, peering down the center aisle of the stalls.

A few horses poke their heads out. Johnny whistles quietly. It echoes through the hollow ceiling. Johnny's tune is returned with another whistle. He follows the sound, quietly marching to the end of the barn.

"Tuor?" he whispers.

Johnny's footsteps are slow and measured as he walks down the aisle. A horse whinnies as we pass. Tuor emerges from the very last horse stall. Bits of hay fall from his white pants.

"What happened to you?" he asks quietly when he sees me in Johnny's arms.

"It's just my leg," I say.

Johnny shoves Tuor outside. We scurry into the shadows behind the stables. A mound of hay, taller than me, hides us.

"Put me down," I say.

Johnny sets me carefully on my feet. I nearly trip but steady myself against the barn wall.

"We have to sneak out on foot," Johnny says. "I have a wagon not far from here."

I remove the key from around my neck and beckon Tuor to come closer. I push the key into the lock on Tuor's shackles.

"Where did you get that?" Tuor asks.

"Long story." I cringe as my knee screams at me.

Talking about the kind gesture that Fairalisa did for me right before I had her arrested isn't a conversation I want to have right now. I turn the key and hear the lock loosen with a *click*. Tuor kicks off his shackles. I then remove his collar too.

"How did you sneak into the wedding?" I ask Johnny as I return to standing. "How did you even know we were here?" My brows scrunch in confusion.

Johnny furtively scans the tree-lined property. "I nicked an invitation off a man. Left him tied up in his carriage. I went looking for you before everything started. When I didn't see you inside, I looked for you outside and ended up spotting Tuor at the stables. That's when he told me you two planned to meet here. Then I saw you at the dinner. I almost didn't recognize you." Johnny's attention falls to my face. "After everything went down, we waited for you. I started getting worried, so I decided to look for you while Tuor waited here. That's when I found you limping across the yard."

"But how did you know we were at this wedding?" I ask in desperation.

"Reed told me everything."

My eyes leave Johnny. I stare at the ground. Reed knew that Johnny was in LilyAye and he never told me? *Why?*

"Where is Reed?" Johnny asks.

I shake my head. "Gone."

"We can catch up later," Tuor says. "I want to get out of this place."

"I agree," Johnny says.

"If they're not letting anyone in or out, then how are we going to get past the wall?" I ask.

Johnny rubs his chin. "We'll climb it."

"How?" I protest, thinking of my knee.

"There's a ladder in the stables that leads to the loft," Tuor says. "It should be tall enough to reach the top of the wall."

"Get it," I tell him.

Tuor runs back inside the stable, leaving Johnny and me alone in the dark. I suddenly feel awkward. I lean against the wall to shift my weight off my throbbing knee. Did he get the letter I left with Ralf? He must have. How else would he know I came to LilyAye? I told Johnny I still loved him in that letter.

My stomach flip-flops. Too nervous to ask him if what I suspect is true, I stand in silence, listening to nothing but his breathing and the rustling trees. Johnny looks down at me. I press my lips together as I meet his eyes. Tuor rounds the corner, a thin wooden ladder in his hand. I quickly look away from Johnny.

"Let's go," I say.

Johnny, Tuor, and I make a run for the border of the Bradac estate. I hobble, feeling the sting of my knee with every step. Hidden behind the stables is a wooded area. We slog through the brush until we find the brick wall that encompasses the castle. The barrier is segmented with two columns connected by a curved wall. Tuor places the ladder at the lowest dip in the curve. The bustle of the city barely permeates the dark woods. The Bradac castle glows in the distance.

"Camilla, you go last so you can swing the ladder over to climb down the other side," Johnny says.

I nod. Johnny climbs up first. He stands at the top of the wall before jumping down onto the other side with a thud. Then it's Tuor's turn. As he reaches the top of the wall, shouting bellows through the trees. I whip my head around to see a line of soldiers standing in the light outside the stables.

"Someone ran that way," a man yells.

"Hurry!" I tell Tuor.

The soldiers dive into the woods. Tuor scrambles over the top and jumps off the wall. I step onto the first rung of the ladder. My knee wavers with every step. The soldiers call out to each other as they comb the woods. I climb quickly.

At the top, I sit and swing my legs onto the other side. Tuor and Johnny are just dark figures on the ground.

"There's something up there!" one of the soldiers calls.

I slide the ladder up toward me. The rustling in the woods grows closer. I set the ladder onto the other side of the wall and climb onto the rungs. Skittering down the ladder to the ground, Tuor and Johnny grab me and we dart away. Johnny holds my hand, practically dragging me through the woods.

We empty into the neatly manicured lawn of the estate next door. Running past the Catahli mansion, we connect with the road out front. As my foot hits the sidewalk, my knee twists again. I scream, stumbling to the ground. Johnny swiftly picks me up and holds me in his arms.

"Follow me," he tells Tuor as he breaks into a run.

We cross the road to the other side. The front of the Bradac castle comes into view. It buzzes with flickering torches and pacing soldiers. Johnny ducks into the nearest alley. Connecting with the next parallel street, he runs the length of it until we're past the castle. Johnny whips left onto the road and then scurries into a side alley, until he stops at a flatbed wagon.

Breathing heavily, he sits me on the end of the wagon. Johnny throws off a woolen blanket covering the back of the wagon and tells Tuor and me to lie down.

"Get comfortable," Johnny says. "These are going to be heavy."

He covers us with the blanket and sets filled burlap sacks on top of the blanket. The pressure builds as Johnny nestles the large, clunky bags around us. The air seems to be sucked out from under the blanket. I huddle close to Tuor and listen as Johnny mounts the wagon and urges his horse forward.

We rumble down the cobblestone street. I feel every bump in the road. Johnny whips his horse, and we drive faster. The noise of the city dies away. He pulls us suddenly to a stop.

The Servant's District.

"Where are you heading?" a man asks.

Lantern light pierces the wool blanket. I can feel Tuor's hot breath.

"Just heading home," Johnny says. I feel the wagon shift as he dismounts.

"What's in the bags?" the guard asks.

Johnny clears his throat. "Feed for my horses."

The soldier tugs on one of the sacks. He tries to slide it off my body but stops. The light from his lantern dims.

"You're clear," the soldier says.

Johnny hops back into the driver's seat and we barrel away. We drive for what feels like hours. The night grows cold. Finally, we slow to a trot. The road is no longer cobblestone. It feels like pebbles, or perhaps a rocky dirt road. The wagon curves to the right. Johnny pulls hard on the reins, and we jerk to a stop. He unloads the sacks and lifts the blanket. I suck in a great gulp of air.

A barking dog causes me to jolt. A baby cries in the distance. Johnny helps me slide off the wagon. Turning around, I see the northern wall of the city towering not far behind us. The wagon sits in a muddy plot. Shacks made of sticks, cloth, and random pieces of wood butt up against us on all sides. We're in the LilyAye slums.

Johnny unhooks his horse and ties her up by a dirty water trough. He then throws a sheet over the wagon.

"Come on," he says, placing my arm around his shoulder to help me walk.

I clutch Johnny as he hurriedly takes us to a narrow building, no better built than one of the sheds at the Bear Gap farm. He unlocks the door, which is nothing more than a wooden flap. We enter a dimly lit room. A woman stands quickly.

"Tuor!" she blurts.

Eve rushes to my brother, pushing past me to throw her arms around his neck. Roehana stands in a shadowed corner of the room. I stare at her awkwardly, my mouth hanging open. Two more women sit on a bench against the wall, huddling close to each other, while another man I don't recognize stands with his hands in his pockets.

I look at Johnny and shake my head.

He smirks and says, "Welcome to the rebel safe house."

***

The two women stand reverently as I enter. All eyes fall to me as if I were royalty. Johnny places me on a tattered, stained couch. I wince as he props my foot up on a wobbly stool. A clump of blankets lies on the floor with a thin pillow. Someone's been sleeping in what I assume is the sitting room. Wind whistles through the big cracks in the walls.

"*This* is the rebel safe house?" I ask.

"One of them," the man says, taking a step toward me. He's pudgy and partly bald, and he's nervously holding a floppy hat in his hands. "There are others throughout the city. Quinten's men don't bother in these areas too much. It's the safest place for us. I'm Ron, by the way." He sticks out his hand to shake with me. I accept, touching his clammy hand.

"This is Alice and Esmeralda." Johnny gestures to the two girls.

Alice is young, perhaps just a teenager, with long inky-black hair that's been folded into a tight braid.

"We were servants together," Esmeralda says, pointing to Alice. Esmeralda, a stocky woman with a rectangular frame, keeps her arm protectively around Alice's shoulders as she speaks.

"How did you get out?" I ask.

"It was very difficult," Esmeralda says. "Most don't make it, but I met a rebel sympathizer in the market, and he connected me with Ron who aided us." She glances down at the obvious shackle bruises on my ankles. "We never go anywhere, Alice and me. It's just far too dangerous."

"It's an honor to meet you," Alice says. Her voice is small and mouse like.

"We know all about what you did in Bear Gap. And we're glad you made it back here alive. Sorry this is all we have to offer you." Esmeralda gestures to the ragged house.

Tuor and Eve slink into a chair, holding tightly to each other while Johnny leans against the armrest of the couch I'm sitting on.

Ron fidgets with his hat. "How did he look . . . when he died?"

For a moment, I'm confused, unsure of what he's talking about. Then, I scan the room and realize this modest group of rebels has been waiting here with bated breath to learn the news of the Supreme Ruler's assassination. My heart sinks. I look to Johnny, who squeezes my shoulder for encouragement.

"It didn't work," I admit, hanging my head. My eyes focus on my fiddling fingers.

"What?" Esmeralda bursts out.

"Please tell us you jest," Ron says, his eyes sullen.

"It didn't *work*?" Eve asks. "What does that mean?"

"The poison that Reed gave me acted too quickly. It killed Quinten's taster before Quinten had a chance to eat it. I'm afraid Quinten still lives . . ."

"Oy," Ron says, rubbing the top of his bare head. He stumbles backward and leans against one of the unsteady walls.

Esmeralda tugs Alice closer to her.

"He'll know it was us who tried to kill him," Eve says.

Roehana speaks. "We're in grave danger if the man we tried to murder is still alive."

"Well," Johnny says, "Quinten seems to think it was the wedding host, who tried to poison him. He's had him and the daughter arrested already."

A chill falls over me and I hug my arms close to my chest.

"So are we in danger or not?" Esmeralda asks.

Everyone looks to me for an answer. I open my mouth to speak, but my throat tightens as I think of Pip and Fairalisa.

"You're a part of the rebellion," Johnny says. His steady voice calms me. "You're always going to be in some danger. For now, it's not obvious that Quinten suspects the rebels directly, but that could change. He may exonerate these other people. Someone at the wedding could point the finger at Camilla, or Quinten could just change his mind. We don't know."

"Where's Reed?" Ron asks.

I purse my lips. "I don't know."

"What do you mean you don't know?" Esmeralda asks.

"He just . . . ran away."

From across the room, Eve scoffs. "Ran away. Big surprise."

"Is he coming back?" Esmeralda asks.

I shrug my shoulders. "I don't know."

"What is it that you do know?" Esmeralda asks. "What are we to do now?"

I don't know. I DON'T KNOW!

The questions race through my head faster than a river over a waterfall. Two of my best friends have been arrested, and our leader has abandoned us. What good is there in killing Quinten now if we don't have someone to take his throne? A crashing noise comes from the back of the shack. Despite my injured knee, I jump to my feet.

"What was that?" I whisper. My body is tense, ready to flee.

"It's okay," Johnny says, grabbing my shoulders from behind.

I look at the other rebel members, who seem undisturbed by the noise of a possible intruder. I twist and look Johnny in his face.

He sighs. "I might as well show you. No point in delaying."

I scrunch my eyebrows together. Johnny takes my arm around his shoulders and hobbles me through the shack. It's a crooked maze of oddly shaped rooms and random furniture. Johnny pulls open a door that leads into a rudimentary kitchen. My breath catches in my throat. Two figures are there; one of them, I'm certain, is a ghost.

The words bubble from my lips before I have a chance to stop them.

"I thought you were dead."

CHAPTER THIRTY-FOUR

"IT'S UNFORTUNATE, I know, but I haven't stopped breathing quite yet," Knox says.

Burn scars coat the side of his face and neck from where the lantern erupted on him during the Bear Gap occupation. He sits at a square wooden table that has a crack down the middle.

"Camilla," Mirabelle breathes, covering her mouth with her hands.

She stands over a big empty pot lying on the floor, which I can only assume made the clattering noise a moment ago. A smoking stove warms the room.

"How are you?" Mirabelle asks, clearing her throat. "Are you—are you well?"

Mirabelle's eyes glisten as she takes in my limp and bloody ankles. I stare at the two of them in awe.

"Why are you here?" I demand, looking from Mirabelle to Knox.

"We were worried about you," Mirabelle says.

"I wasn't worried. I knew you could take care of yourself," Knox says gruffly.

"Did you tell them about our plan, about the letter?" I ask Johnny. I nudge out from under his support and steady myself against the wall.

He takes a deep breath. "I thought they deserved to know."

"No. They don't deserve to know anything about me."

"Camilla, please." Mirabelle takes a tentative step toward me.

"You betrayed me, both of you," I say. "You have no place in my life!"

"We're still rebel members," Knox says in a firm voice. I glare at him as he rises from the table. "When Johnny told us about the mission to assassinate Quinten, we wanted to be a part of it, especially since you banned us from the Bear Gap rebellion."

"You have no right to be a part of the rebellion at all," I say, staring down Knox. "How could I, or any of the rebels, ever trust you? You sacrificed Tuor and me to save your own skin when we were just kids. And you colluded with the very man we're trying to kill!"

My pent-up anger spills from my mouth as I recall everything I've wanted to scream at Knox and Mirabelle all summer.

"*Trying* to kill?" Mirabelle looks to Johnny with a worried expression.

"We weren't successful with the assassination," Johnny says.

"Oh, dear . . ." Mirabelle falls into a chair next to the dining table.

"I want you gone," I say with a set jaw. "I want both of you out of this house and out of the rebellion."

Mirabelle's eyes are sympathetic. "Please, Camilla. I've done nothing but apologize for withholding the truth from you. I . . ." Mirabelle's gaze falls to the scratched surface of the table. "I shouldn't have kept you in the dark. It wasn't fair."

Knox rubs at his graying beard. "I'm not leaving this house, and I'm not leaving the rebellion until Quinten is in the ground."

I press my lips together angrily. "How are you even alive?"

Mirabelle looks over at Knox, a glow on her face.

"It was a miracle," Mirabelle says. "He recovered, slowly."

I press a hand to the side of my head and say, "You were on your deathbed when I last saw you."

Knox grunts as he shifts in his chair. "I remember."

"You were lucky, Uncle," Johnny says.

"No," Knox says. He reaches out and takes Mirabelle's hand in his. "I had a woman who wouldn't give up on me."

My eyes widen at the obvious closeness that has grown between Mirabelle and Knox.

"Give them a chance," Johnny says.

I whip my head to face him. "I can't believe you did this. You brought them here knowing what they did to me."

Johnny rubs at the back of his neck. "You should try to make amends."

I let out a sardonic laugh. "You talk as if I'm the one who transgressed. They deceived *me*!"

"Sit down and let's talk," Mirabelle pleads. "We can work this out."

"Never! I'll never forgive you for what you did."

Tears burn at the corners of my eyes. I shoot Knox a disgusted look before hobbling from the kitchen. I tumble through the rooms, bumping into crates and chairs. My sight is blurry with tears.

I find a door and spill into a bedroom with four bed mats on the ground. My breath comes quickly in my lungs. I brush away the tears, willing myself to stop crying. I fall forward against the shack wall. Balling my hand into a fist, I punch the paper-thin wall and let out an agonizing groan.

Knox is back, back from the grave.

The memories from the day flood my mind all at once. How could I fail this badly? Quinten was mere feet from me, and I couldn't kill him. I've come all this way to LilyAye and only managed to put the rebellion at more risk. My body crumples to the floor. I bury my face in my hands and weep.

I sob silently as I think of Fairalisa and Pip. Where are they? What's being done to them? I can't stand the thought of what their fate will be. Reed has abandoned us, and now, Mirabelle and Knox are here. A fire of rage burns in my belly. How could Johnny bring them here? How could he do this to me?

A knock comes at the bedroom door. It's Roehana. She slips into the dark room, carrying a lantern in one hand and her medical box in the other. She watches me carefully.

"I thought I'd take a look at your injuries," Roehana says as she sets the lantern on the floor near me.

I draw a shaky breath as I wipe my cheeks dry. "Sure."

Roehana kneels to my level. I stretch my legs out on one of the bed mats. She lifts the hem of my white slave dress and inspects the raw skin around my legs, where the shackles rubbed.

"It is okay if you'd like to keep crying," Roehana says. "I don't mind."

I sniffle. "There's no point in it. Crying won't fix any of this."

"Perhaps not, but tears are sadness and anger that's been dammed up in your mind. Eventually you have to let it out."

Roehana rises and retrieves a clay wash basin from the other side of the room. She dips a rag into the water and rinses off my wounds. I recoil from the cold water as it stings my skin. Roehana then carefully pats my ankles with a dry towel and dabs them with a healing ointment.

Roehana speaks, breaking the silence. "One thing about being with the rebels, I have lots of opportunities to practice my healing skills."

I laugh in spite of myself.

"I didn't think I'd ever see you again."

Roehana moves her attention to my swollen knee. As she feels around the bone, I have flashbacks to when I first met her.

"I didn't think I'd ever see you again either, but Eve is very clever," Roehana says.

Her fingers press around the side of my knee. I wince, clutching the blankets on the bed mat. I let go of the breath I was holding.

"How did she convince you to come to LilyAye?" I ask quickly.

"She argued with me until I couldn't refute her anymore. At first, I only agreed to get her to the city gates. Then, she managed to trick me inside the walls. Before I knew it, she had me baptized as a rebel. It's incredible what a woman motivated by love will do."

"How did the two of you find Reed?"

"It took a while. We were very careful in asking people for help. It was Eve who decided to start searching in the slums. The poor have the biggest reason to hate their ruler, she said. If there were rebels in the city, we were most likely to find them here." Roehana sits back on her heels. "The bone is not broken. Just sprained. A few days of keeping your weight off it, and you should feel much better."

"Thanks," I say in nearly a whisper. What Roehana doesn't know is that it's not the pain in my knee that's causing me the real agony.

Roehana digs into her medical box and produces a thin roll of fabric. She snuggly wraps the bandages around my knee. "Eve may have gotten me into LilyAye, but I'd still be spending my days on that mountain if it weren't for you. I would have died alone up there." Roehana peeks up at me with her dark eyes. "It was you who taught me not to shut people out."

Roehana holds my gaze. She heard the argument in the kitchen, I realize.

"You don't understand what Knox did," I say.

"No," Roehana admits as she ties off the end of the bandage. "But I've been living with these people for the last few weeks, and I can see plain as day that Johnny, Mirabelle, and even Knox love you a lot."

I exhale through my nose and avoid Roehana's eyes. She latches her box closed.

"Only you can choose to be bitter. No one else controls that," Roehana says. "You should remember who the real enemy is."

Roehana's words ring in my head long after she leaves the bedroom. I could, perhaps, learn to live side by side with Mirabelle and Knox for the sake of the rebellion. Despite myself, I've grown sympathetic toward Mirabelle and the part she played, but Knox? Forgiveness feels a territory away.

Later, I'm instructed by Eve to stay on the bed mat that I plopped onto and get some sleep. I don't fight it. I curl up and make myself as small as possible. The moment I'm alone, the tears begin to fall again.

Something pokes my head. I pull a clip from my hair, the one that Fairalisa gave me on my first day in the Balley house. I clutch it as a sob escapes my lips. I shiver under the thin blankets. My pillow and hair are wet from crying. Guilt wraps around my neck like a constricting snake.

***

When I wake, the events of the previous day are momentarily absent from my memory, but as I blink my eyes open to the morning sun, the horribleness floods back. I'm still holding Fairalisa's hair clip in my hand. Alice, Esmeralda, and Roehana sleep on the floor next to me. I crawl out of bed. The cold fall air bites at my exposed skin. Someone has left a set of clothes out for me along with boots and a fur-lined jacket.

I hobble on my swollen knee as I strip off my bloody slave dress and wash up. I pull on a knit top and a pair of brown riding pants that are too tight on my hips. They have to be Eve's, I reason. Combing out my hair, I pull it back into a low ponytail. It's grown out long enough that I can do that now. A wooden crutch leans against the corner of the room. *Roehana.* I grab it, then don the jacket and limp from the room before anyone else wakes.

Outside, the sun barely peeks over the city wall. The back of the house is just a muddy plot with a tall rickety fence encompassing it. I breathe in the crisp air and search for clarity in the light of day, but find none. Turning around to face the shack, I wonder if this is what the rebellion has become, just a few people crammed into a house so deplorable that a big gust could blow it over? A horse whinny draws my attention to the other side of the plot.

A shed with nothing more than one wall and a roof sits pressed against the back corner of the yard. I walk through the mud to find a few horses tied up. I recognize Eve's horse and Tuor's. It's then that a pure white mare comes into view. *Shae.* I run to her as best as I can on my crutch and bury my face in her mane.

"You made it, girl," I mumble as I stroke her.

I breathe in the tangy hay smell and run my hand along her neck.

"Eve and Roehana brought her here." Johnny stands at the end of the stable. He leans against one of the wooden posts.

"I can't believe it," I say.

Johnny pushes off the post and comes to stand next to me. He pets Shae, and I wonder if he's remembering the same memory that I am, of the day he gave this horse to me.

"They made it to the rebel safe house before us," Johnny says. "I knew when I saw Shae tied up back here, but you weren't anywhere to be found, that something was wrong."

"I thought I'd lost her when I got captured."

I scratch the spot between Shae's eyes.

"I heard it was a tough trip over the mountain," Johnny says.

I'm suddenly aware of how close he's standing to me.

"Tough . . ." I chuckle. "Yeah, it was tough. How did you and . . . Mirabelle and Knox get here?"

"We were able to take the LilyAye Road," Johnny says. "One of our spies reported back about the checkpoints and told us not to stop at any of the inns along the way because many of them had been compromised by Warwick soldiers. So we dressed up as traveling healers selling potions and ointments. It took us a week or so of mostly riding through the woods, but we managed to make it through the city gates."

I nod. An awkward silence settles between us. The city slowly comes awake as the low hum of chatter and carriages grows around us.

"I'm sorry for yelling at you yesterday." I keep my eyes focused on Shae.

Johnny, wide eyed, looks at me. "An apology? I'm mildly shocked."

I roll my eyes. "I'm trying this new thing where I let go of my grudges and stop shutting people out," I say, remembering my conversation with Roehana.

"Does that mean you'll forgive Knox?"

I groan. "I'm not there yet. I only just started this new way of life."

Johnny laughs as he runs his fingers through his thick golden hair. "After I got your letter, I couldn't just leave Bear Gap without telling them. You understand that, right?"

The letter. *My* letter that I left for Johnny, in which I told him I still loved him.

"I know," I say.

"Once Mirabelle learned that you were no longer safely in the Bear Gap House, nothing was going to keep her from following you. And Uncle Knox, you know how he is. He wasn't going to let Mirabelle go by herself." Johnny shakes his head. "Plus, he's always got debts he's trying to pay."

I want to ask Johnny why *he* came to LilyAye. I want to know what he thought when he read my letter, if he feels the same way. I want to ask him who that woman in his house was, but of course, that would mean admitting that I spied on him the night before I left for LilyAye. I look up at Johnny, those very questions resting on my tongue.

"We need to join together again, Camilla," Johnny says suddenly.

"We do?"

"You should have told me yourself that you were coming to LilyAye. I would have come with you. We need to be in this rebellion together."

"I hadn't seen you since we parted ways at your parents' house last spring. How was I to know you still considered yourself a rebel member?"

"Of course I still consider myself a part of this. Bear Gap seemed quiet. I assumed you'd come to me if you needed help."

"Why didn't you ever visit me?"

Shae shifts on her hooves.

"I thought you needed space," Johnny says, shrugging his shoulders. "We'd just broken up. I thought that's what you wanted."

I let out an exasperated sigh. How could Johnny and I be on such different pages?

"Then . . . how did you find my letter?"

Johnny draws breath and rubs the back of his neck. "Ralf came to my house and gave it to me."

I press my lips together. "He wasn't supposed to do that."

"Yeah, I think he felt bad for me. There was this letter sitting on his desk that I wasn't supposed to read unless I came and got it. How was I supposed to know it was there?"

"Ralf is lousy at keeping secrets," I mutter.

"Hey, it doesn't matter," Johnny says, stepping forward and taking both my shoulders in his hands. "It's a good thing he gave it to me, or I would've never known you were here. Camilla, we . . ." Johnny searches for his words. "We did great things when we were together. The rebellion thrived. We have to do that again. We have to work together."

"For the sake of the rebellion?" I clarify.

"Yeah," Johnny says as if it's obvious.

I exhale, realizing that for whatever reason, Johnny is avoiding a discussion that has anything to do with our relationship. His eyes locked on mine and his warm hands on my body send a burst of butterflies through my stomach.

"All right," I say. "For the rebellion."

CHAPTER THIRTY-FIVE

I SIT, BENT forward with my elbows on my knees, staring across the room at Ron. Darkness blankets the outside so thickly that the flickering candles barely light our faces.

"How long are we to wait for him?" Ron asks, adjusting the floppy hat on his head.

"We have no choice," Esmeralda says. "There's nothing to be done until Reed returns."

The sun has set on the rebel safe house five times since I was first brought here. No one has left the house, and there's been no sign of Reed. Tuor sits on the couch, holding hands with Eve, while the rest of the rebels fill in around the tiny sitting room.

"We can't wait here forever," Knox says.

"Well, what is our plan?" Eve asks.

Ron speaks. "There is no plan. That's the problem."

"We can't form a plan until Reed returns!" Esmeralda says, her voice rising.

"Remain calm," Alice whispers to Esmeralda.

A man shouts at his wife in the house next door. She snaps back at him before breaking into tears and stomping away. It sounds as if a piece of furniture is turned over, followed by a baby's cry.

Esmeralda exhales. "The fact remains, we have no chance of following through with the assassination without Reed's help. Can we at least all agree on that?"

I glance around the room and search their faces for a glimmer of inspiration that doesn't involve Reed's direction.

"I don't see a way," Mirabelle says.

"So then, we have to locate Reed. That's our next step." Eve sits with her knees perfectly together and her back straight as a board.

"He could be hurt somewhere," Tuor says. "Or maybe Quinten's found him."

"No." Knox shakes his head. "Quinten's been trying to kill Reed for years. If he'd caught him, we'd have heard about it."

"It has been oddly quiet," Ron says with an agreeable nod.

"What was the last thing Reed said to you?" Johnny asks me.

He stands near the front door, leaning his back against the wall. I shake my head, searching for words.

"He . . . he just said he couldn't be arrested," I say, holding out my empty hands.

"What did he mean exactly?" Esmeralda asks.

I let my back rest against the wooden chair. "We were being chased by soldiers. I fell and hurt my knee. He came to help me but said he couldn't be arrested."

A dog barks in the distance. The shack creaks as a breeze pushes against its fragile boards.

"Look," I say. "I know everyone in this room wants to see Quinten dead and Reed the new Supreme Ruler, but . . . Reed left me to the soldiers. He probably assumes I was arrested. He might think the rebellion is dead. I hate to say it, but Reed might have abandoned us."

"He wouldn't do that," Esmeralda shouts.

"Then, where is he?" Knox asks.

Knox's question places the room in momentary silence.

"He's our leader," Esmeralda says. "He wouldn't just leave us."

Roehana speaks from a shadowed corner. "If I were him, and the person I tried to kill was still alive, I'd be running as far from this place as possible."

"But doesn't Quinten think it was that council member at the wedding who tried to poison him?" Mirabelle asks.

"That's what Quinten said at the wedding, but he might eventually start to suspect the rebels," I say.

"Maybe Reed's just in hiding, waiting for things to blow over," Johnny says.

I stare at Johnny under heavy eyelids. "For five days?"

"We have to try to find him," Eve says firmly. "Whether he's given up on us or not. We can't move forward until we know where he is."

"So how do we find him?" Tuor asks.

Ron speaks. "Camilla, you're the governor killer, what should we do?"

"You were the closest to Reed too," Tuor adds.

A sigh escapes my lips as I meet the gaze of everyone in the room. I bring my hands to my head, clutching at my scalp, searching for a solution. Would

Reed really just abandon us? He always said he needed the rebels to kill his uncle. Knowing how much he wanted Quinten dead, if we were his best chance to make that happen, why would he leave us?

"Where do you think he would have gone?" Johnny asks me.

"I have no idea." The words spill from my mouth.

Eve purses her lips. She taps her fingers furiously against the arm of the couch, the uncertainty obviously irritating her.

"What about the other rebels in the city?" I ask. "Reed told me he had many supporters in LilyAye."

Esmeralda and Ron look to each other.

"We've never met any other rebels," Ron says quietly.

"But you said there were more safe houses in LilyAye."

Ron hesitates. "That's what Reed told us."

"It's for our safety. Reed's always insisted we stay separated in case one of the safe houses was discovered," Esmeralda says.

"So Reed could be at one of these other safe houses?" Roehana asks.

"Yes," Esmeralda says, nodding. "The problem is, we have no idea where any of those houses are."

Silence fills the room. We've hit another dead end.

"I think we should all sleep on this," Mirabelle says. "It's late, and nothing will be accomplished tonight."

Everyone reluctantly agrees to Mirabelle's motherly advice. I rest my head in my hands as the room clears of everyone except Ron, who takes a seat on his makeshift bed. Eve blows out all of the candles except for one.

"Are you gonna be okay?" Ron asks, shoving his pillow behind his back to sit up against the wall.

I raise my head. "As long as I can save everyone I love."

"Hmph. Good luck with that," Ron says.

I bend my knee back and forth a few times before coming to my feet. The pain in my knee is all but gone, and I don't use the crutch anymore. Turns out, Roehana was right. A few days off my feet, and it's better. But every day I've sat around this house doing nothing has been torture.

Walking like a ghost through the shack, I find myself at the doorway of the kitchen. Mirabelle bends next to a wash basin, scrubbing out an old cast-iron pot. She doesn't notice me at first, but as I step into the room, she pauses her work. Her eyes light up at the sight of me.

"Can we talk?" I ask, resting the palm of my hand against the dining table.

The first real words I've spoken to Mirabelle in months hang in the air like a sweet floral scent.

"Of course, dear."

Mirabelle wipes the suds from her hands onto her apron. She takes a seat at the table and I follow, pulling out the chair next to her. My fiddling hands lie stretched out on the wooden surface. I avoid her eyes, searching for the right opening phrase, but there's only one thing I know to say. "I don't know what to do."

Mirabelle looks at me with a sympathetic tilt. "That's okay. We can't know the exactly correct action to take in every situation."

"All of these people are looking to me, and I don't know what to tell them. My whole plan revolved around Reed being here. He said this was his mission.

It was his idea. I didn't think I'd be the one to lead us through this."

"You led the Bear Gap rebels."

"That was different. Bear Gap is like a tiny speck compared to LilyAye."

"You led a rebellion all the same," Mirabelle says.

I connect eyes with Mirabelle. "Some days I don't even care about the rebellion. I just want to save Pip's and Fairalisa's lives and get out of this city unscathed. We're talking about killing *the Supreme Ruler*."

I say the words as if I'm hearing this idea for the first time. I realize how ambitious and ludicrous this plan really is. "You must see that I was mad for thinking I could do this."

"You're not mad. I saw the rebellion when it was nothing but a few hopeful village men. Over the last thirteen years, I've seen it grow."

Silver strands fleck Mirabelle's sandy colored hair, and the wrinkles around her eyes have deepened since I last saw her in Bear Gap.

"I never thought I'd see the day that the rebels occupied Bear Gap, but you did that," Mirabelle continues.

"Maybe the Bear Gap occupation is all I'm capable of."

Mirabelle grunts in understanding. "Perhaps it is. But if that's all you ever accomplish, that's something to be very proud of. Camilla, the rebellion isn't a movement you want to burn bright and then die away. We have to keep working, year after year."

"Year after year? I just want to make it through the next day."

"Remember that you're not alone," Mirabelle says, reaching across the table for my hand.

I take it, needing desperately the reassuring touch of another person. Pip enters my mind as I recall our conversation on the balcony where she offered her friendship to me. She must have realized by now that it was me who poisoned the pudding and framed her for the assassination attempt. I hold back the tears that lately seem ever present.

"I am sorry, Camilla. For everything that happened with Knox."

Pain and guilt cover Mirabelle's face. It's not an expression I can stand to see any longer on the woman who practically raised me.

"You have my forgiveness," I say.

Mirabelle leans forward and pulls me into an embrace. A tear streams down my cheek as I press my face into Mirabelle's soft shoulder.

"And you don't need to speak those words to me ever again," I say, pulling out of our hug. "I've withheld my forgiveness for far too long."

"We will figure this out together, like we have everything else." Mirabelle tightly squeezes my hands. I nod, shouldering a tear from my eye.

"Do you really believe he's abandoned us?" Mirabelle asks cautiously.

"I don't want to believe it, but I'm plagued by this question. Why didn't Reed tell me that you and Knox and Johnny and Eve were all here at the safe house?"

"You didn't know we'd arrived in LilyAye?" Mirabelle asks.

"No. I saw Reed several times while I was being held as a slave, and he never said anything about you."

Mirabelle crinkles her nose. "Maybe he wanted you to stay focused on what you had to do and not be distracted by what was happening here."

It's a fair argument but not one I believe. Knowing that Eve had returned with my horse would have settled me. Perhaps Reed didn't know that, I reason.

"Men do not think the way that we do," Mirabelle says. "And Reed is a very singular minded person."

"I had put quite a lot of trust in Reed and now . . ." I look down at my hands resting on the table.

"What went on between you two?" Mirabelle asks.

"What do you mean?"

Mirabelle hesitates, then says, "How did he convince you to come all this way without telling anybody?"

I furrow my brows, mildly offended by Mirabelle's question. "I wanted to kill Quinten too. It seemed like the obvious next move."

"But everyone I spoke to said you seemed so content in the new Bear Gap."

Somehow, Mirabelle sees directly through me. Although she's been absent from my life for months, her third eye detects that there was something more between Reed and me.

"He told me he cared for me," I admit.

"As more than a friend and rebel member?"

I nod silently.

"Did you believe him?" Mirabelle asks.

"Why wouldn't I? Am I so unlovable?"

"I didn't mean it in that way, dear. I just meant, do you think he really, genuinely cared for you in that way?"

Uncertainty washes over me. Slowly, over the last few days, I've questioned everything about my relationship with Reed. There's hardly one part of it that seems solid and without question.

"I can't say for sure. At the time, I don't think it mattered if it was true or not. I was just so lonely."

"Oh, sweetie," Mirabelle croons.

"Doesn't matter now," I say, leaning back in my chair. "He's not here anymore."

"The rest of us are still willing to fight, and that's what matters," Mirabelle says.

I cock my head as a thought enters into my mind. "How did you find Reed when you arrived in LilyAye?"

"Oh, well, we obviously thought that you and Tuor were with him, but we had no clue where to look for you. We wandered about the city in our disguises for days until we started asking around at the market."

"We found a man there who was naturally suspicious of us, but he turned out to be a rebel informant. He arranged a meeting between us and Reed. When he saw that we were who we said we were, he brought us here and told us the news that you'd been captured and were currently working as a servant in the house of Lawrence's fiancée."

"Would this man at the market know where Reed is now?" I ask.

Mirabelle jumps back in her chair in surprise. "Well, I don't know. Perhaps?"

I rise quickly from my chair.

"Camilla, dear. What are you going to do?" Mirabelle asks.

"Maybe this man can tell us where Reed is hiding. I have to go see him."

"You can't go to the market," Mirabelle says, standing. "It's too dangerous."

"Don't worry. I won't be going alone."

***

"This is what I've got," Esmeralda says, digging two dress dresses out of an old chest in the bedroom. "Alice and I used these when we escaped. We stole them from our master's wife."

She holds up a midnight-blue ball gown with sheer sleeves and diamond embroidery along the neckline.

"Alice's was far too big on her. She kept tripping and ripped the hem, but this one still looks as nice as the day I wore it."

Esmeralda lays the dress reverently in my arms.

"It's beautiful," I say, touching the dress's pillowy skirt. "And I don't even like LilyAye style."

"Only the best for the lady," Esmeralda says sarcastically. "Ron wanted us to burn the dresses in case the house was ever searched, but I insisted on keeping them. I knew they could be useful to the rebellion someday."

"Yeah, I think this will work."

Esmeralda closes the lid on the chest with a *thunk*. "Is it really the best idea for you to go out there? You were just a servant a week ago. Maybe I should be the one to go."

"No." I absentmindedly smooth out the folds of the dress. For a moment, I imagine I'm back in Fairalisa's bedroom, preparing her dinner dress. "I have to do something. I can't wait around here any longer."

***

It wasn't hard to convince Johnny to go on a mission into the city. He's as stir-crazy as me, if not more. We can't hide in this house indefinitely. I have to find out something about Reed. Knox wasn't fully on board with the plan, but that's the one benefit of me taking the position of leader in Reed's absence. I can overrule Knox.

The following day, Eve helps me into Esmeralda's stolen dress. It fits pretty well, albeit a little loosely around the chest, and the hem doesn't quite cover my toes, which is an issue, considering shoes were not one of the items that Esmeralda and Alice stole from their master's wife.

"I can't wear these boots, can I?" I ask. "People will see them."

"You'll have to wear your slave shoes," Eve says as she loops the buttons running up the back of the dress.

I slip on the flat, white shoes I was given on the day I started working at the Balley house. They're now dirty and scuffed from overuse. The neckline on the dress dips into a V shape. My chest feels exposed and in need of something to cover it.

"Can you do something with my hair?" I ask.

"I'll try," Eve says flippantly.

She forces me to sit cross-legged on my bed mat. The fluff of the dress flows all around me. Eve tugs on my tangled mess. The hair clip Fairalisa gave me lies on the floor nearby. I grab it and hold it up to Eve. "Maybe you can use this. It might sell the lie a little better."

Eve grabs it quickly, then suddenly her fingers stop moving. "This is made of crystal. Where did you get it?"

"Fairalisa gave it to me," I say solemnly.

"The woman who you were a lady's maid to?"

"Yeah." I fiddle with my fingers, fully aware of the irony that a mere week ago, I was helping Fairalisa dress and now I'm the one being dolled up.

"What was it like being in one of those houses?" Eve asks, combing out my hair.

"In ways, it was nice. I didn't have to wonder where my next meal was coming from. My own bedroom was bigger than the house I grew up in, and all I had to do was help Fairalisa with whatever she needed."

Eve tugs on a knot in my hair, and I let out a groan as she combs it free.

"I started to like that life," I admit.

"As a servant?" Eve asks with a disgusted tone.

"It was just nice to not have to worry."

Eve pulls back a chunk of my hair and secures it with the clip. "I think that's the best we're going to do."

I stand, adjusting the skirt of the dress so that it lies smoothly around me in a cascade. It feels appropriate to turn around and gaze at myself in an ornate mirror, but there's nothing like that here.

Instead, I run my hands down the tight bodice and take a deep breath. The diamond embroidery along my chest sparkles even in the bedroom's low candlelight. My arms, covered in a delicate sheer fabric, feel lithe and beautiful.

Eve stands back, inspecting me, holding a finger to her chin. She raises her eyebrows and gives me a cheeky expression.

"How do I look?" I ask.

"Well, the neckline is cut far too low to be modest, but . . . you look pretty good."

A compliment of *pretty good* from Eve is nearly unheard of. I take that vote of confidence and walk out to the sitting area, where Johnny and the rest of the rebels are waiting.

"Be careful, dear," Mirabelle says, a deep crease between her eyebrows.

"Good luck to you two," Ron adds.

Johnny, dressed in the same sharp suit he wore to the wedding, bends his arm for me like a gentleman. He has cleanly shaven his face and combed his hair to the side in a debonair swoop. I loop my arm through his as a rush of nerves flutters through my stomach, nerves that have nothing to do with our mission.

"You ready?" Johnny asks.

CHAPTER THIRTY-SIX

AFTER LEAVING THE horse and wagon tied up outside a tavern, Johnny and I walk arm in arm down the streets of LilyAye. The sky is a dull gray. I wear a long matching cape that Esmeralda gave me to keep warm against the drizzly day. Johnny and I don't go directly to the market. We walk first to the wealthy part of town in order to cross through the Servant's District with less suspicion.

"See up there," Johnny whispers, pointing to a guard perched atop one of the towers. "This is the border where they watch you and make sure you're not a slave on the run."

I nod, knowing Johnny has no clue that I'm keenly aware of these towers ever since I was shot down by one of the guards.

"The trick is to look like we belong here," Johnny continues.

Straightening his back, Johnny tugs me forward, down the sidewalk. He launches loudly into a fake story as we walk into a neighborhood akin to Anthond

Balley's. A soldier paces on the ground below the tower. I plaster a broad smile on my face and laugh wildly at his story. Johnny acknowledges the soldier with the tilt of his head. The soldier bows back at him. My heart races as we continue down the sidewalk as if we live there. I wait with bated breath for the sting of the arrow to hit me in my back, but it never comes.

"It pays to be bold." Johnny exhales.

Maroon banners hang from the lampposts with the Warwick crest emblazoned on them. A horse and carriage barrel down the street, the wheels splashing through a puddle. Johnny and I swiftly cross the road. I try to focus on the mission at hand, but find myself enjoying Johnny's closeness, the warmth of his body, and the image of the two of us as a couple.

The dreary weather has left the square of LilyAye quieter than usual. Spray from the fountain bends as the wind catches it. A girl twirling an umbrella near the fountain flirts with a soldier atop a horse. He seems eager for the distraction. Johnny and I take a right and continue toward the market. The canvas tops of the vendor booths come into view.

The tall wooden platform looms ahead. As quiet as the city center is, the slave auction is buzzing. The auctioneer's sharp voice hits my ears and immediately brings me back to when it was me standing on the stage. My chest tightens, and I freeze on the cobblestone street.

"What's wrong?" Johnny mutters as my eyes stay pinned on the fenced-in slaves ahead.

The panic I haven't felt for days begins to creep up my back. Johnny relaxes his arm, taking my hand and squeezing it.

"Hey," he says softly.

I click back to reality. Clearing my throat, I lift my chin and keep walking. Johnny continues to hold my hand as we take the curve in the road. I'm not sure if he's holding my hand to comfort me or to sell the lie that we're a couple, but I don't care.

Freshly purchased slaves are dragged from the pen to various carts and carriages. The screaming and moaning hit me in the pit of my stomach. I keep my eyes straight and force myself not to look. If I get distracted now, I'll never have a chance to fix the mess I've made.

We slip past the auction and into the market. Slaves in their white garb move through the carts and shops like ants in their colonies. A few other wealthy LilyAye residents meander the market as if this were a rainy-day activity for them.

I'm stunned by the plethora laid out before us. The fishmonger has long silvery fish resting on slabs of salt. The apothecary stand must have hundreds of bottles of ointments and herbs. The deep beating of drums echoes through the market. The music mixes with the floral scents of cardamom and basil. A man yells at me to feel his silky fabric and to take it home with me.

"Stay close or they'll suck you in," Johnny says, bending to my ear.

He leads me through a maze of crated chickens. Then the smell of smoke and paprika fills my nose. Barrels of apples, squash, and pumpkins have been nearly picked clean. Many other produce baskets are completely empty, evidence of the change at the Bear Gap farm.

"Every lady in LilyAye will be wearing these," a woman says, her elbows propped up on the countertop and a sheer veil covering her face.

Beaded necklaces and bracelets hang from the posts and knobs inside her stand.

"No thank you," I say as Johnny tugs me deeper into the market.

We curve around the jewelry stand to the back, where another row of tables and booths are filled with merchandise. A few servants haggle with the seller over a set of silver bangles. Johnny and I enter a large tented area. Long poles stick out of the ground with big pieces of canvas drawn across them. The temperature cools as we slip under the shade of the tent, and I pull the cape tighter over my shoulders.

Tables covered in not only jewelry, but trinkets of all kinds, little wooden statues, charms made out of Catahli, even braided horsehair talismans, fill the inside of the tent. Just outside the tent is a wooden building with a sign hanging from the door that says "Hawthorne Jewels." Johnny takes me up the steps and through the creaky door into the shop.

Inside, it's narrow and dark. The windows are dirty with soot. To our right is a set of steps with a dusty railing. Johnny leads me past the steps, to the back of the shop. There sits a work bench with a short man crowned in powdery white hair, wearing a linen apron, standing behind it.

"Welcome," the man says, a pair of tweezers poised in his hands.

"Hawthorne," Johnny says with a nod.

Hawthorne's face lights with understanding. He slowly sets down his tool, his eyes settling on me. "You're looking well, sir. How can I help you?"

Strips of leather hang from the ceiling of the shop. A thick magnifying glass is bent over a ruby gem resting on a black velvet cloth.

"It's okay," Johnny says. "This is Camilla. She's on our side."

Hawthorne adjusts the spectacles on his scrunched face. "Awfully bold of you to show up here in the middle of the day."

Hawthorne places the ruby in a drawstring bag. He cinches it up and hides it under the counter, as if he doesn't trust us. I notice a symbol carved into Hawthorne's work bench. It looks like a W with a slash through it. The marking on Hawthorne's bench is almost identical to the mutilated brand on the inside of my arm. It's a symbol of the rebellion, I realize.

Johnny rests an elbow on the bench and leans forward. "It's important. We're looking for Reed."

Hawthorn's expression turns to concern. "Is he missing?"

"We haven't seen him for almost a week," I say.

"No, no," Hawthorne says. "I haven't seen him in a while."

"Any word about where he might be?" Johnny asks.

The chatter outside, in the market, is muffled against the walls of Hawthorne's shop.

"Last I saw him was when he came here searching for someone to buy poison from." Hawthorne's voice drops. "I found out the day after the Balley wedding that whatever he got didn't work. Makes sense that you can't find him."

Frustrated, Johnny covers his mouth with his hand. This was our only shot, our only idea at finding Reed. I glance at the door of the shop and then shift closer to the bench, my skirt rustling as I move.

"What about anyone else, any other rebels that might know where he is?" I ask.

Slowly shaking his head, Hawthorne says, "Ron and those women are the only other rebels in the city that I personally know."

"But that marking on your bench, surely that represents the LilyAye rebels."

"The only thing that represents is the frustration I feel toward the crown from time-to-time. If someone asks me for help, I help them, but I don't go looking for trouble."

Another dead end.

"Could he have been arrested?" Johnny asks.

"There's been no word of that, but the Supreme Ruler did set an execution date for those people he arrested at the wedding."

"He has?" I ask.

Hawthorne seems surprised by my reaction. "It was announced in the streets this morning. The Supreme Ruler does suspect they had rebel ties which is why I'm surprised to see you here."

"We didn't know," Johnny says.

"What about the people who were arrested at the wedding?" I ask urgently.

"The three of them are to be executed in the square, two days hence."

The three of them: Anthond, Fairalisa, and Pip. My heart sinks. It suddenly feels like hot spiders are making their way up my chest.

"If I were you, I'd lay low for a while," Hawthorne says. "I know I am."

My knees weaken. I grip the bench for support. I feel a tightening in my chest, as if someone were squeezing my heart.

"Is she okay?" Hawthorne asks Johnny.

I stumble down the hallway, placing my hand on the shop door.

"Camilla?" Johnny calls.

Turning the knob, I spill out into the market, under the big tent. The loud chatter of shouting shop owners fills my ears. I rest the palms of my hands against one of the tables and try to catch my breath. My head feels dizzy. A servant girl skirts around me.

"Are you all right?" Johnny asks, placing his arm around my shoulder.

"I don't know if I can do this anymore!" I shout.

"Shhhhh," Johnny croons into my ear.

"They don't deserve to die," I say, looking up at Johnny with wet-rimmed eyes.

He ferries me away from the tent, past Hawthorne's shop, and down a dark alley. Johnny presses my back against the damp wall.

"They weren't even rebels!" I cry, clutching at my chest. "They had nothing to do with it. I'm the one who deserves to be executed."

"It's not your fault that Quinten had them arrested."

"But I'm the one who tried to poison him at Fairalisa's wedding."

Johnny nervously glances down the alley.

"And now, Reed is nowhere to be found and we have no chance of killing Quinten without his help. We have nothing! Three innocent people will die for something that *I* did."

"There's nothing you can do about that now," Johnny says, desperate to calm me down.

"There is something I can do." My voice is sullen. I tilt my head up to look at Johnny's face as a tear streaks down my cheek. "I can turn myself in."

Johnny's face twists in horror. "What are you saying?"

"I can turn myself in to Quinten. Tell him that I'm the one who tried to kill him at the wedding and that the others had no knowledge of it. He'll believe it because of my reputation."

"Are you insane?"

"I see no other way."

"There's always another way." Johnny spreads his arms wide. "There's never just two choices on the table. There's always a third option."

"What possible third option could there be that would save my friends?" I ask.

"We kill Quinten ourselves, without Reed."

"How?" I snap back.

Johnny presses his lips together. "I don't know."

"See!"

"I don't know exactly, but we'll figure it out!" Johnny grabs me by the shoulders. "We'll go back to the safe house, and we'll find a way. I won't let you turn yourself in."

With my breath heavy in my lungs, I let my body slump. I bury my face in my hands. "I don't have it in me anymore."

Johnny shakes me. "I won't let you walk away from me again."

His voice is serious. I drop my hands and ease forward onto Johnny's chest. He wraps his arms around me. "Promise me you won't do this."

I draw a shaky breath and hesitantly say, "I promise."

"Come on. Let's get out of here."

Johnny grabs my hand and pulls me out of the alley. I feel like a petulant child who's being forced to do something against their will. We pause just outside the big tent. I wipe my face dry and force a pleasant expression. Johnny slips his arm around my waist as if to prop me up. My own legs don't feel sufficient.

"We can do this," he whispers to me.

We. My heart aches when he says that word.

"Ah, sir, I know what you're looking for!" a man behind one of the tables calls. "Take a look at our special collection."

"No thank you," Johnny says quickly.

The seller pulls out a shallow box and whips open the lid to display a row of knives.

"Just for you," the seller adds.

"No thank you." Johnny's voice is stern.

"Wait," I say.

I slip out of Johnny's grasp and step forward to inspect the knives. Lying in the box is *my* dagger, the one that Knox gave me. I stare in awe at the short curved blade and the handle that fits so well in my hand. The slavers must have pawned it off with the rest of our belongings. I snatch the dagger out of the box.

"Whoa there," the seller says with a chuckle. "Looks like the lady's the one who's interested."

"Huh, yeah," Johnny says.

What are the chances that I'd find this dagger again? I wonder as I pull off the sheathe and finger the blade. There must be a reason. I'm meant to fight again. Maybe Johnny is right. Together, we've been able to get out of tough spots before. Together, we've done great things.

Together.

My breath steadies. I look up at Johnny and give him a sweet smile.

"I've been thinking of buying a knife for my brother's birthday," I say with a charming lilt.

"Then you've come to the right place!" the man says jovially.

"But I don't know about this one . . . " I muse, placing the cover back on the blade. "Do you have any others back there?"

"Ah yes!" the seller proclaims. "Let me take a look."

The portly man turns his back on us and bends to a cabinet underneath his booth. I slip the dagger into an inside pocket of my cape, loop my arm into Johnny's, and stride away. We take a sharp turn, disappearing into the market.

***

A new energy pulses through me as we bustle the rest of the way through the market and out of the Servant's District. Something about having my dagger back at my side makes me feel invincible.

Esmeralda bombards Johnny and me with questions when we sneak into the safe house. I tell her nothing but announce to everyone that we're having a meeting in an hour. Slipping out of the ball gown, I put on the clothes that I'm actually comfortable in: pants, a loose top, and boots. I secure the dagger to my belt and decide to attach Fairalisa's hair clip to the lapel of my shirt as a reminder.

Outside the bedroom, I instruct Tuor and Johnny to carry the table from the kitchen into the sitting room. This provokes a horrified look from Mirabelle, but I busy her with the task of having drinks and food for everyone. We might be up late, I tell her. I make sure there's a chair for everyone around the table and plenty of candles in case our meeting runs into the night. I even manage to scrounge up some scraps of parchment and a quill with a half-dried inkwell. It'll have to do.

"Are you going to tell us what you found out?" Eve asks, her tongue sharp.

She sits across the table from me, Tuor on one side of her and Roehana on the other. Knox and Mirabelle sit next to Tuor while Johnny is seated next to me. Esmeralda, Alice, and Ron flank me on the other side.

"Did you find Reed?" Ron asks.

"No," I say. "No one knows where he is."

Esmeralda's gaze turns to the floor.

"And in two days, Quinten will execute the people, my friends, who he arrested at the wedding," I add.

"Well, that's good, isn't it?" Esmeralda says. "Not about your friends, but for us. He's not looking for the rebels."

I can't help but glare at Esmeralda.

"Not exactly," Johnny chimes in.

"Quinten thinks Anthond might have been working with the rebels," I say.

"Oh dear," Mirabelle breathes.

"So he will be coming after us?" Eve asks.

"Maybe he's already looking for us. I don't know," I say. "But it doesn't matter. Quinten will always be trying to end the rebellion. We can't sit around and let things happen to us. We have to act first."

"I agree with that," Knox says.

"But what can we do without Reed?" Esmeralda asks.

I stand from my chair and place my fingertips on the table's surface. "We have to move forward without him. The reality is, Reed isn't here, which means I'm leading this rebellion now."

A smile dances on Mirabelle's face.

"Well spoken," Eve says flatly. "But what's your plan?"

"In two days, Quinten plans to execute Anthond, Fairalisa, and Pip for the attempted poisoning." I take a deep breath. "My plan is, we murder Quinten before the execution date."

Tuor, wide eyed, looks at me.

"How?" Eve asks.

"That's why I've brought this table in here and why I've called this meeting. Together, we're going to figure that out."

"That's it. That's all you've got?" Esmeralda asks.

"Hold on a moment. Why would we risk our lives to save one of Quinten's council members?" Ron asks.

"Yeah," Esmeralda agrees. "Why don't we just go into hiding, maybe leave the city, and wait for all of this to blow over?"

Alice reaches up and pulls Esmeralda's arm down. "Because Camilla cares for these people."

Esmeralda scoffs.

"They're right," Roehana says. "It's not a good enough reason."

"Fine. You want a good enough reason?" I roll up the sleeve of my shirt and show everyone the mutilated Warwick brand on my skin.

"I have a set of scars on my back too if you need to see those."

"What's your point?" Esmeralda asks.

"This isn't just about my friends. This is about ending slavery." I let my eyes settle on Esmeralda. "You and Alice barely got out. What about the hundreds of new slaves that are brought into this city in droves every month?"

"I'm not talking about giving up. I'm just saying let's wait a little bit," Esmeralda says.

"What about the mine workers?" Tuor shakes his head. "Or Quinten's work camps? One more day in those places can mean the difference between living and dying."

Knox leans back in his chair. "You're a fool if you don't think Quinten will do everything in his power to claim back Bear Gap and squash the rebellion here. It might not be tonight, but he's coming for us."

"We can't just exist as rebel members," I say. "We're either working for it or letting the rebellion die."

"We all still want Quinten dead, right?" Johnny asks, peering around the table.

Eve smirks as she smooths down her shiny blonde hair. "If I had a ring for every time someone has asked me that question since I left Bear Gap, I'd be rich enough to be the Supreme Ruler myself. Yes, I want him dead, and I want him dead now."

"I'm tired of hiding," Alice says.

Esmeralda furrows her brows. "Okay fine. We'll do this now."

I ease into my seat and pull up the parchment and quill. "The one advantage we have is being on the offensive. Quinten hasn't found us yet. That gives us a chance to play our hand first, so let's make it a good one. Who has an idea?"

I place the tip of the quill to the paper, poised and ready to write, when someone bangs on the door of the rebel safe house.

CHAPTER THIRTY-SEVEN

ALL EYES DART to the splintered front door. Silence hangs like a foul odor in the air. The banging comes again. Barely a thin piece of wood sits between us and the stranger on the other side. Ron slowly rises from the table as he removes his hat.

"What should we do?" Roehana whispers.

"Remember the plan," Ron says slowly. "Everyone quietly move to your hiding places. I'll answer the door."

The stranger knocks again, a deep banging that feels like it's going to push over the shack.

"Hurry!" Ron urges.

I stand carefully. Pushing my chair back, it makes a tiny screeching noise as the legs rub against the floor. Johnny places a hand on my lower back to direct me out of the room, but before I can take a step, the knob rattles. I pause and turn back to the door. Someone is turning the lock. The stranger has a key, I realize with horror. The knob turns. I whip out my dagger.

The door swings open as Johnny pulls a sword from his belt. A caped man emerges from the darkness.

He steps into the house. The candlelight plays at the edges of his hood. Mirabelle lets out a gasp. The caped man is trailed by two other men I instantly recognize: Lawrence and his father, Captain Ridley Thatius.

"You're back," Esmeralda says as the caped man removes his hood, revealing Reed's gaunt yet stern expression.

I stagger backward, my knife poised and ready. My mind twists to try and understand why these three people would be in the same company. Ridley, dressed in his captain's military uniform, politely closes the door behind him as if he'd simply been invited to dinner.

"What are *you* doing here?" Tuor's eyes are pinned on Lawrence.

Lawrence's brows are pinched in a smoldering, angry expression. He hangs back behind his father.

"We're here to help you," Ridley says coolly.

The blazing Warwick brand on Ridley's chest sticks out, putting all the rebels on edge.

"Who are these other people?" Esmeralda asks as she eyes Ridley and Lawrence.

"They're with me," Reed says.

He removes his cloak, tosses it onto the back of a chair, and plops down at the table as if he were a child being told to sit and obey.

"Are you all right?" Alice asks Reed.

She meekly approaches him. Reed's hair is disheveled, and he's wearing the same clothes he was the night he ran away from me.

"I'm fine," Reed snaps.

"What's going on?" Ron asks, his body visibly tense.

410

Ridley's back is straight, his expression arrogant. "My name is Captain Ridley Thatius. This is my son, Lawrence Thatius, and I assume you're all familiar with Reed." Ridley removes his leather gloves. "You can all put your weapons down. There's no need for that."

"I'll put my weapon down when you explain what you're doing here," Johnny says.

"He means you no harm," Reed says nonchalantly.

"How do we know that?" Eve asks, her nose wrinkled.

"Because I said so," Reed growls.

"Please, everyone, return to your seats," Ridley says. "Allow me to explain my presence tonight."

"I prefer to stand," Knox retorts.

Ridley holds a hand to the breast of his jacket. "Suit yourself."

I cautiously ease back into my seat along with the rest of the rebels. Johnny keeps his sword at his side. Lawrence remains in the corner of the room with his arms crossed.

"Where have you been since the wedding?" Johnny asks, staring across the table at Reed.

He returns Johnny's look with an icy gaze. "I've been trying not to get arrested."

"I'll do the talking for now," Ridley says, placing a hand on Reed's shoulder. "Your leader has been hiding out for the last few days."

Ridley walks to the edge of the table and inspects each of us, one by one.

"What are you doing here?" I ask, annoyed.

"The simple answer?" Ridley asks. "Like all of you, Quinten Warwick is not my ruler."

Eve asks, "Then who is?"

The captain's eyes settle on me. "Do you remember what I said to you in Bear Gap when I came to retrieve my son?"

I whirl back my memory to a year ago. After we rescued Tuor from the execution block, we all hid at Johnny's cabin, Lawrence included. Ridley found us there. I thought he'd come to turn us all in to Quinten, but he said all he wanted was to return Lawrence home to LilyAye.

"You said you served a different Warwick," I say.

Understanding floods me as I turn my gaze to Reed—Reed *Warwick*.

"You wish to see Reed as Supreme Ruler?" I ask.

"Why are you so surprised?" Ridley asks.

His boots make a hollow, clicking sound as he walks across the room and stands behind Reed. "Quinten's brother was as insane as him, if not worse. Reed is a logical choice. More convenient, he's technically next in line to inherit the Warwick wealth as soon as Quinten dies."

"So this is why you've never had me arrested those times you've seen me?" I ask, remembering our encounter at his house a few weeks ago. "You weren't really loyal to Quinten."

"Although I had hoped it wouldn't come to this, I knew I might need you and the rebels someday," Ridley says.

"But you sit on Quinten's council," Tuor says.

Ridley lets out a condescending chuckle as if what Tuor's just said is the most ignorant thing Ridley's ever heard. "I've made a good career for myself climbing the ranks in the Warwick Militia. I owe a lot to Quinten, but just because I advise him on military strategy doesn't mean I bow the knee willingly."

A long sword hangs from Ridley's belt. The handle is an ornate gold-plated design. He rests his hand comfortably over the hilt. "Each of you thinks you want Quinten cut down more than the next man, but I promise, I've been anticipating Quinten's demise far longer than any of you."

"How can that be?" Johnny asks. "How can you serve someone for so long and be so disloyal?"

"I've spent years being his whipping boy and taking his harsh criticism," Ridley says. "Which was never much of a problem. I can work for a man and not care for him personally, but in the last few years, he's slowly dismantled this country. The slave trade has gotten completely out of hand. It's not being regulated anymore. He's distracted, erratic." Ridley draws a deep breath. "And the events of my son's wedding didn't earn him any of my esteem."

"He had your daughter-in-law arrested at her own nuptials," Lawrence says through gritted teeth.

"Yes, son," Ridley says in a calming voice. "The events that took place at the wedding are unfortunate. I know we all hoped Quinten wouldn't be a problem anymore after that night."

"Except for *me*," Lawrence says in a disgusted voice. He taps the tips of his fingers into his chest. "I didn't know anything of this coup, or treason toward the crown. My own father!"

Lawrence glares at the captain from the shadowy corner.

"You're one to talk of honesty and loyalty," Tuor mumbles.

"What does that mean?" Lawrence's eyes flash.

"You've betrayed the rebellion more than once!"

Lawrence marches toward the table, stepping into the light. "That was because my father was pressuring me into family duty, and now I learn it was all a lie."

Tuor jumps to his feet and points a skinny finger at his once best friend. "You said you hated LilyAye. You hated your father. You were willing to do anything to get out of here, yet somehow you found yourself right back in the life you ran away from. You turned your back on the rebellion!'

"Gentlemen," Thatius warns.

"I was *trying* to do the right thing," Lawrence says.

"You chose Quinten over us," I say.

"You're a traitor," Tuor snaps back.

"Tuor . . ." Eve says.

Her face is a sheen of horror as she looks up at him. Like her, I've never seen my brother speak so harshly.

"And now you want to come back with us? Make up your mind who you are." Tuor's lips quiver. He stares at Lawrence as he drops back into his seat.

"I'm not with the rebels," Lawrence spits. "I'm just here to save Fairalisa's life."

"Gentlemen, please." Ridley places his arm across Lawrence's chest, gently nudging him away from the table. "I know my secret motives have caused disharmony with my son and have garnered confusion from some of you. My commitment to appear devoted to Quinten Warwick was deep-rooted. Not even my wife knows my true allegiance."

"Are you saying you're on the rebels' side?" I ask, scrunching my eyebrows together.

"I wouldn't say that. This is more of a 'your enemy is my enemy' sort of situation," Ridley says. "I want to help you assassinate Quinten."

"We're supposed to just fall in line and trust you?" Knox asks.

"*I* trust him," Reed says. "You will all trust Captain Thatius because I do."

"Reed and I are allies," Ridley adds.

Allies?

"Thatius swore me to secrecy," Reed says. "You understand."

"Then, we're to join forces with you?" Ron asks, glancing at Reed for confirmation.

"That would be my desire," Ridley says. He clasps his hands together in front of him.

"Wait," I blurt out. "I saw Reed punch you and spit in your face when we captured you in Bear Gap."

"It was an act," Reed admits.

"I was very delicately playing both sides. I couldn't appear to not be fighting for Quinten, but I was also angling for Reed," Captain Thatius says.

"So . . ." Mirabelle's voice is nearly a whisper. "We never really won Bear Gap? You allowed the rebels to take over?"

Thatius tilts his head from side to side as he ponders his answer.

"Is that true?" I ask.

"It was a bit more complicated than that," Ridley says. "There were many elements of that battle that I had no control over, but I did allow myself and Lawrence to be captured so that the rebels could take over the territory."

Lawrence scowls. "Are you serious?"

Dropping my dagger on the table, I set my face in my hands and groan. The one accomplishment I'd grown proud of has turned out to be a lie.

"Did you know of Thatius's plan?" Knox asks Reed. He sets his foot on the seat of his chair and lurches forward.

Reed purses his lips. "I knew some of it."

"What about you?" I ask Lawrence, my face twisted in disgust.

"Like usual, I wasn't privy to anything," Lawrence growls. "I trusted my father, obeyed the crown like he told me to, only to learn he's a traitor to Quinten."

"We mustn't become distracted with past events," Ridley says, his voice growing firm for the first time in the conversation. "Our focus is singular: killing Quinten Warwick."

Reed leans forward, placing his elbows on the table. His lithe arms are exposed as he runs his fingers through his inky-black hair.

"My uncle is still convinced of Thatius's loyalty, even to this day," Reed says.

"Even after the wedding?" Johnny asks.

"Quinten and Anthond had been arguing over the handling of the rebels for months," Ridley says. "So Quinten believes that Anthond became jealous and enraged enough to recruit his daughter to try and poison him. He told me this the day after the wedding, and the two of us lamented over the treasonous union of our families. It is unfortunate that these people have been blamed for a rebel move, but it works to our advantage."

Lawrence seethes as his father speaks. "Just a little sacrifice of my Fairalisa's life."

Ridley draws breath as he tilts his head toward Lawrence. "You should be pleased it's not you in the dungeons." He turns and faces the rest of us. "Quinten and I had a slight falling out after the Bear Gap incident, but I've regained his favor and retained my position on his council. Quinten trusts me explicitly. I've served him his entire reign, and I've made certain that Lawrence appears just as loyal."

Reed speaks. "He doesn't suspect me for the poisoning either."

"Fine, you want to join forces with us," I say to Ridley. "So how exactly does that work?"

"In case it isn't obvious," Ridley says as he approaches the table, "I had no intentions of revealing my true allegiance to the lot of you, but with the failure at the wedding, it's time we deal with this before Quinten turns a suspicious eye toward me."

"We have a proposition," Reed says.

"Reed is rightfully next in line to be Supreme Ruler," Ridley says. "If Quinten were to die tonight of a fever, all of his wealth would pass to the next male heir, who is Reed. The problem dwells in the manner of Quinten's death. The council carries out the wishes of Quinten's will. If the other council members suspect that Reed has anything to do with his death, there's a provision in Quinten's will that would negate Reed's claim on the throne."

"I'd prefer to kill him myself, but we can't do it that way," Reed says, drumming his fingers on the surface of the table.

"Why not?" Esmeralda asks.

Turning slightly toward Esmeralda, Ridley says, "Reed could assassinate him and attempt to usurp the throne, but that would lead to a war. We'd likely have to fight for years to create stability in Elmyra. The cleanest way to take care of this is for Quinten to either die of something that looks like natural causes, which we already failed at with the poison, or for the blame to be clearly placed on someone else besides Reed."

Silence settles across the table. Ron looks to me. I look over at Tuor and furrow my brows.

"You want to intentionally blame Quinten's death on the rebels?" Knox asks. Still standing, he lumbers into the candlelight. Knox's dim eyes watch Ridley with uncertainty.

"We'd seem a fool to point the blame at ourselves," Roehana says.

"Is Knox right?" I ask Ridley.

"The council only needs to be convinced it was the rebels who killed their Supreme Ruler. Once I'm on the throne, it won't matter," Reed says.

"How would we even manage that?" Esmeralda asks, her forehead creased in concern.

Ridley pulls a chair up to the table and takes a seat. He sits soldier-like with his torso straight as an arrow. "It's quite simple. I have one of Quinten's guards on my salary. He'll give us access to the castle."

"Then why don't you kill him yourself?" Eve asks, a bite in her tone.

Ridley laughs derisively. "I need to be a part of the council that allows Reed to become Supreme Ruler. If they suspect I killed him, then they'll have to replace me on the council before he's given the crown. That could take months. Again, it's too messy."

"The rebels are well known after the Bear Gap occupation," Reed says. His voice sounds exhausted. "The people of Elmyra will believe it."

"I'll have a soldier lead you into the castle," Ridley says. "You'll locate Quinten's bedroom. You kill him. Then allow yourselves to be caught and arrested. The council will receive the news that there was a breach and that the rebels assassinated the Supreme Ruler. In short order, we'll call upon Reed to take the throne. He'll have you released from the dungeons, and you'll be safe. It's simple."

"I don't want to be arrested," Alice says, her voice tiny.

"Do not worry. Only a few rebels need be sacrificed," Ridley says.

"This is madness," Eve says. "How do we know you'd be able to have us released?"

"I'll be Supreme Ruler," Reed says.

"I don't like this plan," Knox says.

"If you can get us into the castle, why can't you provide a safe escape?" Johnny asks.

"An arrest will make the blame more cut and dry," Ridley says. "We'll catch you with literal blood on your hands. There will be no question as to who killed him. With an obvious culprit, our plan comes to fruition quicker."

"There has to be another way," Mirabelle says.

"Not if we're going to save Fairalisa in time," Lawrence says.

"Yes," Ridley agrees. "They're to be put to death in just a few days. The assassination of the Supreme Ruler would be enough to put their execution on hold until Reed is on the throne."

"I will make sure that they, along with any other rebels, are released from the dungeons once I'm Supreme Ruler," Reed says.

"You *will* do this," Lawrence says, looking directly at me. "If Fairalisa dies, it's on you."

Ridley clasps his hands together and rests them on the table. "We have the plan. We have the opportunity.

All that remains is choosing our marks," Ridley says, glancing around the table.

"You want to know who's willing to sneak into the castle, murder Quinten, and then allow themselves to be arrested and placed on trial?" Eve asks.

"Precisely," Ridley says.

Reed glances around the table, a look of anticipation on his face. I think of Fairalisa and Pip, the only female friends I've ever really had. They'll face the execution block in a few days because of me. Alice cowers behind Esmeralda. Mirabelle presses her lips together and silently shakes her head.

"I'll do it," I say.

CHAPTER THIRTY-EIGHT

"NOW, HOLD ON," Mirabelle protests, shooting me a worried look. "Let's discuss this first."

Johnny's head twists in my direction.

Eve speaks. "If we're going to do something this mad, we need to take our time and choose the right people."

"I am the right person," I say solemnly. "I have to go make this right for Fairalisa and Pip."

"I agree with Camilla," Ridley says. "Her name has been in the news often. If the council were to learn that the famous rebel member, Camilla Crim, managed to kill their Supreme Ruler, I don't think there would be a lot of surprise."

"There'd be less of an uproar from the people when I'm crowned Supreme Ruler," Reed adds.

Roehana leans back in her chair, her arms crossed over her chest. "It sounds like the two of you have already chosen Camilla to do the job," she says, her tone suspicious.

Ridley calmly turns to Roehana. "I don't need to be deceitful with you." His chair squeaks as he faces the group again. "Reed and I have discussed the possibility of Camilla being the one to kill Quinten."

Mirabelle whimpers.

Reed's crystal-blue eyes connect with mine. "Only because we think the council would believe it without question."

"She's not going in there alone," Tuor says. "I'm going with her."

"No, you're not!" Eve snaps, clutching Tuor's arm.

Tuor furtively glances from me to Eve. "She's my sister."

"I only just got you back a few days ago!" Eve hisses.

"It's all right. I don't want you to come," I say. "I want you to stay here with the other rebels."

My words rescue Tuor from having to choose between his sister and the woman he loves. Tuor purses his lips in disapproval, but he doesn't fight me.

"I'll go too." Johnny slips his arm under the table and wraps his callused hand around mine. My eyes widen in surprise.

"I'm not going to hang around here while Camilla walks into a snake pit," he says.

Knox grunts as he steps forward and presses his knuckles onto the table. "By Thatius's logic, then I should also be there. I'm a known rebel."

"No," I say immediately. "You're not coming."

Ridley draws breath and looks Knox up and down. "Knox Duffy is a name we've heard around here. Sure." He waves his hand nonchalantly.

I stand suddenly, slipping my hand from Johnny's grasp. "No. I can't trust you, and I don't want someone by my side who I can't trust."

Knox used to look at me with guilty eyes, but right now his expression is nothing like that. His face wears resolve. He stares at me with an unwavering gaze.

"I'm coming. I have to make things right too," Knox says, rubbing the spot on his chest where my mother damaged his heart.

We stare at each other, a battle of wills playing out in front of Thatius and the rebels.

"You enjoy torturing me, don't you?" I growl.

"I'm not playing into your girlish drama anymore," Knox says, taking a seat next to Mirabelle. "I'm the best person to come along with you and Johnny. It benefits the rebellion."

Heat rises in my cheeks. I tightly squeeze the handle of my dagger.

"I'd be fine to send somebody else with you besides Knox," Ridley says. "But I don't think any of the other rebels are volunteering."

I look hopefully around the table, at the others.

Esmeralda speaks. "These people you speak of, Pip and Fairalisa, mean nothing to us. I'd like to help any way I can to see Quinten dethroned, but I feel no rush for such a theatrical plan."

"I'm sorry," Ron says. "I agree with her."

My teeth grind together as I try to maintain my composure. I stare darts at Knox.

"Well then," Ridley says, "it sounds like we have this figured out."

I angrily stick the tip of my knife into the table before easing back into my seat.

"Camilla, Knox, Johnny, you three will meet me at the lower gates tonight, an hour after sunset," Ridley says. "That's about the time when Quinten is making his way into his bed chambers."

"Tonight?" Tuor asks, rubbing the side of his head nervously.

"We can't wait any longer," Reed says.

Ridley stands swiftly. "It has to be tonight, I'm afraid. We must take the Supreme Ruler off guard, catch him unawares." Ridley politely pushes his chair up to the table's edge and adjusts the lapels of his jacket. "Plus, I've played my hand by exposing my true allegiance to all of you. I'm on dangerous ground until Quinten is dead."

"What will the rest of us do tonight?" Eve asks.

"We'll stay here," Reed says. "We won't do anything to draw attention to ourselves, and we'll be fine."

"As long as you lie low until Reed is crowned Supreme Ruler, you'll be safe," Ridley says. He tugs on his leather gloves. "I must be going. My wife expects me promptly for dinner."

Captain Thatius gives us a curt nod before him and Lawrence duck outside into the waning evening sun. The autumn wind beats against the shack walls. A somber mood falls over the table. In mere hours, I will be determining the fate of the rebels and of all Elmyra.

Our meeting breaks up and most of the rebels disperse, except for Reed, Johnny, Knox, and me. We go over the plan several times. Reed assures us repeatedly that we'll be kept safe once he's on the throne. It's only temporary discomfort, he tells us. The continual discussion of being arrested and placed in the LilyAye dungeons makes me extremely grateful that I don't have to survive a night of sleep with this mission's heaviness on my mind.

Still, I manage to agonize over the plan. I consider if this is truly our only option, but after running every possible scenario through my head, I find no other solution. Getting to Quinten is nearly impossible without Reed and Captain Thatius' help.

A raid on the dungeons to rescue Pip and Fairalisa is also farfetched. The dungeons beneath the Warwick castle are so heavily fortified that most who are brought there never see the light of day again. Assuming we could even make it into the castle before getting to the dungeons, which would put us up against hundreds of soldiers. The rebellion simply doesn't have the numbers to match.

So, yes, this is what we must do. This is what *I* must do. I'll sacrifice myself on the altar of Ridley's plan in order to save our country. I try to let the other thoughts swirling around in my mind fall away and focus on this one singular act: killing Quinten.

***

"We're all clear on the plan?" Knox asks as our meeting draws to a close.

Johnny and I nod then the four of us rise from the table.

"Camilla," Reed says in a deep tone. "I'd like to speak with you privately."

Reed watches as Knox and Johnny exit the sitting room.

"What do you want?" I ask.

I lean my hip against the edge of the table and study Reed. His disheveled appearance from days on the run seem to have no hinderance on Reed's cocky attitude.

"Thank you for doing this mission. You're truly more integral than you realize."

"That is what you wanted to speak to me about?" I spit. "You left me injured and exposed, surrounded by soldiers."

"That night at the Bradac castle, I acted out of fear which is unbecoming of a Supreme Ruler."

"I'd agree with that." I cross my arms over my chest.

"You have no idea how grateful I am that you weren't arrested that night."

An awkward silence settles between us

"Is that all you have to say to me?" I ask.

Reed's dark eyebrows cinch together. "What more could I say?"

Staring at Reed, I wait for him to explain himself further. I wait for true remorse to light on his face. I wait for him to give me a real apology. But it's in this moment that I realize I'll never get any of that from him.

"Once Quinten is dead, I'll be going back to Bear Gap," I say before walking swiftly past Reed.

"Camilla," he calls. I turn around to face him once again. "Thanks for all you've done to get me here." He wears a sly smile.

I give Reed a look of half disgust and half confusion before slipping from the room. I'm not sacrificing myself tonight for him. I'm doing it to save Fairalisa and Pip. If we had more time and more options, maybe I'd try to angle for someone else to sit on that throne, but right now, Reed is the best we can do.

A nervous energy now pulses through me as we prepare for the raid. Knox spends the evening sharpening his knives. Johnny tends to our horses. I dress in dark pants and a black tunic. Pulling my hair back into a low ponytail, I still wear Fairalisa's hair clip. If nothing more, it's a reminder of why I'm doing this.

I lace up my boots on the couch as Tuor enters the sitting room. He slides in next to me.

"I don't like that we're doing it this way." His hand is pressed against the side of his head, nervously pulling at his curls. I tie the string laces into a knot before leaning against the back of the couch.

"I know. I don't like it either, but what other choice do we have?"

Tuor rubs at his head. "I should be coming with you."

"No, you shouldn't. Eve is right. You need to stay here—with her."

A smirk spreads across Tuor's lips. "Did you just admit that Eve was *right*?"

"Don't tell her I said that."

Tuor claps his hands together and lets out a lighthearted laugh.

"That's enough," I say as I punch Tuor in the shoulder.

"Okay, okay," he chuckles.

"Stay here. Stay with the rest of the rebels, and make sure everyone is safe."

"What about our pact to stick together?"

My eyes fall to my hands in my lap. "You have to put what's important first in your life. For you, that's Eve. She's your world now." I lift my gaze to Tuor's face. "I used to say that all I wanted was for you to be safe and with me. At some point, I might have to settle for just the safe part."

Tuor puts his hand on my shoulder and playfully gives me a shake. "Do you really think this plan will work?" Tuor's tone turns serious.

"I'll spend some time in the dungeons, and then we'll be reunited, and it'll be different. All of Elmyra will be different. This is what we've been working toward for so long. It's nearly here."

Tuor nods. "Promise you'll come back."

"I'll always come back."

Footsteps echo through the shack. Johnny swings his head around the opening into the sitting room. "It's time to saddle up."

***

As Johnny and I walk through the backyard, to the stables, it feels like the day I left Bear Gap to come to LilyAye. I sense the impending doom of the task before me.

"Knox will be along soon," Johnny says, carrying a torch through the darkness.

My heart skips a beat at the thought of Johnny and me being alone. A flutter of dead leaves falls to the ground as a chilly breeze blows past us. Johnny sets the torch in the sconce on the stable wall. He picks up his horse's saddle and sets it on her back.

"I calculated that it's a twenty-minute ride to the castle gates from here, so we shouldn't delay much longer," Johnny says.

I glance across the stable at Johnny as I secure Shea's saddle. "You know, you don't have to do this with me."

Johnny tightens the buckles on his saddle. He laughs lightly. "And let you go alone with Knox?"

I pause, fiddling with the leather strap of Shae's reins. I've been holding back from Johnny since I

428

arrived at the rebel safe house, but in a few moments, we'll be riding toward Quinten's castle. I don't know exactly what will happen there, but whatever happens, it will change our lives forever.

"Why are you really coming along?" I ask

Johnny cocks his head, confused. "To help the rebellion. To make sure you get out of this alive."

Something about my conversation with Reed has filled me with boldness. I walk around Shae to Johnny's horse. His back is bent, and he's lifting his horse's leg to inspect her shoe.

"Why did you hold my hand under the table today?" I blurt out.

Johnny lets his horse's leg drop. He slowly comes to standing and exhales.

"Yeah, I'm sorry about that," he says, resting a hand on his horse's back.

"Why are you sorry?" I scrunch up my eyebrows.

"It wasn't appropriate. I know that's not what you want."

I shake my head, perplexed. "How do you know that's not what I want? I wrote in my letter that I . . . that I still loved you."

The words spill from my lips, and I hardly believe that I've just said them out loud. For a moment, I forget to breathe.

"Well, yeah, but Reed told me that you two had struck up a relationship during your trip here."

My chest tightens. "He what? He told you that? When?"

"When we first arrived in LilyAye. He approached me and wanted me to know that you were his," Johnny says, scratching the blond stubble on his cheek.

I scoff and scrunch up my face in disgust. Why would the man who treated me so poorly as his girlfriend demand that I was his?

Johnny's voice drops. "And since you wrote that letter before you left, I assumed your heart had changed."

"I can't believe he told you that," I growl.

"Is it true?"

I glance down at my fingers as they nervously twist together. Johnny's horse scuttles on her feet.

"Kind of," I admit.

Johnny raises a questioning eyebrow.

"We had a very, *very* brief encounter on the mountain, but . . ." I shake my head. "It didn't take long to figure out that he wasn't for me."

Johnny rests his elbow on the stable wall. "I'm surprised you actually fancied him."

My expression turns to a frown when I sense judgment from Johnny. I then quickly remember what I saw in Johnny's cabin the night before I left Bear Gap.

Without thinking, I say, "What about that girl you were with in your house?"

Johnny jerks backward away from me. "What are you talking about?"

I freeze, realizing that I've just given myself away. I cross my arms over my chest and contemplate denial, but it all ends tonight. There's no time to play games.

"I came to see you the night before I left for LilyAye. And I saw you sitting on the couch, cozy with another woman. It's completely fair. We aren't together anymore. I just thought, since we're examining my past lovers, maybe we should talk about yours."

Johnny brings a fist to his mouth and bursts into laughter. I hold my arms close to my body as if the tightness will alleviate my embarrassment.

"Well?" I ask.

Johnny moves around his horse to stand fully face-to-face with me.

"That was my childhood friend, Sara," he says.

"Friend…"

"We've known each other forever. Haven't stayed in contact much, but she asked me to help her parents with a leak in their roof and that was her coming over to thank me."

"Oh."

"You were spying on me?" Johnny asks, laughter still in his mouth.

Heat rises to my chest. My cheeks burn. "I missed you, okay? I hadn't seen you in three months, and every night I slept in the Bear Gap House, I regretted the day I ended things with you. The only reason I fell for Reed was because I missed you so much."

The words spill from my lips like a rushing stream. I avoid his gaze, realizing I've just admitted that, yes, I still love Johnny. His laughter stops. A moment of silence passes where only the crickets chirp.

"I didn't know that," Johnny says flatly.

"And if you think that Sara girl was just giving you some friendly appreciation than you are sorely fooled. I saw the look she gave you."

"Camilla…"

"Well, do you like her? Sara? She's beautiful. I would understand."

"No," Johnny says quickly. "She's like a sister to me! When Ralf gave me your letter, I left immediately to come and find you. But then Reed told me about the two of you, so I figured you didn't want that kind of relationship from me anymore. I thought you'd already moved on."

He boldly reaches for both my hands, urgently holding them tight. I tilt my head up. His glistening eyes are pinned on mine.

"If I had known how you really felt, I would have told you that I still love you too. When we broke things off, you said I needed someone more attentive, but you're wrong, Camilla. I only ever really wanted you in whatever state you were in."

A warm flush washes over me, and a smile plays at the corner of my mouth. "You do?"

"I volunteered to come with you tonight because I didn't want you to slip through my fingers again."

I wrap my arms around Johnny's waist. He rests the palm of his hand against my cheek. Johnny's pale blue eyes shine like a beacon to me, a beacon of hope for a better future. For a moment, I feel like I'm back in the quaintness of Bear Gap with him. I lean in, bracing for a kiss, when the back door of the safe house swings open and Knox lumbers across the yard.

***

Johnny and I loosen our embrace. I clear my throat as I turn back to Shae. In silence, Johnny, Knox, and I finish saddling our horses. The rebels gather to watch us leave. Mirabelle gives me a kiss on my cheek as she squeezes me into a hug. I say my final goodbye to Tuor. To my surprise, Knox grasps Mirabelle and gives her a firm kiss on the lips.

Reed watches me. He truly is an enigma. Why would he tell Johnny that we're together, but then seem to not care at all when I told him I'm going back to

Bear Gap? After all this time of knowing him, I still haven't figured him out.

Johnny, Knox, and I are all wished the best of luck as we leave the rebel safe house for the cold streets of LilyAye. Set on a hill, Quinten's dark castle looms before us. It's outside the Servant's District, so we don't have to worry about crossing over that threshold.

Shae's hooves pound the cobblestone street with an eerie echo. The wind whips past me as we gallop urgently toward our destination. LilyAye is quiet. Only a few candles burn in the windows. We ride through the quaint neighborhoods until we come to a stop at an outer wall that protects Quinten from his own people. We stop under a torch along the wall, where Captain Thatius instructed us to.

Johnny inspects the empty street around us. Still sitting atop Shae, I twist my neck to take in the magnitude of Quinten's castle. The full harvest moon casts a white haze across the nearly black facade. Defensive walls and circular turrets encompass the beast of a castle in case of enemy attack.

"Good evening," Ridley says as he approaches us.

A soldier rides behind him. Instinctually, I tighten my grip on Shae's reins. Ridley sits stiffly in his saddle, a commemorative military sash around his horse's neck.

"Fret not. This is Lemund. He's with us," Ridley adds.

"How are we getting inside?" Knox asks in a low voice.

Ridley strokes his pointed graying goatee with his black leather-gloved hand.

"The only reason to bring someone into the castle at this time of night would be if you were a physician tending the Supreme Ruler, or if you were being taken to the dungeons. So, from here, you've all been arrested," Ridley says.

My body seizes at that thought. Perhaps sensing my tension, Shae whinnies and shakes her head. The soldier eyes us. He holds a pile of chains in his hands. Johnny peers over at me. His lips are pressed tightly together. He's clearly nervous.

"You will all dismount and leave your horses here," Ridley continues. "They'll be part of the evidence used against you, proving that it was in fact the rebels who did this horrible thing."

"Come on," Knox grunts. "We're going to be arrested after it's done anyway."

"Hide your weapons too," Ridley says.

I slide off Shae, giving her a quick scratch on her mane before tucking my dagger into the front of my pants and buttoning my jacket over it. The soldier dismounts his own horse. Pulling our hands in front of us, the soldier ratchets a set of shackles on me, Johnny, and Knox. He connects us in a row by a chain so one of us can't run away.

"From this point on, I'll need to remain completely unaware of what's happening. Lemund will take you the rest of the way inside. This is where I leave you," Ridley says.

"How long will we be kept in the dungeon?" I ask.

"A few days, I suspect," Ridley says nonchalantly.

I take a shaky breath. The tightness of the shackles sends a shiver up my back. What am I doing, willingly putting myself in the very restraints I worked so hard to get out of? I force my body to relax.

"Is everyone prepared?" Ridley asks.

Collectively, the three of us nod. The captain then turns his horse around and rides away from the castle.

"Let's go," Lemund says with a low voice.

He mounts his horse and tugs our chains to pull us forward. We wrap around the wall and approach a set of guards at the outer gate. "On our way to the dungeons," Lemund says. There's little questioning. They open the gate and let us through.

We wind up a stone road that leads to the castle. Whether intentional or not, the soldier pulls on our chains harshly. I stumble. The cuffs on my wrists rub against my skin. Breathe, I tell myself as Quinten's castle grows larger. We meet a second set of guards at an inner wall. Lemund gives his name, and those guards let us pass with no issue.

The road, wide enough to fit a wagon, continues all the way to the singular entrance into the castle: a wide-set wooden door.

"I didn't know you were on patrol tonight," one of the guards at the door says.

"Last-minute fill-in," Lemund answers.

"What'd these people do?"

"Caught 'em thieving," Lemund says.

The guard opens the door. "Have a good rest of your night."

We enter into a stone tunnel. Torches rest on either side of the wall. Lemund pulls us into the castle's courtyard. It's a long oval shape with a pristine lawn and a grand statue of Quinten in the middle. The statue, bathed by the night sky, looks to be the color of charcoal.

Lemund dismounts from his horse. He scans the courtyard, then pulls us through a door along the courtyard wall. A carved-out set of stone steps leads into a hazy downstairs.

"This is as far as I can take you," Lemund says, unlocking our restraints. "If they catch me upstairs, I'll be arrested too."

"How will we find Quinten?" Johnny asks, his voice an urgent whisper.

"His chambers are in the section at the back of the courtyard. That's all I know." Lemund hurriedly collects our chains.

I rub my wrists. "I thought you were going to take us to him."

"No. Are you mad? I'm fleeing. I'll be at the city gates before he's dead," Lemund whispers. "As soon as the council finds out what happened, it won't take long for them to figure out which soldier brought you in tonight. I don't care what Captain Thatius is paying me. I'm not taking any chances. Good luck."

Lemund ducks through the door and back out into the courtyard. He leaves the three of us alone in the middle of Quinten's castle.

CHAPTER THIRTY-NINE

"NO POINT IN waiting around. Let's move," Knox says.

He removes his machete from the folds of his jacket. I hold my dagger, unsheathed at my side. We spill out into the night air once again. This time, free of chains. Lanterns illuminate the lawn. We duck low and scurry along the outer perimeter of the courtyard. Knox leads the way. The tall edifice of the back portion of the castle slowly becomes visible through the darkness. Quinten's weather-beaten statue in the middle of the courtyard personifies him as a young warrior.

Throwing his arm up, Knox pushes us flat against the wall to blend in. Up ahead, a man guards the door that leads inside.

"Camilla, you run to the other side and distract him. Johnny and I will get him from behind," Knox whispers.

Silently, I scamper across the courtyard, past the statue, while Knox and Johnny make a rush for the door. I whistle, drawing the guard's attention toward me. He holds his position. I approach, making sure he sees me. He reaches for his sword. I draw up my dagger and begin running toward him.

"Who goes there?" he shouts.

His eyes are pinned on me. I stop short, bracing myself for a fight.

"Halt!" he barks.

The guard raises his sword. Johnny's shadowy outline runs up behind him. He sharply bends the guard's head and drives a knife into his neck. The guard drops to the ground. We drag his body behind a large clay flowerpot, then run to the door, where Knox is waiting, his hand on the knob. We slip inside.

Torches flicker down the castle hallway. Gaudy paintings and massive tapestries cover the walls. A sleepy calm rests over the castle, but my heart is pounding against my ribs. We twist down one corridor to another until we empty into an entrance hall. We huddle behind a stone column.

A wide grand staircase with deep maroon carpet snakes up through the center of the room. Soldiers pace across each of the stairwell landings. They're dressed in thick, silvery armor. A stained-glass window stretches as tall as the ceiling. The moonlight, mixed with the colors of the glass, casts a mysterious purple pall over the staircase.

"Safe to say that's the way we have to go," Knox says, his eyes following the twisted steps. "Those men are guarding something important."

"How are we getting up there?" Johnny asks.

"Surprise attack is our only chance," Knox whispers. "But we have to make sure not to alert the other guards. Stay tight. We'll take them one at a time."

We move to the stairs, quietly pumping our legs up each step. The light pouring in through the window catches on the dust, creating the image of glowing fairies floating through the room. I imagine them as wicked beings, created for Quinten's amusement.

The guard at the first landing hums as he walks in step with his spear. Our footsteps thud lightly against the carpet. We nearly reach the top when the guard pauses and whips around. His spear pointed in front of him, the guard charges at Johnny. Armed with only a short knife, Johnny ducks. Knox slips up behind his nephew and grabs the pole of the spear with both his hands.

The tip of the spear narrowly misses Johnny's head. I make a run at the guard. My dagger collides with his chainmail. The guard grunts as he tries to swing Knox off his spear.

"Intruders!" the guard shouts. "Assistance!" he yells as he battles with Knox for the spear.

Two soldiers from the higher landings barrel down the steps. Knox curses. The guard reaches for his sword with his free hand. I lunge at him, pushing him backward. I wrap my hand around the hilt of his sword and fling it from its sheath. The metal zings through the air.

Johnny slips his knife up and sticks it under the guard's arm, into his exposed soft skin. He lets out an agonizing cry as Johnny pulls his knife out. The spear releases from his grip. The guard stumbles backward against the thick stone railing.

Knox swings the spear around and stabs it toward the two soldiers as they spill onto the landing. Johnny runs to Knox's side. One of the soldiers spots me in the back. He twists his face into an angry scowl and charges me. My dagger in one hand and the guard's sword in the other, I raise up both blades against my attacker. He swings his sword at my middle. I block with my sword and skitter backward.

He strikes me again. I block his blow, feeling the impact shudder down the blade. The hit nudges me a few more steps back. Our swords connected, the soldier pushes against me. My arm quakes as I strain to hold him off. The dagger slips from my other hand and falls with a *thud* on the carpet. I grip the sword with both hands. My back hits the cold, rough railing behind me.

The soldier bares his teeth. I groan as my back bends over the railing. The razor-sharp edge of his sword inches closer to me. My head swims, and my feet lift off the floor. I let out a shrill scream that echoes through the stairwell. I kick my legs. My knee connects with his metal armor. A throbbing pain pulses up my leg reminding me that I haven't fully healed from my fall out of the Bradac castle.

With a burst of energy, I push the sword away from me and knock the hilt into the soldier's nose. Frustrated he latches onto my shoulders, swinging me around. The move causes me to lose grip. My sword tumbles over the railing and lands with a *clatter* on the floor below. I swing my arm, hitting the soldier in the side of his head. His hands grapple for my neck.

"Johnny!" I yelp, but get no response.

Knox lies on the floor, barely moving. Johnny is pursued, down the steps, by the other soldier. I wrestle my attacker's hands away from my neck. He grabs my ponytail and rips my hair. I swing again, knocking him back. I scoop up my dagger. As the soldier charges me, I squat and jab my dagger into his thigh where his armor doesn't meet. Blood gushes over his black boots. I lurch onto my feet, grip his breastplate, and push him over the railing. A moment later, a deafening *thud* floats up the steps.

My breath heaves in my chest. I run to the other side of the landing. At the bottom of the stairs, Johnny is still in a sword fight with the other soldier. My feet pound down the steps. Dagger in hand, I launch myself at Johnny's attacker. He twists and spots me. Just as I'm about to wrap my arms around his neck, Johnny drives his sword into the side of the soldier's stomach. The soldier whirls on Johnny, his sword flying wildly. Johnny backs away, his sword still embedded in the soldier.

I grab the soldier's arm from behind and pull him to the ground. The soldier collapses, splayed out on the steps, unmoving.

"What happened to Knox?" I ask.

Johnny is bent over, his hands resting on his knees.

"He got hit with the butt of a sword."

We rush up the steps and find Knox sitting upright, rubbing the side of his head. Johnny falls on his knees next to him.

"Are you all right?" Johnny asks.

"I will be," Knox grumbles. "Let's keep moving before someone finds this mess."

"Someone had to have heard us," I say.

"Let's not wait to find out," Knox says.

Johnny pulls Knox to standing. The three of us continue up the winding staircase. The moonlight, through the stained-glass window, lights our path. At the top, we run beside a long stretch of railing, then turn into a maze of hallways. We jog for what feels like miles past thick walls and solid doors. I understand now why no one came running to the stairs; our screams were deadened by the layers of walls.

Groping through the dark castle, a flickering glow signals firelight around the next corridor. We sneak down the length of the hallway and peer around the corner to a dead end. Two soldiers stand in front of a cherry-oak double door. Long swords hang from their belts. Torches flank the soldiers on either side. The door cracks open, and the soldiers step aside to let a woman exit into the hallway. She's short and plump, wearing a crisp white apron and carrying a chamber pot.

Knox silently points down the hallway in the direction that we just came from. The three of us quietly retreat and duck into the shadow of an arched doorway. We wait for the servant woman to walk past us, out of sight.

"That has to be the entrance to Quinten's chambers," I whisper.

Johnny's body is pressed close to mine.

"Yes, I agree," Knox says, his voice low.

"We can't take out those soldiers with a fight," Johnny says. "If we're too loud, Quinten will hear us from inside."

"And we have to hurry. I imagine that woman is heading for the steps. She'll see the dead men soon enough," Knox says.

"We have to move now," Johnny says.

His face is fully immersed in darkness, but I feel him ready his knife.

"Wait," I say, grabbing Johnny's shoulder. "Let her discover the dead guards on the steps."

I shift to face Johnny and Knox, glancing down the hallway to make sure we're still alone. "If she sees trouble, she's going to run back up here to where she knows there's a soldier. She'll draw them away from Quinten's door."

"Maybe," Johnny says. "Or she'll alert someone else, and we'll be outnumbered."

"They don't know where we are," I whisper.

"It's worth a try," Knox says.

Johnny steps into the light. His expression is worried.

"But then the soldiers at Quinten's door will still be alive while we're in his chambers," Johnny says. "They'll come back for us."

"Let them," Knox says.

I look up at Johnny and say, "We need to get arrested, right?"

Johnny presses his lips together. Planning to get arrested is against his nature.

"Once we get inside his chambers, we have to be fast," Knox says.

Johnny reluctantly agrees to the plan, and then we do something that is difficult for all of us. We stand in the dark alcove and wait. We wait until we hear the light, thudding footsteps of the servant woman returning to Quinten's chambers. Her heavy breathing is ominous as it cchocs down the hall.

"Help!" she calls out as she runs past us again. "They're dead!"

"What are you talking about, woman?" one of the soldiers asks.

"On the steps!" she screams. Her voice is breathy and choked. "There are dead men!"

A moment later, the servant woman and one of the guards marches past us, down the hallway. Our clock has begun ticking. We move through the hallway, and all of us rush the one guard who remains standing outside Quinten's chambers. I cover the soldier's mouth with my hand. Knox holds him still while Johnny pushes his knife behind the soldier's breastplate. We quietly let him drop to the floor.

Retrieving a key from the guard's belt, I slip it into the lock and crack open the door to Quinten's inner chamber. I carefully close the door behind us. We enter a round vestibule with multiple doors along the wall. A round maroon rug with tassels sits on the floor, and a candlelit chandelier hangs from the ceiling. Knox signals us by pointing with the tip of his sword.

Firelight glows under only one of the doors. We move to that door. Knox rests his hand on the knob. He makes eye contact with Johnny and me, silently affirming that we all know what to do next. He then swiftly turns the knob, and we barge into Quinten's bedroom.

A sharp scream pierces the room as Dina spots us. She's sitting up in bed, a small gold mirror in her hand. Clothed in a nightdress, Quinten rounds the corner of the four-poster bed.

"What is the meaning of this?" he barks. "Guards!"

"No one's coming," I say darkly.

We stand with our weapons outstretched.

"Move," Knox growls.

He directs Quinten, with the tip of his blade, to the other side of the bed. Quinten's face pinches into smug annoyance. He slowly raises his hands and comes to stand in front of us. Quinten's wife lets out a whimper and pulls the covers up toward her.

"Johnny," Knox says, nudging his head in the direction of the blonde-haired woman on the bed.

Johnny roughly removes Dina from the safety of the blankets and ties her up in a gold-threaded chair. Quinten slowly backs away from us. He eyes Knox with a condescending gaze.

"What do you animals want?" Quinten spits.

His forehead creases with deep wrinkles as he snarls at us. I suddenly realize how unimposing Quinten is in his bare feet and shoulder-length graying hair. His face is a sickly shade of white.

"It's time for your atonement," Knox growls, taking measured steps toward Quinten.

Quinten laughs derisively. "Who are you to cast judgment upon me?"

"I'm one of the many people whose lives you destroyed," Knox lifts his machete, the wide blade gleaming in the candlelight. Dina moans from across the room. She's now gagged and tied, and Johnny is standing behind her.

"You decimated my village thirteen years ago and captured my father."

"War crimes?" Quinten chuckles. "That's what this is about?"

Quinten takes a step backward. Knox pursues, matching each of Quinten's retreats with an advance of his own.

"I never saw my father again." Knox's voice is harsh and gravelly.

Quinten stops moving when his back presses against the wall.

"Remember me?" Knox asks.

Quinten's lips curve into a devilish grin. "I don't recall the faces of peasants."

Knox lets out an angry huff of air from his nose, like a bull. I nervously glance back at the bedroom door.

"We don't have time for this," I mutter.

Quinten's body jerks. He quickly lunges for his bureau. From behind it, he pulls out a sword. Ripping off the silver scabbard, Quinten points it at Knox.

"You filthy rat," Quinten says, bending into an offensive stance. "You think you can surprise me."

Quinten whirls the sword around in a smooth, showy movement. Johnny runs to my side.

"I am the most powerful man in Elmyra." Quinten raises his sword and strikes at his opponent. Knox blocks his blow. A deafening *clang* reverberates through the ceiling. Quinten advances, swinging his sword again. Their blades clash together in spirited swordplay. For a moment, I see the warrior Quinten once was. Knox holds Quinten's blow midair. I make a run at Quinten.

"Wait!" Knox shouts. I pause. "Stay out of my way! Both of you!"

I shoot Johnny a concerned glance, but as instructed, we stand back from the fray. Knox grunts as he pushes Quinten. Knox's fiery eyes burn through the Supreme Ruler.

"Why don't I help you remember!" Knox yells, raising his machete again. "I did your bidding for years. Chasing after that witch of yours."

Weapons collide. Quinten falters. He grinds his teeth together as he returns with another swipe of his sword. Knox clips Quinten's blow, swiftly dispatching the sword from Quinten's hand. Quinten looks at his sword lying on the ground. His dry lips are spread in seething anger. Johnny scoops up Quinten's sword.

"Remember me yet?" Knox asks, his breath heavy in his chest.

The snarl on Knox's lips complements the mutilated burn scar on the side of his face, making him appear a true villain.

Quinten snaps his mouth shut and lifts his chin. "Oh, I remember."

"It's time to end this. You're done destroying Elmyra," I say, gripping my dagger tight. "And by the way, I'm Portia's daughter, the girl you tried to use to manipulate my mother."

Quinten freezes, and then his face falls into a sheen of horror. Dina screams through her gag.

"You're Portia's daughter?" Quinten tumbles backward against his nightstand. His eyes widen. He stares at me as if I were death itself. I glance furtively at Johnny.

"Yes," I say, furrowing my brows.

"I see her in you," Quinten says in a daze as if he's noticing me for the first time. He grips his heart.

"It's not her you should be afraid of," Knox says.

With his eyes pinned on me, Quinten whispers, "Have mercy."

The Supreme Ruler falls to his knees.

"You'll find no mercy from us." Knox raises his machete high into the air. In one powerful strike, Knox swings his blade, slicing off Quinten's head so it drops and rolls onto the Warwick maroon carpet.

CHAPTER FORTY

THE DARK RULER is dead.

A clock chimes the hour. Quinten Warwick's body lies lifeless on the floor. Blood oozes from his neck. Dina screams through her gag and wrestles against the ropes. Knox wipes the blood on his machete onto the bedcover, leaving a crimson smear. I urgently turn to the door. We can't look like we're waiting to be arrested, or Quinten's wife could grow suspicious.

"Let's get out of here," I say, leading Knox and Johnny from the bedroom.

Johnny nervously paces the vestibule of Quinten's inner chambers. Dina's cries pierce the closed bedroom door.

"This doesn't feel right," Johnny whispers. "Just waiting around here to get arrested. We have time. We could sneak out of the castle before anyone finds us."

"That's not the plan," Knox says firmly.

I force confidence into my voice as I say, "If we get arrested, then Reed will have an easier claim to the throne."

Inwardly, I agree with Johnny. Waiting for the inevitable is torture and against my instinct.

"We have a witness that saw us kill him!" Johnny says. "We can run out of here, and she'll tell them it was us. They won't suspect anyone else, and we don't have to get arrested!"

On the wall is a bell pull, used to summon the Supreme Ruler's many servants. I consider striking one of the bells to get someone here faster when pounding footsteps roar down the hall. Knox places a hand on Johnny's shoulder.

"Relax," he says calmly. "Our job is done."

I ready my dagger. A battalion of soldiers barges into Quinten's inner chambers. We put up a fight, an act to make us appear surprised at being caught. The soldiers place us under arrest and confiscate our weapons. We're pushed and shoved through the castle to the same set of stone steps that Lemund first brought us to. They lead to the dungeons. We descend into the belly of the castle. The temperature drops to a crisp iciness.

We're led through rocky hallways lined with bars. My eyes widen at the sight of rooms with metal torture devices. We twist and turn, passing cell after cell filled with LilyAye citizens, who, for whatever reason, met an unfortunate fate.

The soldiers stop in front of a large cell with chains hanging on the walls. They swing the metal bars open and take all three of us inside, cuffing us, by the wrists, to the wall. They lock the cell door, murmuring about what will be done with us.

The cell floor is strewn with hay. I sit in what smells like a pile of manure. My arms are stretched tight over my head, causing my shoulders to burn. The metal cuffs rub at my wrists. The air is thick with dust. Knox coughs violently.

The flickering torch in the hallway lights up the specks of Quinten's blood still splattered on Knox's face and beard. He's just ended Quinten's reign of terror in Elmyra, but more importantly, he's avenged the struggle in my life. When I look at Knox, his gaze is soft, his body relaxed. He appears calm.

"Thank you," I whisper. "Thank you for killing him."

"It had to be done, and it had to be done by me."

"Why aren't you more worried right now?" I ask.

Knox pauses as if considering his answer. He then glances around the damp cell. "You know, the original rebels from Bear Gap that Quinten took captive, built this castle. Men like Peter Lindon and my father. I've just accomplished the only thing I've needed to do in my life. I've avenged those men."

Resting his head against the cold stone wall of the dungeon, Knox continues. "I'm done, Camilla. I've confessed to you and Tuor. Somehow, I've gained Mirabelle's forgiveness. And now, I've killed the man who took my father and terrorized me these last thirteen years. I can die now and that would be all right."

I swallow hard. Ever since the day I met Knox Duffy, he'd always seemed a tortured soul. Now when I look at him, I see a man at peace, and I find myself . . . jealous. I stare at the dusty ground. Holding onto my anger against Knox has made me bitter like he once was.

"I hated myself after that day," Knox says, his voice breaking through my thoughts. "Ever since I came face-to-face with Quinten in the woods and pointed the finger at you two as a way to get to Portia, I couldn't stand my own company."

Years of self-loathing have left Knox an older looking man than what he really is.

"I believe you," I say in a soft voice. I lift my head to look Knox in the eyes. "When you confessed everything, I wanted to hate you for what you'd done, but I realize now, I wanted to hate the younger version of you. The person you are now would never do that."

Johnny watches us intently. The rattling of chains echoes down the dungeon hallway. Although Knox and Mirabelle kept the secret of Knox's transgression from me, I can't really blame them. I'd have probably done the same thing. The Knox who sold out the five-year-old Camilla no longer exists. There's no one left to be mad at, which means the grudge I'm holding is only against my own anger.

Knox gives me an approving grunt. "I've never been a perfect person."

"Neither have I," I say, and I think Knox understands, this is my way of telling him, *I forgive you.*

***

Knox, Johnny, and I languish in the dungeons for what feels like days, but I suspect it has really only been a few hours. The cranking of the stretching machine in the torture room grates on my every nerve. Moaning and screaming waft through the hollow corridors. My arms are pinned so tightly to the wall that I can't even cover my ears. The sound of other people's pain starts to fade into the background.

I pull my legs into my body. I never considered what they'd do to us during this time before Reed is crowned Supreme Ruler. We might make it out of here alive, but we might not be fully intact. For now, we're left alone. Occasionally, a soldier or two comes to leer at us. Word spreads fast. We're a spectacle in the dungeons, the people who murdered Quinten Warwick. Yes, the rumors are true, I want to scream.

A band of soldiers barges into our cell and unchains us from the wall. We're taken to another wing of the dungeon. Johnny and Knox are ferried off somewhere else, and I'm placed in my own cell. It's a hollowed-out hole in the stone foundation with rusty bars over the door.

At first, I'm thankful that I'm not chained to the wall anymore, but they've put me somewhere completely by myself. I pace the length of my prison cell. The cries of the other prisoners are so far off in the distance that they sound ghostly. I'm alone, and there's nothing to do. It drives me mad.

Finally, there's a commotion at the end of the hallway. My heart leaps. Could it be Reed or Thatius already coming to get me out? I press my body up against the bars of my cell and strain my neck as far as I can to see what's happening. I peer down the end of the hallway. A crowd of soldiers and prisoners walk in my direction.

A head of shiny blonde hair comes into view. I squint. Eve's hands are cuffed behind her back. She's led past my cell. Then comes Ron and Esmeralda. Alice weeps as she's roughly pushed forward. Mirabelle and Roehana are next to be marched by. Mirabelle's eyes are rimmed red.

"Tuor!" I call out as he passes.

His lips are angrily pressed together.

"What happened?" I ask.

"They found us," he mutters as he's swiftly nudged out of my sight.

I search the hallway for answers. How did they find the rebel safe house? This wasn't part of the plan. Reed said they'd be safe if they laid low during the assassination. It's then that I realize Reed was not among the arrested rebels.

The dungeons grow quiet again, then light yet determined footsteps come from the end of the hall. Emerging from the shadows, the figure of a woman is barely illuminated by the flickering wall torches. She's accompanied by a soldier, but she's not bound in chains like the rebels were. She appears fully in control. Her head is covered by a dark hood. My heart catches in my throat. I stagger away from the bars of my cell, terrified of the apparition in front of me.

This can't be. *How?*

"Unlock it," the woman demands.

The soldier turns the key in the lock. My cell door creaks open. The woman strides inside just before the soldier slams the door behind her. He locks it again and stands at the ready, just outside.

My back presses against the cold wall of my cell. "Why can't you just leave me alone?"

Removing her hood, my mother smiles at me pleasantly. She fingers the turquoise amulet on her chest.

"Why would you want me to? I've come to rescue you," Portia says.

"How did you get in here?" I growl.

"Oh, Camilla," Portia says, folding her arms across her chest. "Haven't you learned yet? I run this country."

"How's that possible?" I protest. "You've been out of Quinten's favor for years."

"Yes, but Quinten's dead now, isn't he? In fact, I think it was you who killed him," Portia says with a smirk. "I tried to get you to join forces with me so we could kill him together, but it looks like you managed it all on your own."

"They'll never make you Supreme Ruler."

My mother's long black cape trails across the dirty floor as she tugs it tighter over her shoulders.

"Ugh," Portia spits. "I don't want to be Supreme Ruler. Having to force a smiling face in front of all of those people, pretending to care. I'd never be good at that. I prefer to operate in the shadows."

Portia slithers farther into my prison cell. She scans the dank wall and ceiling with disgust. "You assumed I wanted to kill Quinten so I could take his position, but really I just needed to put someone else on the throne who I could control. It's much more fun that way."

I shake my head in disbelief. "But the council decides who the next Supreme Ruler is."

"You're correct," Portia says with surprise. "You've learned a lot during your time in LilyAye. Fortunately, I have someone on my side who sits on the council."

My body stiffens, and my heartbeat picks up pace.

"Perhaps you know him?" Portia continues, her red lips a stark contrast to her pale face. "His name is Captain Ridley Thatius."

"You're lying."

"Surely you've learned by now that I don't lie."

"You're pretending to know him to manipulate me," I say, determined not to fall for one of my mother's ruses.

"I needn't pretend, my darling. The only reason Captain Thatius came to your rebel safe house was because I instructed him to. I put the very words in his mouth."

I grit my teeth. "Lies."

"Of course we never planned to make that pathetic plea at the rebel safe house." My mother paces the dungeon cell. "The plan was to kill Quinten at the wedding, but we had that trouble with the poison and…"

"Lies! I don't know what sorcery you used to learn about that meeting or about the poison, but you're lying."

"Poor Camilla," my mother says sympathetically. She bites her fingernail. "I know it's hard to learn you were wrong all along."

My heart pounds in my chest.

"If you really know Thatius, then why are you here? It sounds like you have everything you desire. What do you want with me?"

I straighten my back and wear a stern expression, attempting to save face. Reed. She still doesn't know about Reed, and he's the only one of the rebels who hasn't been arrested.

"I told you before," Portia says. "I want *you*."

"Why?"

Portia saunters toward me. She fiddles with the stone amulet. "You're my daughter. Now that I'm back in control, I think it's time we were reacquainted."

"Never. You'll never have me."

Portia chuckles. "I'm offering you an escape from this deplorable place. I'll take you out of LilyAye to safety. Don't tell me you'd prefer to stay."

"I don't need your help getting out of here," I say firmly, though I feel less than confident.

Portia takes another step closer to me. "It's unfortunate that I have to tell you this, but Reed's not coming."

My heart seizes and I forget to breathe. "What do you know of him?"

"Plenty, my daughter. You see, Reed and Thatius serve *me*. They always have. Quinten wasn't the only one who had spies. I had eyes on him too. Even when we were together and happy, I made sure I had Thatius there to tell me what he was up to." My mother's eyes stalk me like a poisonous snake. "And Reed? We've been entwined since you were just a child."

Entwined? Does she mean—?

My mind spins back to the kiss that Reed and I shared on the mountain. "But he and I were—"

"I told him to romance you. I had to break you away from that boy in Bear Gap. Falling for Reed assured me that you had enough motivation to continue to LilyAye. I had enough trouble when you changed your mind about coming to LilyAye at the beginning of the summer. I was thrilled when Thatius delivered that news, but then you started to waver in your decision. I figured if you had someone new to pine after, Reed would be able to get you to do whatever he wanted."

"I don't believe you," I say through gritted teeth.

"What's so unbelievable about it? Quinten always loathed his nephew. He humiliated him at the Battle of Bear Gap all those years ago. Then Reed and I connected over a growing hatred for the man. And Thatius, he saw the powers I had and rightfully chose to respect them."

"But Reed helped the rebels take Bear Gap. He's been with us, on our side, since the spring."

"Only because I instructed him to." Portia says this as if I should already know. "I'm Reed's ruler. When are you going to understand? He does whatever I tell him to. I told him to travel to Bear Gap and infiltrate the rebels. I told him to watch over you, to influence you. I directed him every step of the way."

"So this has all been a lie? The last year?" I feel all the blood rush from my face.

How could I be so foolish?

"Reed and Thatius have fed you just enough truth to string you along. I'm the one who told Reed to make sure he convinced you to come to LilyAye and help murder Quinten."

"Why?" I scream. "Why do all of that? Why manipulate me like this?"

"Because I need you, Camilla. I need you on my side, and when I approached you in Bear Gap, you wouldn't budge. So I had to find another way. I decided to be efficient in my plotting. I used you and the rebels to take care of Quinten for me, and in the process, I've put you in a situation where all of your loved ones are under my thumb. You have no way out without yielding to me."

I turn from Portia and shake my head. "No. I won't believe it. This is madness, just one of your tricks. Reed is going to be crowned Supreme Ruler, and he'll come for us."

"He'll certainly be crowned Supreme Ruler, as we planned, but he won't be saving you."

I whip around to face my mother and press my lips together angrily. "I told you, I'll never go with you. I don't care what it costs."

457

Portia draws breath. "Okay, fine. I should suspect that any daughter of mine would be impossibly stubborn. I have a new offer."

"I'm not taking any of your offers!" My shout echoes against the stone ceiling.

"You're going to want to listen to this one. You and your band of goons have been caught with sword in hand over the dead body of the Supreme Ruler. Surely, you understand that the fate of the rebels, including you, is death. Reed will order it himself."

I stand, facing Portia head-on with my fists clenched.

"But," Portia continues, "if you come with me, I'll have all your friends safely released. I have the power to do that."

I reach my fingers into my hair, scratching my scalp in frustration. "If you want me so badly, why not just steal me away yourself? Why give me a choice?"

"I won't force you to go. I can't do that," Portia says. "My father took away my ability to decide for myself. I've never wanted to do that to you."

"Why should I trust you?" I ask, stampeding toward my mother. I point a finger at her. "After all the deceit, why would I ever trust you to release the rebels even if I did agree to go with you?"

Portia purses her lips. "I suppose that's for you to decide. What do you say? Will you leave this place and come with me?"

I stare fiery daggers at Portia. "No."

Portia's chest rises with a deep breath. She says nothing as she walks to the cell door and calls the attention of the guard.

"Bring me the boy," Portia says.

My breath catches in my throat. Portia stands coolly in front of me, until a moment later, when the guard returns. His hands tied behind his back, Johnny is dragged in front of my cell bars. He's forced to his knees. His breathing is rapid. I come to the bars and grip them firmly.

"What are you doing with him?" I ask.

Johnny seethes, fighting against his captor.

"Leave with me now and I won't touch him," Portia says.

"We've been played, Camilla!" Johnny shouts. "Don't listen to them!"

"Yes or no?" Portia asks, her voice growing firm and impatient.

"Don't do it!" Johnny says.

"No," I say. My voice shakes. "I won't let you control me anymore."

I watch Johnny with worried eyes.

"Fair enough," Portia says.

She flicks her fingers at the guard, giving him the signal. The guard pulls a switch blade from his pocket. My teeth are gritted.

"I could have done this with Tuor," Portia says calmly with a chuckle. "But truthfully, I'm really interested to see how you'll react with the boy."

I stand helpless as the guard wrenches back Johnny's head by his hair. He takes the tip of his knife and digs it into the corner of Johnny's eye. Johnny lets out an agonizing scream. Blood gurgles from his face. I shriek, covering my mouth in horror.

"Stop!" My voice bellows down the hall.

The guard twists the knife as if he were trying to pluck out Johnny's eye. His yelps bang over the walls of the dungeon.

"Stop! Stop! Please!" I scream.

I turn to my mother and grasp her arms in both my hands. "Make him stop!"

A smirk flickers on Portia's face.

"You won!" I cry. "I'll go with you!"

My mother raises a hand, signaling the guard to stop. He removes his knife. Johnny moans as he bends forward, blood dripping onto the dungeon floor.

"Get him fixed up," Portia instructs.

I stand frozen and stunned as Johnny is dragged away.

"Oh, Camilla, I'm sorry you had to go through this," my mother says sympathetically. She wraps her bony arms around me, pressing my head against her chest. I stare absentmindedly at the pool of blood on the ground.

"I'll take you far away from here," she says, and I close my eyes in defeat.

EPILOGUE

SHAE SHAKES HER head as the late autumn breeze tussles her mane. I adjust the woolen scarf around my neck to block the crisp air. My mother rides up next to me. We're perched atop an embankment a few miles outside of LilyAye. The turrets on the Warwick castle are like branches from this distance. The city wall resembles a dainty fence. No longer are the houses and buildings of LilyAye imposing. They're simply a point off in the distance, a place I was once doomed to live.

Reed was officially crowned Supreme Ruler this morning, just before Portia and I saddled up and left. My mother has accomplished her goal. Like she always does, Portia weaseled her way into my life, mixed it all up, and spewed me out. She preyed on the fact that the rebels and I desired to murder Quinten, and she used that to get me to do what she wanted. I see that now.

Portia touches the tips of her long dark hair before lifting the hood of her cape to cover her head. She grips tightly to her reins. Her lips are spread in a pleased smile.

"I'm overjoyed that you're finally with me," she says.

"Don't talk to me like we're companions," I say.

Portia exhales. "Perhaps not now, but some day we will be."

I shake my head in disgust. My mother manipulated me at every turn. She orchestrated this whole thing. Reed and Thatius were her minions long before I ever started the rebellion. It's sickening to realize I never had a chance.

She put me in an impossible situation so that I had to go with her. I had to face the facts of my situation. I was trapped in the dungeons with Quinten's blood on my hands. My only other option was death by execution. Some moments I wonder if I should have taken the latter. If it weren't for the lives of everyone else, perhaps I would have faced the execution block.

"How much longer?" I ask.

"Patience, my daughter."

I look out over a valley filled with a dense forest and ask, "What is this place?"

"It's the Otsana Wood," my mother says, fingering the amulet on her chest. "It's the beginning of a vast wilderness. They say it stretches all the way to the corner of Elmyra, but I'm not sure anyone's ever actually traveled there to find out."

"The Free Territory, perhaps," I say.

Portia laughs. "The Free Territory is a fairy tale told among people who are too unfortunate to enjoy this world."

I purse my lips. My face curls in disgust every time I look at my mother. Her hands are permanently covered in blood, unable to be scrubbed off. The image of that knife burrowing into Johnny's eye turns my stomach whenever I think on it.

Two flatbed wagons bumble into the grassy knoll just outside the tree line. I sit up in my saddle, alert. Portia and I would be even farther from LilyAye if it weren't for my insistence on seeing this for myself. The wagons pull to a stop. The rebels are squished into the wagons, their hands tied behind their backs and blindfolds over their eyes.

"They'll be released. Don't worry," Portia says, glancing over at me.

The rebels are pulled from the wagons and onto the ground. A Warwick soldier uses a knife to untie the ropes from their hands and rip off their blindfolds. Mirabelle stumbles and reaches for Knox's arm. Tuor holds tight to Eve. I spot Roehana and Esmeralda, Ron and Alice.

"Surely, you understand they'd be fools to go back to LilyAye," Portia says, pulling her cloak over her arms to fight against the cold wind. "One step inside those city walls and our deal is off. Reed could do with them what he likes. And I wouldn't advise returning to Bear Gap. If they'd even survive the journey, Reed will be returning that territory to what it was."

"Back to captivity," I mutter. My mind spins, thinking about Ralf and my father. What will become of them?

Squinting my eyes, I notice a few figures on the grassy knoll who surprise me. Fairalisa is there, along with Pip and even Lawrence.

"Why is Lawrence with them? He was never arrested."

Portia lifts her chin. "Mmm, yes, Lawrence and his bride chose to go with your rebels. Thatius would have protected them, but unfortunately, I think Lawrence said something about finally turning his back on LilyAye. I feel sorry for Thatius. He tried so hard with his son."

"Lawrence truly didn't know of his father's connection with you?"

Portia shakes her head. "No. He's quite innocent."

I smile to myself. Maybe Lawrence has finally figured himself out. I watch as Fairalisa, still dressed in her filthy wedding dress, stumbles onto the grass.

"What will become of Anthond?" I ask.

"Who?" Portia asks, crinkling her nose.

"Fairalisa's father."

"Oh, the old man? He didn't make it. Died in the dungeons, they said. He was too weak."

Portia's tone is disgusted, as if she has an aversion to even speak of weakness.

My heart sinks. *Poor Fairalisa.*

"What about all the other rebels?" I ask. "The ones in the other safe houses."

Portia cocks her head, then gives me a sympathetic look.

"Oh, Camilla . . ."

My mother's horse scuttles on its hooves. She holds firmer to her reins.

"There were never any other rebels," she says. "No one could form a rebellion in LilyAye. You underestimate how much people truly love Warwick in that city. Plus, Reed didn't need the support of the rebellion. He only needed you."

A sigh escapes my lips. I finger Fairalisa's clip, which I keep pinned in my hair as a reminder. The wagons turn around and barrel away from the huddling crowd of rebels. They've been left with nothing in the

464

middle of the Otsana Wood, but they're alive. All it took was to sacrifice myself. I'd do it over and over again if I had to.

"Here, I snatched this for you," Portia says.

From the folds of her cape, she produces my dagger. She hands it over, and I take the smooth leather hilt in my hand.

"You trust me with this?"

"Of course. We're a team now, Camilla. Plus, I know how important a weapon is to a girl."

The group of rebels walk aimlessly into the forest.

"It's time for us to take our leave," my mother says, turning her horse around.

"Where are we going?"

"It's time I brought you home, where you belong."

I glance one last time down at the forest. Johnny walks at the back of the group. He wears a patch over his eye. Urgently scanning their surroundings, Johnny turns his gaze on the hillside where I'm standing. I smile, tears welling in my eyes. He pauses, catching sight of me, and for a moment, I feel him next to me.

"Come," my mother calls, beckoning me to a new life.

THE END

Acknowledgments

Thank you…

To my writer's group and critique partners for suffering through rough drafts of this book when it was truly *rough*.

To my editor, Nicole, for slogging through my mess of a manuscript and polishing it to a shine.

To each member of my advanced reader team for helping me launch this book. You have the special talent of spotting the tiniest, yet most annoying typos. I would look like an amateur without you.

To my husband, Noah, for putting up with 4x6 cards scrawled with plot points, on the floor, couch, and bed.

Pronunciation Guide

CHARACTERS
Camilla: Kuh-mil-uh
Tuor: Toor (like tour)
Roehana: Roh-hah-nah
Gracine: Gray-seen
Fairalisa: Fair-uh-lee-suh
Thatius: Tha-tee-uhs
Ohbolina: Ah-boh-lee-nuh

PLACES
Elmyra: Ehl-meye-ruh
LilyAye: Lilee-eye
Ebertier: Eh-birr-teer
Billage: Bill-ehj (like village)
Rande: Randee (like Randy)

OTHER
Catahli: Kuh-tah-lee

Want to know what happens next?

Camilla's story does not end here. Her story continues in a thrilling sequel.

***

Visit www.emilyfortney.com to explore the entire Camilla Crim series and grab a **FREE** eBook by signing up for Emily's email newsletter.

***

If you enjoyed this book, please leave a 5-star review on Goodreads or the online retailer where you purchased it. Also, pass this book on to a friend. Good books are meant to be shared.

EMILY FORTNEY is the author of the Camilla Crim series. Currently living in Pennsylvania with her husband, Emily is passionate about dark chocolate, Earl Grey tea, and her cat.

Emily absolutely LOVES hearing from her readers! Connect with her over at www.emilyfortney.com

www.ingramcontent.com/pod-product-compliance
Lightning Source LLC
Chambersburg PA
CBHW031026030726
47497CB00004B/1019